USEFUL IDIOTS

Jan Mark

David Fickling Books

OXFORD · NEW YORK

USEFUL IDIOTS
A DAVID FICKLING BOOK
0 385 60413 0

Published in Great Britain by David Fickling Books,
a division of Random House Children's Books

This edition published 2004

1 3 5 7 9 10 8 6 4 2

Copyright © Jan Mark, 2004

Papers used by Random House Children's Books are natural, recyclable
products made from wood grown in sustainable forests. The manufacturing processes
conform to the environmental regulations of the country of origin.

Set in New Baskerville by Palimpsest Book Production
Limited, Polmont, Stirlingshire

DAVID FICKLING BOOKS
31 Beaumont Street, Oxford, OX1 2NP
a division of RANDOM HOUSE CHILDREN'S BOOKS
61–63 Uxbridge Road, London W5 5SA
A division of The Random House Group Ltd

RANDOM HOUSE AUSTRALIA (PTY) LTD
20 Alfred Street, Milsons Point, Sydney,
New South Wales 2061, Australia

RANDOM HOUSE NEW ZEALAND LTD
18 Poland Road, Glenfield, Auckland 10, New Zealand

RANDOM HOUSE (PTY) LTD
Endulini, 5A Jubliee Road, Parktown 2193, South Africa

THE RANDOM HOUSE GROUP Limited Reg. No. 954009
www.kidsatrandomhouse.co.uk

A CIP catalogue record for this book is available from the British Library.

Printed and bound in Great Britain by
Clays Ltd, St Ives plc

For Willy, Lieve, Johan, Jan and Ludo
and all my friends in West Flanders
in the hope that when the time comes,
we may float.

Chapter One

The gale came out of the north-west and struck in the early hours. Across the Isles its progress and approach had been monitored throughout the night as rivers boiled over, monorails and bridges collapsed, roofs disintegrated. In the city canyons, small buildings imploded and storm drains burst while flood alarms blared. Everywhere solar panels were destroyed.

By the time it reached the coast it was at hurricane force. There was no rain left to fall. Under a clear sky it was a dry wind that raced across the low hills, sucking ponds empty, flattening the reeds in the marshes, crushing bushes, felling trees, driving out to sea with a screaming hiss. At the Briease Reserve, between the fen and the shore, windows bellied and buckled with every gust, but the roofs were constructed as they had been for centuries to withstand coastal weather, the tumult of the North Sea, and when daylight came the houses still stood.

The first children who ventured over the dunes to Parizo Beach in the hope of finding sea wrack discovered only what they had lost. The tide was going out, snarling and dragging its way seaward, lunging back to crash sullenly on the barren black shore. The beach had been golden, but in five hours the fearful pressure had scoured away every grain of sand to expose the peat that had lain beneath. Still wet, it glistened oilily under the chill rays of the early sun that crawled across the shore, and the gulls were on it already, strutting, grabbing, seeking what they might devour. The bald beach was empty; the treasure seekers would have to wait for the afternoon tide before anything arrived, the lattermath of the hurricane. The children returned home cold and empty-handed over the sand hills, through the rasping marram grass. The one thing they might have found was as yet no more than a bulge, like a worn cobblestone, scarcely proud of the peat in which it lay embedded. There were to be three more tides before the bulge became a cupola, then a dome and then, as the mumbling sea withdrew, two bony brows emerged from the peat and frowned at the horizon.

Between the first tide and the fourth the children were followed by the adults, who knew enough about coastal fluctuations to take seriously the breathless claims that the beach had disappeared in the night. Before now whole villages had disappeared in the night.

They took the broad view, panning from north to south, from the gaunt causeway of the Chisel to the dim shoulder of the Nox, far down the coast. Today was eerily windless after the night's turmoil; the tide was on the turn, nibbling fretfully at the shore, sucking at the piles of the landing stage. If anything was to be lost they had expected to lose that, but still it strode out into the sea, relic of a former generation.

They had allowed that the children might be exaggerating, but the acres of sand where as children themselves they had run and played, raised ramparts, sunk basins, cut canals, incised sprawling pictograms that would never be seen except from the empty skies, that sand had gone, as if it had never been. Already they were asking themselves if it had been so golden, so soft, the air so warm.

By the time another tide had risen and fallen the mayor of Briease had come down to the beach with the representative from the Bureau of Aboriginal Affairs. They would have been there sooner but when the weather turned violent they had been caught in the fen between Herigal Staithe and Briease Town, and had spent the night cowering in a turf lodge while the wind bellowed overhead.

They had no business on the beach, beyond the business of being present at a time of calamity, and they did not stay long in the scything wind that blew inshore as the light began to fade. They were not looking for skulls, and even if they had been they would not have noticed the ambiguous hemisphere at their feet. There was still little to see. Nevertheless, during the next twenty-four hours somebody did see it and looked it in the eye, and knew it for what it was and had been.

Amandine Turcat was not looking for skulls when she glanced up the beach and sensed that she was being watched from ground level. The only human figures in the whole length of the landscape were herself and her boss, Philippe de Harnac of the Energy Commission, but the feeling of surveillance had persisted since they moored their launch at the jetty and now she knew why. The two black caverns were five metres away, between her and the first grassy outcrops of the dunes, set in their own little Golgotha and peering over the rim of the peat.

De Harnac had walked so directly towards the skull that he might have been aiming at it and his impetus was such that he almost trod on it, stopping short and skidding on the sable surface of the peat. It was his balletic gyrations that had drawn her attention. He did not seem to understand at first what it was that he was looking at. She identified it immediately.

'Are we on Oyster territory?'

'Stop yelling. You don't say that in their hearing.'

She caught up with him. 'Are there any about?'

'With your voice I should think they heard you in Briease. Mind your manners. If they want to be called Aboriginals then that's what we call them, on their territory.'

'Are we on it?'

There was no reason why they should not be on it. The Briease Reserve was crossed by rights of way, should anyone be fool enough to try to follow them, but Amandine was new to the work, head filled with warnings about trespass upon Aboriginal reserves and Aboriginal sensibilities. Honour their boundaries and call them Oysters, that was a good start.

The eye sockets continued to gaze impassively.

'Do you think that's an Oys— an Aboriginal?'

'Hard to tell. Everyone's the same underneath. It must have surfaced after the hurricane and the sea's washing it out.'

'No, they're not – not the same underneath.' Amandine crouched and examined it. 'You can tell a lot from the shape of the skull, racial origins—'

'Which we *don't* tell, as you very well know. I suppose you pick up these subversive notions from your brother.'

'They aren't notions. There is a difference.'

'There was once a political movement that measured people's skulls to determine whether or not they were human. The subhuman ones were exterminated,' de Harnac said.

'That's not what archaeology's about, you know it's not.' Amandine spent much time deflecting de Harnac's insults. He only teased, but it was a damaging tease. 'This is peat we're on, isn't it? What a shame it's not a bog burial – a corpse found in a peat moss. They came up so fresh people used to think they were murder victims and called the Politi, but some were – oh, a thousand, two thousand years old.'

'How can you tell this isn't one?' He found her macabre enthusiasm amusing.

Amandine gave the skull a tentative tap with one fingernail. 'It would be spongy, maybe squashed flat. This is solid bone. Could be recent . . .'

'How recent? This place has been under sand for decades.'

'I don't know. Anyway, I don't think there's any history of finding bog burials in the Briease Moss. It's not acid peat.'

'Your brother would know, of course. Would he be interested in this?'

'Interested? Rémy would give his eye teeth for something like this, a shore burial. And no one's ever dug up a whole skeleton before, not any kind of body.'

'Which is precisely why his depraved choice of occupation was banned for so long,' de Harnac said. 'Digging up bodies has generally been regarded as an anti-social activity.'

Amandine ignored him and knelt on the peat to stare into the hollows beneath the brow ridges. 'What's the procedure? Which authorities have to be informed – *do* they have to be informed?'

'Certainly they do. We assume that we've found a murder victim and report it to the Politi. They can be the ones who decide what to do next.'

'Can they do anything – if it's on a reserve?'

'Federal Politi can, until it's established that it's not a murder victim; which it might be.'

'It isn't, though, is it? Or rather, if it is, it must be an ancient death. I think that's the legal term. Rémy's always *hoping* to find an ancient death. Can't we skip the Politi and go straight to him?'

'No we can't. His activities are barely legal at the best of times.'

'If he could get down here before the Oysters— Aboriginals discover it—'

'If they haven't already discovered it. If they do

you'll just have to hope that they also do the decent thing – inform the cops.'

'Their cops or ours?'

'If it's possible murder, ours.'

'Would they report it?'

'Why not? You may not care for the way they live but they're the ones who suffer for it. They're as law-abiding as the rest of us.'

'Except for the laws they wangle out of,' Amandine muttered with the easy intolerance of hearsay. 'So, whether it's on the reserve or not, the Politi will have to exhume?'

'You wouldn't like to dig it out now and take it with us?'

'Absolutely not. Everything must be left *in situ*, properly excavated.' She seemed prepared to believe that he was offering to hunker down on the peat and grub up the ghastly thing with his bare hands. He would hate to see the brother at work.

'Call him up.'

'Rémy?'

'I'll call the Politi, you call him. I'm sure he can contrive some way of being in on the exhumation. Didn't you say he was still excavating the cathedral site?'

'Not while it's flooded. I'll be seeing him this evening. But what if the Oysters find this first?'

'If they haven't found it yet, they won't now. We're below the high-water mark here and the tide's coming in. It'll be dark before it's on the turn again. Anyway, we don't know if this is on the reserve. What makes you think it might be?'

'Well, it *might* be. You said the town was north of the Parizo wind farm, and the Moss must be on the other side of those sand-hilly things.'

'Dunes. If the Aboriginals are so fussy about their boundaries they should mark them,' de Harnac said. 'What have you been taught about reserves? Roads and monorails run through them, and canals, in the Central Region. If you want you can picnic on Parizo Beach, take guided tours into the Moss. People do.'

'Picnic *here*?'

'Visits to the seaside were once a form of recreation, believe it or not. Remember, till three nights ago, this was all sand.'

At their feet, while they talked, the eye sockets stared beyond them, out to sea. Amandine stooped and patted the smooth bone.

'If it hadn't been for the hurricane it would have stayed buried, perhaps for ever.'

'There is no such thing as for ever on a coast,' de Harnac said.

It was the hurricane that had flooded the cathedral dig. Trenches were filled to their crumbling lips with thick yellow water; ruts had become channels. The Interpretation Centre, with its optimistic sign, DISCOVER ARCHAEOLOGY, THE LOST SCIENCE, was deserted except for its director and a single member of academic staff. On the elevated boardwalk, where last week those few members of the public who had responded to the invitation to see archaeologists at work had watched Rémy Turcat and his team cut into

8

their past through a layer cake of centuries, there were now only a couple of loitering youths dropping small objects into the water. When power became available to commence pumping and the lode of thirteenth-century detritus turned out to be salted with twenty-third-century artefacts, what confusion there would be, what humiliation.

They had been paid to chuck the stuff in and were supposed to be doing it under cover of night. They did not know why, and night was inconveniently dark at the moment, so they stood in the autumn daylight and in full view of Dr Turcat himself, who was watching them glumly from the doorway of the Interpretation Centre. He imagined them to be Oysters, off the reserve, rootless, purposeless, bored, cultivating obscure grudges; unemployed and unemployable. They had no idea who he was, or that they were meant to be ruining his reputation. He knew. On the far side of the Interpretation Centre stood the faithful band of protesters with their screen banner and its revolving message: BAN ARCHAEOLOGY NOW. EXCAVATION IS AN AFFRONT TO CIVILIZED SOCIETY.

Although the sun was still quite high in the sky it never, at this time of year, rose above the glassy heights that surrounded the site, many of them now glassless and swarmed over by robot glaziers and welders on cradles and cables. The Interpretation Centre had lost its roof and, being low on the list of priorities when it came to repairs, was huddled under a creaking patchwork of rainproofing materials. Since the source of natural light had been the glazed pyramid of the roof, and the power was intermittent, Rémy Turcat appeared a lonely troglodyte in the twilight of his cave, attended by the one member of staff who had arrived for work and, workless, was sweeping away the water which continued to well up from somewhere, flotating floor tiles.

'This is the ideal time for visitors to look around,' Turcat said when his sister splashed in followed by her boss, de Harnac. 'A peep into the past, a glimpse of how we used to live, pre-virus. Somehow the species survived for millennia – amazing, isn't it?'

'Not people like us, though,' Amandine said.

'I was joking. The virus only wiped records, not civilization. As they say. Some of us think the records *were* civilization. No, not people like us, more like the Oysters. Have a seat, do. Are you just dropping by or did you want something? A drink? There's plenty of water. Korda here could rustle up something over a candle.' The graduate assistant did not even look up from his sweeping.

The seating was a horseshoe of chairs facing the screen wall, which was obdurately blank and streaked with downward-creeping moisture that rippled with every gust beneath the temporary roof. Amandine and de Harnac took the central chairs, adding to the desolation by their resemblance to forlorn enthusiasts at a poorly-attended lecture. Turcat had recently experienced many such. Of the dispiriting numbers who followed the signs to the dig through the labyrinth of tower blocks, the heights, fewer still responded to the invitation to discover the lost science. In the view of the general public it could remain lost. Archaeology, from what they could see of it, was about being dead. Being dead now was as conclusive as it had ever been. Life might be prolonged indefinitely but no one had yet come up with a way to make it infinite.

'We were at Parizo Beach this morning,' de Harnac said, wishing that Turcat would sit down with them instead of looming from the middle of the floor as if he were delivering the ill-attended lecture, 'checking the damage to inshore wind farms.'

'And how is it?' Turcat asked courteously, but failing to make any connection between his ruined dig, with its half-demolished Interpretation Centre, and the activities of the Energy Commissioners. They were not proposing to restore *his* energy.

'Something extraordinary has happened out there. Do you know the Briease littoral?'

'Miles of sand.'

'Wrong. The sand's gone. The hurricane's taken the whole beach with it.'

'Down to the peat, then.'

'You knew about the peat?' Amandine's disappointment was plain. 'I tried to call you. Why weren't you receiving?'

'I tuned out; I'm not taking calls at the moment.' He gestured towards the trenches: weightier matters concerned him. 'Two thirds of the Briease Reserve is peat moss, and since what is now the offing was once land under cultivation it's reasonable to suppose that the peat extends far out undersea. You didn't come here to tell me that.'

11

'No,' de Harnac said. 'What we found we have to report to the Politi as a matter of law. It might not occur to them to pass on the information to the Department of Archaeology so we tried to inform you at the same time – by which I mean first. You under-stand? But as we couldn't raise you I've delayed the report. I'll have to do it soon, though.'

'It's a whole skeleton,' Amandine said, bouncing up.

'A whole skeleton? On the beach? Just lying there?'

'A skull,' de Harnac said. 'All that's exposed is the – the . . .' He passed his hands over his head.

'Cranium?'

'That's it, cranium, down to the eye sockets. Presumably the rest of it is in the peat, but that is only a presumption. It could be a formal grave, part of a cemetery. It could be a murder victim, whole or just the skull. For all I know it's not attached to a body at all, it could be stuck on a pole. We didn't touch it.'

'I did,' Amandine said. 'It's not a bog burial. The bone is hard.'

'Is it on the reserve?'

'We couldn't tell,' de Harnac said, 'but apparently the Oysters haven't found it yet. The thing hadn't been disturbed but the sea's uncovering it with every tide.'

'When are you going to the Politi?'

'Right now. Once I've done that and attended to the authentication of discovery I can get on with what I'm meant to be doing, which is inspecting the offshore installations.'

'You'll come with us?' Amandine was watching her brother for some signs of the anticipated excitement.

12

'I mean, you won't be able to do anything here for ages.'

'Thank you for reminding me. I can watch those oafs out there trying to damage my credibility, but they've left it a little late. If they wanted to adulterate the dig they should have done it last week while we were still digging. Not that *they* want to do any such thing. Someone's put them up to it.'

Turcat looked out into the thickening dusk. The last flush of sunset was leaving the top storeys of the heights. At ground level they were in near darkness. Only the reflected sparks from a high-rise welder showed where the flooded trenches lay, the wreck of weeks of patient scraping and brushing, a slow, slow race against time. It was the wrong season to begin excavation but he had been given two months before the next height went up, to find relics of what had once spread so prodigiously over many hectares – the cathedral that had stood from 1270 to 2164, almost nine hundred years. Now a commercial tower would be lucky to stand for ten before it was torn down and replaced, and in three weeks the engineers were scheduled to begin sinking the foundations of Mandeville Height, new headquarters of the Parizo Corporation. The trenches would not be pumped out in time nor the digging resume; the Interpretation Centre would not be reroofed but dismantled, its prefabricated walls packed flat for use elsewhere; and by next spring the height would stand where he was standing now, pinning down the past.

In that time perhaps half a dozen new sites might

open up briefly as a building came down, initiating a mad scramble each time to find what lay beneath before the engineers moved in. The lost cathedral was lost again, just when he had known he was digging down to the heart of it, the altar, sacred place of the old religion. Meanwhile a skull, perhaps a whole skeleton, lay awaiting him at Parizo Beach, where only the wash of the tides would interrupt his investigations. No new Canute had yet discovered a means of controlling the tide. De Harnac with his wave turbines and barrages could confirm that.

'No,' Turcat said. 'I won't be able to do anything here. Lock up, Korda.'

They waited while the floor-sweeping assistant went through the formality of sealing the roofless ruin and set off on foot for the Central Plaza, where all municipal buildings were situated, all stricken equally powerless. From their own point of view they could hardly have chosen a better time to report the discovery of a corpse, especially a corpse that promised to be as long dead as the one under Parizo Beach. Criminal elements were taking advantage of the blackouts.

'You can't inspect it now,' de Harnac told the sergeant, in between endorsing declarations.

'We are equipped with night sights,' the sergeant said. He had no intention of taking his night sights outside the city perimeter.

'No doubt, but the thing is under water at the moment – it's between the tide lines. You should be able to get at it just before midnight; after that, late tomorrow morning,' de Harnac said, knowing perfectly

14

well which the sergeant would choose: waste man-hours on an all-night jaunt up the coast to investigate a body that was ninety-nine per cent certain to have been centuries underground, or remain in the city to act should a body turn up only minutes dead.

'We'll go down tomorrow, leave here at o-eight hundred. You will be required to locate and identify.'

'Not necessarily,' de Harnac said. 'This is Dr Rémy Turcat from the Department of Archaeological Research and Excavation—'

'Yeah, yeah, the lost science,' the sergeant murmured, without looking up. He had evidently passed the cathedral site recently. 'I suppose you want first crack at the Parizo body – if it's not a recent kill? I know you people are into skeletons.'

'Dr Turcat's sister works for me,' de Harnac said. 'She was at Parizo Beach this morning. She can locate and identify.'

'I would appreciate the chance to survey the remains,' Turcat said formally, 'and as it's obvious that all work on the cathedral site will have to be suspended I'd be glad to supervise the removal of the— of Parizo Man.'

He sounded pompous but Korda, the assistant who had accompanied them uninvited and unregarded, knew the pomposity was a damper on his flaring excitement. The Parizo body; Parizo Man; it was a little early to risk giving this anonymous collection of bones a name, but it had a certain ring to it, worthy to stand alonside the ancestors: Neanderthal Man, Cro-Magnon Man, Peking Man, Java Man. How much they

15

had lost, how little they had to build on, starting all over again, almost from scratch, with scarcely anything to go by but books.

But the books were untouched, no virus had attacked them, and as a university department they had access to all of them. Tollund Man, Grauballe Man, Parizo Man, the name linked for ever with that of Rémy Turcat. Merrick Korda might contrive a footnote somewhere.

The sergeant did not greatly care about Parizo Man. 'Usually these things surface during construction or you people root them out. Then we turn them back over to the university if it's an ancient death. If you care to come along tomorrow it will save everybody's time. O-eight hundred. Please arrive at seven thirty at the latest. You'll have to pick up a local officer at Eavrey Point.'

They filed out.

'I have a strong suspicion,' Turcat said, 'that unless Parizo Man still has raw flesh adhering, the Politi will turn him over to us with indecent haste.' He was beginning to feel the same lurching, almost nauseous excitement as when he had cornered Professor Ehrhardt after a lecture to show him his first shard, prised out of rubble on a construction site.

A skull, perhaps a whole skeleton. And it's mine, all mine.

Ehrhardt, for all his years in the faculty, all his achievement in founding a department of archaeology, had never had more than a random litter of bones and fragments to boast of. They had passed many wistful hours with photographic records of early excavations in pyramids, kurgans, barrows: the ship burial at Sutton Hoo, the communal grave at La Chaussée-Tirancourt – that glorious riot of crania, jaws and teeth – the orderly plague cemetery at East Smithfield in London. Together they had drooled over reports and rumours from the mainland about bog burials, entire succulent corpses still with hair, finger-prints, faces. Parizo Man had none of these by the sound of it, but if he were not on Oyster land, inside the reserve, he would be Turcat's own, no question. If he *was* on Oyster land then a raid on the beach first thing tomorrow was urgent. The reason that the bog burials remained rumours was that the recovery of human remains was frowned on, especially by the Oysters who still practised interment, and on the whole public opinion in this matter, if in no other, favoured the Oysters. Should the Oysters get to Parizo Man first he would be lost to science for ever.

They departed the building into a night still punc-tuated with flares and sparks from the welders high above. The wind was strong again; Central Plaza trapped and funnelled it.

'So you'll give up on the cathedral,' de Harnac said, 'on the chance that our man is worth a look?'

'It's giving up on me,' Turcat said. 'We had under three weeks left. They'll never get the water out in time. Once the engineers want to start sinking foun-dations, then they'll pump.'

'It won't drain?'

'We're on clay here. You know, once archaeologists had months to uncover a site, *by law*. And for centuries

17

no one would have destroyed a cathedral to put up new buildings.'

'Sacred, were they?'

'Literally. Anyway, they were owned by the Christian churches, although as far as I can make out it was mainly atheists who paid to keep them standing – in the Isles, at least. One by one places of worship were sold off, converted, pulled down. A few survived as public facilities. The cathedrals were the last to go; they were such works of art, but they did not *earn*. In the end, no one could afford to keep them standing and when they began to fall they had to be demolished – incidentally releasing valuable areas of real estate.'

'What do you expect to find when you excavate them?'

'The past,' Turcat said. 'It's gone, lost. History drowned and we pulled up the ladder behind us. Everything you've said proves that.'

'And what do you do with the past when you've found it?'

'You ought to have come to the Interpretation Centre when it was still open.'

'It looked more open than usual,' de Harnac said.

Merrick, who had never supposed that his head of department had any kind of a sense of humour, heard Turcat laugh sadly in the darkness. De Harnac sounded vaguely sorry for Turcat and his little band of delving moles, scratching desperately for what was gone beyond recall. With the future so uncertain, why pursue the past? It was not as if they were going to find any more fossil fuel.

18

'We part here, I think,' de Harnac said, on the edge of the plaza.

'I'll walk on with you,' Turcat said. 'If I'm going to be out tomorrow I'd better get back to the department now.'

'Oh, but the theatre!' Amandine squeaked.

'Are you going to the theatre?'

'*We* are. You're coming with me, remember? I got the tickets.'

'Manda, I can't. You must see how important this is.'

'I do see. I'm coming with you in the morning, aren't I? I *found* it, your Parizo Man. Why do you have to work tonight?'

'Because I shan't be here to do it tomorrow. Can't you find someone else—' He turned suddenly. 'What about you, Korda? Wouldn't you like to go to the theatre?'

Merrick, who was unaccustomed to social chit-chat from his superior, especially chit-chat involving enormously expensive tickets for a live theatrical performance, made a noncommittal noise.

'Do *you* have something important to do too?' Amandine was gallantly swallowing her disappointment. Merrick found the gallantry harder to take than the disappointment.

'No, of course not. I'll come with you,' he said. 'I'd like to.'

'It will be wonderful.' Amandine rallied and glowed. 'A ballet, at the Ayckbourn – you know, the reconstruction? A friend of mine is dancing.'

'There you are, then,' Turcat said heartily and with

19

evident relief, and dived into the darkness behind de Harnac.

The Ayckbourn foyer was crowded when Merrick arrived to meet Amandine. Bereft by the power failures, people who would normally be relaxing indoors in their viewing rooms with their home media had ventured out into the windy darkness, darker than ever they had expected or known, to places of entertainment – videodromes, concert halls, theatres, anything rather than sit at home in the derisive silence. Public buildings were always the first to get their power restored. Merrick's own apartment block, Admiral Height, was on firefly wattage.

There was no evidence that the Ayckbourn management was trying to conserve energy. The foyer was softly but not dimly lit and light poured through the open doors from the auditorium. The crowds were streaming in eagerly. The show tonight featured a ballet, a lost art that attracted a lot more attention than a lost science.

Merrick had never seen a ballet and had only once or twice visited a theatre. He had never seen anything remotely resembling the interior of the Ayckbourn, a lovingly accurate recreation of a twentieth-century playhouse, although he passed its brick and stucco facade from time to time. He peered in at the imitation of Old England, noted the carpet, a floor covering he particularly disliked – it always made him suspect that it might break out in spores – and waited on the steps for Amandine.

Here she came now, flushed and excited, unlikely sibling to Turcat's own dry detachment. It had taken a skeleton to excite brother Rémy. She stood barely a metre away, looking all around. Merrick, accustomed to not being recognized, reintroduced himself. She must have seen him a dozen times before, but he was never more than the graduate assistant, on hands and knees in a trench.

'Oh, *there* you are,' Amandine cried as if she had discovered him by herself. 'I couldn't get here sooner – so sorry. Let's find our seats before we have to start climbing over people.'

He followed her through the foyer and into the auditorium; climbing over people? He began to en-vision a scaffolding to which they would cling, but the auditorium, still showing its ancestry in the old Greek amphitheatres, was raked, with long curving rows of seats. Theirs, predictably, were in the middle of a row and they did have to climb over people. No one minded, shifting amenably; it was all part of the experience.

Amandine was seated next to someone she seemed to know and who looked familiar to Merrick. He had an unnaturally round head with short hair cut in a fringe that made him resemble, did he but know it, the generic medieval villein in department reference works. When he noticed Amandine settling beside him he held out a hand with extravagant enthusiasm.

'How good to see you again.' Merrick knew the voice, fluting, self-assured, too matured for the face it came out of. He had visited the dig a couple of times, asking intelligent questions that Turcat had suspected him of composing at length beforehand. He gave no sign of having seen Merrick before and, of course, Merrick told himself viciously, he *hasn't* seen me before. I'm the guy in the hole, scratching up dirt.

He stared at the red velvet curtains that hung in front of the proscenium stage while Amandine's acquaintance yawned informatively in a carrying voice.

'Have you seen *The Sea Witch* before? The piece they commissioned to open this place, pastiche of classical nineteenth-century ballet, danced on the point. Live orchestra – authentic early instruments.'

The auditorium darkened; the orchestra, positioned in a kind of gully in front of the stage, began playing; the red curtain went up like an eyelid. Pale lights spread across the silhouettes of rocks and out of the shadows advanced a squat shape, scuttling and creeping like a crab. Did it move on its feet or its hands? Was that probing, hesitant limb an arm or a leg? Where was its head? In the mass of its cramped, warped body a dead-white face looked up suddenly and caught the light. A new note sounded; the creature began to unfold, a knee, an elbow, a flexed arm, and stood upright: a woman.

Merrick assumed it was a woman, thin and arachnid, too many joints. Her limbs articulated at unlikely angles, emphasized by the black bodysuit. He tried to imagine what kind of a skeleton lay beneath; it was a dance of transcendent grace and peculiarly ugly to watch, like the face under its wig of straight pale hair.

'Is it a mask?' Merrick whispered.

'No, it's make-up. Traditional. It's a kind of paste. You'll see the others.'

The others did not appear. The solo went on, mesmerizingly horrible. How could human joints, a human spine, endure such contortions? He saw now what dancing on the point involved: her whole weight was carried on the tips of her toes.

Traditional make-up for a traditional dance-drama, a tradition, Merrick thought as he watched, that might usefully have been allowed to atrophy. The bone-cracking woman was a wicked spirit who haunted the seashore and saved a handsome prince from drowning. In gratitude he invited her back to his palace and she, deeply in love, for even the wicked can love deeply, went along in her finery, seaweed mostly, only to find that the prince, too dimwitted to read the signs, had invited her to his wedding.

Here came the prince in his handsome pink face paint and golden wig, with his pink and gold attendants, who disported themselves in various maritime pursuits, fishing, swimming or possibly surfing – it was hard to tell without any water – while the witch scuttled across the rocks, watching them, until the prince slipped and fell, swooning, drowning, and she sprang into the sea and dragged him out, and kept his friends at bay with gestures, since no one spoke, until he breathed again. Then she danced triumphant, disjointed, avid: *He's mine. He's mine.*

The curtain fell as the prince was borne palace-ward and his lovesick witch danced her passion alone on the beach.

23

'It makes all the difference,' said the man with the round head, as the lights went up for the interval, 'all the difference in the world, having an Aboriginal dancer.'

'Who, the witch woman?' said a voice with penetrating clarity from farther along the row. 'She's an Oyster?'

Heads turned, breath was audibly drawn in, and the round-headed man launched into a lecture on Aboriginal sensibilities. Merrick was ready to bet that he too talked about Oysters when no one was listening, like all the tooth-sucking liberals within earshot. Oysters – it just slipped over the tongue. Aboriginal took longer to say and you had to think about it in advance.

In the second act the prince prepared to wed his bride. The scenery was sumptuous, every head was golden, every face was pink, the dancing was fluid and comfortable to watch; these big, well-rounded people did not dance on the point. Into it all irrupted the frenzied convulsed fury of the sea witch, jerking, twitching in thwarted rage, the face immobilized under its plastered maquillage, the body alone conveying jealousy, betrayal, revenge.

The courtiers, naturally, did not notice what was in their midst until she burst into the centre of the nuptials, miming retribution. All shrank in fear. A shimmering guardian-angel character intervened, danced a duel of wills with the sea witch, drove her thence. The party continued.

In Act III the newly-wed princess came down to the sea to bathe and was lured onto the rocks by the sea witch pretending to be some lovable marine creature until those frightful, steel-sprung crab-claw limbs sprang close like a trap, gripped the foolish princess and held her under to drown. Re-enter the guardian angel to engage in another duel of wills that drove the black witch up the rocks, higher and higher, until she cast herself down in a heart-jolting free-fall dive to the floor, dying, dead. Whereupon the princess revived, ascended into the arms of her rosy-fingered prince and everybody danced elaborately and longer than was strictly necessary around the shattered body of the sea witch as it lay broken and twisted, a knee here, an elbow there, head wrenched askew.

When the triumphant royal party had left, the light turned blue. The body twitched, bucked, reassembled itself, and the crab that had advanced on stage at the beginning dragged itself away into the darkness.

The audience, shocked beyond its expectations, rose to its feet, applauding, cheering, and the dancers filed on to bow acknowledgement. Last to appear was the sea witch, on two feet but walking with evident discomfort, like an animal on its hind legs; there was still that suspicion of too many joints.

'Would you like to meet her?' Amandine asked. 'I know her – we could go backstage.'

Round-head, assuming that the invitation included him, declined, saying that he would rather not spoil the magic. Pure Aboriginal art was so *rare*, he breathed preciously. Merrick was tempted to come up with a similar excuse but his brief from Turcat was to accompany Amandine, so he followed her out, wondering what Turcat himself would have made of the performance. After five years in the department he still had no idea of how the head of it spent his spare time or even of where he went when he left work in the evenings. If he imagined him at all, his mind's eye saw him alone with a bone upon which he gnawed absentmindedly, consumed by his work and consuming it.

The Ayckbourn, being the creation of a drama-loving philanthropist and not state sponsorship, reproduced ancient theatre with exhaustive attention to detail. Amandine led the way along narrow passages, down staircases, through tunnels, all lined with doors. There was no room to walk two abreast except at intersections, where they were sure to encounter a dancer flitting between rooms in wrapper and slippers, and everyone had to flatten themselves against the walls and sidle. Most of the dancers had already removed their make-up but their faces retained a greasy sheen and glistened in the wings of the nose.

'Isn't there a terrible flood risk?' Merrick asked, and a woman they were passing made a hasty sign with her fingers, her face pinched with disapproval.

'Shh. You know how superstitious stage people are,' Amandine said. Merrick had not known. She knocked on a door with two names on it: RODRIGUEZ, MASON.

Someone called out and they went in. The room was very bare but brilliantly lit by the illuminated mirror that took up one whole wall. Two women in wrappers were sitting at it, their backs to the door, but their faces reflected in the mirror: the princess and the sea witch.

The princess, her head wrapped in a towel, was polishing away her make-up with a cloth. The other was carving at her face with a strigil, removing thick curls of paint.

'Frida, you were wonderful,' Amandine cried. 'And you, Elena.'

Elena Rodriguez turned and smiled. Cleansed of the princess's pink complexion, her brown face was delicate, small featured, a perfect oval with gently arching brows above dark eyes. As she unwrapped the towel that swathed her head Merrick saw that the rolls and swatches of golden hair were now perched on a wig block to the side of a table. The towel fell away to reveal short charcoal curls.

'It is so *hot* in that thing,' Elena said. 'You would not believe. Frida is so lucky to be able to wear her own.'

Merrick had assumed that the straight lustreless hair of the sea witch *had* been a wig but there was no false head at Frida's end of the table.

The sea witch, who had only raised a hand in greeting, was still carving and scraping. With one swipe of the strigil she sliced off her right cheekbone and began shaving at her jaw. Korda tried not to stare at what was being exposed. Under the paste was not smooth skin but a corrugated strip like the surface of a wheat biscuit. He looked away hastily before Frida Mason should notice that she was being stared at, and joined in the conversation between Amandine and the other dancer, the princess who had nothing to hide beneath her stage face.

But now and again he could not stop his eyes slithering towards the mirror, where more and worse was being laid bare. The pockmarking began below the eye, spreading over the cheek and jaw, down into the pit of the neck, gnawing into the corner of the mouth on the way. Frida, quite unself-consciously, was excavating obstinate morsels of make-up from the scar tissue. With helpless disgust Merrick looked away and saw her feet instead.

The toes were long and knuckly like fingers, the tendons five rigid wires that ran taut into the ankle over knots of callus and bone process. Being over-familiar with the skeleton, having to identify any fragment that he might unearth, he could name every bone in that foot.

'Nine more performances,' Elena was saying, 'then into rehearsal for the next one. *Windows* – it's a contemporary piece, by Laken. So farewell to this muck, thank god. We'll be wearing our own faces.'

'Are you in that?' Amandine asked, seeing that Frida was ready to talk. She was, after all, the one they had come to visit.

'Me? No, I'm only on loan to the company.' Frida turned round to answer and Merrick noticed that the other side of her face was almost unblemished; firm, handsome, as sharply defined, in a way, as the make-up had made it, and without the make-up, just as white.

'*We* can't do the steps on the point,' Elena said. 'No amount of training makes any difference. Frida will be back at the end of the winter season.'

'Will you come and eat with us?' Amandine said.

28

Merrick hoped that this would not be part of his escort duties.

'How could I refuse?' Elena said. '*Windows*, thank god, goes on at the Outer Limits. Full accommodation laid on, and food. This kind of historical nonsense is all very well for a few days, but, my god, the thing's been running on and off for weeks. Next time the Ayckbourn's mentioned I'll look very hard at my contract. Are you coming with us, Frida?'

'No, thanks, I've got to find a steam room fast.'

'Won't you eat first?'

'If I don't get warm very quickly I shan't be able to move at all tomorrow,' Frida Mason said. There was no complaint in her voice, she was simply stating a fact. She wrapped a cloak around herself and limped out of the room; they heard the halting footsteps recede in the empty echoing corridors.

Elena closed the door cautiously before speaking. 'A dancer's life is short but, my god, those people – half-crippled at thirty.'

'She's never thirty,' Amandine said.

'Oysters age so fast.' Merrick was beginning to dislike Elena, with her tapered limbs, plump feet, flawless skin. Everyone had flawless skin, but how did Frida Mason feel as she sat side by side with this beauty each evening, covering up her flaws and uncovering them again?

'What happened to her face?' he asked. It was the first time he had spoken. They looked at him as if they had forgotten that he was there. Probably they had. It was a Turcat failing.

'One doesn't ask,' Amandine said.

'I've never had the chance,' Elena added. 'We've been sharing this room for weeks. We get on well. I'm the official female star of the company, but you saw the performance. Everybody knows who the real star is and no one begrudges it. We all suffer for our art, but we don't go through what she does – which is why she was engaged. Only an Oyster could dance the sea-witch role. All the moves are authentic and completely impossible for anyone else.

'But we've sat beside each other at this mirror for four weeks of rehearsal and two months of performance; we've put on our make-up, we've danced together, we've come back here and taken it off again. I've never once found the right moment to ask about her face and she's never mentioned it. I could have bitten my tongue out when I called the make-up muck just now. It's not muck to Frida, believe me. And you've seen how thick hers has to be. Thicker than mine – and *I* have to change colour.'

She laughed, and Merrick liked her a little better after all. 'What do you talk about?' he said, and wondered how well Amandine, who claimed to know Frida, did in fact know her.

'Nothing,' Elena said. 'Nothing that does not concern the dance, the costume, the make-up. Aside from that we have nothing to say to one another – that is, she has nothing to say to me. Why do you think they call them Oysters?'

On Parizo Beach the tide had risen and fallen, risen, and was on its way out again. As the water receded it left behind a wrack of shells and weed, floating debris of the storm cast up on the sloping peat bed of the beach, around the watcher on the shore. The eye sockets were now half-exposed and into one scuttled a little crab which, fitting neatly, drew in its claws and settled down, and the buried face stared on, up the moonglade.

Chapter Two

The police launch was built for speed, not comfort. Once out of the estuary it bounced from crest to wave crest as if someone were playing ducks and drakes with it.

'Motion sickness decreases with age,' the officer from Eavrey Point bawled cheerfully at his passengers, Rémy Turcat, who was vowing that any further trips to Parizo Beach would be made overland, Amandine, too cheerful and eager to care about the discomfort, and Merrick Korda, who had assumed that he would be expected to turn up. Turcat had neither welcomed him nor turned him away; he was expected.

The Nox lay far behind them; the low coastline, spooling out of the horizon, lay to the left, broken only by dunes and, above them, the rotating blades of the turbines on the Parizo Corporation's wind farm. It was a fine autumn day, bright and mild, even on the water. The beach was deserted. The helmsman steered the launch alongside the wooden stairs of the jetty and cut the engine. The officer sprang out, up the steps, and ran confidently onto dry land. Turcat and his party followed uneasily, disoriented by the sensation after hours on the water that the boards were swaying beneath their feet.

'Is this where you came ashore?' the Politi officer asked Amandine. 'Have you got co-ordinates?'

'I don't need them,' Amandine said. 'I can see it from here.'

The beach inclined smoothly from the edge of the water to the foot of the dunes. Halfway between the two margins an ochre-brown tump broke the glistening surface. A seagull perched on it.

'Are we on Oyster territory or not?' Turcat said.

'I'd say not, but it's a close thing. Not that it makes much difference. A body is a body and we have to investigate whether it's an ancient death or not. Anyway, the Oysters will have other things on their mind, right now. Briease Township must have been flattened the other night.'

'Hasn't anyone been to find out?' Amandine said.

You could have asked your Oyster friend last night, Merrick thought.

'If they want help they'll ask for it soon enough,' the officer said. 'Then they can complain that it wasn't offered.'

The seagull screeched and took off. The four of them stood looking down at the skull.

'He's coming up,' Amandine said.

'He? Could be a woman.'

'Not with those brow ridges,' Turcat said. 'Adult, you can tell by the sutures.'

'I know that much,' the officer said pettishly. He took out his scanner and applied it to the skull. Turcat and Merrick watched enviously as its insect proboscis took the minute core sample and read it for comparison with records. The officer moved away as the results came through.

'No match,' he said, turning back to them.

'No match at all?' Turcat was trying not to sound over-eager.

'Nothing; which means that either he was born during the Anarchy and managed to evade registration afterwards, or he's pre-Anarchy, in which case we'd have no records. He's not listed as a missing person or a criminal, so as far as we are concerned he doesn't exist. You can have him, Doctor. Ancient death.'

Turcat was looking almost coy. 'I suppose there's no chance . . . I mean, it wouldn't do any harm, and it would be of enormous assistance to us—'

The officer cut in severely, as to an impertinent child that was pushing its luck. 'I'm surprised to hear you even suggesting it. DNA records are strictly for forensic purposes and no other. You know why.'

'I'm sorry. Forget—'

'You lot always try it on,' the officer complained. '*I've* worked in the city . . . bones . . .' he muttered self-righteously, unstrapping the cutting equipment they had brought with them.

Merrick was responsible for the tools employed in the more delicate investigations that would follow the excavation, and a contour-cloth bag to carry home Parizo Man.

Amandine sidled up to him. 'Why won't they let you access DNA records?'

'In case we use them to trace ancestry, racial origins. Which is what we *really* want to do, of course. I think it happens on the quiet, on the mainland, but they're especially strict here.'

In some respects, he added to himself. It did cross his mind that the dates did not conform to his definition of ancient, but it would be foolhardy to argue. Parizo Man was theirs. They were being handed him more or less on a plate.

They marked out a rectangle, well clear of the supposed outline of the grave. 'On the assumption that the skeleton was buried in a reclining position,' Turcat said.

'The angle of the head . . .' Merrick ventured.

'What about the angle of the head?' Turcat's own head snapped round. He regarded Korda as little as he did his own shadow: it was always there beneath him; he did not expect it to speak.

'It looks more as if it was buried sitting up.'

'Or standing,' Turcat said, validating Merrick's suggestion by appropriating it. 'I don't know of any island culture that buried its dead in either position – but we dare not cut in too close, we might sever a hand or a foot. It can easily happen.'

'I do know what I'm at,' the officer said. 'I probably disinter more *whole* bodies than you do, Dr Turcat.'

The surface peat was rock hard. They drilled and sliced before they could dig, but then it came away cleanly as they worked a trench around the perimeter of the supposed grave until the skull was emerging

35

from a plateau two metres long and one wide, and it was safe to work away at the sides to determine where the extremities might lie. All the while they operated the eye sockets watched them dispassionately.

Turcat began with his trowel to cut away carefully at the lower end of the block.

'What are you looking for?' the officer said, only mildly curious, anxious to leave. He was not obliged to assist these ghouls.

'Toes,' Turcat said.

'He doesn't seem to have any. Maybe someone's had his feet off already.'

'This body isn't reclining,' Turcat said. 'It may be flexed, in a foetal position, sitting, standing – possibly it's not there at all. Parizo Man may simply be Parizo Head.'

It was Merrick, trowelling from the other side, who found a kneecap, a little distance from where the chin must be.

'You were right.' Turcat looked across at Merrick and had to acknowledge him. 'He must be sitting, knees drawn up' – Merrick exposed a second patella – 'feet together . . . staring out to sea.'

They all turned and stared out to sea in sympathy.

'I wonder if he died sitting,' Amandine said, her eyes big with tears ready to shed for the unknown departed. 'Waiting for his friends, for a ship that never came.'

'Depends how long he's been here,' Merrick said. 'He might have been a long way from the coast when he died.'

Turcat's head came round again to look at him curiously. Three nights ago Parizo Man had been under sand, under sea. In less than three hours he would, if left where he was, be under sea again. However, if he had sat down to wait in the hour of his death, he would not have been sitting on the shore but several kilometres inland, looking out across a stream, a road, a field, resting against a grassy bank perhaps. Had he simply died, been killed and left where he sat, or had he paused to rest at the moment of some cataclysm – a storm, a surge, a lightning strike?

'Well, what are you going to do with him?' the officer said. 'What sort of a procedure do you people have?'

'If we don't get him out now we'll have to wait for the tide to rise and go down again,' Turcat said. While they had been digging the sea had continued its stealthy return. 'Look, he's sitting. We need only a small block round him – a cubic metre, less. Half that. Can't we undercut and get him out?'

'Him, yes. Not the peat. Put that lot in the launch and you'll have us over, the first wave that hits.'

'But you've got lifting gear.'

'And I'll use it to lift him out for you. I'm not using it to lift him into the launch.'

'But what did you think we were going to do?'

'Shovel him up and take him back in that bag. Isn't that what it's for?'

'Not as such—'

'I didn't imagine you were planning to take half the beach with you.'

'We'll have to keep the block. We don't know what we may find in it – might be full of clues, so might

37

the digging. Look, if you can help us get him above the tide line we can manage the rest ourselves. I'll call back to base and tell them what we've got. They can arrange for proper transport. I'll pay for it myself if I have to.' He began to walk away.

'Where are you off to? *Help*, you said. I'm not wasting Politi time on university work.'

'He's calling Professor Ehrhardt,' Merrick said, taking up a cutter again. Amandine seized a trowel and with one energetic swipe came near to shearing off vital Parizo parts.

Turcat reached the end of his conversation, wheeled and came back.

'We've got about an hour and a half,' he said, looking at the sea. 'Professor Ehrhardt's arranging a boat. If we can get the body out now it ought to be back at the department tonight.'

The officer went out to the launch and returned with the helmsman and the lifting gear. While they erected the windlass Turcat and Merrick slithered into the narrow trenches and reassembled the contour-cloth bag around and under the block of peat. Amandine laboured back and forth between the sea's edge and the excavation, fetching bucketfuls of water to souse the cloth, which hardened on contact with liquid into a rigid casing around the block. It was an outdated paramedic device for immobilizing fractured limbs, and invaluable for contriving instant containers. Amandine's bucket had been a fabric bag before she dipped it into the sea.

There was not quite enough cloth to cover the top

of the block and the skull, which seemed to ignore their attentions with disdainful eyebrows until Merrick extinguished it in his coat, while the block was lifted from its bed and manoeuvred by the five of them into a sheltered cwm under the dunes. Then the officer and Turcat sat dickering over documentation, one abdicating responsibility, the other assuming it, while the foam crept slowly towards them and the helmsman pointed out that the launch was now riding dangerously close to the level of the jetty.

'Are you just going to leave him here?' Amandine's question cut across the murmured conversation like a gull's squawk.

'No one's likely to steal him,' the officer said, with some truth, 'and he's not going anywhere.'

Turcat was doing a head count: the helmsman, himself, the officer, Amandine—

'Korda, you can stay with him. We ought to be back within four to six hours. Any problem?'

Merrick shook his head; left on a deserted beach with a skeleton encased in a block of peat for six hours? On Parizo Beach, with the Briease Moss at his back, and Briease Town at its heart, and the population of that town who might have a number of reasons for displeasure should any of them decide to visit the beach? It was highly unlikely, in fact, that a coastal settlement had suffered much damage in the hurricane; no reason at all why beachcombers should not be out in pursuit of their gainful employment. What was he supposed to do if anyone came and challenged him about Parizo Man's resurrection?

'No problem.'

Merrick had been putting away the tools. He handed them to Turcat, who handed them back. 'Improve the shining hour, Korda. The tide's not up yet, look in the pit.' He might have been instructing a robot, the kind that cleaned drains.

The party walked out along the jetty and climbed aboard. The engine barked into life and the launch first headed seawards then turned to starboard and sped away south like a dart skimming the surface. When the sound of its passing had died away the beach was silent except for the roll and crash of the sea advancing, advancing, and the cries of sea birds. Only Amandine had turned to wave goodbye.

Six hours alone with the skeleton. Merrick had not wanted to touch it with anyone watching. Turcat would have forbidden it – Parizo Man was *his* man – but Merrick had worked on enough digs to forecast what had to be done and how. Amandine had been all impatience to uncover the face; the policeman had imagined that the peat could be hacked away by the trowelful. Merrick knew that what lay ahead were hours of scraping, dusting, chipping, an infinitely slow liberation, the painstaking erosion, flake by flake, that would show them what they had saved from the sea. He longed to begin, but Turcat's last words had been, 'Look in the pit.'

The pit was barely hip deep and the sea was already closing in around it. He took a trowel and, leaning in, began to scratch at the sides and base. Anything that Parizo Man had had about his person at the hour of his death would, presumably, still be about his person, deeply impacted: perhaps his belongings, perhaps a knife in his ribs; but there might be something else lying about.

He scraped and probed gently, forgetting where he was and only occasionally thinking to glance up at the strange hairy sand hills, the dunes, but he saw no movement save for the shifting in the wind of the marram grass that bound the sand together, birds alighting and leaving. It was at the precise moment when his trowel struck wood that the first trickle of water slithered down the side of the pit.

Don't hurry, don't hurry, he told himself, but could not help making more determined strokes with the trowel point. He seemed to have uncovered the edge of a box with – here came another rush of water, more of it this time – a box with a metal plate of some kind fixed to it, deeply corroded. He had freed one corner; the end of it almost filled the base of the pit and it continued underground at the seaward end, longer than it was wide. If only he had more time, but while he thought of time passing, it passed. The sea was now around the lip of the hole, sneaking up, slipping in, leaving a little of itself behind as it retreated, next time daring to advance farther. Soon the pit would be as flooded as the cathedral trenches; then immersed, unreachable, until the tide went out again. There was nothing else he could do here now.

He knew what the situation was. The site possibly was on the reserve and the Oysters might legitimately claim that archaeologists had no right to dig there without permission which probably they would not have given; but because of Politi involvement Turcat had been able to avail himself of the rare, unprecedented opportunity to excavate a whole human skeleton in perfectly legal circumstances. And along with it he'd got a block of surrounding material which might contain all kinds of unguessed-at goodies; it would be taken back to the laboratory and they could work on it at leisure. But the conditions were not ideal. If Turcat had stopped to think, he might have calculated, as Merrick was calculating now, that at high tide the water would still be less than two metres deep above the excavation. Given time they could have constructed a coffer dam around it and excavated at their own pace, over a wider area. If Turcat hadn't been in such a mad enthusiasm to get at his skeleton he might have thought of this. It had been the first thing Merrick had thought of as he walked up the beach behind his superior, but behind his superior was where he always walked. Turcat did not welcome suggestions.

And, after all, they might be on the Briease Reserve, although if they were not they could have found themselves contending with the Parizo Corporation which, having given its name to the beach, might be proprietorial about it. He cleaned the trowel, returned it to its carrying case and retired to the foot of the dunes to sit beside Parizo Man.

It was impossible to tell what condition he was in, but even from the little of him that was exposed, cranium and kneecaps, it was clear that all they had here were bones. Amandine's surmise that it could not be a bog body had been correct. Bodies found in peat bogs were famously intact, from skin through to the stomach, even the last meal still in that stomach, undigested. A heart, a brain would survive, but not the bones; they would be reduced to sponge and the whole corpse squashed flat. From the evidence of the staring skull, this had not happened.

Beside him, from the edge of the contour-cloth, a crumb of peat dropped to the ground. Even in the light salt-sea wind the matter was drying out. Would a little illicit fretwork around the edges catch Turcat's attention? And even if it did, it would be too late to do anything about it, and if it was done properly, done well, even Turcat could not complain.

He took out his own knife, a small illegal imple-ment, and stroked it gently against the block. Little beads fell away, the kind that would drop off naturally as the peat dried. With the thinnest blade of the knife he tickled at the kneecaps, a sliver, a molecule, an atom, nothing that could not be attributed to nature's attrition.

His nose almost level with the surface, he detected movement in the left eye socket and for a clammy moment thought the thing was looking at him. Out of the socket came a little crab, no bigger than his thumbnail. It skittered across the block, its small dislo-cated universe. He scooped it up on the knife blade, tossed it into the foaming ripples, now only a few metres away, and returned quickly to the block. He had seen something else, something that no one had

had the time or the opportunity to notice. Although the peat was pressed into the lower halves of the sockets it was possible to make out that the right was smoothly concave at the rear, as if modelled with the casual but accurate twist of a thumb. Just above the level of the peat in the left eye socket was the suspicion of a fracture, even a hole, that could not be the superior orbital fissure. He explored tentatively with the tip of the blade. A new scratch, even a hair's breadth of a scratch, would be evidence of his depredations, but his instincts were correct. The blade slid softly in. The bone wall of the socket had been pierced.

He replaced the knife with his little finger, investigating the puncture with no more than the tip of his nail, which was describing an arc, perhaps part of a circle, of which eighty per cent was still buried. At some time something had entered Parizo Man's head through his left eye. Whether it had ever come out again was a question he dared not attempt to answer.

He could answer it if he were prepared to face down Turcat's wrath, but that might entail the loss of his job. It was a high price to satisfy mere curiosity – no, intellectual curiosity. Were he not curious he would not have applied to join the department in the first place, but it would be rank insubordination and there was a chance he might do some damage. He knew that he would have to wait to find out if Parizo Man had suffered a post-mortem penetration of his skull or whether there was, as Merrick suspected, a shattered exit wound in the back of the head. What he might have here was not simply an ancient death but an ancient murder.

Well, when the mystery was uncovered he would at least have the satisfaction of knowing that he had been on the scent all along. He might even risk indicating the hole in the eye socket to his irascible boss. He folded the knife and put it away. He would do no more than he had been told to do: look in the pit, which was now past looking into for several hours, and watch over Parizo Man.

As the policeman had said, Parizo Man wasn't going anywhere. If felons had an eye on him they would be as visible on the empty beach as Merrick was. No boats were approaching. To remove himself from temptation's reach he stood up and walked away from the peat block, the beach, the sea, to scramble through the loose sand and marram grass, up the cwm to the summit of the dunes.

The view on the landward side was as empty as the beach. Marshy and flat, the green turf was glazed with pools, bristling with clumps of rushes. About a kilometre away the pools grew larger, narrower, longer; standing among them, birches, alder, low-growing shrubs that thickened into the distance to become woodland. To the right the land rose a little but trees concealed what lay beyond. He knew he was looking at the great peat moss of Briease and that somewhere in it dwelled those Oysters with whom he ought to feel some kindred or affinity; but there was no evidence of human life.

Then a movement between two belts of trees caught

his eye, a steady indefinable twirling as if a turbine had spun loose and was wheeling across the landscape, but it lacked the triangularly regular thud of a turbine's three blades and it was too far, too fast, to identify. There was another, and another – windmills? wheels? moving at speed – now they were gone among the trees.

There had been no sound, the motion as insubstantial as that of winged insects. All he could hear was the wash of the sea, the thin high calling of marsh birds, the faintest rattle of wind breathing through the marram grass, and over all the steady turbulence from the groves of pylons on the wind farm that was felt rather than heard. But now he looked up. The sun was dropping through the western sky towards the birch trees, although there was plenty of daylight left. But it was turning pale, the light was cool and diffused, the air grew colder. Looking round at the beach, he saw that the eastern horizon had vanished. A sea fog was coming in.

Who would return for him now? If anyone had yet left the estuary they would surely turn homeward or put in to shelter. Unless the monorail was back in action, the station open at Eavrey Sound, twenty kilometres away, the nearest route back was by the highway that skirted the far side of the Briease Moss. He did not know how to cross it, how to begin to enter it. If he could make his way to the town he might ask for help, but he did not know how far, which way. And how would he account for his nefarious presence on Parizo Beach? One thing everyone knew, so he knew too, by hearsay, as everyone did: only Oysters born and bred could find their way through the marshes and the Moss. He might as well walk down the beach and into the sea as try to traverse it even by day, and the light was thickening.

In any case, there was no question of leaving without Parizo Man and he was going nowhere, encased in his shroud of peat. He still sat, unsurprisingly, where Merrick had left him by the case of tools at the foot of the dune.

Bodies had emerged from bogs as far back as anyone could remember. Merrick had seen pictures of the earliest ones, dark-brown slumbering victims of guessed-at ends: murder, execution, sacrifice, accident. They lay, always they lay, prone, supine, flexed, extended, whole. The guardian of Parizo Beach was none of these things. They would not know what he was until they freed him from his shroud, but while the light lasted Merrick could scrape, just a little.

It was too dark now to continue, night and fog combining into soup. Merrick waited, feet drawn up, back against the dune, until he noticed that he was sitting exactly as his companion sat, had sat at the moment of his death, sat now perhaps hundreds of years later. And had *he* argued with himself that someone would come for him soon?

No one was coming for them now. An hour ago Turcat had muttered in his ear that seagoing conditions were impossible for small craft.

'Tell me about it,' Merrick said rudely, emboldened by distance.

'If they improve we'll be along in the morning.'

'And if they don't improve?'

There was no answer. The receiver fell silent. He tapped the stud in his earlobe, an atavistic response to malfunction, as once people had kicked recalcitrant machines. It produced no result; the stud was not malfunctioning. Turcat had said what he had to say and cut out. When Merrick called him back there was no reply.

No one else had troubled to get in touch; there was no one he could call. He was used to being invisible but not so invisible that he was forgotten. Anyone but Turcat would have recalled that he was alone, without food or shelter. Turcat had lived too long among bones, which needed neither. How satisfying it would be to leave a really coruscating tirade in his office message bank; how satisfying now, how short-sighted.

True darkness had fallen by the time the tide reached its high point and the temperature had fallen with it. In the murk he hollowed out a little grave in the dunes where a natural cleft had formed between two clumps of marram. He would not be as well sheltered as on the landward side of the dune, but to cross over would be a dereliction of duty, abandoning Parizo Man, the one reason for his being there. As the cold increased, his clothes were acclimatizing to contain his body heat and in any case, years of exposure to wind, rain, ice, sleet, snow on Turcat's excavations had rendered him hardier than the average citizen who dived into the souterrain at the first chill breath of winter.

He pulled up his hood and lay down to sleep in the sandy depression. It was hard to believe that this time last night he had fretted in the over-warm auditorium of the Ayckbourn Theatre, watching a landsman's impression of life on a sea coast.

The tide was on its way out again. He did not see the fog lift at midnight, the moon shine down on the figure that kept its watch beside him. When a third party appeared and stood a while in the moonlight surveying both of them, still he did not stir, and never knew it.

When he woke it was light and clear and if his night in the grave had given him bad dreams he did not remember them. People who knew what he did for a living, even if they did not actively disapprove, assumed that his daily contact with the world of the dead must inflict him with nightmares and a queasy waking conscience. But this morning he was only hungry and unbearably thirsty. The night was over, the sun well above the horizon, the sky cloudless.

He eased his way out of the grave and walked down the beach to meet the incoming sea. The other grave where they had excavated yesterday was filled with water but the tide, in its coming and going, had done a little excavating of its own, and the sharp edges of the cut peat were sucked smooth.

An hour later, sooner than he had expected, he heard the sound of a marine engine and made out a dark speck to the south, where the Nox shone white in the sunlight. As it approached he walked out along the jetty, waving, and saw that behind the boat was another, smaller craft, with only one occupant. The first boat, a substantial, high-sided vessel, contained Professor Dieter Ehrhardt, who held the Chair of European History, Turcat and Paul Tudor, another low life form from the department, hauled along, no doubt, to help Merrick with the shoulder work. In the second boat was the tiresome round-headed man who had sat beside Amandine at the theatre.

Tudor was first on to the jetty, even before the helmsman had moored securely. Turcat and Ehrhardt followed more cautiously and they all processed along the boards, leaving the round-headed man to his own perilous devices.

'Who is that guy?' Merrick hissed to Tudor. 'Do you know him? What's he doing here?'

'He's the Briease representative from the Bureau of Aboriginal Affairs,' Tudor said. 'Orlando Mirandola.'

'He's not big enough to have a name that long. What do we call him?'

'Don't make jokes, he could be trouble,' Tudor said, under his breath.

'Why did they bring him along, then? Is that my breakfast you've got there?'

Tudor handed over a flask and canister. 'No one else thought of it.'

'Of course not. I'll remember you in my dissertation.'

'We didn't *bring* him along. You weren't forgotten last night—'

'Turcat came through to say I'd have to wait.'

50

'Then things got awkward. This Mirandola called in demanding to know what was going on and when we left this morning he tacked himself on behind us.'

'What do you mean, he wanted to know what was going on?'

'He already knew about the skeleton.'

'How? You mean the Oysters had found it too?'

'Listen, if it's on Oyster land – don't let *him* hear you calling them Oysters.'

'I never call them Oysters.'

'If it's on their land they have to give permission for its removal and he has to authorize it.'

'But we *have* removed it. Isn't that why Turcat's come back for it?'

'Yes. You'd think, wouldn't you, that there'd be a few Oysters around, if they're so worried about losing it. Is that it, up there by the sand hills?'

'Go and have a look,' Merrick said. A high-pitched yawning voice came boring up the beach towards them: Orlando Mirandola, already causing trouble.

'This is highly questionable,' he was saying. 'Absolutely contrary to statutory practice. Nothing should have been removed without prior consultation. I don't know how many regulations have been violated. By rights I should insist that you return the remains to the site of discovery until proper authorization has been obtained.'

He had reached the edge of the pit. 'Where is it?'

Turcat indicated the block of peat. 'Which regulations in particular? Exactly? De Harnac and my sister discovered a human burial. They reported it to the

Politi – I trust you don't regard that as a breached regulation?'

'They were morally and statutorily obligated to inform the Reserve Police—'

'Why?' Turcat said. 'We are not on the reserve here. Where precisely does the reserve begin? If there's supposed to be a boundary I don't see it.'

'Just one centimetre inside the boundary—'

'Yes, but so far as we know it may be one centimetre *outside* the boundary. In any case, they reported it to the Politi, who came out the following morning with an archaeologist, me, who was given permission to excavate.'

'By persons with no authority to give permission. I insist you return it.'

'Don't be ridiculous. This is the first shore burial we've found.'

Ehrhardt weighed in diplomatically. 'You must see, Mirandola, that conditions here are not what any of us is accustomed to. The body had to be exhumed by law. Even if it had not obviously been of interest to us the Politi would have had to remove it anyway. The site lies below the high tide mark. Twice a day it's under water. The remains can't be examined here. Did you find anything else?' he said, addressing Merrick and turning slightly so that he stood between him and Mirandola.

Merrick tried not to move his lips. 'The sea is starting to wash out the sides of the hole. There's a wooden box down there, I can't tell how big.'

Turcat glanced into the water-filled pit. 'That idiot won't see it yet.'

The idiot had been strutting up the beach to examine the body but stopped instead to look at Merrick.

'Who is this person?'

Merrick assumed that Mirandola would recognize him from their encounter at the Ayckbourn but Mirandola had been too occupied larging it among the balletomanes to notice him, it seemed.

'He's my graduate assistant,' Turcat said.

And not even worth naming, Merrick thought. Mirandola swept on by to view the skeleton. They heard his cry. 'It has been *interfered* with.'

'Why has he got himself involved?' Turcat demanded. 'Has he got any authority to stop us? He can't really force us to put it back, can he?'

'Possibly,' Ehrhardt mused, 'but he's on his own at the moment. Two of us, these two lads, Tudor and—?'

'Korda.' Did anyone remember him?

'– and that bruiser with the boathook who brought us here. I presume he's on your side.'

'You're not proposing violence?' Turcat said primly.

'Of course not, but Mirandola isn't in a position to do anything but declaim at us. Later, if he's got the energy and the patience, he can legally insist that our man is returned – *if* it turns out that he is on Briease land. Although if, as you say, he's pre-Anarchy, they've got no claim on him at all.'

'What about the box?' Merrick said. He could see that Ehrhardt was dying to go fishing for the box but dared not go anywhere near the pit while Mirandola was exercising his rights on behalf of his Oysters. No one was likely to see it now; the tide was drawing near.

'A few more days of this and the sea will do our excavating for us. There may be more than one body,' Ehrhardt said.

'*How* did Mirandola know what we were doing?'

'While inspecting storm damage with the mayor he saw what he thought might be a skull. Presumably someone of the Oyster persuasion saw what you were up to yesterday and word must have got to him. Doesn't he look like someone waiting for The Word? Any real or imagined insult to the Aboriginals and it justifies his existence.'

'Nothing else does,' Turcat said sourly as Mirandola bobbed up under his elbow.

'I strongly advise you to come with me to Briease and make representations to the mayor.'

'Isn't that what you're for?' Turcat said.

'You do not understand,' Mirandola said passionately. 'You do *not* understand Aboriginal reverence for the dead. Archaeology may be a lost science in the United States of Europe, but these people have never lost touch with their past.'

'Well, they certainly lost touch with this bit of it,' Ehrhardt said, strolling over to the block of peat and patting Parizo Man on the head. 'If it *is* theirs. We're taking it back with us, and if it subsequently turns out that this excavation is on the Briease Reserve then I'm sure that the BAA will have the authority to get it returned. I'm equally sure that your friend the mayor will be impressed by the reverence with which we treat it. Are you going to Briease now— Look out!'

Mirandola, skipping about to get his balance before launching into his next attack, stepped back a pace and teetered on the slippery lip of the pit, arms wind-milling as he struggled to stay upright. They all stepped forward to grab him, all noting with satisfaction the certainty in his eyes that they were united in the intent to push him in.

Whatever he had been going to say remained unsaid. Instead he relieved himself of a few more standard protests, exchanged a last look with the sightless eyes in the peat block and stumped away up the dunes.

Merrick followed him. 'Is that the way to Briease?'

Mirandola did not bother to look round as he answered. 'It's the quickest way for those who know it. I wouldn't advise a stranger to try it.'

Merrick watched him slither down the landward side of the dune. A few metres from the foot was a ditch or a trench, almost hidden in the yellowing long grass. He crossed, apparently by a plank bridge although Merrick could not see it, clambered up the far side and, without looking back, struck out across the green carpet of the marsh.

Watching him Merrick was glad he had not tried it himself yesterday, and reluctantly admitted that Mirandola had been right when he said it would be inadvisable for a stranger to try it. He clearly knew exactly where he was going, but his route never ran straight for more than four or five metres. He made acute-angled diversions, circuitous oxbows, sometimes around a pool or to skirt a clump of rushes or a bilberry bush, but more often for no discernible reason. Either he was putting on a demonstration of his arcane knowledge for Merrick's benefit, or he had a genuine reason for avoiding what looked to Merrick like smooth green sward. He had obviously done it before, and often.

As Mirandola approached the nearest belt of trees and became hard to distinguish, Merrick started to turn away, back down towards the shore, but as before a faint movement caught his eye. From among the alders, where he had seen it yesterday, emerged the enigmatic twirling thing, heading towards Mirandola, making detours like him, but faster and straighter.

Perhaps it was some kind of a swamp demon come to drive him to his doom. Merrick peered and blinked and peered again, but in the instant of his blinking the twirling thing had ceased to twirl and all he could see, with difficulty, was two human figures, Mirandola and another. And then, soon, he could see no one.

'Let's burn his bastard boat while he's away,' said Ehrhardt, down on the beach.

Chapter Three

They could see him more clearly now, whittled out of the peat block down to the arm bones on the left side. Merrick had been hoping that Turcat would share his curiosity about the skull, thereby coming to share his speculations about how Parizo Man had met his end, but Turcat was going in laterally. He wanted a whole profile of the skeleton's position before he began to dismantle it. Ehrhardt came down from time to time to see how things were going. Both men were in a desperate hurry to learn as much as they could before Mirandola tried to put a stop to the work by reclaiming their prize on behalf of his Aboriginals.

'He's unlike anything we've encountered before,' Turcat said. 'The oldest bodies on record have been horizontal, in various positions.'

'By record you mean our photographic archive,' Ehrhardt said. 'Here in the faculty? Is that really all there is?'

'Since Comfort and Joy, yes. I got everything I could out of the stacks but it all corroborates what I said. Peruvian human sacrifices were found sitting, but not inhumations.'

Merrick had seen the photographic archive and the rare books in the library stacks and knew that Turcat was right. Parizo Man gazed moodily ahead, leaning back, one arm at his side, while Turcat and Merrick scraped and squirted at the peat, freeing him millimetre by millimetre. If only Turcat would get at that hole in the orbital cavity that Merrick was sure they would find. When was he going to start on the skull? All that could be seen so far was the merest hint of cheekbone, the hinge of the lower jaw, the gentle bulge of the parietal bone.

At comparable speed Ehrhardt negotiated with various authorities for retrospective permission to excavate, complaining that in the past, by which he meant centuries ago, the discovery would have been greeted with excitement; news media would have clamoured for information. He and Turcat knew that the only people likely to be remotely interested were the Oysters, and daily awaited a deputation from Briease.

When it arrived it was a deputation of one, Orlando Mirandola. Merrick, coming up for air at mid-morning, found him sitting in the reception area glowering at the information wall, which was relaying its customary obsession with the weather. Every time Mirandola crossed his mind, which was frequently, he thought of the flooded pit on Parizo Beach, the wooden box, the possible treasures awaiting them out of reach. Mirandola, true to his word, had lodged a formal complaint. The department had excavated Aboriginal land without permission and desecrated the dead. Then he gave Turcat and Parizo Man their first publicity by rehearsing his complaint, fully and often, on newscasts.

'What kind of barbarity are we returning to,' he had demanded, 'when graves can be broken open with impunity, corpses laid to rest for eternity by trusting relatives hauled out and hacked about in the name of science?' If this were science, he iterated, better it stayed lost. Had they made no moral progress since the days when such things were taken for granted, encouraged even? Digging up ruined cathedrals was one thing, but human remains? They'd be eating human flesh at this rate, he implied.

Merrick ducked back down the stairs before Mirandola could turn his head. Turcat, nibbling methodically at the great trochanter, registered his return without looking up.

'Break over already?'

Merrick had been out of the room for barely thirty seconds but time ran on different gears down in the basement.

'I've only just stopped work. Mirandola's up in reception.'

'What does he want?'

'I didn't ask, he didn't even see me. I thought you'd want to know before I had to say anything.'

Turcat did not praise his tact and forethought. The hand wielding the scalpel remained stationary, centimetres from the bone. 'Find out if he wants to see me or Professor— No, wait, I'll go.'

He brushed past Merrick, pressing the scalpel into his hand as he went by. Merrick took this as a silent command to carry on with the work, but deciding to misunderstand for once, he waited until Turcat reached the top of the stairs and then followed him halfway to where he could hear without being seen if Turcat left the door open. It stood ajar. Merrick went all the way up, and by leaning against the wall could see Turcat's back and the three-quarters profile of his visitor.

Turcat was dissembling smoothly. 'I didn't know you were on the premises. I've been half-expecting a visit.'

'Good day,' Mirandola answered levelly. 'Have you found anything interesting yet?'

'Every cubic millimetre is interesting.'

Merrick wondered why exactly Mirandola was there. He did not seem to be working up to one of his harangues. Turcat intended to find out.

'Have you got the peat off yet?'

'About twenty-five per cent. There's no telling what we may find buried with him.'

'Grave goods?'

What does he know about grave goods? Merrick wondered. What does he know about anything? What is he trying to find out? Does he want to know something that Turcat doesn't want to tell him?

'Possibly grave goods if it dates from a period when such practices were current – pre-Christian at any rate. The pagan dead were given food and personal possessions for the afterlife. Weapons even. Their horses might be sacrificed and buried with them.'

'You're expecting to find a horse?'

Turcat ignored this. Merrick thought it might be

60

worth adding to the records: *13 October 2255: Orlando Mirandola made a joke* – or was it a joke?

'Also hunting dogs,' Turcat continued imperturbably. 'Sometimes warriors, wives, concubines to provide their lord with every comfort in the afterlife – it would *be* a life, you see. More of the same only better, not some vague spiritual hangover. Many cultures believed that the soul must make a journey across a river to reach the land of the dead and money was buried with the corpse to pay the ferryman: a coin or a pearl might be placed in the mouth. That is broadly what we mean by grave goods. But it's possible that our man wasn't actually buried—'

'He buried himself?' Two jokes in as many minutes; what could he be on, toxic frogs?

'He may have died in a remote spot, in a snowdrift perhaps, although we can't tell. His clothes don't appear to have survived – or he died stark naked.'

'In a snowdrift? Couldn't he have been sunbathing? He was on a beach.'

'It's unlikely to have been a beach then. He could have been kilometres inland. The position of the body doesn't suggest burial as such.'

'You can tell that much?'

'Much more.' Imperceptibly the conversation was thawing. After all, Merrick thought, these are educated adults, not two kids having a quarrel. Who could be educated and not curious? 'Do you want to come and look?'

There was something disarming about the way Mirandola jumped to his feet. Although Ehrhardt and

61

Turcat habitually referred to him as the little bastard he was taller than he seemed and obviously older than he looked. The littleness was in his officiousness, but there was no sign of that now as he followed Turcat down the staircase to the basement laboratory.

Having assumed that this would be the last thing that Turcat wanted, since he had gone up with the intention of heading Mirandola off, Merrick had only just time to dive back down the stairs, but when the two men walked in he was assiduously scraping.

The underground room was lit carefully to keep the temperature low and a fine spray played over the block of peat where Parizo Man lounged on the central workbench. At night he was swaddled in wet cloths. Turcat did not want random bits dropping off as the soil dried out.

'He's so small.'

'That's an illusion – the way he's sitting. And he's been a little compressed – think of the weight he's been under: peat, sand, water. But by the length of his femur – the thighbone – we reckon he must have been close to two metres when upright.'

Mirandola's hand went out involuntarily and Merrick twitched the scalpel out of the way as he withdrew it sheepishly.

'You can touch,' Turcat said kindly, as if to an overexcited child.

He did not actively want to, Merrick could tell, but eventually Mirandola laid a tentative finger on the acromion process of the shoulder blade.

'How long will it take to get him out completely?'

'Days, at the rate we're going. I told you, it's not just him, it's what he may have with him.'

'The grave goods.'

'Your words, not mine. That's what I was explaining upstairs. If he wasn't in a grave as such, there won't be any. But he may have had things with him: money, weapons, food.'

'Will that have survived?'

'The food? No, unless it was meat on the bone.'

As they continued to ignore him, Merrick resumed his scraping. He might have been an item of basic equipment, something that needed very little maintenance, for all the notice they took of him. He was used to it from Turcat but he had met Mirandola socially at the theatre and adversarially on Parizo Beach. The man might at least have acknowledged his presence. How could Mirandola tell he wasn't worth looking at?

'How old is he?'

'That's going to take time. It's still possible to carbon date but we don't have the facilities here. I'd have to take samples and send them to Paris or Cracow.'

'Carbon?'

'Radioactive carbon, naturally occuring in all living matter, including you. Its decay can be measured. With luck, though, his right hand, if he has one, will be clutching a diary with, say, the thirteenth of October nineteen seventy-eight written up but nothing on the fourteenth—'

'Why nineteen seventy-eight?'

'Any date would do, twenty twenty-three, twenty-one seventy-eight – which is more likely.'

'How old do you *think* he is?'

'I can't begin to guess; I mean that literally.'

'Really? Not even a guess?'

'Guessing is not what we do. Why is it so important – to you?'

'It will be very important to the Aboriginal peoples.'

Now we're coming to it, Merrick thought. *Scrape. Scrape.*

'But only, presumably, if it turns out that the body was on their land. Has anyone taken measurements yet?' Turcat, by his voice, was also on the alert.

'Yes,' Mirandola said. 'The area has been thoroughly surveyed.' The little bastard was back, a full head shorter than the eager young man who had gazed at the emergent skeleton, and inflating as they watched with self-importance. 'Any further discoveries will be excavated under the jurisdiction of the Bureau of Aboriginal Affairs. By Aboriginal archaeologists.'

'There aren't any!' This tactless remark was wrung from Turcat by the dread, evidently, of what might pass for an archaeologist among the Oysters, and what one such might do.

The wooden box, Merrick thought. *Scrape. Scrape. Scrape.*

'Now, how would you know that?' Mirandola said. 'These prejudiced assumptions are what Aboriginal peoples have had to battle against for decades.'

'Is there a Mr Archaeologist among them?'

'Is that meant to be funny?'

'Oh, come on.' Turcat's voice was rising. 'Their names – Cartwright, Cooper, Thatcher, Glover, Ploughman

. . . do you imagine they've ever made a glove or thatched a roof? Do you know what thatch is? Do they?'

'The reason the reserves were established was because these people, their forebears, wanted to keep what was historically theirs: names, currency, weights and measures—'

'Language?'

'Everyone speaks it.'

'I'm surprised they didn't demand a law forbidding the rest of us to.'

'Folk customs—'

'*Folk customs?* Like what? Dancing round tree trunks in spring? Lighting bonfires in autumn, roasting effigies? Sacrificing virgins?'

'They don't do any of that. I'm shocked to hear a historian suggest it.'

Merrick too was faintly shocked. He excused it on the grounds of Turcat's anger and anxiety about the fate of his skeleton at the hands of the little bastard. Turcat, however, had a different grievance.

'I'm not a historian—'

Mirandola droned on, 'In recognition of the suffering and suppression they had endured at the hands of the federal authorities they were finally granted recognition as a distinct race. They are proud to call themselves Aboriginal, the First Nation.'

'Inglish. So proud that they live in a swamp and pretend to be Anglo-Saxons. Distinct race? They're practically a different species. What's so special about being Inglish? With the size of their gene pool they

65

soon will be a different species. What are they trying to do, breed themselves back into Cro-Magnons?'

'I would have thought an anthropologist – isn't that what you call yourself—?'

'You just called me a historian. I thought you meant it as an insult.'

'– an anthropologist would understand. You study human history. They live it.'

'They imitate it. Exactly *who* is proposing to excavate Parizo Beach?'

'That's really none of your business now,' Mirandola said, glistening slightly with self-satisfaction.

Merrick heard a pleading note enter Turcat's voice. 'But I could work alongside them—'

'Guiding the poor primitives with your superior knowledge? They don't *want* you working alongside them. Do you ever ask yourself *why* archaeology became a lost science? Because people came to recognize it for the disgusting desecration it is. Disturbing the dead and worse – worse' – he was incoherent with ardour – '*putting them on public display.*'

'You were keen enough to come and have a look,' Turcat said.

'I am not the public.'

'The public is millions of Orlando Mirandolas. So, if your Aboriginals are so revolted by the thought of disturbing the dead, why do they want to dig up the beach?'

'To see what is there. Not necessarily bodies.'

'But it's an impossible site, under water twice a day. They don't know how—'

'Neither do you.'

Gotcha, Merrick thought. *Scrape. Scrape.*

'There may not be anything else to find.'

'So your interest in the site will be at an end, will it not, Dr Turcat? As it will be in any case when he' – Mirandola waved towards Parizo Man – 'is returned to his origins.'

It took a moment or two to sink in. 'They're going to put him back?'

'You don't imagine my visit today was to see what you were doing.'

'Why did you come down here, then?'

Mirandola ignored that. 'I came to inform Professor Ehrhardt that he will shortly be summoned before a magistrate, who will examine submissions from both sides. Given current legislation I don't think there's any doubt that the department will be required to surrender the skeleton and everything found with it.'

'Not to be buried on the beach.'

'It will be treated with respect,' Mirandola said. 'And given a proper burial according to Aboriginal rites. Where, I really couldn't say.'

Turcat had just enough fight left in him to mutter, 'Is Professor Ehrhardt expecting you?'

'No, I had just asked to see him when you came up the stairs; I'd been told to wait.'

'How long?' Malice was poor consolation for what Turcat must be feeling but there was method in it. Merrick saw what he was getting at at the same time Mirandola did. They had been in the basement for a quarter of an hour at least.

'Ten minutes.'

'And no one knows where you are? Shame. He'll have left by now. He had to be at the Senate Height by eleven hundred.'

'Can I catch him there?'

'If you know where to look. I can't help you, I'm afraid.'

'You did this on purpose,' Mirandola said, losing several centimetres more.

'Did what? Lured you down here with promises of history and hot sex? I didn't even know you were in the building.'

'You must have known.'

'How could I? You trot off to the Senate. I'm sure someone will be able to find Professor Ehrhardt for you, if you really do want to see him. Admit it, you could easily have contacted him through the usual channels – as the court will. You didn't have to come here at all, you just wanted to find out what I was up to.'

'And you showed me.'

It had been a serious mistake to show him, Merrick was sure. Turcat had seen that Mirandola's interest was genuine, evidently hoping to convert that interest to sympathy for the advancement of science. Whatever he had converted it to, it was not sympathy.

When Mirandola had taken himself away up the stairs, Turcat picked up a scalpel and advanced upon Parizo Man. Blade poised, he stopped and looked across at Merrick.

'*Festina lente*,' he said. 'Do you know what that means?'

'It's Greek? Latin?' Merrick's Latin and Greek were largely biological. *Festina lente* might be an anatomical term such as acromion process and great trochanter, which he had learned as he uncovered the bone structures they named.

'It's Latin: make haste slowly. That's what we have to do now, Korda. If the arguments go against us and our man is confiscated we're going to get as much out of him first as we can. Cut him free, examine him, take samples, date him. Deconstruct, reconstruct. We might even determine what he looked like. Once there were specialists who could rebuild a face from a skull. All this may be impossible after the court proceedings and judgement.'

Merrick seized his chance. 'Just from a skull?' He leaned forward and looked fully into the eye sockets, holding his gaze theatrically until Turcat showed signs of noticing that he had seen something. 'There's a – a – this orbit, the left one, it looks as if it's been fractured.'

'Are you trying to account for damage inflicted by yourself?' Turcat inquired.

'I haven't touched it,' Merrick lied, 'but come round and look. Could it be a wound?'

Crowding Merrick out of the way, Turcat directed a slender beam of light into the socket. For the first time Merrick saw clearly that he had been correct all along. The peat bed still came halfway up the sockets, but the upper surfaces had been thoroughly scoured by the tides. The small cavity that he had suspected, on the left side, was clearly visible.

'It's a puncture, isn't it?' he said.

'It seems to be.'

Merrick was sure that Turcat was even now rewriting the last few minutes to exclude him from the discovery so that he could point it out to Ehrhardt as his own. In Turcat's view, Merrick had as it were gone off at the right moment like the flood alarm system.

'It could be what killed him. Maybe a shot – the bullet might still be in there. And if it isn't' – he could feel Turcat's irritation radiating from him like heat but bashed on regardless – 'there'll be an exit wound at the back, won't there?'

He moved round to look, as if for the first time.

'There's nothing showing above the surface. The gun must have been fired at a downward angle – by somebody taller – or he was sitting when he was killed, looking up.'

'Gun? Somebody taller?' Turcat was filing it all away for future reference. 'Stop hypothesizing. We haven't got time. Extrapolate from facts. Let's get at the facts.' Even while he spoke he was making delicate tweaks with his scalpel into the eye socket. Merrick hovered, not daring to hope. 'Well, get on with it,' Turcat said.

'What procedure?'

'Just start at the top and work down, keep going, think of those Oysters swarming all over Parizo Beach, digging like badgers, no clue about what they're destroying as they go.'

Seeing that Turcat had taken possession of the eye

70

socket Merrick understood that he might move round to the less interesting bit at the back.

'Do you think they've started digging?' He started scraping.

'I don't want to think.'

'There's that box I saw—'

'Oh, don't go *on*,' Turcat said in anguish. 'So few resources, so little money, such a small staff, and everything carried on – under *siege*.'

Scrape. Scrapescrape. Scrape. Scrape.

Everything carried on in the face of public opinion that ranged from apathy through disapproval to downright hostility. Mirandola had not spoken only for himself when he'd indicated that there was a world of difference between digging up a cathedral, dislodging a few bones in the process, and exhuming a whole skeleton.

An earlier public's opinion had closed the museums; looking at the dead, imprisoned for that purpose in display cases, had no place in the twenty-first century. It had gone the way of gladiatorial combat, bear-baiting, fox-hunting and public executions. And since it was the mummies, the bog bodies, the shrunken heads and skeletal remains that had attracted the spectators and the funding, the doors closed. Voyeurs could sate their prurient curiosity in cyberspace. Everyone else was left to believe in the disgust they were told they had felt. The bodies had been returned to their countries of origin, where these still existed, and reinterred. Sculptures and artefacts went with them. Then the great empty buildings that had housed the collections came down as the cathedrals came down, and the sum of the knowledge of those spacious times lay packed flat in the university stacks and there stayed until Professor Ehrhardt, learning that a tower was due for demolition to make room for another tower, had taken advantage of a spell of weather inimical to builders to plead for a chance to see what lay beneath.

That had been fifteen years ago. He had not been a professor then, only a lecturer in an undersubscribed specialism, history. But he had posted an invitation to fellow academics and students: *Help rediscover archaeology, the lost science.* One of the few who had responded was a young graduate, Rémy Turcat.

Now Ehrhardt ruled history, Turcat had his own department, a few staff, a few students. It was mainly because of the department and its reputation that the Senate, half-embarrassed by its activities, had seized the chance to turf out the entire faculty from the main university complex, which was why they all huddled together in a state of general inadequacy, Ehrhardt on the upper floors, Turcat on the first floor and the basement of a twanging structure, Millennium House, also known as Foster's Folly, two blocks behind the Central Plaza and leased by the administration for unpopular overspills like themselves and the faculty of early religions. The building had a preservation order on it as a Structure of Historical Importance, otherwise known as a Pile of SHI.

'Preserved as a warning,' said the dean of engineering, 'never to build something like that again.

72

Anything that can go wrong will go wrong. QED.'

As Merrick scraped at the back of the head he risked an occasional look to where the face of Parizo Man was surfacing under Turcat's scalpel, but even the eyes, free of their casing, told him nothing more than he had surmised. The back of the left socket was pierced by a round hole. When they got down to the jaws they would uncover a deceptively cheerful rictus, but he knew from pictures that, even with the skin on, the face in death was no guarantee of the manner of that death. Tollund Man, from the drowned peat bog of Denmark, eyes closed, lips slightly pursed, spoke of pious repose, an easy end, belied by the halter around his neck that had strangled him. Others of his kind smiled peacefully above slit throats; a young girl pinned under a stone seemed no more than asleep. One woman's limbs had been pegged down with crooked stakes before she was covered with branches. Had she gone into the peat cutting alive? What had her last sight been?

Scrape. Scrape.

And then, nothing to scrape.

Turcat, hearing his exclamation, skipped to his side. 'I knew it!'

Who knew it? Merrick inquired silently. He had uncovered what he had been expecting. Turcat, so far as he knew, had not been expecting anything. The back of the skull lay exposed, seamed by the sagittal suture, where the parietals met, down to the occipital bone, but there was no occipital bone. The parietals ended in ragged crenellations; below them was nothing but impacted peat. As Merrick watched, powerless to intervene and repossess his area of operations, Turcat scooped recklessly at the peat.

'Took out the cervical vertebrae as well.'

'What did?'

'The bullet.'

'It was a bullet, then?'

'Shot through the eye,' Turcat said, and ushered Merrick round for an official view of the hole in the eye socket.

Turcat leaned forward and addressed the skull. 'Well, I wonder what you were up to when they caught you?'

All court business had been suspended during the power failures and there was a backlog, giving them perhaps six days at most with Parizo Man. In spite of Mirandola's insistence that the Parizo body was a matter of the utmost urgency, the magistrates disagreed and it remained at the back of the queue. The Briease representative of the Bureau of Aboriginal Affairs had to content himself with denunciations on newscasts.

Assistants were co-opted, the idea being that Turcat and Merrick might operate shifts and get some rest, but neither of them could bear to be away from the basement for long, returning jealously at every opportunity. Turcat declined Ehrhardt's offer of assistance; Merrick resented Tudor taking a turn. From somewhere Turcat obtained a folding bed, itself an object of archaeological interest, and set it up in the stockroom that led to the flood escape.

Merrick, who had supposed that Turcat would jump at any opportunity to oust him from the basement, came to realize that his work must be valued since he was the one, of all the assistants, who got to take turns with the bed. He would have been prepared to sleep on the floor under a bench. Turcat's indication that whichever of them was free should make use of the bed pleased Merrick almost more than a rise in salary would have done.

They were cutting down to the pelvic area when they made the discovery. Hourly, more facts were coming to light. Without the earthen shroud to support it, the skinless skeleton was being transferred, bone by bone, to an adjacent light table and laid out like a kit, ready for assembly: at one end the skull with its lower jaw standing in front of the upper like the prow of a boat, occupying the space vacated by the missing cervicals. Down from that the dorsal and lumbar vertebrae were lined up with a collarbone and shoulder blade either side and the disconnected ribs, with the three long bones and the whole hand of the left arm, the humerus only of the right. The left arm had been lying extended by the side of the body, the right was bent across what would have been its lap.

Every stage of his deconstruction had been recorded photographically. Parizo Man had not been sitting peacefully when he died; he had not been prepared for death and he had not been prepared for burial. Merrick was forced to admit that Turcat had been right to go in from the side, for scrap by scrap they had uncovered the profile of the dead man, leaning back as if against a sloping surface. The remains of the sloping surface had yielded minute splinters of bone, the relics of the blasted skull; most of them would still be embedded in the peat of Parizo Beach if the sea had not already washed them out. His lower jaw had hung gaping. No one had bothered to support it – or perhaps he had died screaming.

On one side of the skull were laid out three bent and blackened hoops which Merrick had picked out of the peat where the ears would have been, but he had found no communications stud. Two rings that had encircled the phalanges of the left hand now lay beside it. Below the lumbar vertebrae was a gap calculated by Turcat to allow for pelvis, sacrum and thighbones; then two lower legs, tibia and fibula of each, crowned with the kneecaps, the tesserae of each foot laid out with exemplary care.

'I said we'd treat it with reverence,' Turcat murmured, nudging the right big toe into position with a spatula.

'Professor Ehrhardt said that,' Merrick remarked daringly. Their eyes met briefly and Turcat's face broke into an unexpected grin. He tapped the toes.

'*This little piggy went to market* – where have I heard that?'

'*This little piggy stayed home*,' Merrick said. '*This little piggy had roast beef, this little piggy had none. And this little piggy went wee wee wee all the way home.*'

'Where did *you* hear it?' Turcat asked curiously.

'I must have read it somewhere.'

'But you were singing it.'

'Then I must have heard it. Where did you come across it?'

'Can't imagine.' Turcat had no need to imagine. No one was going to query his suspiciously intimate knowledge of arcane Inglish nursery rhymes, but he might even now be filing Merrick's own suspiciously intimate knowledge as a mark against him in the future. 'Come on,' he said. 'We're on the last leg now, literally. Remember, reverence at all times.' Success was making him frisky. No pun had ever crossed his lips in Merrick's hearing.

As the skeleton grew on the light table, Parizo Man had been whittled down to a skimpy clod of earth which contained his pelvis and sacrum, the bones and hand of the lower right arm and his two femurs, the long thighbones that rose at an angle of forty-five degrees like the drumsticks of an overcooked chicken. They were working on a femur each, almost at the point where the bones could be lifted away. Turcat was farther in; Merrick's femur supported the right hand; the right elbow protruded on Turcat's side. In the event Merrick had to pick out the whole hand before he could get at the thigh; its great trochanter had been twinkling at him almost from the beginning. He eased it out to dust it over a tray and laid it punctiliously alongside the right thighbone on the light table. The skeleton was almost complete, lacking only its pelvis, sacrum and coccyx, the vestigial tail. He went straight back to the depleted block but already the friable soil, dried out now by warmth and handling, was falling away unaided to reveal the twin pelvic crests and the sacrum wedged between them. Also revealed was a little crescent of solid substance that was not bone.

He took up the spatula again and began etching around the object; a pebble, a claw . . . ? As soon as he touched it he knew he ought to be using a brush.

'What have you got there?' Turcat, sensing his hesitation, was at his side.

'I don't know. It's just started to show.'

Not long ago Turcat would have nudged him aside with a word if not with an elbow, and taken over. Now he simply held out a brush and directed his light at the place where Merrick was working. 'Keep going.'

It was glass, the base of a tiny phial less than a centimetre across, and as it fell into Merrick's cupped hand something else fell with it, a crusted whitish sphere the size of a pea.

'Ball bearing?'

'I don't think so – keep going – careful.' Turcat picked up the sphere with forceps and took it over to the light table. Merrick brushed with agonizing restraint at the place from which the objects had appeared. The remains of the phial came next – had *he* cracked it with some ill-considered movement? – one end sealed. Whole, it would be no longer than the top joint of his forefinger, and inside it, large enough to be wedged into place, were four more of the spheres; *fossilized* peas?

As Turcat came back the door from the staircase opened and Ehrhardt walked in.

'Found something?'

Turcat faced him; the little orb, now brushed clean and smooth, rolled in his palm. It was not wholly white, but creamy, flushed pink on one side as if sun-ripened, tinged with blue on the other.

'I think we have a moss pearl.'

'By god, so you have,' Ehrhardt said. 'Where—?'

'From the pelvic cavity,' Merrick spoke out of turn, but the find – pearls, peas, ball bearings – was *his* find. 'Under the sacrum.'

'Don't be facetious.'

'He isn't,' Turcat said. 'That's exactly where we found it.'

'Surely a myth—'

'That it grew there? Oh yes.'

'There are four more, in this.' Merrick held out the broken phial.

'In the pelvic cavity?'

'Why did you think I was being facetious?' Merrick said.

They turned and looked at him. Ehrhardt harrumphed apologetically. 'Thought you were trying it on. There's a tasteless old calumny which I did not expect to hear repeated, certainly not in my own faculty, that moss pearls grew in Oysters – of the kind we have living in the Briease Moss. In fact, between the onset of global warming in the late twentieth century and the loss of the Gulf Stream in the twenty-second, the Fiji clam and other tropical molluscs began to establish themselves in British waters. With the cooling of our seas they disappeared

79

again. You can tell a moss pearl by its colouring, distinctive, unique, but it grew in one of the Ostreidae, not in homo sapiens. I believe the things were first observed in the twenty-one forties. Now, look at these teeth.'

He strode towards the light table and Turcat, buoyant with elation, bounded after him. Merrick followed sedately as Ehrhardt picked up the skull and jaw in either hand.

'No erupted wisdom teeth – the rear molars – so he's old but not *that* old; historically, I mean. He was probably under thirty when he died. The enamel will tell us a lot – it never changes after childhood, even in the grave. We could find out the composition of the water he was drinking as a child – once we could have done. As to his dates, perhaps twentieth century – wisdom teeth were becoming rare by then. So, late twentieth to mid twenty-second centuries, at an educated guess.'

Which is not at all the same as a mere guess, Merrick thought, recalling Turcat's words to Mirandola. 'Is that good news or bad?' he said.

Turcat's adoring gaze at the teeth wavered.

'From our point of view,' Ehrhardt said, 'not very good. If he was prehistoric or even pre-twenty-first century, we could argue that the Briease Moss and of course the Briease Reserve did not then exist. The bureau could counterclaim that if he was Ancient British or Ancient Inglish or whatever they like to think they are, he's obviously Aboriginal, but we might get away with it. If he went into the peat in the last hundred years or so they'll say that since he's on their land he's definitely one of theirs. We're going to have to argue this every step of the way. Those pearls have really complicated things.'

'Why?' Merrick said. Apart from the skeleton itself, the pearls were the only interesting thing they had found.

'Look at our man, big tall fellow, no deterioration of the bones, or fractures, except for the obvious.' He poked his finger through the punctured eye socket and waggled it. 'He doesn't look Aboriginal unless he's a very early example, much too strapping. So he is, by his teeth, no more than, say, three hundred years old, and by the pearls, no less than a hundred and ten. I don't think he's an Oyster but I wouldn't know how to prove it. The pearls moreover suggest that he had some connection to the Moss.'

'He wasn't wearing an ear stud.'

'You mean you haven't found one. Those things disintegrate.'

'What's the very youngest he could be?' Turcat said.

'Can't tell yet.'

'Doesn't it depend on where he was buried?' Merrick asked.

They looked at him as though he were mad.

'That's the one thing we do know,' Turcat said.

'No, we don't. He might have died in a ditch and been covered up naturally. He could have been buried on the beach.'

'Unlikely. That would make him very recent. Why do you think so?'

'There's a box in the pit we dug. Suppose he was burying it, got disturbed, murdered—'

'Who saw the box?' Ehrhardt said.

'The murderer didn't. He left it there.'

'I think Professor Ehrhardt means last week,' Turcat said heavily.

'Oh – I did. Unless the pit's been drained since, I don't think anyone else has.'

'Describe it.'

'I didn't get much chance to look. It was wooden – I could only get at one end, one corner. He must have been sitting on it, but it was long, the rest of it was still buried. It had some kind of metal label on it, corroded.'

'Any theory about what it might be?'

'In the old fictions,' Merrick ventured, 'people buried valuables in boxes . . . buried treasure.'

'We used to bury our dead in boxes,' Turcat said.

'So we did. Coffins. Could our friend have been a grave digger? I wonder. We've got maps upstairs,' Ehrhardt said. 'Let's go up and see where he could have been. I wish we could afford to get you viewing facilities down here.' He turned suddenly to Merrick. 'And you, what's your name?'

'Merrick Korda. I've been working here for nearly five years.'

'Inglish, are you?'

How could he tell? 'Way back,' Merrick said.

'Not local? That's all right, then. We wouldn't want a conflict of interests. Rémy, make sure you're properly secured down here.'

'Lock up, Korda,' Turcat said. Merrick, checking the flood escape door and extinguishing the lights, heard them discussing him as they went upstairs.

'I never thought of him being Inglish,' Turcat said. 'What makes you think so?'

'Oh, there's something about them . . .' As well as his personal affront Merrick felt shocked by Ehrhardt's unscholarly prejudice. 'That air of perpetual resentment . . . there's a word for that sort, malcontent. Still, he's obviously assimilated. You know what Oysters are like, smaller, unhealthier – not surprising, given the environment. And so *white*, positively fungal . . . Diseases we haven't seen in centuries still break out. But it's their choice, they fought hard enough for it.'

'Diseases?' Turcat said.

Skin diseases, Merrick thought.

'And problems with the joints. Think how inbred they must be. They rarely marry out.'

Breeding themselves back to Cro-Magnons, Turcat had said to Mirandola, more to annoy him than anything else, but he might well have been near the truth.

In Ehrhardt's office Merrick blanked the windows. As Turcat's assistant he had a perfect right to be there, but he sensed that the more menial he appeared the less they would mind his presence.

They turned to face the screen wall and the first map came up. It was familiar to them as historians. Very few people outside the faculty would have identified it with the modern state they knew as the Rhine Delta Islands.

'The old woman riding on her pig,' Merrick said without thinking.

'The what?'

'That's what the British used to call their outline,' Turcat said.

Merrick went to the screen and traced the coast with his finger. 'Here's her bonnet, Scotland, the pig's head is Wales, the front leg is Cornwall. Back leg's Kent and the rump is East Anglia.'

'Which is, of course, no longer there,' Turcat said.

Ehrhardt superimposed the current map of the RDI over the first so that they could see exactly where the North Sea had gnawed away at the pig's rump, leaving a ragged peninsula. By degrees, so that they might observe closely, he enlarged the East Anglian section, or the section that showed the absence of East Anglia, until the entire screen was filled by the Briease Moss and Parizo Beach. Under the sea a phantom tracery of roads ran like arteries beneath the skin, punctuated by dots and occasional polyhedra with names alongside them, the drowned villages and towns that had once stood far inland. Ehrhardt erased them, leaving only those eastward of the present coastline. They went to the screen and studied it closely.

'Of course,' Ehrhardt said, 'this had been going on for centuries. Even by the middle of the nineteen hundreds there were remains of settlements on the beaches, villages known to be three or four kilometres out to sea. Now, here's the Nox . . . the Eavrey wave barrage . . . Parizo wind farm . . . our site must be about here.'

84

The screen melted again to enlarge the area where Ehrhardt's finger had been resting: a crossroads, a dozen or so black rectangles to denote buildings and a square surmounted by a cross.

'Church,' Turcat said; 'church with a tower.' He read out the legend. 'Yexham St Peter; and that went under in twenty-one forty-nine.'

'That wasn't a bad estimate,' Ehrhardt congratulated himself. 'Well, Korda, what do they have around churches?'

'Do?'

'Don't your people still have churches?' Ehrhardt said. 'There's one at Briease, I believe, although I can't imagine what they use it for.'

'I've never been to Briease,' Merrick muttered sullenly. 'I've never seen a church – only foundations. What did they have round them?'

'Graveyards,' Turcat said, and Merrick, who knew this perfectly well, cursed himself for not guessing what Ehrhardt was after. 'Cremation was reintroduced here by the end of the nineteenth century, common by the end of the twentieth. Also by the end of the twentieth century the idea of green burials was catching on, not in a graveyard or cemetery but in open countryside, woods; cardboard coffins, everything returned to nature as fast as possible. No notion of trying to preserve the corpse for future resurrection, although people did evince a peculiar attachment to their vital organs, almost like the ancient Egyptians.'

'Canopic jars?' Ehrhardt said.

'Not quite, but there are records of people holding separate funeral services for errant viscera after autopsies. Still' – Turcat paused impressively – 'at that time it was still acceptable to bury the dead in wooden coffins with a metal plate on the lid. So, our man downstairs probably was rooting around in a graveyard. Who'd shoot a grave digger?'

'They might shoot a grave *robber*,' Ehrhardt said. 'The pearls—'

'The box— coffin hadn't been opened,' Merrick said.

'So far as you know. Say he's been observed, caught in the act. Whoever catches him kills him and fills in the grave again, burying him with his crime. The pearls could be loot from elsewhere. He's in a graveyard. He may have been at more than one coffin already.'

'And his killer never knew he had them?'

'You found that phial in the pelvic cavity. He may have swallowed it in panic. Over the years it's worked its way down.' Ehrhardt smiled. 'Guard those pearls, Rémy, and you' – he jabbed a finger at Merrick – 'not a word outside this room. Those things fetch a fortune on the antiquities market and this department's like a magnet for black marketeers. Remember that brass *memento mori* you found when they rebuilt Galleria Station? We were offered millions for that, from half a dozen sources.'

'Korda, we'll need manifests of those maps, get them scanned,' Turcat said. He turned back to Ehrhardt. 'I'm told it's the Brandenburgers who keep the black market going. They'll collect anything.'

'Anything that shines,' Ehrhardt said. He lowered his voice. 'You're absolutely sure you can trust him?'

Turcat's reply was even lower. Merrick did not hear it.

Chapter Four

He lay, all 1.89 metres of him, on the light table in the basement laboratory. One after the other the whole of the history faculty had been down to look at him, while he was there to be looked at. Not everyone approved but no one passed up the chance to see him, Turcat's Parizo Man.

In the stockroom his few secrets were stored in protective cases, the bone splinters, the rings and ear hoops, the pearls. They had found no traces of clothing. 'Strip,' he had been told at gunpoint. In the darkness – they were sure it had happened at night – he had hidden his loot in his mouth and swallowed it, either as a last desperate attempt at concealment, or by mistake. Bone samples were sealed and ready for dispatch to Paris-Sorbonne for dating. The capsules containing the records of his emergence awaited editing before being made available to interested parties, should any party show an interest.

'If Mirandola stirs up enough curiosity we could open our own channel,' Turcat said; 'round-the-clock viewing of the whole operation from the first day on Parizo Beach to the moment we put the coccyx in position.'

Merrick doubted that even a fellow enthusiast would be sufficiently enthralled to sit it out to the ultimate tail bone. People wanted a good long look, *one* good long look. Ideally Parizo Man would be laid out, as he was laid out now, but in a display case, custom built, well lit, in congenial surroundings with other human relics for company. A special building could be erected for the purpose; they already had a word for it.

In the meantime the only channel anyone in the department was watching was the one relaying court proceedings. Unlike a criminal case where physical evidence had to be presented, Mirandola's demand for the skeleton to be returned to the Briease Reserve, countered by Ehrhardt's application for retrospective permission to have excavated in the first place, was conducted entirely on screen. Ehrhardt was arguing his case from his own office. Merrick and Turcat sat in Turcat's office watching the debate. Mirandola pleaded eloquently for Aboriginal rights to their own dead. Ehrhardt appealed to common sense and brought in the Politi sergeant to back up his assertion that the skeleton would have had to be exhumed in any case. He did not mention the pearls. The magistrate seemed concerned only with the site, which was definitely at the Briease end of the beach, but might be under the jurisdiction of the Pan-European Coastal Authority. After listening to hours of dispute she adjourned her decision.

'Who the fuck are the Pan-European Coastal Authority?' Turcat exploded. 'Have you ever heard of them? I don't believe they exist. They're a myth, like the Brandenburgers. Someone's invented them just to give us grief.'

Merrick made inquiries and learned that the Pan-European Coastal Authority had existed for almost two centuries under various acronyms and was currently overlord of the Energy Commission's offshore operations. This made no difference, though, to the fate of Parizo Man. All they could do now was wait upon the magistrate's decision.

Ehrhardt was with Merrick and Turcat in the stockroom, studying the map manifests, when word came down to them from an assistant that judgement had been delivered. Before they could begin to ask which way it had gone they heard voices coming down the stairs from reception, followed by a peremptory knocking on the outer door and sounds of confrontation in the stairwell.

'I don't have means of access,' someone was protesting.

'Then you had better call Professor Ehrhardt immediately.' Mirandola speaking.

'Shall I see to him?' Turcat said, with murder in his eye.

'No, I'd better take this call myself,' Ehrhardt said. 'If this is what I think it is I'll have to be involved. We may be about to lose our man. If there's anything you think you can hold back, shut the door behind me and sort it out. Then leave by the flood escape.'

He went out. Merrick fetched a cloth bag from under the bench and soundlessly they tumbled everything in, communicating by gestures, listening intently to what was going on in the laboratory beyond the door. The outer door opened. Ehrhardt's rapid assessment of the situation had been correct. The magistrate had delivered her verdict on the excavation. Mirandola was relaying his triumph in a carrying voice.

'The corpus in question is to be surrendered immediately to a representative of the court, this person here, along with all artefacts and related material from the trespass and illegal excavation on Parizo Beach until such time as proper investigations have established the provenance of the said corpus.' He was evidently reciting from a document.

'Is that *it*?' The officer of the court had seen Parizo Man.

'Related material?' Ehrhardt said. 'You mean, you want the dirt back?'

'Where is it?'

'Somewhere in the city sewage system, I imagine,' Ehrhardt said. 'I assure you, if there had been anything of interest in it we would have kept it.'

'And where have you put what you have kept?' That was another voice: how many of them were out there being kept at bay by the lone professor; how long before their attention turned towards the stockroom door?

'Your remit extends only to the said corpus, I believe.' Ehrhardt was stalling masterfully. Turcat dropped a box and turned green as Merrick fielded it before it struck the floor.

No one had answered Ehrhardt. By the silence they gathered that he had hit on Mirandola's one weak spot; no one knew what they had removed from the skeleton, but the silence was of no help to them. Turcat was relying on the cover of conversation, or better still a blazing row, to open the door into the flood escape.

'All artefacts and related material.' Mirandola's voice was rising to a shout.

'*What* artefacts? Show me a list.'

Several voices broke out together. Merrick dived at the flood door.

'How do you propose to remove the skeleton, officer? In a *bag*?'

'What do you keep in that inner room, Professor?'

'I don't keep anything in it. This is Dr Turcat's department.'

'Where is Dr Turcat?'

'Why are you here, Mirandola? You seem to have had advance knowledge of the verdict—'

'Why are *you* here, Professor?'

They paused just long enough to hear Ehrhardt improvising rapidly, and partly for their benefit, in the circumlocutory jargon he was picking up from Mirandola. 'I was checking the flood precautions as regulations require me to do, in person, during the first week of each month, it being concomitant upon my doing so that my faculty is permitted the use of these premises in a preserved building and as such not covered by the provisions of the Integral Escape Planning Act of twenty-one ninety-eight.'

This was quite possibly a fact, although it was not the first week of the month and Merrick had never seen Ehrhardt or anyone else checking the flood escape, but even if it were not it would account for the unbarred door when Mirandola forced, or talked, his way into the stockroom. The cases and bags were now in the single carrier. Turcat took it from Merrick and ushered him through, pushing the door closed behind him until it just touched the frame.

The staircase was unlit and would have to remain so. They groped their way up to ground level, which they told by the number of steps, on and up into the sealed area which must, again by the steps, be halfway to the next storey.

'Do you know how to get out?' Merrick whispered. That thought had only just occurred to him. Flood drill was mandatory in all public buildings but he had never been in the basement when the alarm sounded.

'First thing we're taught,' Turcat said.

'No one taught me.'

There was was still no sound from the stairwell behind them but Ehrhardt must have had to admit his visitors to the stockroom by now. Merrick heard the hiss of watertight seals released, a door sigh open. A dim automatic light filled the chamber where they stood, barely a metre square. He wondered what would happen if the basement flooded while full of people, but the flood escape was there only to satisfy government requirements. No one seriously expected it to work like the terrifyingly efficient system in the university stacks.

Automation took over now. The door opposite opened immediately onto a staging where the emergency raft was moored in space at the rear of the building, left over from the time when buildings had fronts and backs. Conventional steps led down to ground level.

'Now what?' Merrick said, as they descended.

'I re-enter by the back door, a quaint device which unfortunately Mirandola will know about from his time spent hanging out with Oysters. Still, he doesn't even know I'm here today, so I might get away with it. He doesn't know you're here either. Get lost.'

'Where?'

'Use your initiative.'

'What are you going to do?'

'Find a place to put the artefacts and related material and cook up a story about why they aren't where they ought to be. I have a matter of minutes. Go away. Show up for work tomorrow – no, make that Wednesday, and with luck, no one will miss you. Goodbye.'

'Give them to *me*. I can—'

It was too late. Turcat had already accelerated to the corner and vanished around it. Merrick dared not raise his voice to repeat his suggestion, and he could not remain here in case Mirandola and his mob decided to come up the flood escape and check on Ehrhardt's story. It seemed sensible to go in the opposite direction from Turcat. Hugging the side of the building he turned the corner, then another, and found himself at the top of the steps in front of Millennium House.

For some reason there was a large number of people milling about at the foot of the steps and some on them. At the main door was a Politi officer, a hard-looking nut in riot gear. He could scarcely be expecting a riot, since he was alone, and in any case the crowd was too few to constitute a riot.

Merrick's first instinct was to retreat but he had taken the corner quickly and his momentum was carrying him forwards, among the people on the steps. If he suddenly stopped, turned, made to leave, it would be the hawk-eyed cop who spotted him, the security eye that recorded him.

'*Crime against humanity,*' someone bawled in his ear. '*Insult to Aboriginal peoples and a crime against humanity.*'

He had walked into the middle of a demonstration. The few persistent zealots who had picketed the cathedral dig, veterans of that group which had convened on the day of Ehrhardt's first excavation, had, since the inundation of the site, shifted their theatre of operations to Millennium House. He noticed them every time he came in to work, crying their slogans and accosting apathetic passers-by. But this was different; not hugely different but significantly. Now there were twenty or thirty chanting in unison instead of half a dozen. Either public indifference had melted in the fierce heat of their indignation at Rémy Turcat's heinous crime (against humanity) or someone had been mobilizing reinforcements. It was a pity that Turcat had not come out this way too. The last place Mirandola would seek the missing artefacts and related material was among this bunch, especially as he did not know what the missing artefacts might be.

It was at this moment that Mirandola appeared in the entrance accompanied by another Politi officer and, Merrick saw with alarm, Dr Turcat. He took up position behind a placard-carrying man and yelled in concert with the rest, 'Ashes to ashes, dust to dust. From earth we came, to earth we must return.' That was a new one. Nobody here would be returned to ash, dust or earth. 'Crime against humanity!'

What did they imagine Parizo Man looked like? Still fresh and moist with the bloom of life as if only recently deceased? At the sight of the new arrivals in the doorway a voice called out, 'There he is! Turcat the desecrator. That's Turcat!' A chorus of hoots and howls went up. Turcat, who had been maintaining either cool detachment or brazen effrontery – depending on how you regarded him – looked taken aback by the ferocity of the invective. Turcat the Desecrator; as if he were a revenant from the distant past when barbarians sacked Rome, Alaric the Visigoth, Attila the Hun. Merrick, looking round, saw that the crowd had thickened in the short time since he joined it. Even if Turcat had been arrested or pulled in to assist with inquiries, he must be glad of the police presence. He could never have expected his work to have stirred up so much protest and Merrick, who got out more, frankly doubted if Parizo Man were anything other than the flimsiest of excuses for civil unrest. Possibly there was a riot squad parked out of sight, ready for the trouble that none of them had expected.

Was Ehrhardt under arrest too or was he still being

harried by the rump of Mirandola's party in the flood escape, while Turcat had been outflanked and intercepted on his way back to his office? He could never have had time to reach it. The court official was now in possession of the bag of artefacts and related material.

Mirandola and his officers were on the steps now with Turcat among them, ignoring the demonstrators and striking out towards the Central Plaza and the Politi HQ. From that direction a group of home-going workers was coming towards them, en route for the monorail station. Intent on getting back before another power failure paralysed the system, they trudged unheeding through the demonstrators; accustomed to a few, they did not notice that the numbers had swollen.

The whole business was being recorded, of course, but there was no obvious reason why he should not be outside his own place of work. Only Turcat would have recognized him, might even have seen him as he came down the steps. Mirandola might have recognized him if he had ever looked at him, which was why Turcat had told him to stay out of sight, but anyone might ask questions if Turcat's willing assistant were identified as someone who protested against the very work he was engaged in. As two or three people jostled past him, vanguard of hundreds, he turned and, in joining the current, ceased to be part of the demonstration, becoming instead one of the home-going workers, heading for the station.

No one would be taking any notice of this lot, early-shifters, essential but unremarked, returning to their homes in the dormitory belt to sleep away the remains of the day, or whatever maintenance staff did with themselves when not maintaining. He could easily pass for one of them. If not for the foresight of his grand-parents he could easily have been one of them.

Any maintenance staff employed at the Metropole Station must be sleeping on the job. There were no welders at work here and only a couple of unsuper-vized inspection robots, crawling around testing for stress fractures. The station had been badly damaged in the storm and was invisible now in a plantation of scaffolding, with tunnels among the stilts. The elevator shafts declared unsafe, access to the platforms was by way of metal stagings that clanged hollowly beneath the tread of resentful commuters. Unlike airship travel the monorail was free, so restoring it to normal effi-ciency would be a very low priority. The service had been reduced to a dozen cars a day each way, running to severe speed restrictions, but one was drawing into the north-bound platform as Merrick reached it. He had not been aiming for the northern route, rather the southern city loop, from which he could transfer to the souterrain transit and make his way home, but the group he had joined at Millennium House and stayed among bore him along with it and into the car. He rarely used the service himself and did not have time to check the destination, but as things stood, north was as good as south.

The driverless car started with a jolt and advanced unsteadily, crooning to itself. Passengers avoided looking at each other for fear of communicating the unspoken thought, What if the power fails again while we're between two stations, six metres above the ground?

The battered city lay below them. When working on the cathedral dig Merrick had raised his head from time to time to see a car glide swiftly between two towers, reflected as it receded or approached in the windows on either side, so he knew where to look out to catch a glimpse of the abandoned trenches, but although the car, moving at a third of its normal speed, gave him plenty of time to look down at his former workplace he saw nothing but an armada of earth-moving equipment converging on the area where he and Turcat had been excavating. Farewell to the cathedral for another ten years at least.

On the opposite side of the car someone was already asleep, head lolling against the window glass. Merrick's casual glance, in the act of turning away from the lost excavation, became a fixed stare. He had seen that long light hair before. The ravaged right jaw was hidden against her shoulder. Frida Mason had ended her engagement at the Ayckbourn and was presumably going home.

Merrick hoped that she was planning a good rest. In spite of the erratic movement of the car, which jarred her head against the window hard enough for him to hear the thuds, she never opened her eyes. The car had already stopped and started several times before one of its halts coincided with a station and people got out. Merrick began to wonder whether he ought to follow suit, and what he would do when he left the car. It was instinct that had led him into it, and he had been following Turcat's injunction to get lost until it was time for work on Wednesday. He did not know what degree of loss Turcat had had in mind. Already he had been thwarted by Mirandola; the artefacts and related material were in custody. If Mirandola were to remember that Turcat had an assistant, Merrick's disappearance might cause more speculation than otherwise. The Politi could be at his height right now, questioning the neighbours. He personally had nothing to hide. He ought to go home.

Another stop, another start, another station; he looked up and Frida Mason raised her head simultaneously. Meeting his eyes she nodded pleasantly. Used to being recognized, he thought, before recalling that no one who had seen her on stage in that cheesy paste mask would ever recognize her in the flesh, and amended his thought to, Used to being stared at.

He looked away, out of the window. They were far enough from the city centre now for him to see wind turbines on the horizon. They were leaving the dormitory belt, passing among the high-rise farms. He had expected a display, or a voice, that would-be soothing moo that one might use to hypnotize robots, spreading alarm and despondency in every elevator and public vehicle in the state. The muffled intermittent drooling must be all that was left of it. Now that he came to think about it, there were surprisingly few people still on board if this were a local service. The car might be going all the way to Eavrey Sound or beyond, in which case it would not necessarily stop at every station on the line. He must get off at the next one and make his way back.

When the car halted he leaped up.

'This isn't a station,' Frida Mason said.

'It's not?' he said stupidly, and sat down again.

'We passed the last station a few minutes ago.'

'I thought you were asleep.'

'You feel the doors open at stations.' She did not remark upon his tacit admission that he had been watching her.

'When's the next one?'

'Your guess is as good as mine. Tomorrow, at this rate.'

'I meant, where?'

'Eavrey Sound. This is an express. I think that used to mean a vehicle that moved very fast without stopping.'

'This won't stop again till Eavrey Sound?'

'Don't be daft, it's stopping every ten yards. But there aren't any stations between here and Eavrey. Then Norge, where I'm going. Where are you going?'

'Eavrey Sound, I suppose,' Merrick said.

'Well, never mind, you'll probably be able to get back some time next week.' Her eyes closed again. She was either asleep, like a cat, or terminating the conversation.

Norge, he knew after seeing the maps, was beyond the northern fringes of the Briease Moss. Merrick had not thought of her literally hailing from the Moss, living in it, an Aboriginal, an Oyster. Still, they could not all be diseased inbred bogtrotters. There were several working in the faculty of early religions at Millennium House, although he could not foresee a day when an Oyster held a professorial chair or won a seat in the State Assembly. You had to assimilate in order to advance, didn't he know it? And there was something about them, Ehrhardt had said, even the assimilated ones. What could it be about him? He did not share the Oysters' susceptibility to premature ageing and problems in the joints.

Elena Rodriguez had said they were crippled by dancing at thirty; Frida, not yet crippled, must be a few years shy of that, but she looked thirty. There was something unyouthful, hard-edged about her, and if not diseased, then at some time prey to whatever had eaten into her face.

The car lurched into motion again, stopped with a jerk and then resumed its spasmodic trundling, as if on wheels. Frida gave up trying to go back to sleep, or pretending to. Merrick, now looking studiedly out of the window, saw from the corner of his eye that she was stretching, quite unself-consciously, in spite of the fact that now everyone within range was also *not* looking: left leg, right leg, left arm, right arm, ankles, wrists; rotating her head, flexing shoulders. Merrick thought again of a cat, although, unlike a cat, she seemed unable to stay in one position without seizing up.

'Stiff?' he said, when the performance was over. She was still extending and retracting her fingers and, by the undulations inside her shoes, her toes as well. If she had a tail, he thought, she would be lashing it

102

from side to side. He knew people who affected to believe that Aboriginals had tails.

'Very stiff. I overlaid this morning – had no time to exercise. Ran for the car, ought to have guessed it would be an hour late. Dared not miss it – you never know when the next one will run.'

'Do you have to be in Norge by any particular time? I could call ahead.'

'So could I,' Frida said, 'but I'm not expected. They'll know what state the line's in.'

'You live in Norge?' he asked disingenuously.

'No, at Briease. In the fen.'

'The fen?'

'You call it the Moss. We call it a fen.'

Merrick knew people who would as soon claim to live in a sewer as admit to coming from Briease, but Frida seemed to see no shame in it. He said daringly, 'You're an Aboriginal?'

Frida's smile took on a satirical dint at one end. 'Oyster,' she said. 'You know right well I am. I remember you too, you know.'

Someone remembered him. 'From the theatre? I didn't think you would. We were only there – in the dressing room – for a few minutes.'

'Ah, but you were with someone I know.'

'Amandine. Her brother's head of my department.'

'Amandine is one of those bright young things who think it's chic to fraternize with Oysters – don't look so shocked. *I* can say it – but don't you think of trying. And what department would that be; at the Energy Commission?'

'Archaeology, at the university.' As soon as he said it he realized that an Oyster was the last person he ought to have told. He would have been safer trading on her assumption that he worked with Amandine. But she must know what Amandine's brother did for a living; perhaps she had thought he would lie about it. He held out his hand, hopefully, open. 'Merrick Korda.'

'Winifrid Mason. Frida will do.' She extended her own arm and Merrick was shaken to find himself grasping a handful of bones and sinew; it was as if Parizo Man himself had reached out to greet him. 'What on earth made you come backstage?'

'Amandine invited me. I went to the theatre with her because her brother couldn't go.'

'And you couldn't refuse the invitation, huh?'

'I didn't want to spoil the magic.'

'No, watching us carve our faces off must have broken the spell.'

With knobs on, Merrick thought, cursing himself for not seeing where the conversation would lead, and deeply thankful that he was still sitting to her left with the width of the aisle between them, although each had shifted companionably to the side of the seat.

The car had stopped again on the edge of a wind farm. On Merrick's side the view was seen through the pylons of the turbines across hectares of arable land to low hedges, then the sea, grey and flat today under a sunless overcast. Frida looked out towards a stand of aspens behind which lay the road to the north-west, its sparse traffic flickering between the trunks. Small rain began to spit fitfully against the windows like handfuls of thrown gravel.

'What will you do at Eavrey Sound?'

'Try to get home again.'

'We ought to have reached it by now. At this rate' – the car hiccoughed and jumped forward – 'it'll be dark before I get to Norge.'

'How will you reach Briease?'

'Oh, that's not a problem. It's annoying though to pass so close and not be able to get off. The rail crosses the road just inside the edge of the fen.'

'Won't the Assembly allow you a station?' Surely Mirandola could bore the Assembly into submission. 'It wouldn't take much work, would it?'

'The Assembly has been trying to give us a station for years,' Frida said. 'Our council has rejected it. And since it would be on reserve land, the Assembly can't do a thing about it.'

'Can't they build outside?'

'Of course, but who'd use it?'

'You'd use it, evidently,' Merrick said.

'Ah, but who'd build a monorail station just for me?'

Up ahead, in the leaden distance, the low bulk of Eavrey Island rose darker against the sky. The car stopped, started, stopped again. Merrick looked across at Frida and saw that she had fallen asleep in the brief lull in their conversation, her head hanging forwards, hair swinging across her face.

The announcer crackled into life with a feeble eructation and informed them that owing to structural damage to the rail supports they would not be going forward to Norge but would terminate the journey at Eavrey Sound.

Frida opened one eye and observed, 'It looks as if we'll each have a long walk home. Have you seen any cars going south?'

'You'll walk from Eavrey?'

'It can be done. There's a tramline along the north shore of the sound and I can walk from the point to Parizo Beach; or I can cut through the fen.'

'Are there roads?'

'For them that knows them. Not what you'd call a road.'

The car eased forward and from behind the shoulder of Eavrey Island slid a mistier outline, the Nox, last reminder of the power that had once fuelled the land that lay under the sea. Only the top of the turbine hall remained visible, a strangely rectilinear silhouette in the soft eroded landscape.

'What will you do if you can't get back? There's an overnighter at the station.'

'I'll stay there if I have to. How long will it take you to get home?'

'By tram and along the beach, three to four hours, if the trams are running. About a couple of hours through the fen. I'll see what the weather's like when we get out. And I have to take the tides into account.'

'The beach isn't passable at high tide?'

'If I didn't know it I wouldn't risk it at any tide, and you can hardly tell what you're going to find from one day to the next. Quicksand – you know what that is?'

The car was sliding into Eavrey Station and rain was

beginning to fall heavily. The remnants of the platform canopy squeaked and flapped dismally overhead
as they disembarked with a dozen others onto
windswept concrete. Frida was hung about with
luggage: a backpack, a flat metal box under her arm
and a creaking wicker basket in her other hand. It was
the kind of thing some people kept in their living
rooms for decoration as examples of native crafts.
Merrick had never seen anybody using one before.
She refused his offer to carry anything.

The overnighter stood opposite the station but as
they reached ground level Merrick saw that the
building was roofless and boarded over with metal
grilles.

'You won't be staying there,' Frida said.

A roadrunner was parked outside the station by a
sign advising that transport would be provided for
anyone needing to continue their journey to Norge.
There was no provision for idiots who had not meant
to come this far in the first place, and no one to ask.
While Merrick was searching for information Frida put
down her luggage and went to speak to the driver of
the roadrunner. Merrick noticed that although no
longer limping she walked awkwardly over a hard
surface.

Frida returned while he was still staring towards
Eavrey, hoping for lights in the murk.

'He says he'll set me down on the edge of the fen.
Do you want to come too?'

'To Briease?'

'Why not? Unless you'd rather camp under the

station. He thinks there'll be nothing back to the city now until nine o'clock at the earliest, perhaps not then.'

Six hours at least. Why not go with her? Turcat had told him to get lost. Where better to get lost than in the Briease Moss?

The doors of the roadrunner moaned together in discord with the whine of the motor unit as the vehicle ambled away from the station. The road, not much more than a lane, ran straight across flat countryside, flatter still beneath the rain, until it met the highway. It was moving at about ten kilometres an hour, but at least it kept moving steadily through the dregs of the afternoon, flat fields to the left and to the right the distant boundary of trees that marked the edge of the Moss.

Frida was asleep again. Merrick, sitting on her right, had a close view of the ridges and craters in her skin. A burn? Necrosis? Why didn't she do something about it?

The rain had moved seawards by 17.00. The western horizon was rimmed with yellow, and out of the window of the roadrunner Merrick saw the sunlit struts of the monorail curving towards them. Where the elevated track crossed the highway the driver halted the vehicle and called back, 'Who wanted to get out here?'

'We do!' Frida, suddenly less asleep than she had seemed, scrambled her belongings together and they struggled to the door in an atmosphere thick with hostility at yet another delay to the interminable journey.

As soon as they were out on the roadside the driver yelled, 'I hope you know what you're doing!' slammed the doors dramatically and the roadrunner crawled away again. With a little effort they could have overtaken it.

'As you do,' Frida said.

'Do what?'

'Hope I know what I'm doing.'

'I'm sure you do.'

'No you aren't. But you ought to trust me, I grew up here.'

That might be an excellent reason for not trusting her. Merrick thought of what Mirandola had said about ways through the Moss: 'I wouldn't advise a stranger to try'. And Frida herself had said that there were roads for those that knew them. 'Not what you'd call a road.'

Frida caught his expression and laughed as if he had spoken aloud. 'You needn't start worrying yet. We're on firm ground for a while. That's why the road and rail cross here.'

The lengthening rays of the sun followed them down a straight track, clearly marked with wheel ruts, at first level with the grassland on either side where large slow white cattle grazed, then rising on a causeway to run between straggling hedges.

'Is it like this all the way?'

'You wish. This track serves the farms, and Herigal village.'

'Will we stay at the village?'

'I don't think so. I might leave the luggage if I can't get a boat.'

A boat? What sort of a boat? Merrick was beginning to feel both his ignorance and shame for it. For all the loose talk in the department and elsewhere about Oysters, he knew nothing of the interior of the Briease Moss, having always associated the word with hectares of brown bog in which one sank knee-deep with every step, or the treacherous stretches of brilliant green that lay beyond the dunes to hoax you in and suck you down, like the quicksands on the shore between Eavrey Point and Parizo Beach. And now Frida told him it was not a moss but a fen. Even stranger to think that it had once been cleared land, inhabited, farmed and above sea level; dry.

The hedges were growing taller; there were trees in them, trees beyond them. The sun was hidden and the way seemed darker. It was also softer underfoot. Frida was bounding along now in spite of the load she carried, literally in her element. How soothing this spongy carpet must be to those tortured joints and muscles.

'Do let me carry something.'

'Oh, sure, if it bothers you.' She passed over the wicker basket. 'Clothes. Not heavy.'

'What's in the tin?'

'Make-up – stage make-up. I like to use my own.'

The face again. 'What sort of a boat can we get?'

'A punt.'

'Won't that take a long time?'

'Oh, it will, it will. We'll be mostly travelling through old peat cuttings, two – three feet of water in places. Then for a way on the river.'

Two feet? This was one of the old ways the Oysters had fought to preserve: imperial measures. Inside the reserve, he'd heard, people had reverted to trading in pounds and ounces, shillings and pence and the pound sterling, a proud totemic ideal. They were said to worship it. Pennies were known as peas, which set him to thinking of the five nacreous peas that Parizo Man had carried in his guts.

The courts would have them now if Mirandola had not abstracted them first. He put artefacts and related material out of his mind and looked with foreboding at the prospect of a journey through the darkling fen in a punt.

The track turned suddenly, then again, and on rounding the second bend became a street with small houses, cottages on either side, a modest wind turbine rearing up behind. A few people, dressed for manual work, were making their way home. Greetings were exchanged. Some seemed to recognize Frida and nodded incuriously at Merrick. They must be able to see that he was not one of them, but evidently they did not care or wonder why he was there, or if they did they were not greatly worried about it.

Or perhaps they could see that he *was* one of them, in that indefinable way that Ehrhardt had nebulously described . . . 'There's something about them.' But what did he and they share except common ancestors? And again he gave thanks to his own far-sighted forebears who had quit their ghetto before it became a reserve, pausing on the way only to prune their name from Cordwainer to Korda.

At the far end of the village street the trees crowded together again and in place of the hedges grew tall reed thickets. A row of widely spaced wooden posts stood along the edge of the track and two had stout ropes hitched about them. As they came close Merrick saw long flat-bottomed boats basking in the reeds on the other ends of the ropes.

'Ah, what luck,' Frida said, in that tone that made certain remarks sound as if she meant exactly the opposite. She dropped her pack at one end of the farther punt and laid the make-up box carefully beside it, motioning Merrick to load the basket.

'Whose is it? Are you just going to take it?'

'Common property.' Frida was squatting by the foot of the mooring post, against which was propped a square of purple slate. She patted the grass with a flattened hand until she located a lump of chalkstone. On the slate she wrote: *3.40 p.m. Monday. Mason to Briease Town by the Vyzel Cut.* Then she turned it over.

'What's that for?'

'So it's known who has the punt, and where it's going, and by which way. An itinerary,' she pronounced laboriously, as if to one who might not know the word. 'Like a flight plan, only not in the air.'

'How will anyone know you've written on it if you turn it over?'

'Because the punt will have gone. It may rain.'

Merrick, standing by a vacant post, turned over the slate at its foot. *5 a.m. Sunday. Plowman, South Turf Bank by the Hazel Carr then Briease Town by the Vyzel Cut and the Niven.*

They still went by a twelve-hour clock in the Moss and that clock was set in antiquity to Greenwich Meantime, two hours behind the rest of Europe. They travelled by punt and wrote by hand with chalk on slates. He envisioned the coming journey ending in a circle of mud huts. And they used these reeds to roof their cottages. Turcat had been wrong about that: there were thatchers in the Moss.

'What's this Vyzel Cut?'

'Part of the old land drainage system, dead straight, as good as a highway, between two bends of the Niven.'

'Which is?'

'A river. Get aboard and sit down – up at the prow, face the stern, unless you don't want to talk. Give me the quant.'

'The what?'

'The pole – that pole there.' It was as long as the vessel, lying the length of it. He held it up.

When he was settled Frida stepped on to the end of the punt and cast off the mooring rope. One thrust of the quant and the punt swung out of the reeds on to the black water. Alder boughs leaned down and almost touched the surface; the reeds rose up on either side like railings. Down on the water it was perceptibly colder and much darker. The sun still lit the tops of distant trees but soon the alders closed in and they seemed to proceed through a tunnel,

113

moving in dark silence broken only by the sound of the quant as Frida drove it into the bed of the waterway, stooping when the branches scraped over-head, then standing to stab again. Merrick did not speak. What had possessed him to accept this stranger's invitation so unquestioningly? What proof had he that they were in fact following the route so sketchily described on the slate. He wished very much that he might try calling Ehrhardt, but even if he were not overheard his private mumbling would be insulting. And he could imagine Ehrhardt's responses: 'On a *punt*? In the Briease Moss? At nightfall? With an *Oyster*?'

Just what he was thinking himself in fact. Turcat had told him to get lost; there was a limit to how lost he wanted to be.

The punt was nosing into a channel that was scarcely wider than its beam by the brush of reeds and branches on its sides. He could no longer see what he was touching and could only dimly make out Frida's labouring figure by her white shirtsleeves.

'Shall I take a turn?' It seemed only proper to offer.

'Do you know how?'

'Is it difficult?'

'If you don't know how.'

'This is narrow. Why have we left the Vyzel Cut?'

Frida snorted and a bird answered close by. Soft scurryings and splashings in the reeds echoed the sound. 'That wasn't the Vyzel Cut, just the Herigal Channel.'

'Where are we going, then?'

'This runs to the Cut eventually but we won't make it by nightfall.'

He was sure they made another turn before the punt stopped moving. He could see by the glimmer of white that Frida was securing the rope to something, a tree trunk perhaps.

'You must have known that.'

'That we would never reach Briease tonight? Of course I did.'

'What are you going to do?'

'We'll stop over at a turf lodge. There's one here, a few yards away. Switch on your torch.'

'I don't have a torch.'

'Do you not? You must have something – your clever city technology. Don't you glow in the dark?'

'If you remember, I never intended to be out after dark. I certainly didn't intend to be out here.'

'Ah, no.' Did she sound sceptical? 'We'll have to make do with this, then.'

A light flared at the end of the punt and steadied to a glow.

'What's that?'

'A hurricane lamp.' It looked to him like a wick in a glass chimney, contained in a wire cage and swinging from a handle. A hurricane would make short work of it. 'Follow me.' The light caught her in the act of stepping off the punt and catching at a branch with her free hand.

Merrick followed on to the pulpy bankside. In the seedy yellow gleam of the lamp he saw that they were on a narrow tongue of land, carpeted in low-growing vegetation and cleft abruptly at one side by another stream or cutting. Ahead was a small cabin built of peat blocks, not high enough to stand up in.

'Welcome to an Oyster overnighter,' Frida said and pulled open the wooden door to let him in. The door was in two halves; when the bottom one was shut the top formed a window. 'Do sit down.'

The floor was beaten earth and cold.

'What's it really for?'

'A shelter, as you can see. For peat cutters, coppicers who can't get home at night, for travellers like us. For strangers who don't know how close they are to Herigal Staithe. They could get in deeper than they know and be lost for ever, drowned, frozen,' she said cheerily. 'These lodges are everywhere. Somebody sees one, they'll stay put until daylight. Not that that's a lot of help if they're lost.'

'Can we light a fire?'

'No. Peat burns for ever once it catches alight. You'll be warm enough, won't you, in your clever city coat? Have you got any food?'

'*Food*? I wasn't expecting to picnic.' He had been expecting to eat, as usual, in the laboratory stockroom. His lunch was still there, if Mirandola hadn't confiscated it.

'Nor you were. Well, that proves you're no Oyster. We never venture anywhere without a night's provisions.'

'Even in the city?'

'Not many of us live in the city. And I knew I might be here tonight. We don't share your trust in technology.'

116

'Whose trust in technology?'

'Europeans. You *are* European, aren't you?'

'Aren't you?'

'Angles,' she said, 'or as it pleases you to call us, Inglish.'

Curious, he thought, how no one had ever wanted to be called Saxon.

She was taking something out of the backpack. 'We'll share. Close the upper door, the lamp will soon warm the air in here.'

The darkness outside was *so* dark. As he reached out to close the upper door Merrick saw a blue ambiguous flickering, whether distant or close he could not tell. 'Someone's coming.'

'Are you expecting someone?'

'There's a light.'

'Probably foxfire,' Frida said. 'There's a lot of rotting wood hereabouts; or maybe a wandering wraith.'

'A *what*?'

'The fen is full of them, since the beginning of time, misleading poor fools to their doom who think they are following a lantern. It's called the light of fools, ignis fatuus.'

Merrick felt a cold grue across his back. Hair prickled. 'The Moss hasn't been here since the beginning of time. It hasn't even been here two hundred years,' he said.

'Methane, then. Marsh gas, spontaneously combusting. How very dull. Where *were* you going today when we met?'

The statement segued so smoothly into the question that he almost told the truth.

'Home.'

'Where do you live?'

'Admiral Height, not far from the Ayckbourn as it happens.'

'Downtown. You wouldn't have been able to get there by the monorail, would you.'

This was not a question. There were no stations on that side of the Central District that he could not have reached faster on foot. He lived there because all university personnel lived in the area. It was five minutes' walk to the main complex and little more than that, in the opposite direction, to Millennium House.

And what had it got to do with her?

'I don't often use the monorail at all. I got on the wrong route. I was visiting friends, first.'

'Before going to Parizo Beach?'

This gave him such a jolt that he could not answer, could not even think of some platitude to bridge the gap while he constructed his next evasion although it was, this time, the truth.

'You *are* going to Parizo Beach?'

'No, I'm not. Wasn't. I got on the wrong car. I never meant to go all the way to Eavrey.'

'But now you've got this far, wouldn't you just like to look?'

'What at?'

'Don't you know?'

She knew. All this time he had assumed that she was

unaware of his connection to the Parizo excavation. Had Amandine said something? He abandoned his pretence. 'I thought we'd taken out all there was to look at.'

'I may only be an Oyster, but if I were an archae-ologist and I'd found a body, I'd take a good look round to see if it was alone.'

'I'm only a graduate assistant. I do what I'm told.' *Get lost.*

'And never ask questions?'

They could go on fencing like this all night. How could he not have seen what was coming? Glib, duplic-itous Frida Mason, winning his trust with a frank approach and the fact that she lived and worked among Europeans. He had relied on the kindness of a stranger. It had not taken a wandering wraith to lure him into the Moss.

On the other hand, why should he have suspected a ballet dancer of fell intent? Because she was an Oyster, that was why, and she had him where she wanted him, lost and benighted in a dangerous unknown waste. No one knew where he was – he scarcely knew himself; all those names were unfamiliar, mutations of older names, Herigal, the river Niven, the Vyzel Cut. He could not even remember seeing them printed on the maps. They might be names that only the Oysters used. Out there the peat fen waited for the unwary, baiting its traps with smooth inviting sward by day and the flickering marsh gas by night, and what went into a peat fen might never come out.

Where was this turf lodge where they crouched on

its spit of terra firma, and was the spit attached to solid ground or was it an island? Would the sun ever rise again?

'On Parizo Beach,' she intoned, 'on the land of our fathers, is a pit, three feet by three feet and two feet six across. Until last week it was a grave—'

'We don't know that.'

'You dug a body out of it and you don't know if it's a grave?'

'Oh, come now.' Merrick began to find his footing. 'After what has happened on this coast in the last two hundred years? You believe that every corpse that surfaces was buried according to prescribed funeral rites? Thousands have drowned over the years. During the Anarchy thousands more were slaughtered. There were mass graves not forty kilometres from here.'

'Wherever a body has lain, that is a grave,' she said, and brought her hand down flat on the lamp chimney. In one second the flame went out. 'And if it is found on our land,' the voice continued in the utter blackness, 'it is one of ours.'

'Look,' Merrick said, 'when he was first found he was mistaken for a recent burial—'

'A skeleton? Recent? Eaten alive by crabs, you thought?'

'Comparatively recent, possibly a murder victim. As it turned out, he wasn't recent, but the Politi had to be informed and he had to be exhumed. That's the law, federal law – which extends to the reserves.'

'But why was no one at Briease informed?'

'They were.'

120

'Yes, at third hand, by Orlaaaando.' The word became a yawn, very appropriately, he thought.

'Can't we talk about this in the morning?' Merrick seized the advantage quickly. He was tired, Frida must be exhausted. He could not even bring himself to ask, out of politeness, 'Would you like to have sex?' He doubted strongly that she would, and Oysters might not regard it as the courtesy it was intended to be, in case of a misunderstanding when it was too late. After all, these people still went through a ritual of marriage.

Another yawn. A laugh. 'Yes, we'll talk in the morning, if you like. You won't be going anywhere, will you?'

The same thought that had occurred to Merrick as he sat beside Parizo Man on the fog-bound beach. For very different reasons, no, he would not be going anywhere.

Chapter Five

Light squeezed through the narrow gap between the
two halves of the door, a sharp morning light, enough
to show Merrick, on waking, that he was alone in the
hut.

On all fours he shoved the whole door open and
looked out on sunrise over the Briease Moss. The sun
itself was out of sight but it was bright enough and
still low enough to illuminate the surrounding woodland, an encircling infinite palisade of birch and alder.
He must be close to the heart of it on this narrow spit
or eyot, little more than two metres wide. A few strides
away a rope knotted about a birch tree confirmed the
presence of the punt, but there was no sign of Frida
Mason.

Birds were calling over the Moss. How long, how
far had they travelled last night through the
labyrinthine channels? In a straight line Herigal village
could not be far, only straight lines did not exist here
– except for the fabled Vyzel Cut; straight as a highway,
Frida had said. If he took the punt and kept going
would he come to it or would he be lost in the watery
maze? Remembering the twists and turns of last night's

journey he could not hope even to retrace the passage to Herigal Staithe, however close it might be.

The undergrowth was ankle-deep, prickly and clutching, rooted in centuries of decay. He went over to the edge of the land and looked down into the punt, seeing what he had failed to miss in the hut. Frida's basket and make-up tin were stowed amidships. The only things missing were the backpack and Frida.

Was it safe to call out? The lurking fear that she had risen during the night, perhaps to relieve herself, and slipped into the water was receding. Without disturbing Merrick she had got up, loaded the punt and gone off with the backpack – and the quant. There was no need to contemplate going anywhere: the long pole that propelled the punt was also missing; why? To make sure he stayed put, that was why.

Where would anyone hide a quant? He looked at the slender, light-starved verticals of the tree trunks. Just planting it upright in the earth would hide it. The eyot appeared to end less than three metres ahead. He edged around the side of the hut and began to walk carefully in the other direction, but after a dozen paces the ground started to slope, grew soft under-foot, then sodden. His shoes squelched and reciprocal belches and slurps came from the surrounding morass as if something were being happily digested.

He was as lost as Turcat could have wished. Would getting in touch with him or Ehrhardt compromise his loss? No one was trying to reach him. He disen-gaged his right foot from where it was rapidly sinking and, grabbing at trees, levered himself back to safety.

As he came again to the hut he heard another sound, not far away but unidentifiable, something approaching, and looking up to the end of the eyot he saw a creature bounding towards him through the trees in great swooping, swinging leaps.

It was not coming directly at him – each leap was at a sharp angle to the last – but he was the target. Before fear overwhelmed him, while he was still listing places to hide, he saw that it was Frida Mason, vaulting across the waterways with the punt pole, at alarming speed, too fast for Merrick to make out how she handled it, how she knew exactly where to place it, where to land as she swung from it, how she was pulling it out of the earth behind her, running it through her hands and plunging it down ahead without ever pausing.

He had seen it done before, the spinning windmilling thing that had come out of the Moss to meet Orlando Mirandola. This was how the Oysters negotiated their marshy terrain, flying from one firm spot to the distant next without having to make the laborious detours that had turned Mirandola's ten-minute trot into a half-hour's trek.

The last leap brought Frida on to the eyot, landing squarely on the centre of it, only a metre or so from the hut. She grinned briefly at Merrick, laid the quant across the punt and unhooked the backpack from her shoulder.

'Where have you been?' He kept the question casual, as if she had slipped out of the room for a moment.

'Back to Herigal – to fetch breakfast.' Frida was not even slightly breathless, although the fair skin of her left cheek was flushed with healthy effort.

'Back to Herigal? How long did that take?'

'About ten minutes each way,' Frida said. 'Less, probably.'

'It took us an hour at least last night; nearer two hours.'

Frida was unpacking hot bread and a can of coffee from the backpack. 'On my own and without luggage I'd never travel by punt.'

'We could have stayed in the village last night.'

She did not answer, even to explain that there would have been nowhere to stay, if that were the reason. He thought he knew why Frida had made sure they spent it instead on this isolated isle. He had received his first lesson on the realities of life in the Moss.

'When we've eaten we'll get started.'

While they breakfasted the sun rose higher, gilding the tops of the birches. The only sound was the gurgle and splash of the fen, breathing, murmuring, farting to itself. When a bird called, the smallest high note echoed through the trees.

'Leave the can in the lodge,' Frida said, 'and the lamp. The next one through can return them.'

'More property in common?'

'If we looked out only for ourselves no one would last long in a place like this. Do you think we get planning permission for the turf lodges? They're built and repaired by anyone who has a little time to spare because anyone might need them.'

They descended to the punt and immediately everything but the yellowing leaf canopy was hidden by the reeds; there was no time for a farewell look at the little turf hut on the eyot among the birches. Frida cast off, dug the quant into the stream and they were moving again.

Merrick wedged himself athwart the seat in the prow so that he could see where they were going without rudely turning his back on Frida. By daylight the water was a rufous brown. Here a ditch broke the line of reeds, there a channel ran off at an angle, sometimes with a block of ashlar standing at its mouth. Where had they got those from in this wilderness of pulp?

'Stepping stones?'

'*No.* You don't walk on them, ever.'

'Milestones?' He had once dug up a milestone. Surely Oysters still travelled in miles.

'They mark still water,' Frida said. 'We're on a stream here that runs into the Niven. There's a current even if you can't see it. Any doubt, you send a float ahead.'

'What about at night?'

'We send candles. Look in the reeds, you may see burned-out floats.'

He looked but saw only rotting leaves and recognized the source of the pervasive smell of decay. Then the reeds ended abruptly, then the trees, and Frida's steady poling brought the punt out into an open area where they seemed to be travelling across the turf itself, so high was the water level, so low the land. The only things proud of the grass were fans of rushes. In the distance two fen vaulters raced across the land-scape, poles rotating, then it was back into the woods, among the cuttings, the peninsulas, eyots, causeways, the little turf lodges perched on their scraps of dry land. A sudden unexpected thud of feet gave only a few seconds' warning and Frida ducked down as a vaulter sailed over their heads, calling out a greeting as he went.

It was the sole word Merrick had heard spoken since Frida had told him of the floating candles, two hours ago. She had nothing to say to him this morning. When a man mysteriously glided by in the opposite direction, on a parallel waterway, he and she exchanged acknowledgements only with lifted hands. It was not until Merrick noticed the quant that he real-ized that he too was in a punt.

There followed another long featureless stretch of silence before Frida said, 'We're coming to the Cut.'

Again the trees ended as if sheared. One final thrust into the ooze and the punt shot into the middle of a waterway six metres across. As Frida had said, it was as good as a highway, dead straight between scrubby sloping banks. Her stance on the stern platform altered; she was now steering as much as propelling.

'Are we going against the current?' Merrick asked.

'I'm going against the tide,' Frida said. 'You're sitting still.'

'Can I help?'

'Of course you can't.'

His experience of water was limited to the city parc lake. 'Where's the tide coming from?'

'Where all tides come from. I told you, this was a cut in the Niven before the Niven changed course. It's tidal this far up and the tide's coming in.'

She was speaking of a past long out of reach, but after the tortuous progress through the Moss it was undoubtedly a short cut. A little song purled through his head: *Row, row, row your boat, gently down the stream* – where had that come from? *Merrily, merrily, merrily, merrily* . . . He had forgotten the rest of it.

Then reeds appeared again at the edges of the water, the banks were crumbling and the current, by Frida's efforts with the quant, running stronger.

'We're coming to the river now.'

Trees reared up on each side. The passage narrowed. Merrick could see the river bed, weedy and close; the punt made a sharp turn, a hundred and eighty degrees. Frida pirouetted around the pole, lifted it, ran to the prow, which had become the stern, and drove it in again. The vessel was out in the middle of the river, which was narrower than the Cut, winding gently between its margins where the trees grew as densely as before. There were no banks: the fen had reasserted itself on either side.

Up ahead buildings began to appear, not the mud hovels Merrick had expected but cottages, brick-built, flint-faced; stout wooden sheds, beyond them the upper storeys of bigger houses with tiled roofs above which the tips of turbine blades idly rotated. Across the river ran a serviceable bridge on concrete pilings, but before they reached it Merrick felt the punt swing again, nosing towards the trees on the right hand and they shot under the branches from sunshine into half light, once more in a narrow cutting.

'Was that Briease up ahead?'

'The outskirts, yes. We aren't going to Briease.'

'Where, then?' Out on the open water in the spacious Cut, on the leisurely river in sight of human habitation, the dark suspicions of the night had seemed ridiculous. They crowded back now in the hushed echoing channels of the Moss.

On a bank, a little above them, squatted a turf lodge. Merrick's thoughts returned to the one they had left earlier, hours earlier, where he had stood alone, perhaps abandoned, on the eyot, wondering where Frida had gone and on the verge of taking advantage of her absence to call Ehrhardt. If only he had acted sooner. Even if Ehrhardt had not replied there would at least have been a record of his attempt to make contact. Would anyone ever know how he had been lost?

'Don't you want to visit your excavation?'

'This way?'

'Why not? This is the way to Parizo Beach.'

Merrick had assumed that they were headed inland again, but almost at once the trees thinned, the sun shone through and beyond the birch trunks he saw the flat green marsh and the scruffy outline of the dunes, where last he had watched Mirandola picking his way towards what might have been this very place. He heard the sea.

Frida was manoeuvring the punt into a reed bed. 'Leave all the gear, we'll come back this way. Now, we've got to cross the merse; it's not far but don't be fooled. We can't go in a straight line so walk exactly where I walk.

'Why are we taking the punt pole?'

'I'm taking the punt pole.' Frida looked over her shoulder and leered. 'If the mood takes me I can vault out of here and leave you to sink.'

Merrick supposed it was a joke. Following his guide he now understood what Mirandola had been about, making his gigantic loops and parentheses around rushes and bushes. Where Frida trod the grass was flattened for a moment, long enough for Merrick to plant his foot in the same spot. Once, experimentally, he stepped aside and water foamed over his shoe.

'I heard that,' Frida snapped. 'Don't bugger about.'

They maintained a steady walking pace, the steadiness of caution. Clearly Frida knew precisely where she was going but she was taking no risks. With her own safety or mine? Merrick wondered.

'You couldn't vault across this, could you?'

Frida neither looked round nor answered. Instead she raised the quant, took three steps forward and flew upwards, swinging around the pole as it reached vertical and aiming for a place at an angle to her trajectory. Landing, she turned the quant, ran and sprang again, coming down two or three paces behind him.

'Now you're stuck,' she said.

'How can you tell where to land, where to put the pole? You're not going to leave me here, are you?' Another joke, he hoped. 'I didn't say anything to offend you, did I?'

'Of course not.' Frida shouldered the quant, caught up with and overtook him. 'But it doesn't hurt to know, does it?'

'Do you learn these paths by heart?'

'They change all the time. We learn to tell by looking, mainly by the colour of the grass, the length of it, even the species; by the light on it – not the same dry as wet, different again if it's waterlogged. I can read it as easily as you read your books. There's a ditch here – you can cross on that plank.' She did not need the plank. 'We're on sand here. Look out for vipers.'

'What?' One peril threatened as another receded.

'They like to sunbathe in the dunes. They won't attack unless you annoy them.

'Like us, really,' she said.

He heard the sea and the cacophony of gulls that was part of the sound of the sea, and as they crossed the marsh it had been augmented by the resonant whispers of the wind farm to the south. It was not until they came over the dunes to the beach that he realized that he was also hearing the sound of heavy machinery.

Subconsciously he had assumed that it was lifting gear on the wind farm, restoring the damaged pylons, but as he located it as coming from seaward he saw the source of it; a dinosaur head rose against the sky, fangs glistening, and plunged downward in a death-dealing surge. It was a robot backhoe, on caterpillar treads, scooping jawfuls of peat out of the beach where he and Turcat and the Politi officer had laboriously disinterred Parizo Man by hand. Instead of their modest pit there was now a room-sized hole, three metres deep. This was the kind of operation now going on at the cathedral site and this was just what Turcat had been afraid of; had said as much to Mirandola. 'They don't know how to do it.'

And Mirandola had said, 'You could guide the poor primitives with your superior knowledge.'

Mirandola, the last person he wanted to see, was standing by the side of the excavation and those surrounding him were, presumably, the poor primitives. One of them was relaying orders to the backhoe, two were staring down into the pit to monitor its progress. Several others had gathered around a row of long wooden boxes. No one had yet noticed Frida and Merrick coming towards them.

As the sound of the backhoe drowned their approach Merrick had time to look at Aboriginals on their own land. Mirandola's sarcastic reference to poor primitives had implied anthropoids clad in rabbit skins and chipping at the soil with stone axes or antlers. The backhoe was old but functional, efficient, and what they were doing with it was more damaging than anything inflicted by flints or antlers.

They did not look primitive in the anthropological sense, but they were short, thin, the tallest a scant one metre eighty. Their faces were the greatest betrayal, lined, weathered, blighted by the same sort of eruptions that disfigured Frida's; and white. Merrick had never seen so many white faces in one place. Few of them, he knew, would see out their tenth decade and it was impossible to guess their ages, but they looked old, particularly the ones wearing eyeglasses hooked over their ears. For all that they seemed active enough, two of them lifting the wooden boxes with ease.

He recognized those boxes. One of them must be the box he had started to uncover on the day they first hurried to unearth Parizo Man before the tide forestalled them, not beginning then to guess what it might be. There was no doubt about its purpose now. Turcat's surmise had been correct; they were standing on the site of a graveyard.

Mirandola looked like a mere youth among the Oysters, although he seemed to have been attempting protective mimicry. Merrick took in at once that he was dressed in the costume of an Oyster, the dark trousers, waistcoat and collarless shirt affected by Aboriginal men and women alike – everyone here, including Frida, was wearing it. It was little different from what everyone else wore, but the fabrics were coarser and their manner of wearing it made it look like a traditional national costume. They all had ear studs, though.

Frida went over to the nearest Oysters and instantly became one of them, so Mirandola, turning, saw only Merrick. He stared, trying to place him.

'What are you doing here?' If Mirandola had identified him in any way it was only as one who was not an Oyster. Oysters had every right to be there. But he continued to stare. 'Don't I know you?' he went on, before Merrick could answer.

'He's with me, Orlando.' Frida turned from her conversation.

'Why?'

'Why not?' Frida, who was still carrying the quant, laid it down as if making a formal declaration. I have a wide circle of friends, she seemed to be saying. I don't need you to vet them.

Merrick saw an opportunity. 'We met at the Ayckbourn,' he said.

'You met Frida Mason at the Ayckbourn?'

'I met *you* at the Ayckbourn. Frida was dancing.'

'I remember.' Mirandola did not relax noticeably. Merrick was sure the man recalled him from somewhere else and was trying to work out where. Give him time and he probably would. Meanwhile he was in no position to start checking up.

The backhoe, rolling up and down on its tracks, bucked and growled as the teeth struck stone. There was a shout from the pit. Merrick looked down and saw a man in a helmet, gesticulating from below.

'Stop digging!

'Hello, Dad.' Frida was at his side, waving down. 'What have you found?'

Mason Senior returned his daughter's greeting with an abstracted wave and turned his attention to the man controlling the backhoe.

'We've hit a wall, Stan. Can it be the church?'

Stan swarmed down a ladder at the side of the excavation. In a satchel on his back were several rolls of what looked like paper. The two men selected one, studied it, conferred. Stan yelled up, 'How long have we got?'

'Two hours, maximum.'

Stan shot up the ladder again. 'We've hit the south wall of the churchyard by the look of it. Now we cut north-east, for the church.'

The backhoe curtsied and crawled forwards, skirting the edge of the pit, made a four-point turn on the far side and lunged its head into the hole again.

Merrick watched, aghast and envious. He knew they were racing the tide but this was construction, not archaeology. The sea was two hours away. If they had started digging at first light, about the time he had awoken in the turf lodge, then this enormous hole was the result and out of it they had rescued, or untimely ripped, eight coffins that were ranged in a row above the tide line.

And yet, he thought, if only we'd had a backhoe at the cathedral, not one of the monsters that dug out foundations for the heights but a manageable machine like this baby that we could have operated ourselves. Why don't we have one? It was painful and almost shocking to think that Aboriginals had access to better equipment than a university department.

But what damage might they not be doing? Three of the coffins had splintered lids where they had been forced open. Surely no one had tried to prise them off with the backhoe? Since everyone's attention was focused on the excavation he sauntered across to look more closely.

The gouges and splinterings were not new. Whatever had caused them had done so long ago. If Ehrhardt was right, this was what Parizo Man had been doing when someone with a gun had surprised him in the act. So where—?

While he was inspecting the coffins two or three people had wandered away from the pit. One of them was Frida.

'Someone here would like to meet you,' she said, touching him on the shoulder. 'You saw my father, down the hole. This is my uncle, Edwin Shepherd, mayor of Briease. Ed, this is Merrick Korda, from the university.'

Shepherd held out his hand. His face was as lined and pockmarked, freckled and scarred as the rest, but he had a vigorous, healthy air. Merrick took his hand.

'You must be the one who dug up the body,' Shepherd said pleasantly.

Merrick was so winded by this announcement that for a moment he could not answer, only gaze nervously past the Oysters to where Mirandola was standing by the pit in an attitude of supervision, although no one was taking any notice of him. So close to the droning backhoe he was out of earshot.

'How do you know?'

'You were observed,' Shepherd said.

Had Frida planned this, pausing on her excursion to Herigal to call ahead and alert her uncle to what she was bringing home with her? He was on his own, faced with a bunch of Oysters and someone who had taken up cudgels on their behalf. They looked as if they could handle their own cudgels.

'We were assisting the Politi,' Merrick said.

'Oh, I don't think so. Wasn't it the other way round – they were helping you?'

136

How much had the observers observed?

'We could have been looking at a murder victim – a *recent* murder victim.'

'Recent as in last week, for instance?'

'Recent enough to have been a recorded missing person,' Merrick said. 'The body had to be recovered. The Politi knew that if it was an ancient death my department would be interested.'

'Isn't it Dr Turcat's department?' This poor primitive was unnecessarily well informed.

'I work for him. We would never have dug here if the Politi hadn't been going to do it anyway.'

'Wouldn't you?' Shepherd continued to sound affable. 'But it was an error to have gone ahead without informing us in Briease – a discourtesy, anyway.'

Which of course it was. 'We didn't think we were on reserve land. I'm not sure that we are.'

Mirandola, making one of his silent, well-oiled approaches, appeared beside them. He looked Merrick full in the face. 'I know you!'

'We met about ten minutes ago,' Merrick said.

'No, I know where I've seen you.' He turned to Shepherd. 'This man is an archaeologist!'

He might have said rapist for all the contempt invested in the word.

'I know,' Shepherd said. 'He helped dig out the body.'

Mirandola deflated, but only slightly. 'You could get him for aggravated trespass.'

'We didn't think we were trespassing,' Merrick said, and saw a chance to cover his tracks at the same time by denying his presence at Millennium House when Mirandola came calling yesterday. 'The matter is before the courts right now.'

'*No it isn't.*' Mirandola almost left the ground in vengeful glee. 'Ehrhardt applied for retrospective permission to *have* excavated, and permission to extend the excavation. In the opinion of the magistrate such permission can be granted only by the Pan-European Coastal Authority. The Bureau of Aboriginal Affairs is also applying to the Pan-European Coastal Authority for repossession of the skeleton.'

'On the grounds that it's an Aboriginal. We don't think it is. The bones can be dated—'

'No they can't. Not by you. You obviously don't know what's been happening. The Parizo body has been confiscated and all further work on the site prohibited.'

'So what are they doing?' Merrick, remembering to look shocked and dismayed, noticed that Mirandola had made no reference to artefacts and related material. 'That looks like work on site to me.'

'Aboriginals can do what they like on Aboriginal land,' Mirandola said.

'If it is their land.'

'You question the court's decision?'

'On what grounds did it decide? The Moss isn't stationary, you know, it's growing all the time. What happens when it moves on to the wind farm? Reaches the city? When Parizo Man went into the peat the Moss was probably half the size it is now.'

'You don't have a leg to stand on,' Mirandola said.

138

Considering that he had failed as completely as Ehrhardt had in his attempt to recover the skeleton, he was taking his defeat remarkably well. Further argument was halted by a yell from the pit.

'Here's another!'

Several people who had tacked themselves on to the fringes of the dispute turned and hurried back to the excavation, Mirandola with them, leaving Merrick and Shepherd alone together.

'Why do you want him so much?' Shepherd said.

'Who?'

'Parizo Man, as you call him.'

'Why do you?'

'He's ours, one of us.'

'How do you know?' Merrick said. 'If you murdered me now and buried me on your land, would I be yours?'

The backhoe had fallen silent and his question rang out across the beach. All heads turned as if giving it serious consideration, then bent to the business in hand. Shepherd went to look and Merrick followed.

A ninth coffin was being hoisted on cables over the side of the hole. This one had been violated more thoroughly than the others, the lid smashed lengthways with savage blows so that a ragged cleft ran from one end to the other. The interior was packed with earth, hiding whatever else it might contain.

'How do you think that happened?' Merrick said to Shepherd.

'Someone tried to dig it up. Someone like you?'

'Someone tried to dig it up soon after it was buried,

139

perhaps. Have you ever seen us at work? We scrape and chip and dust, we use spatulas, brushes – not mechanical diggers. And we don't discard anything.'

'Meaning?'

'Someone tried to break open those coffins to get at whatever they thought was inside.' He beckoned Shepherd out of Mirandola's range. 'Tell me, why did you start digging?'

'The same reason you did; curiosity about the past, our past.'

'Did you know what you were digging for?'

Shepherd put his head close to Merrick's. 'Meaning?'

'You said you watched us dig out Parizo Man. What did you see?'

'I said you were observed. Not by me.'

'Who, then?'

'Orlando—'

'No, he didn't show up till next morning.'

'Someone must have told him.'

Not the way I recall it, Merrick thought. 'So no one looked in the hole to see what I'd found before the tide came up?'

'No, but as soon as you'd all left next morning I went and had a root around myself. The hole was full of water, of course, but I had a pole with me. I could feel something solid down there, harder than the peat. We baled out and saw the coffin. Is that what you'd found?'

'Only I didn't realize what it was. Did you?'

'Oh yes,' Shepherd said. 'We still use them.'

140

'Is that allowed?'

'Aboriginals on their own land . . .'

'Of course. Has Mirandola told you how Parizo Man was found?'

'Sitting up.'

'Sitting up and leaning back. I don't think he was buried.'

'He was a long way down for someone who hadn't been buried.'

'He was in a grave, but it wasn't *his* grave.'

'Whose?' Shepherd said.

'The coffin's – whoever's in it. You know – I know – this was a churchyard. One body per coffin, one coffin per grave, right?'

'Generally speaking. Sometimes on different levels.'

'Top level's the only one that matters. New burial, something worth having in the coffin, and I don't mean the body. Someone goes back to the grave at night, reopens it and smashes his way into the coffin. Look at those four, they've all been broken into. Our man died in an open grave sitting on a coffin he *hadn't* broken into.'

'Are you sure?'

'I found it, remember.'

'How did he die, then?'

'Someone disturbed him; he'd been shot through the eye.'

The graven lines on Ed Shepherd's face rearranged themselves into a diagram of pleasurable excitement. One touch of murder made the whole world kin.

'And then the grave was filled in?'

'And then the grave was filled in, possibly also burying the murder weapon – although whoever did it may not have thought that he had anything to hide – and whatever the robber was using to break into the coffins.'

'Would that have survived?'

Merrick looked at the crowd around the pit, the busy backhoe grumbling and gnawing again, and the new dune of earth that had been cast out of the hole.

'If *we'd* excavated, chip, scrape, brush, we'd have found it. We don't gouge out whole cubic metres in one go.' His despair conquered his envy. 'God knows what you've chucked out – didn't you know about that?'

Shepherd looked stricken. 'No – the tide—'

'Yes, the tide, which will shortly wash away that heap and flood the pit. It doesn't matter how big the hole is, there's enough sea to fill it. What are you going to do about that?'

'Pump,' Shepherd said. 'We're used to that, believe it or not. Then we start again when the tide goes down.'

'Taking with it anything that may be in that heap of spoil. Leave the excavation. Use the backhoe to shift the spoil above the tide line. You've got about an hour to clear it, then we can take our time sifting through it.'

'We?' Shepherd said.

'Will you work with me?'

'The question is, will we let you work with us?' Shepherd said over his shoulder. He was running towards the pit, calling to the backhoe operator. There was a brief discussion, then the backhoe reversed, crawled around the pit and, tossing its head coquettishly, sank its teeth into the mound of spoil.

'Don't make another heap,' Merrick shouted; 'spread it out!'

'Why?' someone asked.

'So we don't have to *burrow*.'

'We?' Mirandola was coming back, palpitating with rage. 'Haven't you people done enough?'

'Do you know why the spoil's being moved? I suppose you thought you were saving time with that machine. Archaeology's not about saving time.'

'I thought that was exactly what it was about.'

Merrick privately considered that this was rather clever and pictured a new sign to hang over future excavations: HELP SAVE TIME BEFORE IT'S TOO LATE. 'You can laugh at the way we work but we find things. We never discard anything. You've no idea what may be in that pile of earth. Nor have I. We can go through it. In the old days priceless information was lost by grave robbers. They only wanted treasure.'

'Grave robbers? Unlike yourself.'

Archaeologists never knew for sure what they might find, but grave robbers knew exactly what they were looking for – treasure. Of the nine recovered coffins four had been forced open and one had been in the process of being forced open when its predator had been stopped with a shot to the head. Most twenty-second-century burials had been simple affairs, he knew. Centuries had passed since people had been interred with grave goods, and yet these dead, in their simple wooden coffins in their quiet rural churchyard, had gone to their graves with something that others had believed worth digging them up for; something worth risking death for, worth dying for.

All this while no one had tried to contact him. Turcat quite possibly could not; Ehrhardt might not even have missed him. More to the point, no one was looking for him; ironically, the only person who knew where he was, Mirandola, did not know that he was worth finding. Almost he might not exist.

Almost, in respect of Parizo Man, he did not exist. Security at Millennium House would have a record of his arrival, but not his departure through the flood escape, and he could not honestly remember when he had last entered the building since he and Turcat had taken up residence to work on the body. Better still, there was nothing particularly unusual in this. Turcat's staff came and went randomly. While they were digging for the cathedral Merrick had not reported to base more than two or three times in four weeks. If there was an equation here, he was not part of it.

When he went back he would have much to report. The mound of earth was now distributed across the beach, above the tide line, the sea was pouring into the excavation and the backhoe was scurrying up the beach ahead of the advancing tide.

'When you said you could pump,' Merrick said to Ed Shepherd, 'what sort of a timescale did you have in mind?'

'We could empty this volume in, oh, an hour,' Shepherd said. 'That'd still leave us ten to dig in.'

'And tomorrow you'll dig as big a hole again?'

'More, now we know which direction to go in.'

'Double the volume, and the next day triple. *Three* hours to pump it out, eight to dig in. You see what I'm getting at, don't you? The bigger the hole the less time you'll have to work in it. In the end you'll have just enough time to empty it between one tide and the next. Are you trying to dig up the whole churchyard?'

'We have to preserve the site.'

'Preserve it? That's *preserving* it?'

'We wanted to protect our own.'

This nonsense from a sensible man alerted his suspicions all over again. They might be seeking to protect their own but in the process they were wrecking the site. Someone had suggested digging before the archaeologists returned and so they had dug, to save their Inglish ancestors from the wicked Europeans, thwarting said Europeans as a bonus. That had been the real reason, he was certain, and even more certain that, to start with, the disinterred coffins had been of no more interest to them than the scattered soil; and yet, now apprised of the situation, Shepherd was intrigued. He wanted to search for clues.

'You're never going to be able to excavate properly here unless you build a coffer dam.'

At least Shepherd knew what he was talking about.

'It wouldn't be difficult – you've got the technology, haven't you? Planks. The point is, why do you want to excavate at all? Why are you bringing out the coffins?

Mirandola's gone to law on your behalf because we dug out – perfectly legally – someone who should never have been here in the first place, but you're hauling these coffins up – for why? Whose idea was it? Who's looking for what?'

Shepherd was looking at him, suspicion and doubt etched into his expression. These people with their lines and wrinkles, their faces could be read like maps, like graphs. They could conceal nothing.

'We were told—'

'Who told you?'

'The bureau made it known that there was nothing to stop us excavating.'

'Why did you want to excavate anyway? I mean, is it something you've always secretly longed to do? If so, why not do it sooner? You didn't have to wait for a department and funding, did you? Aboriginals on your own land . . . You could have *blasted*. No one would have stopped you.'

Shepherd said, 'Did you come here to tell us this?'

'No, I didn't intend to come here at all – I got on the wrong monorail. Frida brought me with her, it wasn't my idea. But now I am here, tell me, what do you think you're doing?'

While they were talking they were picking over the spoil left by the backhoe.

'Are you going back to the city today?' Shepherd asked.

'I needn't.' Unless Turcat decided to call him he needn't. Even if he did call it might be impossible to comply.

146

'Then stay at my house, we need to talk.'

'We? Mirandola?'

'Not Mirandola. I'll keep him occupied for now. You go back the way you came with Frida; she'll deliver you safely.'

'Will she? Are you going to tell her to?'

Shepherd looked puzzled. 'You tell her. Are you not friends?'

'We met for the second time yesterday.'

'Why did she bring you here?'

Merrick had been asking himself that very question at intervals since they had left the monorail at Eavrey Sound, and the question grew more unanswerable every time he asked it. 'She said, so I shouldn't be stuck at Eavrey Station.'

'If that's what she said it's probably true. We aren't as devious as you seem to think. Tell her I've invited you to stay. She'll believe you.'

'Which way are you going back?'

'The quick way,' Shepherd said. 'We have roads, although you may find that hard to credit. How do you think we got the backhoe out here?'

'What about Mirandola?'

'What about him?'

'Is he staying?'

'Not with me. Look, Briease is a town, not a long-house. We have streets. There's no reason to suppose you'll meet him even if he does stay. There's no reason why you shouldn't be here, is there?'

'Legally, no, but he might wonder.'

'He's already wondering. Let him. Look, he's got

his head in the hole, get over the dune now and I'll send Frida after you.'

Merrick did not want to leave the plentious promise of the outspread peat, but unless another storm blew up, bringing an exceptionally high tide, and there was no sign of that happening, he could return to it later. And the urgency of discovering what it might contain was easily matched by Shepherd's own urgency, aroused by nothing more than Merrick's own question about why the Oysters were so eager to excavate and, in the process, destroy what they might find.

Mirandola indeed had his head in the hole, kneeling on the edge, insecurely braced by bent arms. Two men behind him were silently making kicking motions. Merrick nodded to Shepherd, stepped back and took a run at the dune. There were rough tracks winding up it and as he aimed for one, the wiry marram grass closed in round and behind him. He did not stop or turn until he had reached the summit, stumbling and slithering in the loose sand. The group on the beach was still assembled around the excavation; he could not distinguish one from another, or even see Frida, but he turned again and ploughed on down the landward side towards the deceitful green carpet of the marsh.

And here he would have to stay until Frida came after him. Ought he to have trusted Shepherd, who might merely have wanted him out of the way while he conferred with Mirandola; who might be assuming malevolently that he would not wait for Frida but with fatal impetuosity strike out across the marsh towards the trees or in the direction, wherever that might be, of Briease itself?

It must be to the right, although it was concealed by trees. At the worst he could follow the line of the dunes to safety. Shepherd had spoken of roads; if they had brought the backhoe to the shore by road that must be the way from Briease. He tried to envision the maps, but the old map was easier to remember than the new one. Why? Because of the organic purpose of that reticulation of roads, linking towns, villages, farms, that had been settled for good reasons of aspect, water supply, defensibility; each of them a first choice, not a last ditch. Somewhere nearby the Niven must flow into the sea. If he followed the dunes to the estuary he could turn inland and follow the river, wade, swim if necessary, hire a boat, steal one even.

There was a scuffling in the dune above him, the marram grass shrugged and rippled and Frida came out beside him.

'Fraternizing with the natives?' she inquired.

'Doing what?'

'You seem to be getting a taste for our company; last night in a turf lodge with me, now you're planning to stay in one of our houses with my Uncle Ed.'

'Does he live in a turf lodge?'

'In a modest hole in the riverbank,' Frida said. 'Now, keep a civil tongue in your head or I'll vault.'

'I was thinking about that,' Merrick said as they struck out across the marsh. 'There must be more direct ways to Briease.'

'There are, but I left my gear in the punt and the punt is hitched to that alder up ahead.'

It was no longer up ahead, but it had been when they started out and would be again no doubt when they had completed the detours.

'I'm not fraternizing, as you call it,' Merrick said when they were well out into the marsh, too far to be heard by anyone coming over the dunes. 'Your uncle wants to talk about the excavation.'

'With an expert?'

'I never said that.'

'Proceedings certainly changed tack when you showed up. One minute they're digging through to the earth's core, the next moment operations are suspended and what was a hole is spread out all over the beach.'

'Above the tide line. Couldn't you see what would have happened if they'd left that heap where it was?'

'The sea would have done the spreading for them.'

'We keep everything we find in our digs. Anything your people found came out in sodding great chunks, thrown in a heap, and half of it would already be on its way out to sea by now.'

'You're taking over the supervision, then?'

'I'm not. If your uncle thinks I can tell him anything I'll tell him. Otherwise I'll be asking for the fastest route out of here.'

'Back to the city. Why *did* you get on that car?'

'A mistake, I told you.' It had been a mistake to board a car at all, to board that particular car, which made it all the more galling that she clearly did not

believe him. And he could not account for her suspicion. She was, after all, as far as he could tell, a dancer,
nothing more.

A dancer who worked in the city, an Oyster among
Europeans. That alone might account for suspicion,
but hers, surely, could be no greater than his. He was
convinced that whoever had come up with the idea
of excavating Parizo Beach had done it with the
express intention of destroying the site.

Chapter Six

Frida took the punt back the way they had come earlier, although he did not know this until they re-entered the Niven where they had left it. He recognized the view of the bridge which must carry the road that Shepherd had spoken of.

'Where does that go?'

'The road? To Norge.'

'All the way?'

'Why not? We aren't bound by statute to travel by punt and pole. We have vehicles.'

'The backhoe?'

'Roadrunners, bicycles, a few cars, probably more cars than you'd find in the city per head of the population. If the rail had been running to Norge yesterday, that's the way I'd have come. It's only a few kilometres. You don't get out of your city much, do you?'

'Hardly anyone does,' Merrick said humbly. The humility was stirred by the scene that was unfolding in front of him as they passed under the bridge. He had never imagined . . .

It was like looking through one of the photographic archives at Millennium House, from the Antediluvial period: landing stages, wharves, warehouses, shops, homes; no blocks or heights but big solid houses of two, three storeys, row houses with retail premises beneath them and, looking down over all, twin sentinels: the wind turbine and the tower of a church. It could not be anywhere near the size of Turcat's cathedral, but with a tower that high it must be a considerable building of its period. Then he had to ask himself, of what period was this place?

The boats moored at the wharves were seagoing craft.

'Freighters?'

'Trawlers. We have fishing rights; federal law.'

The estuary lay spread before them, sparkling under the noon-day sun. There were buildings on both banks, as far as he could see.

'How many people live here?' He recalled last night's glum prediction of mud huts and Shepherd's sardonic remark about a longhouse.

'About four thousand in the town, maybe two thousand in the villages and the fen. Don't talk now, I have to get out of the tideway.'

The punt swung to the right into an enclosed basin with small boats moored all round. Frida steered the craft against the farthest wall, to a vacant mooring ring where a wooden ladder, flush with the brickwork, ran up to ground level. She secured the rope and skipped up the ladder, while Merrick passed up the baggage. As he followed her an extraordinary sound rolled over the roofs and the water, deep musical notes, four of them repeated four times with a slight variation, then a pause and then, portentously, a single note in a lower key.

'One o'clock,' Frida said, seeing him look for the source of the sound. 'It's the church.'

'That's a clock?'

The last sonorous note was still vibrating.

'Haven't you heard one before?'

No, he had not. He had heard *about* clocks that struck, bells that rang to tell the hour, but no, he had never heard one. He had never in his life been anywhere such a thing was needed.

'Don't you have timers here?'

'Of course we do, but we like our church clock.'

'It's a real church?'

'No, it's a three-dimensional projection.' Seeing that he was half-prepared to believe it she laughed and shook her head. 'It's real enough. I'll show you some-time.'

'But you don't use it?'

'We polish it occasionally.'

'Seriously, no one practises religion here, do they?'

'Aboriginals on their own land . . . There are no Christians, if that's what you mean. It's a fine building. We have uses for it.'

'And the churchyard?'

'Yes, we use that, too.'

Shepherd had said as much: coffin burials. 'Are you going to reinter the bodies you've just dug up?'

They were walking now along a narrow lane between low walls and fences, beyond which each house stood in its own little parc. He knew what they were called:

154

back gardens. Frida was leading the way but she paused and slowed down.

'Reinter?'

'Bury them again.'

'I've no idea what's going to be done. It has nothing to do with me. I haven't been here for weeks.'

'But you know what's been happening.'

'We communicate with smoke signals.'

Merrick, almost involuntarily, put a hand on her arm and she stopped altogether.

'Look, I'm sorry if I'm giving the impression that I think you're all living in the past—'

'You do.'

'I don't mean to. I've never been on a reserve. It's just that you – your people – have opted out – elected to go without certain advances, advantages – in order to live as you choose. But I don't know what they are.'

'I think you're beginning to find out. The trouble with archaeologists is, they don't know any history.'

They walked on. 'That's not true,' Merrick said. 'The department is part of the history faculty. History was my specialism before I started working with Turcat.'

'History of what?'

'World history, European history, history of the Union, the Antediluvian period, the Anarchy . . .'

'History of people?'

'That's anthropology.'

'Are any of you anthropologists?'

'Dr Turcat – don't you know him? You know his sister.'

'I don't know him. Is it being an anthropologist that makes him so interested in corpses?'

'We don't see many corpses – we don't see *any*. Usually, all we turn up are bone fragments. Finding Parizo Man was a bit of luck.'

'Was it?'

'You think we ordered up the hurricane specially? It was pure chance that the skull came to light.' But was it pure chance that Rémy Turcat had got to know about it?

Frida turned aside at a gate in the fence beside them. As they argued their way along the lane he had been taking in how insecure these buildings were. The cottages at Herigal Staithe had not looked much more substantial than the turf lodges and he could not rid himself of the fancy that they were not real at all but imitations put up to amuse tourists, the inhabitants of which retired to apartment blocks when the rubbernecks had gone home.

But these were real houses, functional, solid, built for living in, and yet anyone, it seemed, could do what Frida herself was doing, opening the flimsy wooden gate with a mere flick of the thumb, walking up a concrete path through the little private parc and, stopping only to knock perfunctorily, pushing open a door that led directly into the building. There seemed to be no code, no key, no scanner. He could not get into his own apartment, even into his own height, without pausing for the doors to recognize him. He looked round for an eye but if one existed it was very well concealed.

'What are you searching for?' Frida was noisily dropping her belongings on the tiled floor.

'Security.'

'We are our own security.'

'There's no record of who goes in and out?'

'You need only one hand to count who goes in and out of my family's house, one finger to count for Ed.'

'You live as a family – together?'

'We are a family,' she said patiently. 'People lived for a long while like this without coming to any great harm. Ed's lived alone since my aunt died. They were a family too.'

'Can you just walk in here when you like?'

'I knocked,' Frida said.

'But nobody answered.'

'Nobody's home. Ed's still on the beach, I suppose.'

'But – *anyone* could get in.'

'Who'd want to?'

'You have no crime?'

'One of the advances we've elected to live without? No, the advance we elected to live without in this instance is surveillance. My apartment in the city – the one I've been living in while I've worked at the Ayckbourn – it has a record of every person who has ever lived in it, how many times they went in and out, who they brought with them, how long they stayed, a record of every visitor, maintenance worker, every ancillary robot – it must be like that where you live, where you work. Nobody needs that information but it's there, it keeps growing. And when you go to the theatre, the parc, to a shop – if anyone wanted to they could access every building you'd ever been in from the moment you were born, and when, and for how long. The same for me when I'm in the city, but not here. That's part of our charter; we choose what to record of ourselves.'

He was looking around at this building, designed for the use of an adult family. The nearest thing he knew to a family was Turcat and his sister – did they share an apartment? The room where he stood was apparently used for food preparation and he could see through an arch into the next room, where conventional chairs and sofas, low tables, suggested a leisure area. Between the two was a lobby and a stair-case to the next storey. Did Shepherd own *both* floors?

'Go on up,' Frida said. 'There's a spare bedroom on the left, washroom straight ahead. Ed'll be back soon. I'll see you.' She gathered up her bags and was heading for another door in the next room which, as he could see through the glazing in it, led directly out into the street.

'Where are you going?'

'Home. Make yourself comfortable, have a drink. Goodbye, Merrick.'

She stumped down the short path to the paved way that served as a road, turned and smiled maliciously at his discomposure.

'That's right. I enticed you here for a special purpose and now I'm leaving you to your fate among the savages.'

'Fate?'

'Human sacrifice, naturally.'

He stood in the doorway looking out at the quiet street, the houses opposite and the vast sky. Half-consciously he examined the door frame, the masonry surrounding it, the little overhanging brow of a porch, but he could find no evidence of surveillance. Either they really did have none or it was so sophisticated that it surpassed anything he had ever encountered.

It was not a subject to which he had ever given much thought until now, when he was so conscious of its absence. Unless they breached federal laws, many of which must coincide with their own customs and taboos, Aboriginals on their own land were free to conduct their own affairs in their own way. If they chose to exist without centralized surveillance then they were presumably free to do that too. But what had they paid for that choice; had they all chosen?

He went back to the kitchen area, examining panelled surfaces until he found a refrigeration unit, took out a can and went into the front room again. The quiet was eerie, no maintenance hum and no sounds coming from outside, although one of the windows had a hinged panel that stood slightly open. He had prudently concealed from Frida his surprise at seeing a screen wall and it looked straightforward enough, although he might have expected to find knobs and dials. Sitting to face it he called up a news channel.

Instantly the whole wall was heaving with people, the room reverberated with the frenzied yelling that issued from their gaping mouths. He reduced the volume and sat transfixed, can in hand, watching what looked like a fullscale riot in progress, definitely in progress for the timer on the screen read 15.34. In the background was the familiar frontage of Millennium House. Then the view was blocked by an opportunist rioter holding up a placard that filled the whole screen for a few seconds, madly scrolling mad sentiments: BAN ARCHAEOLOGY. DEATH TO ALL RACIST NATIONALIST BASTARD ARCHAEOLOGISTS. TURCAT MUST DIE.

The picture jumped to another cam angle, catching a charge of armoured Politi vehicles, but the words, imprinted on Merrick's retina, burned across the screen. RACIST NATIONALIST BASTARD ARCHAEOLOGISTS. TURCAT MUST DIE.

A week ago, two weeks ago, a few bedraggled die-hards picketing the cathedral; yesterday maybe two-score belligerents; and now this. How had something which few people even bothered to think about, much less care about, suddenly inflamed this incandescent mob?

A commentary strap ran along the top of the screen. *Amid accusations of anti-federalist subversion demonstrators have taken to the streets to protest at the activities of certain university elements in stirring up nationalist sympathies.*

Academics had a reputation for being out of touch, but whatever had caused this eruption should not have escaped their notice. The resurrection of a long-dead grave robber could scarcely have ignited the conflagration. What were they actually protesting about? If they, whoever they were, felt really outraged about exhumations, why were they not at this moment converging upon Parizo Beach?

160

'Aren't you glad you're not there?'

Ed Shepherd had come in by the street door unheard above the racket and stood at his side.

'What's going on?' Merrick took the volume down further.

'I'd say you're better placed to answer that than I am. Who are those people?'

'I don't know. We've always had protesters opposed to the retrieval of human remains; they hang around our digs, two or three usually, never more than half a dozen. We know them all by sight. They have moral objections – they think bones are the thin end of the wedge; next we'll be laying out fresh corpses for display.'

'Well, it's happened before. Wait there, I'll get a drink and join you.'

While Shepherd was out of the room Merrick killed the screen, but not before he caught the tail end of another surtext: . . . *an inquiry into the funding of archaeological activities.*

'We've never displayed fresh corpses,' he said when Shepherd came back and settled at the other end of the divan.

'Not fresh perhaps,' Shepherd said, 'but wasn't that why the museums were closed in the first place? Public revulsion at seeing the dead used for entertainment?'

'Museums were for education.'

'How educational is looking at a corpse?' Shepherd wondered. 'I mean, clearly it educates *you* because you're educated to learn from it, but don't tell me the general public want to look at human remains in order

161

to increase their knowledge and improve their minds.'

'And don't tell me,' Merrick said, 'that public revulsion closed the museums. It was public indifference did that, when the curators removed the human remains and there was nothing left that anyone wanted to see. That's what happened, you know.'

'I do know, in fact,' Shepherd said. 'As we did not entrust our knowledge to electrons we escaped Comfort and Joy.'

'What do you know about Comfort and Joy?'

'Mainly, as I said, that we escaped it, the virus that swept across Europe and devoured all historical records after the Anarchy.'

'It was the Black Death of viruses,' Merrick said, 'and it swept through the universities of Europe. It was very surgically aimed.'

'Who aimed it?'

'No one knows. Blame the Brandenburgers.'

'Who are?'

'No one knows that either. They're to blame for everything. They probably sent the hurricane.'

'Did it come at Christmas by any chance, your Black Death?'

'Just before the midwinter holiday,' Merrick said, 'which goes back much farther than Christmas.'

'I dare say, but "tidings of comfort and joy" are words from an old carol, a Christmas song. People still wish each other well at that season, don't they? *We* do. Who could resist a message bearing tidings of comfort and joy, especially after a civil war. Who could resist opening it? *All over Europe.* And at one stroke, everything lost.'

'We still have books,' Merrick said. 'Photographs.'

'*You* do. A lot of people would consider them lewd and perverted – and would pay a fortune to get hold of them.'

'We get plenty of indecent proposals. We could sell practically everything we dig up.'

'Ye-e-es,' Shepherd said. 'Turcat the Desecrator must be regarded as Turcat the Pornographer in some quarters. Why must he die? Frida knows his sister.'

'How did you know about that – the death threat?'

'It was on yesterday's newscasts too.'

'Oh shit; was I?'

'What are you accused of?'

'I didn't mean on a placard – no one knows who I am. On the newscast.'

'I didn't notice you. It would have been about six p.m. You must have been in the fen by then.'

'I suppose they can't fake them?'

'The newscasts? What a suggestion. You think it's a virtual riot? But I don't think that's necessary. From what Mirandola's been saying it's genuine enough.'

'It's all got out of hand so fast. What did Mirandola say?'

'That there is a groundswell of public opinion against what your department is doing.'

'Was it Mirandola who put you up to using the backhoe?'

'Why should he? He came out yesterday to have another look at the pit – the one you dug. We'd already got the first coffin out – the one you found. He said that the department had been forbidden by the court to return to the site and that the Parizo corpse—'

'It's a skeleton. You've seen it.'

'No, I haven't.'

'Not all of it, no. But you were with Mirandola when he first saw the skull; inspecting storm damage, weren't you?'

'Did he tell you that?'

'Not directly, but I understood he'd been with the mayor – that's you.'

'We didn't see any skull. The first I knew of it was when we had word that someone had been digging up the beach.'

'Why didn't you stop us?'

'Because we didn't find out until you'd gone.'

'From Mirandola.'

'Yes.'

'He walked across the marsh to tell you about it.'

'I don't know how he got here but, yes, he came to see me.'

By the slowest possible route, Merrick thought. 'Frida says you communicate by smoke signals.'

Shepherd tapped the stud in his ear. 'We communicate the same way that you do.'

Quite, Merrick thought, so why does Mirandola have to cross a marsh to do it face to face? He could have called out enough Oysters to stop us without moving a step. He said, 'What did he tell you yesterday?'

'That the remains had been sequestrated. No one could get at them, not you, not us, until the matter had been decided. We couldn't imagine why this was taking so long – could you? Anyway, Orlando said there

164

was no reason why we should stop digging on our own beach unless some coastal authority ordered us to.'

'And whose idea was the backhoe?'

Shepherd did not answer immediately. He went into the utility room, where Merrick could hear him scrabbling about with doors and drawers, everything manually operated. After a few minutes he came back with more cans and a tray of cold food which he placed on the table between them.

'The backhoe,' Merrick said.

'I don't remember who suggested it. We called a council meeting. It was mentioned that, the hole being where it is, the tide was always going to be a factor, that we would always have to work quickly. I suppose the backhoe came up then.'

'Don't you make recordings?'

'It was an informal meeting – after all, the excavation doesn't affect the town as a whole. And we do keep records, not recordings. They're called minutes. But not at this meeting.'

'So someone proposed using a mechanical digger to save time. When Mirandola told Turcat that you might continue the excavation yourselves, he offered to help, and Mirandola said that you could manage perfectly well on your own.' Merrick paraphrased diplomatically, editing out the comment about poor primitives. 'And Turcat said, "They won't know what to do."'

'Did he?' Shepherd said.

'He was right, wasn't he? You don't know what you're doing. Do you even know why you're doing it?'

'Didn't you leap at the chance to dig up the beach when you knew there was something under it?'

'Turcat leaped. I came along to help with the spade work.'

'So you're utterly uninterested?'

'Of course not.' Merrick tried to recall wild enthusiasm but what he had mainly felt was relief at getting away from the cathedral. 'I was interested, but it *is* my job.'

'So were we interested, discovering that our history was within reach. Don't you understand me – of course you don't. Until you came here, had you ever been out of the city – no, I don't mean to the mainland. You don't know your own island, do you? This is the first time you've ever really seen the coast. You think you're on the edge here. We know that our past is under the sea. You dig for history; we didn't know we could, we thought it was gone for ever.'

'It will be,' Merrick said, 'if you keep enlarging that hole. You have maps – the same ones that we've got, probably. Didn't you know the village was there, the church, the graveyard?'

'Miles of the offing are mapped,' Shepherd said.

'The offing?'

'From the shore to the visible horizon, that's the offing. The sea has eaten away at this coast for centuries, long before the Flood. The Isles are on the rim of the continental shelf, rocking up and down. Thousands of years ago you could walk across from the mainland, before the Channel cut through. Out there, under water, countless villages, towns, roads, all mapped.'

'I know. The church you're digging up is St Peter's, Yexham.'

'And we knew that. What we didn't know was how near the surface it is. It was assumed it must be much farther down, that the sand was deeper, and then the sand all vanished in one night. How could we resist digging?'

'But you did, didn't you? Resist. You weren't exactly gagging for it. How long was it before you even dug out the first coffin?'

'Only a few days back. We carried on where you left off. The problem was the tide. You're right. We didn't know what we were doing.'

'I'll tell you what you've done, you've destroyed the site. We'd love to use mechanical diggers in the city, but we don't have access to them. But if we did, we'd know exactly where to use them, how far down to cut – to the centimetre. The backhoe in, what, five hours, has chewed up tonnes of peat and anything that might be in it—'

'And if you hadn't come along it would have been washed away. All right' – Shepherd frowned, but amiably – 'you're the hero, the man who saved the past. What are you getting at?'

'The site was destroyed on purpose,' Merrick said. 'Not by you, or Frida's father or Cousin Stan or the other guys. By whoever suggested using machinery to excavate. I wish you could remember who it was.'

They returned to Parizo Beach by road. Where it ended, at the dunes, they were high enough to look out over the Niven estuary to the far shore, where the sand hills gave place to a long shingle bank sweeping northwards.

'The Chisel,' Shepherd said.

The tide was on the way out again, leaving a swimming bath where the excavation had been. Above it, at the foot of the dunes, lay spread the contents of the hole. Shepherd had equipped them with hand forks from a selection of tools in a small outhouse, hung tidily on the walls beside stacks of red clay pots.

'What do you use all these for?'

'We grow things,' Shepherd explained kindly. 'In our gardens.'

On the beach they employed the forks to turn over the lumps of peat, beginning at one end of the scattered spoil.

'This could take months,' Shepherd said.

'Exactly; excavation should take months. If you *had* to use the backhoe you ought to have taken out one scoop at a time, gone through it like this and filled it in again. For instance, when we had Parizo Man in the lab we sifted every grain of soil around him – that way we found the bone splinters from the exit wound in his skull. Some of them; the rest are in this lot. Which reminds me, what's happened to the coffins?'

'They've been taken to the church.'

'What do you plan to do with them, open them up and see what's inside?'

'I think we can guess at what's inside.'

'You could have guessed that without digging them up.'

'They were there,' Shepherd said. 'What would you have done?'

'That would have depended on what we were looking for. In the middle of the twentieth century, in London, there was massive destruction after the wartime bombing – you know about that? When they started to rebuild, huge areas of land were cleared for the first time in hundreds of years, and over the next half-century the original Roman city came to light – streets, temples, an amphitheatre. Then there were the Saxon strata, the medieval strata, monasteries, plague cemeteries. People had the knowledge then to read the evidence. They could see how people lived, how they died. All that's been lost.'

'Comfort and Joy.'

'And the sea. We'd have to dive for London now. We're starting again from scratch. If we'd dug here, looking for coffins, it would have been because we expected to find them, and we wouldn't have been looking at all unless we thought they could tell us something.

'Put it this way, our maps, your maps, tell us that there was a village here, a church, a graveyard. We could have calculated how deeply it was buried by finding out first of all when it was flooded. Actually we know – twenty-one forty-nine. It's not a well-documented era, from your point of view.

'You don't imagine that everyone went into the ground in twenty-one forty-nine? There can't have been much room left in the churchyard by then, it would have been in use for centuries.

'Before the court confiscated Parizo Man we were going to have him dated. To find out when *he* went into the ground – because what he was doing, we think, was grave robbing. Your coffins haven't told *you* anything, but they've told me plenty. Parizo Man never got into the coffin he was sitting on; he was shot first. But now I see that four other coffins *had* been opened, coffins that must have contained something worth getting out. And if our department had been excavating we'd have gone down centimetre by centimetre, millimetre by millimetre, checking the levels of the coffins; which were damaged, which intact. I wouldn't mind a look at those coffins before I leave – all we can hope to find here is perhaps the tool he used to smash his way in, or the weapon that killed him, or maybe he had something with him.'

'What sort of a thing?'

'For a start, a bag or container to carry away whatever he hoped to find. He might have been working at night – in fact, we're sure he was. He'd have had a light of some kind.'

'Would things like that have survived? What about his clothes? What was Parizo Man wearing when you found him?'

Merrick stopped probing and paid attention.

'Did he go grave robbing nude by the light of the silvery moon? He may have had good reason but I can't imagine what it was. Not even shoes? Surely there'd be something left?'

'Unless the body was stripped. We did think of that.'

'Somebody robbed the robber?'

170

'They were looking for what he'd found, perhaps.'

'But he hadn't found anything. He never got into that coffin.'

'Maybe it wasn't the first one he'd broken into that night.' Merrick kept his voice level. Shepherd was travelling on his own train of thought.

'He'd have had to be a fast worker. He's just opened a fresh grave. Were they dying like flies that he had several fresh graves to get through at the same time? An epidemic?'

'Suppose it was summer,' Merrick said. 'It's hot work, he's not wearing much. The guy who killed him strips off what the corpse is wearing—'

'Or maybe,' Shepherd said, 'he forces him to strip at gunpoint and then shoots him.'

'Why?'

'He wants to know what he's got on him. Then the killer goes through the clothes, finds nothing and throws them back in the grave along with the axe, or whatever it was, and the gun—'

'Which if *we* had been excavating we'd have found, instead of pronging about in this heap.'

'We have plenty of time now,' Shepherd said. 'We can prong about, as you call it, for weeks, if we like. Have you no idea what he would have been looking for?'

'Why, have you?'

'We can't do much here now, the light's going,' Shepherd said. 'This might be the moment for you to take your look at those coffins in the church.'

* * *

171

Merrick thought again of the cathedral. He had seen pictures of it standing in a landscape that had changed beyond recognition and he had known its dimensions intimately, the length of nave and chancel, the depth of the crypt, the height of the tower. The church at Briease was not built on the same lines: there were no transepts; it looked more like an ancient Roman basilica. The tower was at the western end, not at the crossways, and it was many times smaller, but standing in the road, looking at its outline against the twilight sky, he thought he might be experiencing the same sensations as one would have done gazing up at the cathedral when it stood, designed to draw the eye upward by people who had believed in a heaven above.

'Did you put it up specially?' he asked.

'It already stood here,' Shepherd said. 'Why should we have built it specially? You think it's a replica installed to amuse visitors?'

That was exactly what Merrick had been thinking; the whole town had a recreated look about it.

'We build to please ourselves,' Shepherd said. 'Likewise, what pleases us, we keep. This is why we are here, to please ourselves. Is there a church still standing in the city? Is there anything older than fifty years?'

'The place I work in, for a start. There are apartment blocks in the suburbs—'

'I've seen them,' Shepherd said. 'Shelving. Do people love their apartment blocks so much that they take to the streets to protest when one is going to be torn down?'

'They don't have to, they'd be rehoused.'

'On another shelf? We like what we have, we preserve it, we keep it. We like the church. We keep it.'

'You can afford to. There aren't many of you and you've got plenty of room.'

'Have you any idea what we afforded?'

Shepherd opened the heavy wooden door at the foot of the tower, unlocked, like every other door in Briease, and put on the lights by laying his hand to the wall, another manual operation.

In use as a civic building the church's interior was sectioned off by glass partitions at ground level, but from where they stood at the west end Merrick could see clear to the high east windows as he looked up at an uninterrupted perspective of beams and vaulting. Two thirds of the way along, a wide flight of stone steps elevated the floor area from the nave to the chancel and through the glass screens he saw what was in the chancel. Nine coffins lay in a row on the flagstones.

'Why were they brought here?'

'It seemed the most appropriate place. Coffins were brought into churches for funeral rites; sometimes they were left overnight. Monarchs and great leaders lay in state, often for days.'

'You don't still do that?'

'No. As soon as the cause of death is determined we bury immediately, often on the same day. The fact that we still use coffins is immaterial.'

A corridor ran along the south side of the church,

one wall glass, the other stone. Merrick noticed that they were walking on memorial tablets set in the floor.

'How do you get everyone into the churchyard?'

'We don't, there's a cemetery extension.'

'Do the dead lie beneath these stones we're walking on?'

'Not our dead.'

In the chancel the nine coffins lay at their feet.

'So, what do they tell you?' Shepherd said.

'What do you want to know?'

'I didn't say *I* wanted to know anything. What do they tell *you*?'

'Can't learn a lot just by looking. I'd want to know, is there anyone still inside?'

Shepherd started perceptibly. 'What makes you think there might not be?'

'Well, we'll assume that the sealed ones still have bodies in them, but the ones that have been opened, are they full of corpse or full of mud?'

'Are you suggesting the grave robbers were stealing the corpses?'

'That's what they were doing back in the early nineteenth century,' Merrick said. 'They were called body snatchers. Doctors had to practise on real corpses in those days, to learn anatomy. Before that was legal they used to rely on people to steal them. Now I don't think Parizo Man is so old he might have been a body snatcher. If we still had him we could date him. If we had the bullet that killed him we could date that, but we shan't find it since you chewed up the beach.'

174

Shepherd did not rise to that.

'It's unlikely that it was the bodies he was stealing so it must have been something in the coffins – what could that have been, do you think?' And how did he know which coffins to open? Were they all on the same level?'

'I think so.'

'We'd have known so. All right, say it wasn't an epidemic, they didn't all die at once, but maybe a couple did, close together. Parizo Man knows that some coffins will contain things worth salvaging, worth breaking into a grave to retrieve. Was there a tradition around these parts of burying the dead with valuables, jewellery, that kind of thing?'

'How far back are we talking?'

'I've no idea, but these are from a Christian churchyard. We'd know accurately if we could have had Parizo Man dated. I could always take a sample of one of these guys.'

'No you could not. You aren't taking anything.' Shepherd spoke authoritatively, reminding Merrick that even in so small a community the mayor must be a person of consequence.

'I meant, it might be done; if you were interested. Has anyone looked inside?'

'No, it's not something we do, disturbing the dead.'

'Except when someone suggests tossing them about a bit with earth-moving equipment. Are you at all curious, any of you?'

'I am,' Shepherd said. 'What do you think will be inside?'

'Skeletons, I'd guess. The wood's pine, not oak, isn't it?'

'Not many people would have gone in for oak – it was so rare.'

'I doubt then if anything's been preserved except the bones. Decay would have set in immediately after burial – well, immediately after death, to be precise. Maybe rings, jewellery.'

'Which one do you want to look at?' Shepherd spoke so matter-of-factly that Merrick did not immediately grasp what was being offered.

'You'll open one? Do you know which was the first out – the one Parizo Man was sitting on?'

'Why that one?'

'Because *he* thought it was worth opening but never got the chance. Whatever was in the four damaged ones will have gone. The other four may not have contained anything worth taking. Do you know which one it was?'

'It's the wet one, isn't it?' The glass doors of the chancel had opened, silently stirring the cool air. Frida was standing in the opening.

'How did you know we were here?' Merrick asked, instantly alert.

'Our house overlooks the churchyard walk,' Frida said. 'I saw the coffins go by a while ago, then I saw the lights go on. What are they going to look at? I asked myself.'

'I suppose you want to watch,' Shepherd said.

'Naturally. It has to be the wet one; it was exposed to sea water – sodden as opposed to merely damp.'

Merrick dismissed memories of elaborate preparations and precautions in the basement laboratory. 'Are we just going to open it?'

Shepherd had identified the coffin. 'We'll need trestles. Korda, look at these screws. Can we get them out or shall we cut through?'

Evidently they *were* just going to open it, with the same insouciance that they had dug it up; Aboriginals on their own land. He went over and examined the metal fittings. They were eaten almost away and the wood itself was so warped that lid and coffin appeared to have been twisted in opposite directions by giant hands. What would Turcat do? What would Turcat say when he found out? Turcat might never find out.

'What would you do if I weren't here?'

'Wrench the lid off with a crowbar,' Shepherd said, 'Except, if you weren't here we wouldn't be doing it at all. I'll get a crowbar – the caretaker's sure to have one.'

'You don't want to watch this,' Merrick said to Frida, when Shepherd was out of earshot.

'Oh, I do. Where else would I get to see a skeleton?'

Her undisguised curiosity shocked him a little. This was why museums had removed human relics from public display, because such display had come to be regarded as offensive, and the interest it aroused offensive, but was her curiosity any more offensive than his?

'If you people are going to go in for archaeology you could always start digging up your own cemeteries. Build your own museum – Aboriginals on your own land . . . that would bring in the tourists. Sights to be seen you'd see nowhere else.'

'We don't particularly want tourists,' Frida said, 'and they're always disappointed when they come to Briease. They expect us to be living in wattle and daub, eating raw fish and cantering through the fen bringing down rats in our teeth. For some reason they've been led to expect that we all live in the fen. Sometimes a party is taken a little way in, they see a turf lodge or two, some vaulters, and go away fairly happy, but the magic has been spoiled. They've already seen the town. The only things that live up to their expectations are us. We look just as decrepit as they thought we would.'

Nonplussed, he groped for an answer. Did Oysters truly believe they looked decrepit? Before he had to say anything Shepherd returned with a long steel implement that must be the crowbar and two wooden frames that he set up a metre apart.

They lifted the coffin on to the trestles and stood looking at it. Shepherd held out the crowbar.

'You're the expert. You open it.'

'I wouldn't use one of those. I don't know what we'd use.'

'Given your methods, a hairpin, probably,' Shepherd said. He prowled around the coffin looking for a promising place to begin.

'It might not be a skeleton,' Merrick said, to lighten the atmosphere. 'It might be a saint.'

'A what?'

'In the old religion, some people believed that if a

body didn't decay after death the person must have been a saint, up in heaven with god.'

'Did they keep digging them up to see how they were coming along?' Shepherd asked.

'In some cases, I believe, yes,' Merrick said. 'But it wasn't random selection – only people who might be expected to be saintly. Then the corpse would be raided for holy relics – I'm talking of the twentieth century here, not the tenth. All that insistence on the soul – and yet it was the body they really worshipped. Do you think that lid's going to come off in one piece?'

'Won't know till we've tried.' Shepherd squared his shoulders, inserted the end of the crowbar into a promising aperture and levered cautiously. At the first pressure the lid of the coffin rose up, flipped and crashed to the floor, setting up an audible shimmering in the glass-filled space. Frida was seeing her first skeleton, Merrick his second. He did not know how experienced Shepherd was in viewing the dead.

The silence was loud in the chancel after the crash, as the the three of them stood gazing into the open box. There was residue, which Merrick knew should be retained, sifted and assessed and knew, equally well, would not be; but in spite of its recent upheavals and disturbances the occupant lay as if arranged, bone by bone, as Parizo Man had been on the light table in the laboratory. The ribcage had collapsed, the lower jaw dropped, but as far as Merrick could tell, every other bone was in place, down to the phalanges of hands and feet. The arms lay extended at the sides; the body had been buried after the custom had been

179

abandoned of crossing the hands on the chest. The teeth were worn but in good condition and all present except for the four rear molars, the wisdom teeth. The forehead was near vertical with no supra-nasal prominence; a woman, in late middle age, he considered.

While he was making his rapid and automatic assessment, the other two were simply staring. Frida uttered a distressed whisper, her hands to her mouth.

'I said you wouldn't want to see.' No matter how many models, pictures, diagrams you had been shown it was still a shock, that first encounter with what lay beneath, the framework on which you were constructed, which housed the brain, cradled the gleaming viscera, caged heart and lungs; reminder that inside the leather-bound human lay a smiling mockery, the *memento mori*: *Remember you must die*.

Frida whispered again, 'Died screaming.'

'No, no. Common error, nothing like that. The jaw' – he hooked his finger under the symphysis and waggled it – 'it's hinged. When there's no muscle to keep it in place it falls open. Once, when bodies were laid out for burial a cloth was tied round the head to keep the mouth shut.' But Parizo Man might well have died screaming. 'Don't you still do that? You practise coffin burial.'

'We don't prepare corpses,' Shepherd said. 'Our funerals are simply disposals of the dead. As soon as death is confirmed the coffin is brought, the body is taken away for burial.'

'You don't mourn?'

'Oh, stop collecting data,' Shepherd said. 'Of course

180

we mourn, but we don't need the departed there with us. *You* mourn, I suppose, when you lose someone, but your vaporizers are even more efficient. Don't the departed depart in seconds?'

'Is that too quick for you?'

'We don't have the technology is all.'

'You could still cremate.'

'It's banned, you know that.'

'Aboriginals on their own land—'

'It's not our own air, though. We don't break the law.'

'All right, enough ethics,' Merrick said. 'Frida, are you feeling ill?'

'I wasn't expecting that *gape.*'

'Believe me, it happened post-mortem. After death. She was an elderly woman. If we were going to follow proper procedure we might even find out what she died of. What procedure are we going to follow, Ed?'

'I hadn't thought that far ahead. Why would you want to know what she died of?'

'Because that is what we do. We know what Parizo Man died of and look how much we've deduced from that. If it weren't for what we know about him we wouldn't be here now looking at her.' He tapped the skull. 'If I lifted this out we might find the cervical vertebrae severed – she could have been beheaded. She seems to have died with her bones in very good condition, no sign of osteoporosis, but if we dug around a bit we might find signs of arthritis. These are conditions that have been phased out.'

'Not entirely,' Shepherd said.

181

'Oh yes, they have. Just as the great killer diseases were made extinct, smallpox, cholera, AIDS, tuberculosis . . .'

'Grant you the killer diseases,' Shepherd said, 'but don't imagine that all the afflictions the flesh is heir to went the way of smallpox.'

Merrick did not know which afflictions he was referring to specifically, but thought they might include baldness, myopia, dental caries and whatever it was that had scarified Frida's right cheek or pitted Shepherd's own face. He changed tack.

'We opened the coffin to find something, didn't we? To find what Parizo Man was looking for. Is it here? How much are you prepared to disturb the bones to find out?'

'What makes you think the bones need to be disturbed?'

'Because whatever we're looking for is out of sight. This isn't Anglo-Saxon, no gold torques and shields, no Danish belt buckles; no grave goods. Could something be hidden underneath?'

'Underneath, no,' Shepherd said. 'Inside. Forget your grave goods. It wasn't grave goods.' From a pocket he took out a stylus and with an infinite delicacy that Turcat himself could not have surpassed, he began to probe among the tarsals and metatarsals of the left foot.

'Why there, in particular?'

'Got to start somewhere. Am I doing this right?'

'If we're not taking the bones out, yes, I suppose so.'

Shepherd had slid his free hand under the os calcis,

182

as if fitting a shoe. The little bones scattered into his palm where he turned them over with the stylus point. 'Nothing there. Shall I put them back?'

'It's your skeleton.'

'Right, back they go.' He laid the bones in the silt and lifted the right foot. Merrick and Frida watched. Did Frida know what Shepherd was looking for? But he saw it before they did because he had seen one already, and he saw where it was before the foot disassembled. Between the cuneiform and third cuboid, at the root of the fourth toe, lay something that was not a bone, a cloudy sphere with a faint mauve sheen, perhaps five millimetres across.

'Ever see one of these?' Shepherd extracted it and held it up between thumb and forefinger.

'A pearl,' Merrick said, 'or is it? Aren't pearls white?' He had evaded the question.

'Occasionally black. This kind are always variegated.' Shepherd placed the pearl carefully in Merrick's outstretched hand and ran his thumb up the crest of the shin to where the patella crowned the joint between tibia and femur. He lifted the disc of the kneecap and in went the stylus again, while his hand scooped beneath the joint.

'Here's another big one.' It *was* a big one, twice the size of the first and less rounded, an oblate spheroid, slightly pitted, like a face. 'I'll tell you how she died,' Shepherd said. 'In great pain.'

'But how did they get in there?' Frida was asking no questions, Merrick noticed. Had she known what to expect?

'They just grew. You know how pearls grow.'

'Yes – but in shellfish—'

'That's right,' Shepherd said, 'in shellfish. Why do you think they call us Oysters?'

Chapter Seven

By night Ed Shepherd's living room could have been in any city height or apartment block, five, ten, twenty storeys up. Blinds covered the windows, ambient light glowed through the walls and ceiling, the screen was tuned to a mountain landscape – somewhere in the Himalaya, judging by the contours, Merrick thought, as cwms and cols flowed by, somewhere utterly unlike the place in which he was spending a second unexpected night: in a peat moss at the edge of an island in the Rhine Delta that teetered on the lip of a continent, a place that was sinking even as he watched the mountains soar. Yet in this quiet cocoon there was no sense of earth beneath the floor, of moist earth, threatening subsidence. The seas were supposed to have ceased to rise. Lost cities, St Petersburg, Venice, London, Stockholm, were lost for ever, but what remained was held to be safe.

He thought of the sea defences that the sea itself had thrown up as if to say, 'These being mine I can breach them whenever I choose': the scrubby dunes with their marram tufts, the Chisel where the water rasped and dragged at the shingle, and he thought of all that lay behind them, cowering below sea level.

Frida had gone to her family home near the church; three generations, daughter, parents, grandmother, associating in leisure time, the idea of which surprised him as much as anything had. How old were they all? It was impossible to tell. Non-Aboriginals who looked like his host would be approaching their centuries. He did not think Ed was anywhere near so old.

But the food they ate, different from what he was used to, was still food, no better or worse. Shepherd was heating a meal in the utility room now. Merrick recalled Frida's comment about raw fish, which was more or less what he had imagined they would be eating.

On the low table in front of him stood a shallow pottery dish, the size of his palm, lined with dried moss. In the middle of the moss lay three pearls, the two that Shepherd had found in the skeleton's foot and knee; the third extracted from the wrist of its right hand, midway in size between the other two, its cream complexion smoked blue.

There might be more, but Shepherd had called a halt when it grew dark, not wanting to draw attention to their activities by using the artificial light which in the glass-filled interior would have drawn interested spectators like moths, as it had already drawn Frida. The coffin was off its trestles now, lying on the floor again with its eight companions, the lid replaced. Frida had suggested that Shepherd take it home with him. Shepherd said he drew the line at that. The only place to put it was in the shed, where anyone might see it. Get a lock, Merrick thought.

He inferred from all this that Shepherd was operating on his own and that what he was doing might be censured or even banned by the community customs of which he was in a way a legislator.

Who else served on the council? From his imaginary *mélange* of troglodyte shamans in smoke-filled sweat lodges Merrick was distilling an impression of people who acted in much the same way as the metropolitan councils and with a considerable degree more autonomy. Also with a culpable disregard for records. Who *had* thought of the backhoe?

Shepherd came in with dishes and a bowl of sauce which he put on the table beside the pearls, making them look edible. Merrick examined his dish, each compartment piled with vegetables to be skewered and dipped in the sauce.

'I assumed you don't eat meat, not many of you people do.'

'Do you?'

'When it's available.' Shepherd switched the screen from the Himalaya to a newscast and accelerated it through foreign affairs, defence, finance, to local, whittling that down to the Eastern Region where they learned that protest demonstrations had been brought under control and, again, that an inquiry into the funding of the archaeology department was being set up.

'Doesn't it strike you as strange that something as insignificant as your outfit has to be investigated at federal level?' Shepherd said. 'Excuse me, I don't mean to be insulting, for all I know you lead the field, but why should anyone care where you get your money from?'

'Particularly as we have so little,' Merrick said sourly. 'We work on a shoestring. Apart from Turcat there's about a dozen people like me, two ancillaries and maybe forty students. Very few people are interested in what we do.'

'Change that to a few people were very interested. A hell of a lot seem to be interested now.'

'All right, try this for size,' Merrick said. 'The interest's been aroused, as far as I can see, by Parizo Man. No one outside the faculty would have known about Parizo Man if Mirandola hadn't kicked up a storm about him and gone to court. Did you insist on that?'

'Did who insist on what?'

'On court action, after you knew what we had dug up. We were observed, you say. Why weren't we run off the beach then, if you thought your mud was being interfered with?'

'You had police protection.'

'No, we had a couple of Politi officers who were checking to make sure it was an ancient death. If we'd been asked to stop digging they wouldn't have intervened once they were satisfied about the age of the body. Who turned it into a legal issue?'

'Yes, that was Mirandola. He said that any excavation on our territory was an infringement of hard-won Aboriginal rights.'

'And did you – I mean *you*, Ed – did you leap up in righteous indignation and demand legal action?'

'Not me personally.'

'Then who, personally?'

On the screen Professor Ehrhardt, life-sized, was addressing an unseen interviewer. He was standing in front of a picture of Millennium House, to establish his identity and allegiances. Shepherd raised the volume.

'We have nothing to hide,' Ehrhardt was explaining. 'This is a small, specialized area of an academic discipline, and the funding is also very small, whatever the source. It is a *purely* academic discipline,' he reiterated, with peculiar emphasis, 'and in that respect no different from corresponding departments in Berlin, Budapest, Vienna, Paris, Cracow – universities throughout the Union.'

The unseen interviewer broke in. 'Paris-Sorbonne has a whole faculty devoted to this – discipline, has it not?'

'It does, yes.' Ehrhardt sounded wistful, Merrick thought, at the notion of funds available to support a whole faculty.

'A lot of people,' the interviewer persisted, 'find it quite incomprehensible that anybody should wish to underwrite an area of research that is generally held to be unnecessary and, indeed, wholly discredited.'

'I regard an interest in one's origins as natural,' Ehrhardt said, but Merrick thought he was failing to see where the questions were leading. 'As to discredited, I have to protest at such usage. I think you mean discreditable, although I can't agree with you on that. Some people regard our findings as distasteful. Some people. A few.'

'An interest in one's origins . . .' The interviewer brushed aside the rebuke. 'Are you referring to nationality or race?'

'Neither,' Ehrhardt said, but he looked disconcerted. 'By origins I mean the past. So much of our past has been lost to the sea, to the reorganization of agriculture, the concentration of populations into cities – this is true of all states in the Union with low-lying coastlines. The whole of what were once called the Low Countries have gone.'

'But not their populations. Professor, there are in the Rhine Delta Islands certain areas designated Aboriginal Reserves, where large numbers of people have re-established their right to be called Inglish.'

'Perhaps twenty thousand altogether. Relatively small numbers compared to the population – and not only in the RDI. As you well know—'

'Following their lead other states followed suit, similar reserves set up throughout the Union to reintroduce nationalist taxonomy – French, German, Danish – and, more questionable still, the claims to be recognized as non-territorial nations: the Dutch, the Flemish—'

'Are you suggesting some kind of separatist movement?'

'Professor, there *is* a separatist movement,' the interviewer explained, in the tone of one who had not expected to have to explain. 'We've seen it before;

the most powerful nation in the world fragmenting into dozens of dissociated states as a result of anti-federalism.'

'You're surely not suggesting that the United States of Europe is going the same way as the United States of America?'

'Are you implying that it could not? As a historian—'

'Out!' Shepherd cut the power abruptly and the blank wall faced them, shockingly vacant. 'Have you the faintest idea what is going on?' he said.

'It's all happened so fast,' Merrick said. 'They seem to think we're conspiring to divide people into nations and races again.'

'Isn't that what archaeologists do, though? Isn't that what they used to do, take a bone, a hair, a tooth, date it, prove that the owner was a man with arthritis who grew up in the Isles but was actually a Bulgarian with an Irish grandmother who died aged seventy of a heart attack two thousand years ago? Isn't it true that you can identify a person's race from the shape of his skull?'

'We don't talk about race, haven't done for centuries.'

'We could start again. Nationalism would just be a beginning.'

'You can talk,' Merrick said; 'if anyone's nationalist, you are.' And while we're on the subject, why so pale and wan? he thought. 'You can see the way that guy's thinking – the interviewer. First of all reserves spring up all over the place with people like you in them, calling themselves Inglish or Dutch or German, then the idea spreads, and the reserves spread, and the numbers start to grow: instead of twenty thousand Inglish there are forty thousand, eighty thousand.'

'All this being fuelled by people like you, providing proof of identity, digging up the past. Isn't that what those two were arguing about?'

'Don't let us argue about it. You can't believe it was the interviewer posing those questions off his own bat,' Merrick said. 'That was an agenda.'

'Whose agenda?'

'Whoever, for whatever reason, has conjured riots out of nothing on behalf of a subject that practically no one cares about – or even knows about. How long has Mirandola been your representative?'

'About three – four years. Since 'fifty-one.'

'Who did you have before that?'

'A guy called Shiva Gupta.'

'And did he spend his time jumping up and down yelling about who owned the rights to a strip of beach between the tide lines?'

'We didn't see much of him – I wasn't on the council then. But I doubt if there's a soul in Briease who doesn't know Mirandola by sight or sound.'

'So what did Gupta do to justify his title?'

'He was mostly concerned with housekeeping – like his predecessors: were our doctors properly qualified practitioners? Did our burial customs contaminate the water supply? Energy, agriculture and fisheries – he got our fishing zone extended.'

'Suppose he'd been your representative when

Parizo Man was discovered, what would he have done?'

'Nothing, probably. I'm sure he'd have waited till Arthur Thatcher – he was mayor then – asked him to do something. No one asked Mirandola, remember. He acted first and told us afterwards.'

'How do you know no one asked Mirandola?'

Shepherd shook his head as if he had water in his ears. 'There's something going on here. This wasn't what I wanted to talk to you about at all.' He leaned forward and picked up the dish where the three pearls lay in their nest. 'You have seen these before, haven't you?'

'Yes, I was lying. How did you know?'

'Because moss pearls are famous and valuable. It seemed very unlikely that you wouldn't have come across them.'

'I don't mix with people who wear any kinds of pearls,' Merrick said. 'I'd heard of moss pearls; I'd always assumed that they were like – well, moss agate.'

'Moss agate's got little veins in it, it looks like moss. We still find it on the Chisel sometimes. The pearls are from the Briease Moss, as you call it. They aren't just valuable, they're priceless – and it's illegal to trade in them. That was one of the stipulations of the Aboriginal Status Act, although it was too late by then.'

'Too late for what?'

'In a minute. Where did you come across them. Why did you lie?'

'Because of where I came across them and how. I wasn't sure that what you were showing me were genuine – sorry, no offence, but I didn't know. We've got five of them back at the department, if they haven't been confiscated. We found them in Parizo Man.'

'*In* him? Like these were, in the joints? Then he is one of us.'

'Not in the joints, in the pelvic cavity in a glass phial – which is probably why ours are in better condition, none of these pits or little ridged areas. That was the first clue we had that he might be a grave robber. He didn't grow them, he was swallowing them.'

'You found him with a belly full of pearls and you weren't sure he was a grave robber?'

'We didn't know they were moss pearls – well, yes, Turcat did but he didn't know where they came from. We thought they might have been jewellery, ripped out of their settings – rings, brooches – by someone who didn't care what they looked like, only what they were worth.'

'It wasn't the look that was prized, it was the thought of pearls that had grown inside human beings. They are unique.'

'Why don't we know about this?'

'People are good at forgetting what they're ashamed of. It was a shameful episode, suppressed, wilfully forgotten, like the Irish Famine, Britain's involvement with the slave trade in the eighteenth century. But it was stopped when the facts emerged.'

'You said it was stopped too late.'

'There's a complaint which I'm sure your kind don't suffer from called gallstones, chalk deposits in the gall bladder. That's how our ancestors regarded the moss pearls, painful internal growths to be expelled as fast as possible; waste matter; pathological phenomena. But the idea of *human* pearls – people started to pay to acquire them. And when the trade in them became illegal the price rose, steeply. And when the cause was identified and a cure found, the supply stopped, until someone thought of a way of restarting it.'

'What are you talking about?' Merrick said. 'These things were grown on purpose?'

'When temperatures began to rise at the end of the twentieth century all kinds of life forms that had only ever been found in the tropics began to establish themselves in what had been temperate zones. The malaria mosquito was one of the first, in New York – not our New York, the American one. In the last century, after the Anarchy, marshy areas became infested with a species of horsefly; its bite caused sepsis, deep infections, especially where the bone is close to the skin. They could take months to heal and these calcium growths developed in joints; wrists, ankles, elbows – even the spine. Some were small, a millimetre in diameter. Some weren't – the largest I ever heard of was fifteen millimetres. Finally they erupted and the pearl was forced out.'

'Why didn't anyone do anything? Surely surgery—?'

'Because, to start with, it didn't afflict city populations. It was only when it broke out in urban parks that anyone acted. We were marsh dwellers, outlaws, subhuman, the first to suffer, the last to be treated. But eventually a vaccine was developed, and insecticide saw off the horseflies – but as I said, too late. Too late for us.'

'You don't still suffer, do you?'

'No; we have protected status, don't we? But by then the pearls were fetching enormous sums. It's even said that some people endured terrible suffering to cultivate a – a pearl of great price. Then they'd sell it and leave the fen. Even now not everyone wants to live in a reserve, even with protected status. But that was their choice. Once the vaccination programme was under way the pearls stopped forming. Someone, some people, thought that this was a great pity. They started substituting horsefly venom for vaccine; concentrated. The pearls became very big, excruciatingly big.'

Merrick had picked up the largest pearl, the ovoid from the knee joint, and was trying to imagine the agony of this thing growing in his body. He could not; he had never known agony, he did not have the data to imagine the enormity of such pain. He said lamely, 'They were infecting people deliberately?'

'Most ordinary pearls these days are farmed, in oyster beds. As I said, why do you think we're known as Oysters? They farmed us.'

'Was Parizo Man a farmer?'

'That depends on his dates. You could still be useful in that respect. He might just have been an opportunist who knew who had died with pearls in their bones. Or he could have been a farmer who culled his victims when they were ready. An opportunist would be older, earlier than a farmer. Can you date him?'

'No one can do anything with him, he's been sequestrated, remember?' Merrick said. He was feeling

196

nauseous, almost faint. He could not imagine the pain, but the calculated callousness that fed on that pain; almost that was beyond him too.

'Thanks to Mirandola.'

'Eh?'

'Thanks to Mirandola you've lost the body,' Shepherd said. 'And so have we.'

'Unless he eventually persuades the court to decide in your favour. I wonder if he will. But it doesn't really matter which Parizo Man was.'

'It could to us. Because an opportunist might have been one of us.'

'Inglish. And a farmer would be European – you hope. But it couldn't happen now. You said the horsefly was extinct.'

'So was smallpox officially, but as I understand it, nations liked to keep a bit on the side, just in case, for defence purposes, I believe. We took ourselves out of the restructuring programme in order to *be* ourselves, in order to be Inglish, to go on being Inglish. We were just unlucky that after the Anarchy our people retreated to this area. In the North Isles they live on high ground, but what we had we kept and this' – he stroked the pearls – 'is what we paid for it.

'And now we're left alone, or rather, we were. But think about what you said just now, numbers swelling, other states being forced to recognize Aboriginal Status.'

'You think you're being seen as a threat?'

'With your connivance – your department's

connivance. You're not just retrieving the past, you're retrieving nationality, race. Something that was once seen as merely prurient is now looked on as a menace to civil stability. No one would have cared about Parizo Man if Mirandola hadn't gone to law. You'd have taken him away to your laboratory and – and what would you have done with him then?'

'He'd have joined the other bones in the end. We have quite a collection.'

'Who'd have known about him?'

'Only the department and the faculty. Those pickets who hang around our excavations never knew he existed.'

'Until Mirandola made his presence known. Strange, isn't it, how we always come back to Mirandola.'

Mirandola returned to haunt him in the night. Through the open panel in the window Merrick heard the church clock at intervals and the wash of the sea against the shore, regular as a slow pulse.

Why the backhoe?

Why did Mirandola always time his appearances just too late to make action effective? Why did he *appear* at all? He wore a communications stud and so did Ed Shepherd. All the Oysters had them.

Ed did not think that Mirandola had seen the skull himself, but whoever had seen it must have informed Mirandola immediately, and whoever had observed the excavation had done likewise, but Mirandola did nothing immediately. His information was always relayed after a time lag that allowed certain events to transpire.

It was almost as if Mirandola had wanted the skeleton removed in order to go to court over it, meanwhile ensuring, through some stooge or collaborator, that the site on Parizo Beach was laid waste. Why? In case the court decision went the wrong way? Because he had seen or heard about what Shepherd was unearthing and wanted to make sure that nothing else was found. He must have had a shock when they ended up with nine coffins instead of one; probably he had not known that the site was a graveyard. Did he know about moss pearls? In any case, Parizo Man was a MacGuffin; it was the publicity Mirandola was after, and he had got it. Why?

Merrick left the bed and closed the window panel, cracking his knee against a piece of furniture in the dark. Was that what a moss pearl felt like? He stubbed his toe returning. Nothing was quite where he expected it to be, a little lower, a little smaller. Shepherd's house was not a habitation of dwarves but the Oyster scale was tangibly lesser than his own. He had been easily the tallest person on the beach aside from Mirandola, whom he always perceived as stunted. Ed Shepherd shared his own academic interest in the Parizo mystery, he was clearly no separatist, but he was, all the same, one of these slight white people who had gone to inconceivable lengths to keep themselves slight and white.

And not all of them were happy living on reserves. What did they get up to without their centralized surveillance? Why had Frida brought him to Briease?

And why was the source of the department's funding about to be investigated?

Even with the window closed he could still hear the clock's swingeing tally of passing time. 'Show up for work on Wednesday,' Turcat had said. Tired but hopelessly wakeful he saw that Tuesday had turned to Wednesday. If it took him as long to return as it had taken him to get here it could be Thursday before he managed to reach Millennium House.

God rest you merry, gentlemen, let nothing you dismay . . .

Where had *that* come from?

He got up as soon as he heard Shepherd moving about and met him in the utility room.

'I have to go home. What's the quickest way?'

'For you?' Shepherd said. Merrick guessed that for an Oyster there would be many ways; Frida had had alternative routes in mind. 'Do you need to go as you came, in secret?'

'I didn't come in secret. It was a genuine mistake.'

'But you were trying to get away from – what?'

'I'm not certain. I was told to get lost.'

'And you got more lost than you intended. Well, if you think you can go back openly I'll take you to Norge and you can ride the monorail. It's fully operational again. There are roadrunners but they're slow.'

'How shall we travel?'

'I don't know what you call them, we call them cars. In the days when people travelled overland in large numbers the roads were crowded with them – they ran on petrol then.'

'I ought to say goodbye to Frida before I leave,' Merrick said, mindful of still unanswered questions.

'I'll pass on your good wishes,' Shepherd said. 'Eat now and I'll be ready to leave when you are.'

The car was a basic vehicle but it moved at three times the speed of the roadrunner. They cruised out of the parking bay down near the staithe and over the bridge. Merrick craned his neck to watch the town disappear behind him. Unlike the city, rising skyward and visible from many kilometres away, Briease settled back into the Moss as into a bed. Within minutes the only clue to the existence of the place was the blades of the turbine as the tips followed each other in endless pursuit on the horizon.

'What will you do when you get back?' Shepherd asked.

'I've been told to turn up to work,' Merrick said. 'That means the department, Millennium House. I don't know what we'll be working on, though.' He thought of the vacated basement, the empty light table.

'What about the pearls?'

'Which ones?'

'Yours – from Parizo Man.'

'The court ordered Turcat to hand over everything, all artefacts and related material. There aren't really any artefacts, just a few metal fragments.'

'And did he hand them over?'

'He didn't want to, we were trying to get them away,

201

but the next time I saw him he was in custody or near as dammit. The court officer had all the records and other stuff, it was in a bag.'

'Could he have kept the pearls?'

'I don't know.'

'Does he realize how valuable they are? He could fund your department into the next century.'

'How can I get in touch with you when I find out?'

'Same way that you'd contact anyone else. I'll give you my code.'

Norge rose from the landscape ahead of them, a cluster of verticals but lower than the city skyline. The monorail station was on the outskirts, a car ready to depart southward.

'Keep me posted,' Shepherd said on the platform.

'What are you going to do?'

'Keep looking through the spoil on the beach, find that axe, if it's there. And find out who had the bright idea about the backhoe.'

Without warning the doors slid between them, severing their conversation, and the car swept out of the station in contrast to the spastic progress of the last journey he had made in it. Merrick had no time even to wave goodbye but instead he took a seat on the left side of the car and looked his farewell over the flatlands towards the trees at the edge of the Briease Moss. The town itself was invisible; at that distance he could not even make out the church tower or the turbine, although occasionally he caught sight of the sea, a thin streak of pewter in the early light.

The trees grew more thickly, yielding no clue to what lay beneath, but he was waiting for a particular view and was ready for it. From the right the twin parallels of the highway clove the fields, straight as the Vyzel Cut. When the monorail crossed it he looked down to the place where he and Frida had left the roadrunner; below him was the causeway to Herigal Staithe, then it was gone and moments later he saw the sun catch the top of the Nox, and the contours of Eavrey Island, and shortly after that the car decelerated and slid into the partially repaired station at Eavrey Sound.

The air was clear today. He could see the waters of the sound and the tram track running along the northern shore. That was one way back to Briease. The conventional and easily monitored route was the one he was taking, by monorail and roadrunner via Norge, but there was a third. Now it was possible to make out that towards the coast the Moss was not so very distant from the sound. The South Turf Bank must lie in that direction.

Minutes out of Eavrey and the towers and heights of the city glittered against the sky. The car was full now, people standing. Life and work were returning to normal, but as the car sailed above the suburbs and began its sinuous progress between the shining buildings he started to wonder what kind of normality awaited him at Millennium House, and wished he could prepare for it.

He did not look out for a nostalgic glimpse of the cathedral site and would not have seen it if he had.

Mandeville Height had already sunk its roots into the souterrain, an excavation beyond his wildest imaginings.

The repairs to Metro Station were no nearer completion but destination screens were functioning again, screens that would have told him, two days ago, that he was headed in the wrong direction. What would have happened if they had been there to set him right? If he had simply gone home he might well have received a visit from the Politi and joined Turcat in custody. He would certainly be more ignorant than he was now. And where was Turcat?

Ought he to go home first? There might be information in the message bank. He might have had visitors, the place could have been searched; but he doubted it. It was still possible that aside from Turcat and Ehrhardt – who had trouble remembering his name – no one knew of his involvement. Mirandola knew of his involvement but not the extent of it. Strange, as Shepherd had said, how we always come back to Mirandola.

The way home overground would take him past Millennium House anyway. The last time he had seen it had been in the picture behind Ehrhardt, in contrast to the day before on the newscast when it had been thronged with Politi, rioters, demonstrators. Now it was practically deserted except for the familiar protesters with their placards carrying out their peaceful picket as though nothing had happened, their messages still discreet demands for prohibition rather than incendiary death threats. Merrick found it difficult to believe that the riot had taken place.

It was easy enough to clear and clean a public space, but he would have expected some signs of damage to the relatively fragile fabric of Millennium House if to nothing else. Could the whole incident have been artificially contrived? That too would be easy enough. Quite possibly there had been no riot, but now that the idea had been trailed in front of the viewers there might well be a real one.

He knew the pickets by sight; he had virtually grown up with them. It was like running into old friends, true believers, not a fly-by-night rabble who turned out to see the fun, or cause it, but the ones who had haunted every excavation he had worked on – the cathedral site, the Galleria Station extension, the castle, the museum before that; all the way back probably to the day when young Dieter Ehrhardt had first stuck a trowel in the earth and opened up the belly of history.

He had to pass them to ascend the steps. As if by tacit agreement pickets and archaeologists never spoke to each other, one side meeting the other side's silent protest with silent indifference. Beside a woman whom Turcat had once described as protesting before there was anything to protest about, Merrick halted.

'Were you here yesterday night?' he asked, without preliminary introduction. Maybe she would not remember having seen him before either. He was the object of her protest, no more, nothing personal; he might have been a robot.

'No,' she said, 'we only picket in working hours.'

'Why's that?' Vaguely he had imagined them standing in the rain all night, like caryatids, still there in the morning.

'No one would see us otherwise.'

'They'd have seen you yesterday, all over the Union. Did you watch the demonstration on the screen?'

'That was nothing to do with us,' she said quickly.

'Wasn't it? Organized protest against archaeology?'

'We weren't there.'

She moved away from him; god knew who he might be, asking questions. Her comrades edged in the same direction. He reflected that if they themselves were better organized they could have faked their own riot and broadcast it. But the riot, real or fictional, was nothing to do with them. Presumably, though, their activities had given someone a good idea.

He walked up the steps and in at the double doors. There was no one around to welcome him in or turn him out. The lights were on in the elevator but the door to the basement laboratory was closed. He did not want to try it under the watchful eye of the security cam only to find it locked. He must look purposeful. He went into the elevator and took himself up to the first floor.

Turcat was in his office; Merrick could see him through the glass wall, back turned, hunched over a pile of manifests.

'Well, don't stand in the doorway,' Turcat said without looking round. In his left palm he cradled a hand screen on which, evidently, he had tracked

Merrick's progress through the building. He crooked a finger over his shoulder. 'Your timekeeping is abominable,' he said. 'Still, now you're here you might as well have this; you were asking for it.'

He nudged at a book by his elbow lying closed on a slipcase that identified it as coming from the library stacks, a treatise on mummification by L. Vanderkerckhove. Merrick had asked for no such thing and as he picked it up he saw a sheet of paper inserted between the pages. *Take this to the library now. Senate Height bar 10.05.* The writing was an unpractised scrawl, but he could read it.

'Anything else?' Merrick tried to sound subservient and insubordinate at the same time.

'If there was I'd have said so.' Turcat waved him away without looking up. Merrick slid the book into its slipcase and closed it. He left the office and walked back to the elevator, knowing that Turcat was watching him on the hand screen. Was anyone else watching him? Having spent time among people who wrote things down by hand as a matter of course, it took him a minute or two to register what Turcat had done, passed a communication that circumvented a possible third party.

Did he really think he was being bugged? Their eyes had not met once. Turcat was usually brusque to the point of rudeness and between them they had sketched a scene of routine unfriendliness without a hint of complicity.

No one intercepted Merrick on the way out. He walked casually down the steps, past the pickets and across Central Plaza, the slipcase in his hand held protectively against his chest. The content was valuable anyway, being a book. He began to wonder what was in it.

That was a ridiculous idea, as ridiculous as Turcat's paranoia, or so he would have thought three days ago. Was it possible that someone was following him? As usual, at this hour of the morning, there were few people about. Only two or three were walking in the same direction as he was and only one of those was behind him. He entered the university precinct, strolled round the tree-encircled lawn – how artificial these trees looked compared to the ones in the Moss – and sat down on a bench. The person who had been behind him walked straight past without looking. He opened the slipcase and took out the book, removed the message, read a few paragraphs, looked at the photographs. He had half-expected to find a section hollowed out, a secret cache of artefacts and related material, but the book contained nothing except pages and the slipcase contained nothing but the book. Turcat had simply given him a reason to go to the main complex without saying anything. Was that why he had failed to make contact earlier, because he suspected an eavesdropper?

The university stacks had once been a library in the old sense of the word, with books on open shelves to be taken down and read. Now it was in the undercroft of the Senate Height and there was nothing in it but storage units with an area at one end set aside for on-the-spot reference, the whole system automated and waterproofed. It was said that you stood more chance of surviving a flood in the stacks than anywhere else in the city.

He went down in the elevator and entered the underground hangar, passing into an environment where lights and temperature were controlled. The stacks themselves, three metres high and five long, were compressed into a solid block. He held the slip-case against the scanner, not knowing where it belonged, and the scanner told him. Soundlessly the block split and the units to his left moved on tracks, leaving a gangway between the shelves perhaps seventy centimetres wide. Near the far end a tiny green light indicated where the book should be replaced. It was well above his head but he stood below it and a section of the floor rose to lift him to the required level. As the book touched the shelf the green light went out, the section sank back into the floor. As soon as he had walked out of the gangway the room recorded his progress and the stacks, sighing slightly, moved together again to seal hermetically around the sixteen-metre perimeter. Not one drop of flood water would ever sully the books inside.

As he left he thought regretfully of those rooms full of open shelves where one could stroll and browse, take down a book at random, stand reading it, put it back, take another. The stacks were a resource but there was no joy in using them. They were a great tomb filled with treasure, a sepulchre piled with riches and sealed away like the resting place of a pharaoh.

At 9.50 he went up to the restaurant bar. He rarely

used it as it was not convenient to Millennium House. Given the quality of the food it was a wonder that it, too, was not underground, but the architects had had large ideas and it was housed in a cantilevered glass hemisphere that sprang from the side of Senate Height, fifteen floors up. The view took one's mind off what was on the dishes.

The place was almost empty; it was too early in the day for crowds to gather. He was not hungry – Shepherd had sent him away with a good breakfast – so he bought coffee and sat on a banquette by the window wall where he was easily visible from the entrance, looking down over the precinct. At exactly 10.05 Turcat came in, bought a drink and joined him.

'Well, where have you been?'

'The stacks.'

'So I should hope. I meant, where have you been for the last two days?'

'You told me to get lost. I got lost. I went to Briease.'

Turcat looked incredulous. 'You did *what?*'

'You may be glad I did, but it wasn't on purpose. I saw you come out with Mirandola and his mob so I tried to disappear without attracting attention, joined the people who were going to the station. I meant to go home by a roundabout route but I got on the wrong car, the express to Norge. Because of the power failures it stopped at Eavrey.'

He explained his meeting with Frida without going into detail and, feeling suddenly jealous of what he knew, précised his journey to Briease. 'We called in at Parizo Beach. The site has been destroyed.'

'How destroyed?'

'The Oysters have been doing some excavation of their own, with a backhoe.'

'Oh shit – how much damage?'

'As regards our hole, complete. The hole is now about thirty cubic metres and, at the moment, full of sea water.'

'What did they think they were doing?' Turcat's tone was almost tearful.

'They didn't think. But there's nothing you can do about it. The foreshore is their land and they can do what they like on their land. That's statutory.'

'What have they found?'

'We don't know yet. I got them to stop digging and to move the spoil above the tide line – if I hadn't been there the whole lot would have been washed away. Now' – he ploughed on before Turcat could butt in – 'tell me, what happened to the bag?'

'Don't tell me what to tell you,' Turcat said furiously. 'What bag?'

'The one we took out by the flood escape when Mirandola and the court people turned up with the sequestration order; the artefacts and related material.'

'I was ordered to hand them over.'

'And did you?'

'I hadn't much choice.'

'You had five minutes. I saw you come out under arrest.'

'Escort – I wasn't arrested. Five minutes wasn't enough. I ran into them, I was carrying the bag, it was

211

confiscated. But they didn't know I'd been in the basement so I wasn't charged with feloniously making off
with court property.'

'Everything confiscated?'

'We went through it item by item. I had to explain
what everything was, to a bunch of idiots who hadn't
a clue what I was talking about. I could have made up
names for all of it.'

'They must,' Merrick said, 'have recognized the
pearls.'

Turcat looked at him as if seeing him for the first
time. Given the nature of their working relationship
it might very well be the first time.

'Now I see what you're getting at.'

'Did you hand them over?'

'Hand them over? Have you any idea of what they're
worth?'

'You're going to sell them, then?' As Shepherd had
said, worth enough to fund the department into the
next century.

'I didn't mean that – but, my god, those things are
as rare as phoenix eggs. They're priceless. On the
antiquities market—'

'I wish you hadn't said that. It's illegal to trade in
them.'

'I'm not going to trade in them.' Turcat was almost
spitting. 'But I wasn't handing them over to those
cretins.'

'Do you know why it's illegal? Do you know where
they come from?'

'Oh,' Turcat said, 'you've been in the Moss. They

fed you the old myth, pearls grown in the human body.'

'It's a myth, is it?'

'The rarity is the colouring—'

'No, it's not. The rarity is the source. They do come from the human body. I've seen them taken out.'

'Oh, spare me . . . You've been taken for a ride, and I don't mean on the monorail. Remember the louts who used to salt our trenches? What can be taken out can be put in. Never mind the pearls, they're safe. But have you any idea what's been happening since you took off?'

'The riot, yes.'

'How? You were in the Moss.'

'I was in Briease. It's not what you think there. It's not what I thought. They don't live in huts, it's a town. They're educated people, some of them. They have screens, like us – but look, *was* there a riot?'

'Was there a *riot*?'

'We did think it might have been . . . concocted.'

'No, it was a riot and yes, I think it was concocted, but not in the way you mean. Thirty-six hours of protest and then the riot – quite a small one in its way. If there's another, or any further sign of civil unrest, the department may be closed down. As it is, there's already talk of stricter controls on what we're allowed to excavate, especially as regards human remains. Not just us, throughout the Union.'

'And an investigation of department funding.'

'That's Dieter's province,' Turcat said.

'What's the problem – with the funding?'

'As far as I'm concerned, it's practically non-existent.

213

That's the problem. And just as it was about to be increased, it's dried up altogether.'

'Because of the inquiry?'

'Because of Mirandola and his court order – look' – Turcat quivered with irritation – 'this doesn't concern someone at your level.'

'It does now. Who else knows what I know?'

'Well, who does?'

'That wasn't a riddle. *No* one else knows what I know, even you don't. I excavated, I helped exhume, I found the pearls – and I've been in the Moss. It does concern me. What has Mirandola to do with the funding?'

'It's a matter of cause and effect.' Turcat had apparently accepted his credentials. 'He doesn't have anything to do with it directly. Dieter started the department with reluctant permission from the Senate – *very* reluctant, it was that contentious – and allowed to excavate only if he could raise the money for it outside the university. He was put in touch with a publishing house, Incunabula. It was privately owned, the director was interested in archaeology although he kept fairly quiet about it; he offered a basic endowment with the pledge that there would be more if anything really interesting turned up.'

'By which he meant human remains?'

'Yes, and on the rare occasions any did, the money was increased as promised. But you know how little we've got to show for fifteen years. Parizo Man looked like big bucks – and now we've lost him. Satisfied?'

'Three questions: is the same guy still running Incunabula?'

'Oh yes; Peter Bilderdyk.'

'And why is he so interested in human remains?'

'The same reason as we are, probably, though more in DNA than dates.'

'Why?'

'How should I know? Some private maggot, a passion for the past, wanting to know if a skull is common-or-garden European or identifiably Spanish or German – Dutch, in his case, or Estonian. There's been a Dutch presence in this part of the state going back hundreds of years. Incunabula was the name given to the earliest printed books, from before the sixteenth century. It refers to anything coming from the very beginning.'

'Aboriginal, in fact,' Merrick said. 'It sounds harmless enough. If this Bilderdyk has got money to spare and wants to push a little of it our way, why shouldn't he? Was Professor Ehrhardt supposed to keep him supplied with saucy photographs of bare bones in return?'

'There's no need to be frivolous,' Turcat said. 'Somebody obviously does think there's a reason why he shouldn't, possibly the fact that if he does have access to DNA records it's illegal. We supply him with bone samples. What he does with them is out of our hands. There's more at stake than our department. Every university in the Union with an archaeology department is being investigated – and that includes the big boys, Cracow, Paris-Sorbonne. Most of them have got more to lose than we have, on account of their support from whoever funds them being greater than ours – because they find more. Very few states are as short of space as we are.'

'Third question—'

'Fifth question. I'm counting.'

'What does Incunabula publish?'

'Not books, as such. Mainly short works of an antiquarian nature – I'm quoting. Ancient languages, origins of European peoples, migrations.'

'A rich man's toy?'

'He can't make much from it.'

'Is he an anti-federalist?'

'How should I know? He might be. There's no law against it.'

Not yet, Merrick thought.

'What have you done with the pearls?'

'Why do you keep harping on about them?'

'Aren't you curious? About where we found them? Parizo Man had them in his guts.'

'And you believe they grew there.'

'In a glass bottle? No, he was stealing them. He was a grave robber. We worked that out before I went to Briease. But he wasn't taking them out of the coffins, he was taking them out of the bodies.'

'I think you're being used,' Turcat said. 'Inveigled into the swamp and fed a preposterous story which you swallowed whole. They saw you coming. A useful idiot.'

'I tell you, I saw—'

'What did you see?'

If he went any further he would have to tell Turcat about the coffins and what they had found in the one that Parizo Man had been about to open. Better for now, perhaps, to keep what he knew to himself.

'Nothing, forget it. Why did you get me over here?'

'To bring you up to date in relative privacy. You never know who's going to burst in on you at Millennium House. You can have the rest of the morning off – I suppose you'll need to go home, but I'll want you at work on time this afternoon.'

So Turcat no longer felt secure in his own domain. Merrick watched him leave the bar, pausing to greet incoming colleagues, the ones he regarded as equals.

It was not a camaraderie exactly that existed among them, rather an air of inhabiting the same plane, one far above the plane Merrick lived on. And yet, as Turcat left, Merrick thought he detected a frisson in his wake. Those he had spoken with were looking at each other with carefully expressionless faces. There goes Turcat the Desecrator, Turcat who must die. Nonsense, obviously, he could imagine them thinking; but no smoke without fire.

None of them was looking his way.

But on his own plane he had acquaintances, if not friends. Outside the department there were people he could call colleagues of his own, people he had met as undergraduates, on the rare occasions that undergraduates met. There was Joris Tieltman in the biology laboratories, an entomologist. Merrick had not seen him for months.

Outside a hard rain was falling. He crossed the concourse to the elevators and descended to the souterrain, where he could take a tram home, just in

217

case Turcat's hypothetical spy was waiting for him in the precinct. When last heard of Joris had been living in the same height as himself, although on a different level. There was no reason to suppose that he had moved away unless he had been promoted out of the Admiral Height milieu. Why should they not meet for a drink sometime, sometime very soon?

The underground tram tunnels oppressed him. Waiting at the Senate stop he recalled the high sky above the Briease Moss, the sense of infinite space, the uncontrollable sea that would not be quieted or stayed. No flood would ever penetrate these sealed vaults where the metropolitan population could travel from home to work to leisure without ever setting foot in the open air. In the winter months many thousands did just that. Merrick felt the earth pressing beneath and around him, the weight of the city above. When the tram stopped again he got out and took the nearest elevator to the surface and walked the rest of the way home through flurries of sleet, taking grateful account of every cold breath he inhaled.

He did not seriously think that anyone would have searched his rooms. Each floor of his height was two-tiered; some were built around a central pool or garden. His level, being one of the cheaper ones, had a ball court, and his apartment, being one of the cheapest on that level, was on the lower tier, looking out on to the enervating sight of people exercising for the good of their health.

Indoors everything seemed to be as he had left it, but he owned little to leave lying around. He never

218

prepared food in his utility room, preferring to eat at the commissary across the court. The screen wall was no barer than the other three – he had never been one to hang pictures. The divans were tidy, cushions propped in the corners. If someone had been there they could have ransacked the place without leaving any trace. The only thing to ransack was his communications system, and if that had been tampered with he would have no way of knowing unless the tamperer had been so maladroit that they had wiped information.

He took a can from the cooler, remembering Ed Shepherd's preparations for a meal, the easy informality of the meal itself, the casual clutter, the sheer number of possessions. What could the Masons' house be like with four of them in residence? What did they do for privacy? How bare this room looked now; what kind of a nonentity would live in it, had lived in it for five years without leaving a trace of personality? No wonder no one ever remembered him. How ironic that he should have been drawn to archaeology as a profession because it seemed to offer a chance to work with other people.

He was not good with other people. He burned with embarrassment to think of his arrogant exchanges with Ed Shepherd, a man at least old enough to be his father, arguing, back-answering, issuing orders. Well, he had learned his interpersonal skills from Turcat, and Shepherd, no doubt, expected nothing better from a European.

He called up Joris Tieltman, discovered that he had

219

ascended to Waldemar Height, near the parc, left an invitation, before accessing his own message bank. It was empty. However long it was since he had last been here, and he couldn't reckon how long that was, no one had tried to get in touch or, if they had, thought it worthwhile to leave word for him.

The Masons might lack privacy, but what was privacy save a euphemism for something far less desirable?

Chapter Eight

'*Tabanus bovinus*,' Joris pronounced. 'Horsefly, indige-
nous to the Isles, preferred habitat, peat bogs.
Discovered in centres of population at the beginning
of the twenty-first century. Bloodsucking female of the
species could cause in humans a swelling the size of
a tennis ball. *Tabanus bovinus Rex* appeared in the early
twenty-second century, still flourishing in peat bogs.
That's the one you're after.'

'How big was the swelling?'

'What arcane questions you archaeologists ask,' Joris
said. 'Initially, not very big, easy enough to mistake
for a gnat bite – you know what that is?'

'A gnat, yes.'

'But the infection caused agonizing swelling if it was
in a joint; abscesses formed with solidified cores. They
were called pearls.'

'Someone having a joke?' Merrick said.

They were sitting in the garden bar on the eighth
floor of Waldemar Height, where Joris lived. Zoologists
earned more than archaeologists, being of some use
to the community.

'It was no joke if you got bitten, those things could

fester for months. All the horsefly wanted, of course, was blood for egg-laying purposes – that's why the female was the problem. Properly, I suppose, she ought to be *T. bovinus Regina*. A vaccine was developed but the people most at risk refused to have anything to do with it – the bogtrotters. They seemed to believe it would compromise their pure blood.'

'Was that really the reason?'

'That or some other superstition. In any case, they preferred writhing in agony to any kind of prophylaxis.'

'So what happened in the end? To the horsefly?'

'The usual, for those days. A dedicated insecticide wiped it out.'

'It's extinct?'

'Absolutely.'

'Except for a few specimens kept on the side in case of need?'

'*Need*? What possible need could there be for a horsefly?'

What possible need had there been for anthrax, and yet humanity had been strangely reluctant to let go of it.

'Well, you said vaccination – presumably the vaccine was developed from the *tabanus* venom?'

'We don't keep the flies, we keep the eggs, frozen.'

'So if, mysteriously, there was another outbreak of *Tabanus bovinus Rex* you could immediately defrost the eggs, incubate some females and extract the venom?'

'Don't be ridiculous,' Joris said. 'The vaccine was synthesized once its composition was known.'

'So why are you keeping the eggs?'

'It is contrary to biological ethics to bring about the total extinction of any species,' Joris said piously. 'You should know that.'

'Every little virus must have its day, eh? So the eggs are kept for old times' sake – along with the smallpox, the HIV and the anthrax bacterium?'

'You're in the wrong department,' Joris said. 'Ever thought of changing disciplines? As I've heard it, your department's about to close.'

'Only if those idiots keep rioting about human remains.'

'Useful idiots.'

'By which you mean—?'

'By which I mean, they're idiots because they're rioting over something they know nothing about and don't give a toss anyway. Useful because if I, say, wanted to close down your department, which I don't of course, but if I *did*, I'd threaten closure if there was any further civil unrest and then send out my useful idiots to cause it. That would be very cynical of me but it would work.'

'You're not in espionage on the side, are you?'

'Does any rational person believe that the general public, which normally exhibits signs of awareness only if the global economy threatens its favourite brand of cannabis, could really be so incensed by the exhumation of a skeleton that they'd threaten to lynch an academic? Have you got anything to do with Parizo Man?'

'I helped excavate him.'

'Well, watch your back,' Joris said. 'You never know, someone might think you're a threat to civilization as we known it. *Prosit.*'

Halfway across the plaza on his way home, Merrick started to become aware of unaccustomed noise, foot-steps, voices, then, before he could begin to be curious, a shattering crash and the sound of a minor explosion. Walls took on a red glow, he smelled smoke. At the same time a dark figure loomed in front of him, armed cap-a-pie like a medieval knight.

'Stop!'

He stopped, hands rising automatically.

'Where are you going?'

'Home. Admiral Height.'

'Not this way. Where have you come from?'

'Waldemar Height.'

That seemed to satisfy him. 'You'll have to go round by the Assembly or take the souterrain.'

He did not argue. Arguing with a riot cop was not done and behind the man, if there was a man inside the armour, he saw a robot response vehicle rolling across the plaza in the direction of Metro Station, on the way to which stood Millennium House.

The armour waited until he turned and took the longer route home, hearing all the way the escalating roar, the crash of glass breaking, the muffled exhala-tions that were explosions. His experience of riots was gleaned from foreign newscasts and video-fictions, but he would have expected a riot to develop more slowly, to, well, *develop*, with numbers swelling until a crowd became a mob and all sense of self was subsumed into the mass instinct. There should surely be people hurrying to join it, or to escape from it, running street battles, hand-thrown missiles, peripheral damage. This was shaping up to be another remarkably self-contained outrage, assembled and detonated on the spot. He was surprised to feel no alarm and depressed at feeling no surprise.

A fat man would have deflated. Turcat seemed to have imploded, his bones compacted violently, the skin sucked in against them.

His department sat around him, morosely expectant. Merrick was seeing people he had not met for a year, perhaps longer, who had been extracted from their particular nooks of research in the building and elsewhere, to hear what Parizo Man had cost them. Ehrhardt was not present, having responded to a courteous request to assist with inquiries.

'The skeleton, as you know, has been impounded with all artefacts and related material. It is being held by court order until such time as we can put together a case for recovering it,' Turcat said. 'There is no guarantee that such a case would be successful.'

'If it isn't?' someone said.

'Theoretically the Bureau of Aboriginal Affairs can counterclaim because the court has decided that the bones were found on the Briease Reserve. What it comes down to is a jurist deciding that the final say lies with the Pan-European Coastal Authority, a bunch of bureaucrats who seem to have been convened solely for our inconvenience, who probably, on a whim, can decide in their turn whether Parizo Man is ours because we found him, or the Oysters' because he was found on their land. We are fairly sure we have evidence that he was not Inglish but we can't prove it because we would need to test the bones and date them.

'There is of course more. There is no law that actually prohibits excavation. It's not encouraged but it isn't illegal; we'd never have come this far if it was. The Aboriginal Status Act stipulates that unless they are contravening federal legislation Aboriginals on their own land can do as they please. There is, as I said, no law against excavation or, more precisely, exhumation. I've been informed that certain persons in Briease decided that since a hole already existed they might as well enlarge it. They excavated with a backhoe' – there was a faint stir of dismay among his audience – 'not a very large backhoe; in fact it's the kind of thing we ourselves would have liked to use under certain conditions, had we been able to afford it. But we would have known what we were doing.

'What it comes down to,' he exploded, 'is that the fucking Oysters have dug out an enormous excavation *below the tide line*, the consequence being that the site is completely destroyed. It's full of water.'

He gave himself a few minutes to recover and the others to digest what he had told them, in the knowledge that he was about to tell them something worse.

'The result of all this is an upsurge in public feeling against our activities. Those of you who have assisted at digs will know that we've always had our oponents and you'll know just how much of a deterrent *they've* been. All that's changed. There has been an inexplicable reaction to the Parizo case. You will have seen that, just entering and leaving the building. If you've been watching newscasts recently you'll know that the pickets have become demonstrations, demonstrations have become riots. We are now under notice that if there is any further unrest as a result of our activities the department will be closed. This is, I might add, completely out of our hands. If we sat here for the rest of the day, doing nothing, there could still be another riot tonight. There almost certainly will be in the near future.

'Professor Ehrhardt and I are therefore acting speculatively. On the assumption that the department will be closed down you'll be absorbed into the history faculty: research, teaching, administration. No one will lose their jobs. I have to warn you, our source of funding is also under investigation. If this looks to you like a vendetta, there is no need to say so; it looks like that to me, too. You'd better get back now to whatever you were doing and instructions will be relayed. Korda, you stay here.'

No one seemed surprised that he had been singled out; he must be known to work with Turcat. Then he reflected that to most of them his name meant nothing anyway. Their business was not with the living. Wave a bone or a potsherd at them and they might react. Introduce yourself as a fellow life form and you could be met with a look of blank incomprehension.

227

The room emptied. Merrick was left alone with Turcat.

'That's not the worst of it,' Turcat said. 'If they are feeling really bloody-minded they may get an order to confiscate everything we've ever collected, on the grounds that it offends public decency. *Everything.* Because of *one* skeleton.'

'Do you buy any of this?' Merrick said. 'The offence against public decency, the mortal insult to Aboriginal peoples, the inquiry into funding? The accidental destruction of the site?'

'It wasn't accidental?'

'It was done in all innocence but it didn't happen by accident. Did you see the interview with Professor Ehrhardt a couple of nights back, after the first riot? He must have told you about it.'

'Of course I saw it.'

'Didn't it strike you that the interviewer was asking some very odd questions? Nothing to do with the riot and not much to do with Parizo Man. He led with the funding, and what he was mainly interested in was separatism. Weren't we, the department, stirring up an unhealthy interest in people's racial origins?'

'This state has always had an unhealthy obsession with nationhood – the first to establish reserves, the first to recognize Aboriginal Status. When the RDI was still the British Isles, United Kingdom, a nation state, they held out against joining the first union – the Common Market – then they held out against a common currency; *then* they held out against federation. And when they finally did join a federal Europe

228

they did their damnedest to break it up. They say there are more separatists here than in the whole of the rest of the Union.'

'That's what the interviewer was getting at,' Merrick said. 'Anti-federalism – what it did in the Americas. Is that what is at the bottom of all this? All right, Incunabula funds our department; who funds all the others? Who funds Incunabula?'

'Don't sound off here,' Turcat said. Merrick could not tell if he was completely uninterested in the argument or simply being cautious. 'I only asked you to stay so I could tell you what your work would be, will be, if we are closed down: second year undergraduate supervision; specialism, political history of western Europe before, during and after the Anarchy – that applies to the Brussels administration as well as the effects here and in France. It was our Anarchy, after all, but it had repercussions. You'd better bone up on your enviro-geographical history as well.' He waved Merrick towards the door. 'I don't think you'll be wasting your time.'

Merrick stood in the corridor and watched Turcat sitting at his desk, staring at the floor. He must stop cataloguing Turcat among the unworldly fools of academe who could respond only to bones and potsherds. He had directed Merrick to the single subject it was currently worth pursuing.

He was allocated a roomlet, the partitioned end of a corridor which had to be reached through storage space. It had no screen – he would have to use his own. Western Europe was his original specialism; he did not think he would have to bone up on enviro-geographical history until he discovered how much he had forgotten. The fastest way to find out would be to check on the kind of work that second years were producing these days. They might be far ahead of where he had been at that stage. He settled down to audit a batch of presentations.

After half a morning he discovered that they were precisely where he had been at that stage, seven years ago, with one major difference. The facts were regurgitated dutifully but without a hint of curiosity. Everyone knew what they were talking about and only that. It was his own curiosity that had led him to Turcat and the archaeology department, the persistent voice that nagged him: Why? Why?

The dutiful facts trolled through his head: the global warming, the melting icecaps, the retreat of the glaciers, the rising seas, the loss of the Gulf Stream, alongside the Federation, the rise of the separatists, the armed militias, the Anarchy, the imposition of the United European Peace-keeping Force, the final reabsorption into the Union of the two peoples who had most threatened its infant years, the Franks and the English, nation states who loathed each other because they were so alike.

But no one asked why. What moved this bunch of sullen isolationists, still obsessed with the loss of their currency after a century, to skulk on their dwindling islands while the North Sea and the Atlantic sucked away at their substance on both sides? No one asked why they had engineered a ruinous civil war and courted invasion while the rest of Europe extended its boundaries and mended its fences. And no one asked why, after peace was restored and the Isles reabsorbed, the obsessives had turned their backs on prosperity, health, progress, had retreated up hills and into swamps in exchange for the right to call themselves English, castigating their fellow countrymen for betraying the cause and accepting integration. Their language had conquered the world, it was conquering space; everywhere that mankind spoke, it spoke in English; the word lived on. But that was not enough for the rebels; they had to *be* English.

Or Inglish, as it was derisively written.

As their forebears had seceded from the Union so they had seceded from health programmes, clinging to the miseries their ancestors had suffered on the grounds, presumably, that they were Inglish afflictions ordained by evolution. Physical pain, deformity, injury must be endured, not cured, and the evidence of that was in their bones and on their faces. Their sight deteriorated, their hair fell out, their teeth grew crooked and decayed, they died before they needed to, and for what? For the satisfaction of being able to go to the grave saying, 'I am Inglish.'

It was not only second-year students who did not look past the edges of their own subject. Turcat knew about the moss pearls but not where they came from. Joris knew where they came from but clearly did not believe they were pearls.

Ed Shepherd and no doubt the rest of Briease knew

where the pearls came from, descendants as they were of people who had preferred to let these things grow in them rather than take the poisoned chalice of European medicine. They had gained Aboriginal Status, their wretchedness had won for them the right to be called Inglish. And they were called Oysters.

He himself knew all these things and did not believe them to be myths. In a way he regretted inciting Shepherd to open the coffin in private. If Turcat had been there and seen for himself the pearls nestling obscenely among the bones . . .

It could still happen. The Parizo site was ruined but the map had shown an extensive cemetery; it had shown many cemeteries. Aboriginals on their own land, that tract of bog that was for ever England, could dig again. There was nothing to stop them at the moment.

Merrick disengaged from the litanies of history and began to look ahead. Neither Ehrhardt nor Turcat had seen beyond the immediate obstacle, the closure of the departments. The next step might be legislation, never before considered necessary, to halt all excavation throughout the USE, in which case it would become illegal on the reserves as well. They seemed to be of the opinion that the investigation into sources of funding was just another excuse to suppress the discipline, but what if it was more than that? Suppose the suppression of the discipline were the excuse, and the real intention was to uncover those who made it possible, and the reasons for their doing it.

Turcat had said something at the meeting in the Senate bar which had been working away at the back of his mind ever since. When Ehrhardt had first obtained permission from the university Senate to set up a department of archaeology, he had been put in touch with a publishing house, Incunabula. *How* had he been put in touch with Peter Bilderdyk? When? After permission had been granted and he started looking round for a sponsor, or before? And what had been the nature of the putting in touch, especially if it had been pre-emptive? Not 'I hear you are thinking of resurrecting the lost science of archaeology, I'd love to help,' but '*I'm* thinking of resurrecting the lost science of archaeology. You do the spadework and I'll pay for it.'

That was only Incunabula and Ehrhardt. After the department meeting he had started to question Turcat and Turcat had cautioned him to stop. 'Who funds the other departments? Who funds Incunabula?' He had meant nothing by the second question, it had followed thoughtlessly as a rider to the first, but was that the grit in the oyster that started the pearl? Was there a common source of funding, processed through front organizations like Incunabula?

This was one part of the diagram that lacked a link with the others; the name of Orlando Mirandola did not feature – but there might be a line to it. If excavation were to be banned by law it would take time; even emergency legislation took time. Closing the departments could be effected quickly on the grounds that they were the cause of civil unrest. There had been no civil unrest until Mirandola went to court over Parizo Man.

That put Mirandola in the picture again, but what would have happened if the hurricane had not cleared the beach and Parizo Man had remained buried?

He tried to remember how the information had come to them; by a very circuitous route, as far as he could make out, via Amandine Turcat, who had a friend among the Oysters, Frida Mason. He had told Ed Shepherd that no one outside the department had known about Parizo Man before Mirandola went public but that was not quite the case. Amandine and Philippe de Harnac had known.

Abandon that line – except for the idea of chance. Chance had sent the hurricane, chance had revealed the skeleton, but it could have been a chance that Mirandola was waiting for, had been awaiting for four years. His predecessor at the Bureau of Aboriginal Affairs had been a low-key character, so low-key that Ed Shepherd could scarcely remember what he had done, but Mirandola was high-profile; he kept Aboriginal Affairs in the public eye, making sure that people were aware of what went on in the Briease Moss. The other guy, Gupta, what would he have done after the hurricane? Consulted precedent, told the council at Briease that if they felt like digging up the skeleton there was nothing to stop them. But someone, not necessarily Mirandola, had made sure that Turcat found out about it first. Was there a Mirandola on every reserve, waiting for the chance that might not come, conspiring to bring it about?

He would have to see Amandine. He had to see Shepherd, or speak to him. Amandine did not answer

234

his call. The bank invited him to leave a message; he declined, no messages. Ed Shepherd was answering.

'Ed, any progress to report?'

'I was going to call you – we found the axe.'

The axe ought to have been a priority, but one word diverted his attention. 'How many of you are searching?'

'Oh, half a dozen of us now: Stan, Alfred Mason . . . actually I found it. It isn't very big, not much more than a hatchet. And the haft – I'm sorry about this – it's in two pieces. I know what you're going to say. Don't say it.'

'The backhoe.'

'Alfred found the broken end. He was throwing it out till I realized what it must be. Then we started looking for the rest of it, and the blade.'

'Anything else get thrown out?' Or secretly removed from site. It was not his affair what they did with what they found, and even as he prepared to feel exasperated he knew that he no longer cared very much about the axe, or its handle. All that he needed had been found already.

'Nothing else.'

'What about the . . . things?'

'We've cleared out the chancel,' Shepherd said.

'Where did you put them?'

'Where they're supposed to be.'

He'd buried the buggers.

'All of them?'

'Yes.'

'With everything?'

'I kept what we found, just the three.'

Why were they talking so obliquely? He couldn't mean that they'd kept three coffins; he had to be talking about the pearls.

'We've got to get the *things* back together again.'

'I don't think that's going to be possible.'

'It must be, Ed. I'm coming to see you – is that all right?'

'Any time, but—'

'Friday. I'll see you then.'

He could just picture them, stomping around on the beach, scavenging haphazardly through the spoil with no clear knowledge of what they were looking for, what they might find, what it was when they found it, and at least one of them perhaps the unknown observer, still observing.

This time he was certain he was being followed. At first, as before, he dismissed it as paranoia. There was no need to put a tail on anyone – centralized surveillance would monitor his progress from corner to corner; he would never be out of sight of a lens whichever way he went. The only reason for a live tail would be that whoever was after him suspected that he might be going to a place where no surveillance equipment existed. They were, of course, absolutely correct.

A guilty man, a man with a secret, with something to hide, would take evasive action, thereby betraying his guilt. An innocent, on the other hand, who saw no harm in his activities, would make no effort to cover his tracks or throw someone off the scent because it would never occur to him that there was anything suspicious about his behaviour. Merrick walked straight to Metro Station.

How could he tell there was someone behind him? They were never audible, he heard no footsteps; they were never visible, he scrutinized every plate-glass window as he approached and no one paced into view. He attributed the certainty that there must be someone behind him to the fact that until his visit to the library he had never before had the sensation that there might be.

The car to Norge was half empty and when it reached Eavrey Sound he was one of only three people who did not disembark. Two got on. On leaving Eavrey the Moss became visible, brown and yellow in the autumn sun. He tried to imagine what it was like down there. The recent drop in temperature had brought a heavy leaf fall and through the branches he occasionally caught a glimpse of light on water. Was it *wet* water, or frozen now in the pools and cuttings? He was familiar with ice from many wintry windswept digs, but not ice on waterways. He could only suppose that it was like the skating rink at Galleria Height. The city parc lake was heated, likewise the pavements; nothing in the city ever froze. How did the Oysters negotiate their channels in winter? Perhaps they too skated. He wished he had taken the opportunity to learn to skate.

Sunshine lit the heights of Norge. Leaving the station alone, the other four passengers having continued on the suburban loop, he found the roadrunner terminus, where he was faintly surprised and amused to see Briease posted as a destination, like any other. An hour later, after traversing the flat Anglian peninsula, the vehicle drove over the Niven bridge and drew up in an open square surrounded by houses, retail outlets and a building which, by its size, must be the council hall.

It stood in a walled yard. As he watched a door opened and a small child came out, running, followed by two more, a cluster, then a stream, spreading out around the yard, yelling, jostling, chasing each other until there were sixty or seventy milling about, reminding him of nothing so much as bacteria multiplying under a microscope. This must be where the Oysters acquired their habit of socializing in large numbers, in school, all of them educated together in one building. He stood by the wall, watching them, until a couple noticed him and stopped running to stare back at the lone unaccountable adult.

But he *was* a lone adult; he had not been tailed. The only passenger on the roadrunner, he had not been followed or apprehended because in the scheme of things he did not matter enough. Dr Rémy Turcat had been very publicly hauled in for questioning and Professor Ehrhardt had followed him. There was no profit in making an example of Merrick Korda; his was not the face of subversion or conspiracy. He was in effect faceless. If he were to be arrested in the middle of the city, and his arrest aired throughout the Union on a newscast, the only response would be, 'Who's he?'

But he was going to draw attention to himself here whatever he did, for it came to him gradually as he looked about him that he did not know his way around Briease. He could find Ed's place from the church, but from the square he could not see the church. He did not want to ask directly for Ed – but Frida lived near the churchyard. She must be known to have friends outside the community, and fans too, probably. He went into a shop that sold leisure aids: the shelves were lined with cannabis products of every kind, from resins to leaves and seeds to grow your own, tobaccos, pipes, papers. More sophisticated hallucinogens were in glass-fronted cabinets. He had chosen well: this was the kind of place everyone would come to.

'I'm looking for Frida Mason's house,' he said to the assistant. This then was how Oysters employed themselves, doing work that at home was the province of machines and robots. She came outside with him into the square, where the roadrunner was leaving, and told him the way. 'Up Weavers Street, left along The Holms, across Sydney Street – you can't miss it.'

He thanked her and set off, committing the names to memory. How odd, to name the roads instead of the buildings, but unlike the city the roads were few, the buildings many. At home the walkways around each tower and height, such as his own, were Admiral North, Admiral East, South, West. In the souterrain where the service vehicles plied, the roads were numbered. Here the names were posted at street corners, on little wooden uprights, and before he was halfway along The Holms he saw the church tower and, having gained the churchyard, knew that he could backtrack to Shepherd's house.

There was no one about – they must all be at work, gainfully employed at whatever employment they contrived for themselves: selling things in shops, driving roadrunners, teaching little children. If they had surveillance equipment, although Frida said they did not, well, he was a tourist, a fan, come to see the famous Aboriginal dancer in her famous Aboriginal home, and while he was here in this picturesque corner of it, by the churchyard, he might as well do a little convincing rubbernecking.

He had seen a part of it when he last came here with Shepherd, and his Antediluvial studies helped him interpret what he saw as he began his circuit of the churchyard. It was no longer possible to make out the perimeters of the graves but each was marked by a headstone, all of them so weathered that the lettering was illegible, surviving, where it did, only as runic indentations.

Yew trees grew on three sides of the church, but not to the north. That was traditional and could be linked to the fact that many Christian churches had been built on sacred sites of an older religion. These trees were of immense age; they might predate the church. The grass on either side of the shingle paths was kept cut, yellowish in its winter dormancy. Ornamental bushes such as one might find in a parc had been planted among the headstones. So must St Peter's Yexham have looked before the sea took it. The backhoe had unearthed no headstones. Either they had been pounded into sand or possibly none had been erected on such fresh graves. He knew they had been fresh because Parizo Man had sought the pearls of the newly dead.

He had entered by the gate at the west end; at the east end the graves were recent, few more than fifty years old. The dates were still visible: 2154–2225, 2138–2217, 2119–2197, such little lives; and the names: Smith, Mason, Thatcher, Glover, Plowright, Cordwainer.

Cordwainer; surely a coincidence. He was losing faith in coincidence. Could he really have relatives here in Briease? His people had come from the north originally, losing their tails like tadpoles: Cordwainer, Corder, Korda, a name with no obvious provenance. They had had no interest in national identity, or rather, they had had it and lost or abandoned it, discarding the name as arbitrarily as they had acquired it. Cordwainer the leatherworker had been up for grabs like Cooper the barrel-maker, Mason the builder, Smith the smith. He heard Turcat in the basement laboratory jeering at Mirandola: 'Has any of them ever made a glove, thatched a roof?' Easy for Turcat, he came from a long line of Turcats.

A coincidence, then, but a tiny hook that engaged with this place.

In the flint wall at the eastern end of the church-yard a gate led into the current cemetery, where Aboriginals on their own land continued to conduct their archaic burials. The new stones here were not stone but some kind of resinous compound, the names

241

and dates clear to read. He walked among them, more Masons, Smiths and Shepherds. In the last row, beyond which lay uncut grassland, were nine recent hummocks with a wooden post at the head of each like the road signs. On the crosspieces had been cut the words ONE UNKNOWN. Christian graves had once been marked with crosses. Perhaps these were in deference to those below who had originally received Christian burial, or perhaps it was the most efficient way of joining two lengths of wood.

The church clock chimed and struck three times, 15.00 hours or 17.00. Should he loiter here, mosey around town a little now that he had his bearings? Or was it time to see if Shepherd had come home yet? He did not know what hours these people kept, if Shepherd had a job as such, if he returned to his house straight after work, if he worked on Fridays. As mayor he might have council business. The whole trip might have been useless. Still, people here did not lock their doors.

Shepherd had not locked his. No one called out to Merrick as he crossed the paved way and walked up the short front path, the strips of earth on either side now empty of plants and turned over for the winter. He knocked, and when there was no reply, he opened the door and went in.

The room was much as he remembered it, and warm, which made him appreciate how chill it had become outside, how inadequate his city clothes, which were not designed to adapt to this coastal weather so late in the year. Relaxing, he reclined on the sofa facing the screen wall and ordered up a national newscast. Nothing was happening at Millennium House; no one else he knew had been arrested, although arrested was never the word used. Attention had turned to Burgundy.

He had not been aware of an archaeological department in Dijon and, as it turned out, nor was there. The latest controversy was the presence in the region of a non-territorial nation, the Flemings, sluiced out of their Low Country home and now living as Aboriginals on the south-eastern slopes of the Plateau de Langres. Being non-territorial they had no historic region into which to retreat as the Oysters and other Inglish had.

Along had come a fairy godmother. The presenter intimated that the whole revelation was a fairy tale which a liberal and gullible government had swallowed whole. The godmother was one Eva Wassilievska, industrialist and landowner of unimaginable means who, out of the kindness of her heart – the sarcasm was becoming positively elephantine – had awarded to the displaced Flemish in perpetuity and *for no personal gain* a tract of land on which to establish themselves in order to petition for Aboriginal Status.

Since this must have happened fifty or more years ago and had to be common knowledge among those who had an interest in knowing it, Merrick could only wonder at the presenter's air of ominous excitement.

'But,' said the presenter, as if divining his scepticism, 'there is evidence that Eva Wassilievska was a founder member of the Brandenburg Consortium.' *So there* hung in the air.

It was the first time that Merrick had heard the Brandenburg Consortium mentioned by serious people – if the presenter could be counted as a serious person. Previously it had been barely more than a joke, archetype of all conspiracy theories, the shadowy movers and shakers who were reported to be behind all civil disturbances, dedicated to promoting unrest in the interests of breaking up the Union. They were reputedly scion of the oldest families in Europe, monarchies and aristocracies long forgotten, with names that had supposedly died out by the middle of the twenty-first century: Habsburg, Hohenzollern, Bernadotte, Romanov, Windsor. They were generally held to be a myth since the principalities and monarchies to which they were attached had become republics, then states. Few believed that they existed save as deranged individuals with pathologically long memories.

The only people to take them seriously were conspiracy theorists, who were genuinely convinced, or deluded, that the Union was under constant threat from anti-federalist agitation. Merrick had not imagined that the government harboured many such.

Brandenburgers, said the presenter, were known – *known?* – to be fabulously wealthy; many of them were financiers with global connections, able to divert vast resources to causes that seemed likely to further their own interests.

Who funds Incunabula?

Given the miserly dole that Incunabula had made available to Ehrhardt it seemed unlikely that it was on

244

the receiving end of vast resources; the presenter was saying as much, without mentioning Incunabula by name, but might this not be evidence of a cunning plan? Rather than putting glaringly large sums at the disposal of subversive elements, thus drawing unwelcome attention to them, was it not more subtle and effective to deploy the vast resources over a wide spectrum, sowing the seeds of insurgency in unremarked back gardens, here and there, rather than planting a whole prairie in plain sight?

Very cunning, very subtle; surely no one rational could believe a word of this wild surmise? The phrase 'Reds under the bed' came to Merrick, the panic that had gripped the old USA in the mid-twentieth century when it was generally believed that the nation had been infiltrated by communists. The greater the number threatened, the greater the perceived threat; no one in the city left their doors unlocked as people did here in Briease. He saw the whole Union in hysterical turmoil, barring its doors, blocking its ventilators and suffocating in terror.

'How long have you been here?' Ed Shepherd had come in through the back way and was standing in front of him.

Merrick stood up. 'Since, er, three fifteen. I'm sorry, Ed, I had to see you – I didn't want to say too much over the air.'

'Glad you're here,' Shepherd said. 'Sit down, have a drink. What are you watching?'

'The news. Do you people have any contact with other reserves?'

'In the Isles, yes; not on the mainland. Most of them have reverted to their own languages. A representative there really has his work cut out. He has to learn the lingo and act as interpreter. Orlando only has to cope with our funny accent.'

'There's a place in Burgundy, France, granted to a group of Flemings as their territory – no, not granted. It was given to them. By a Brandenburger. That ring any bells?'

'The Brandenburg Consortium. You mentioned it last time you were here. Nothing to do with us.'

'You may think not, but I wouldn't be too sure. Our department is run on a shoestring, I told you, but it's the same with nearly all of them, everywhere. They're funded extramurally; some get more than others but no one gets much. Our shoestring was provided by a publishing house called Incunabula. From what the guy on the news was saying, Brandenburgers have great wealth which they use to foment unrest – does this begin to make sense? I know it's ridiculous, but does it begin to make sense?'

'Where do we come in?'

'The unrest takes the form of nationalism. Archaeology gives people a key to a nationalist past. The very idea of Aboriginals is nationalist. Giving the Flemings a land to which they had no hereditary links is nationalist. The RDI was the first state to recognize Aboriginal Status, and Briease was the first reserve, wasn't it? Who paid?'

'Who paid for what?'

'Political lobbying is expensive. Who paid for yours?

246

Someone with plenty at their disposal must have taken up your cause, or were the Inglish enormously wealthy a hundred years ago?'

'Of course we weren't. In those days everyone really did live in the fen.'

'So someone took pity on them and promoted the idea of Aboriginal Status out of pure disinterested charity? Or did someone see what that status might eventually lead to? Judging by the resistance to the idea, the government of the time must have seen what it might lead to.'

'You think it was an early Brandenburger plot? Did the Brandenburgers pay for Mirandola to go to court over Parizo Man?'

'No, quite the other way round. Mirandola's working for the government.'

'Of course he is, it's a government post.'

'That's not what I meant. He didn't go to court to get Parizo Man back for Briease – he did it to cook up a public excuse for stopping the excavation and investigating the department and then investigating its funding, and then banning the practice of archaeological excavation throughout the Union. That's why he got you to destroy the site when the coffins started to turn up, in case you – or we – found more than we were needed to find. Did he get you to bury them again or was it your own idea?'

'His, but we'd have done it anyway. Look, have you got *any* proof for all this?'

'No, but you said yourself, all roads lead to Mirandola. I've been travelling some of those roads and there he sits in the middle, waiting, waiting for four years, and when he gets what he's been waiting for, he *uses* it. We've all been used. Useful idiots.'

'What's in it for him?'

'He's doing his job, isn't he? As far as I can make out he was instrumental in letting us know about the skeleton; and we got it out for him. Useful. He got the site flooded – by you. Useful. Now the whole thing's blown up in just the way it was meant to. We've lost our science again, you stand to lose your special status. Any idea of what might happen then?'

Shepherd was silent.

'How much does it mean to you to be Inglish?'

'Does it mean anything to you to be European?'

'It's what I am, I don't think about it.'

'We think about it all the time; we think about what was done to us, designated subhuman, *used*.'

'Used – oh, to farm the pearls. Yes, used again. I don't think many people believe that now, but they might save you yet. I went to the graveyard. Mirandola doesn't know what we found in Parizo Man. Does he know what we found in the coffin?'

'No.'

'Did you open the others?'

'No.'

'It's likely that excavation will be made illegal, and that applies to the reserves as well. But it hasn't happened yet. We could dig again on the foreshore or we could open the graves in the cemetery.'

'What for?'

'We have records of everything, every dig, from start

to finish. We had Parizo Man coming up, me and Turcat working on him in the lab, me finding the pearls. That's all been seized but we could record finding some more if we could get hold of a body that contained them.'

'No, we couldn't . . . there might not be any more.'

'But you've kept the three we've found. If we exhume the old lady we found them in, DNA testing would prove that the pearls came from her bones.'

'I thought that was illegal.'

'For any but forensic purposes, yes. But I might know a way of getting it done, only we'd have to move fast.' Let Bilderdyk risk his neck for once after years of Ehrhardt supplying him with proscribed material.

This silence was even longer. Finally Shepherd said, 'Were you planning to stay the night?'

'If you'll have me.'

'Then tomorrow I'll show you something that is unknown outside the fen, because I trust you. I may be quite wrong but I think you are on our side.'

'I'm not on anyone's side,' Merrick said.

'So for all I know you could be a double agent working for Mirandola?' Shepherd said. 'And don't pretend to be outraged, you know it's perfectly possible, anything's possible. We're finding it hard to trust each other. No one knows who suggested using the backhoe. Mirandola didn't find Parizo Man so one of us must have told him it was there.'

'You think you have a traitor in your midst?'

'He may not see himself as a traitor,' Shepherd said. 'He may have been used too.'

'Well, say I'm on the side of truth,' Merrick said. 'I know, it sounds like self-righteous arrogance, but it's true. My job is looking for the truth, there's no other point in doing it. I *am* on its side, and I say the truth is in those coffins. Why did you change the subject when I talked about opening them?'

'I didn't change the subject,' Shepherd said. 'We can reopen the graves if you like, but you won't find anything in the coffins. They're empty.'

'What about the one we opened in the chancel, then? That wasn't empty.'

'None of them was,' Shepherd said. 'But they are now.'

Chapter Nine

The sun was not yet up when they left the house by the back gate. Merrick had thought they would go down to the staithe but Shepherd turned right along the lane that ran behind the gardens.

'How are we going to get across the Moss – the fen? I can't vault.'

'By punt. We don't usually bring them to the town staithe. There's another, this way.'

It would not be the way he had travelled with Frida. The lane petered out into a muddy track, slippery under a slick of ice. As the sky grew lighter Merrick saw white rims on grass and twigs, a milky skin over puddles and pools on each side of the track that ran between banks of yellowing reeds. On his left the sun was rising out of the sea, over the dunes. The sky was a depthless green-blue and to the west stars still hung in the remnants of the night. Behind them lights were coming on in Briease. The new sun touched the tips of the turbine blades and the metal bird that pivoted on top of the church tower. Ahead the leafless twiggy trees blushed red. He could not remember the last time he had watched the sun come up; he began to wonder if he ever had and marvelled at the speed with which, once free of the horizon, it rolled into the sky.

The path turned to run beside a stream, where a lacy frill of ice hemmed the reeds at the water line. He knew they had reached a staithe by the row of posts along the bank, most of which had punts attached. There were the slates at the foot of each post. While Shepherd walked to the end punt to leave his itinerary, he turned one over. *E. Turner to Herigal Staithe by the Hazel Carr. Tuesday 11.30.* Turner? The man who worked a lathe.

Shepherd beckoned to him from the punt, where he was casting off the mooring rope. 'Do you want to try?'

'Try what?'

'Punting; you might find it useful some day, and this is a good place to practise – only a foot or two of water.'

'Which way are we going?'

'Into the fen. You follow this stream till I tell you to turn – no,' he said patiently, 'you do it from the stern, the back end.'

Even standing up Merrick could not see above the bearded heads of the reeds, but the punt was easy to propel in the shallow torpid stream.

'In a few minutes we come to a mere, open water, no more than two feet deep. On the far side the fen begins. I'll guide you into the cut.'

The reeds grew so thickly that he did not see the mere until the prow of the punt nosed through them and they swept closed behind him. He looked back

252

and saw no trace of the stream he had left; he would never find it again unaided, and without Shepherd to guide him he would never locate the cutting he was supposedly heading for.

Shepherd's guidance consisted of hand signals which he learned rapidly to interpret. The Oyster was living up to his name this morning, morose and uncommunicative, making Merrick reluctant to ask questions. He did not want even to chance saying, 'What happens if I get it wrong?' but on the far side of the mere the rampart of reeds was less dense and he saw that Shepherd had directed him exactly into the mouth of a waterway scarcely wider than the punt.

Then they were among trees, the spindles of birch. Birch was one of the few trees he could name with confidence; the other was alder. This was definitely not the way he had come with Frida but the scenery was looking familiar, the spits of land in their ragged scrub, the turf lodges. He poled on, obeying Shepherd's terse gestures. When they came to a cutting that ran diagonally across theirs Shepherd said, 'You know how to find the current?'

'Put in something that floats and see which way it goes.'

'At night you need a candle float. Never go into the fen without a light.'

Merrick supposed that Shepherd had lights about him even though it was only an hour past sunrise.

At three hours past sunrise Merrick knew that alone he would not find his way out of the maze. At first he tried to memorize what he was passing, but bank followed cut followed eyot, all to his ignorant eye identical. From time to time he saw the white stones that Frida had warned him not to walk on because they were not stepping stones. Now they were becoming more numerous; he saw them gleam like skulls as he glided by, still faithfully following Shepherd's directions and asking himself if this was madness.

He had once, that last time, suspected that Frida was taking him to a place of no return; he had thought that of cheerful, sarcastic, conversational Frida. Shepherd had shed all his friendly ease. He might be silently enjoying the thought of allowing the idiot to punt himself into a trap from which he, with the aid of the quant, could literally spring himself.

The punt jarred against land. Merrick feared that, letting his concentration slacken, he had misread a signal and driven them into the bank, but looking past Shepherd he saw that the craft was nosed into a kind of bay apparently cut out to receive it. They were alongside a turf lodge, larger than those they had seen before.

'This is as far as we go,' Shepherd said.

'Where are we?'

'The Hazel Carr, but the name doesn't matter. What I want to show you has to be seen. It would lose something in the telling.'

They climbed up the bank to the turf lodge. Merrick knew that what he had taken for silence before had been no such thing. This was silence, here, now, more solid than the trees, more solid than the earth on which they stood, as if the Moss were one great vacuum from which all sound had been sucked. Even their breathing seemed an invasion of the stillness.

'This is a wake house,' Shepherd said, indicating the turf lodge. 'Do you know what a wake is?'

'Awake?'

'No.' Shepherd sighed. 'Look around, do you see the stones?'

'I've seen them before. Where do you get them from? There's no natural stone here.'

'From fallen buildings, I believe, ruined churches in the fen.'

'Frida told me never to walk on them – they aren't stepping stones.

'They are markers, lyke stones. They mark still water.'

'What about floats—?'

'Still water where boats may not pass,' Shepherd said. 'You know, you don't have to date Parizo Man, any of us could do that. He must have been one of the last of his kind. While the seas were still rising and the pearls were still growing, Parizo Man came out to rob the graves of the newly dead. He was caught and stopped; that was the work of one vigilante, in one parish. It must have been happening all over the region, not just here but across the peninsula, people who were prey to pearl farmers in life and grave robbers in death, living in agony and violated in the grave. You think interment is antiquated, don't you?'

'You're the only people I know of who practise it. I believe on other reserves they make arrangements to use the local vaporarium.'

255

'Ah, yes, and the bereaved are given a little bottle of condensate, the remains of the departed. Merrick, you must know, of all people, that there are other ways of disposing of the dead. Cremation, mummification . . . think what we're standing on.'

'*Bog burial?*'

'Fen burial. It's a natural resource,' Shepherd said, 'and a tradition thousands of years old. You needn't whisper, we don't have any special reverence for the area, we just take care not to vault or punt over those places where—'

'But they were sacrifices – garrotted, throats slit, heads bashed in – some of them were drowned.'

'You really think we go in for human sacrifice? Would it interest you to know that what you had for supper last night was human flesh?'

'All right. I'm sorry.' The stillness of the place had been shattered. There was no point in pretending reverence.

'They used to say we married our sisters, got high by licking frogs – when there were still frogs. Things like that have always been levelled at fenlanders. We are known to bury our dead in the earth; it seems unnecessary and faintly unhygienic to Europeans, but essentially harmless so long as we don't contaminate our water supply. And what can you expect from bogtrotters?'

'But why, for god's sake. Why in water?'

'Why not? These aren't bog burials in the sense you're thinking of. Thousands of years ago the British buried their dead in water – the gateway to the next world. When Parizo Man and his colleagues began smashing open graves to get at the pearls, people abandoned interment and turned to the fen to guard their dead in the old way.'

'Understood. Why do you still do it?'

'Why not? How long does it take for an action to become a habit, a habit to become a custom, a custom to become a tradition? How old are you?'

He had to think about it. 'Twenty-seven.'

'Age doesn't mean much to you people, does it? And in twenty-seven years, how many habits have you acquired, little meaningless private rituals that would leave you feeling oddly uncomfortable if you didn't observe them? Fen burial began as a desperate resort of the beleaguered, the oppressed; then it became usual, acceptable, seemly. We could not trust anyone to honour us alive or dead, so we committed our dead to a place where no one but ourselves would come and let the authorities laugh at our cenotaphs. That's why our representatives are always able to confirm that we are not contaminating our water supply. They're testing the wrong water. It's not illegal, you know.'

'What isn't?'

'It's not illegal to bury the dead in water. I know that no one has ever thought to ban it because no one knew that anyone actually did it, but we aren't breaking federal law.'

'And all this has gone on under Mirandola's nose?'

'Of course it has. We buried the coffins from Parizo Beach but we brought the bones here to lie with our people; their people too. You could open any grave in our cemetery since twenty-one fifty and you would never find a pearl or evidence of a pearl. You won't even find a body.'

They sat in the wake house to eat lunch.

'It's not sacred,' Shepherd said, sensing Merrick's reluctance. 'It's called a wake house because this is where we wake the corpse, a small party to send it on its way. I believe you have your parties after the vaporization. We have ours before we say goodbye.'

'Hardly parties,' Merrick said.

'We find strange things in the cuttings, and in the springs. You'd love them – coins, mostly; jewellery, ornaments, sometimes weapons. People have always paid tribute to water. Not that it's done them much good in the long run; water goes where it will.'

'They still do – pay tribute. Even in the city fountains people throw tokens. No one knows why they do it. Has anyone ever found out what you do here? It's a hell of a lot of people to be keeping a secret.'

'It's not a secret, it's something we don't discuss. How many of us do you know, or rather, how many did you know before you met me and Frida?'

'There are a few in the building where I work. I couldn't say that I *know* them.'

'People don't. We aren't shunned exactly, we just don't seem to mix. There's something about us . . . Who cares what we do here?'

'The government is beginning to. What do you suppose is going to happen if you lose your protected status?'

'We'll do what we did before. Retreat into the fen and survive unprotected.'

'Is that going to be as easy to do as it is to say?'

'Some may choose to assimilate. I told you, not everyone is happy with things as they are. In fact, some of the younger ones are quite desperate to get away.'

'Such as, perhaps, the one who tipped off Mirandola about the skull on Parizo Beach. This didn't happen because of *you*; the whole thing was a lucky accident. It's not the numbers here, it's the numbers throughout the Union. If the Brandenburgers exist, if there is a mass movement, this action against our department is meant to stop it before it really gets under way; small beginnings. Some of the mainland reserves are big, rich and probably armed. There have been standoffs. The government will do anything to avoid armed conflict. My guess is that legislation will be introduced to end Aboriginal Status and people will be expected to integrate. Those who don't will be left, as you say, to survive.'

'And go back to being subhuman.'

'You never answered my question last night: what does it mean to you to be Inglish?'

'You answered it yourself: it's what one is, the tap root, the anchor, the name itself. Don't names mean anything to you?'

'How long has your family been called Shepherd? I looked at the gravestones at Briease, all those names derived from things that no one does any more. How many sheep do you herd, personally?'

'Our road to the past was broken. We had to build bridges.'

'Do you despise those who burned their bridges behind them?'

'We don't despise anyone. We want only to be left alone to be what we are.'

'Does your birth rate exceed your death rate?'

'What has that to do with anything?'

'It could be the basis of the problem, nothing to do with the Brandenburgers. The Brandenburgers may be a fleabite, a distraction, another excuse. If your numbers are growing exponentially – not just yours, all the reserves' – that may be the real issue.'

'We could always revert to eating our young,' Shepherd said.

'Where do we go now?' Merrick asked when they left the lodge to return to the punt.

'Where do you want to go?'

'I might as well get back to the city. What's the closest the Moss comes to Eavrey Sound?'

'About three miles; five – six kilometres.'

'Is that the South Turf Bank?'

'No, beyond that. Why do you mention the South Turf Bank?'

'I've seen the name on the slates. I thought there might be a staithe there on the edge of the Moss.'

'The people of the South Turf Bank never leave the fen. Anyone who travels there is taking a body for burial. You might call the Bankers our undertakers.'

'Would they, the Bankers, know where the Parizo skeletons went?'

'We could ask. Why did you want to go that way?'

'I told you, I thought there would be a staithe.'

'Not along the southern edge. The nearest one is Herigal, where you went with Frida.'

'That's the only way in?'

'You can get in anywhere. How far you get after that is anyone's guess.'

'Can you take me to the nearest point to Eavrey?'

'Why not go back the way you came?'

'I may not be able to use that way again. I need another route.'

'You think,' Shepherd said, as they stepped back into the punt, 'that after two journeys through the fen you'll be able to find your way alone? Those of us who've lived in Briease all our lives still need help to tell our way.'

'The floats, the lyke stones?'

'They are the obvious ones; there are dozens of others we've learned to observe. Only those who live in the fen can do without.'

'Frida said you can read the grass as I read books.'

'She was right. And how long did it take you to learn to read? All right, I'll get you there. It'll be dark before we even reach the South Turf Bank but we can stay the night and you can walk on to Eavrey in the morning.'

South Turf Bank was a village in a clearing, stockaded with trees, not quite the circle of mud huts Merrick had once imagined, but enclosed, mysterious, over-hung with smoke from the peat fires that diffused the pungent scent through the woodland. The Bankers were what he had expected all Oysters to be, wary and unamiable, but Ed Shepherd, the mayor of Briease, was known to them. Beds for the night were offered. When they had eaten, Shepherd went aside with an elderly man and conferred for a while. Merrick, watching discreetly, conjectured that he had made a request, or a proposal, that had struck the other as profoundly distasteful. At one point it looked as if so much offence had been caused they might be ejected from their lodging to shift for themselves in the night. Finally the old man departed pacified, shaking hands with Shepherd but casting looks of superstitious unease at Merrick.

'What did you ask him?' Merrick said, when they were alone.

'What you wanted me to ask,' Shepherd said. 'Did he know where the Parizo bones were buried and if so, could we have some back, please?'

Merrick thought of the man's disgust and horror, his parting gesture to avert evil. 'I take it the answer was no. Didn't you say you had no special reverence for the area?'

'*We* don't.'

By morning a fog had come in from the sea and frozen into white crusts on every blade and twig. The dwellings on the South Turf Bank were crouching hulks in their own private miasma of sea vapour and peat smoke. The windows were dark under the low-browed roofs of packed reeds, the work of thatchers. Perhaps the rest of them did make gloves and barrels. Alfred Mason might be a builder after all.

When they boarded the punt Shepherd took up the

quant and Merrick did not argue. In spite of their easy passage yesterday his arms and shoulders ached, making him appreciate how fit these undersized, disease-ridden swamp dwellers must be compared to his own healthy self; and he did not, in any case, want the responsibility. The leaden fog enclosed them like wet, freezing quilts; the progress of the punt seemed more sluggish as it crawled through the brittle reeds. In the wider cuttings the ice was visible on either side of the vessel, broken away by their passing. Merrick saw the leaves trapped in it as if arranged by human hands and preserved in resin. He had not known what nature could do unaided, although it had done its worst with the South Turf Bankers.

'They look upon themselves as guardians of the dead,' Shepherd said. 'It doesn't engender much gaiety among them. They are the ones who erect the stones, conduct the bodies from the wake house, lead the mourners, make new cuttings when needed. They don't come to Briease; they are born in the fen and they die here, and as to their own funerary customs, I couldn't begin to guess. Don't ask – don't ask me anything. I need to concentrate. We've taken a wrong way.'

Merrick wondered how he could tell but did not ask. 'Sorry.'

'Not your fault – I'd have done it anyway, very likely. It would take a Banker to know his way in this.'

All the while the fog writhed and warped about them. Then as stealthily as it had arrived it withdrew, trailing tattered shrouds behind it through the trees,

263

and in an instant there were no more trees, only rushes, white pools and ahead, emerging distantly from the misty cerements, the outline of Eavrey Town and, on the right, the confident sweep of the mono-rail track.

Shepherd stopped poling. 'You'll have to walk from here. I can take you to the edge of the merse; after that you're on your own. It's firm going, across farm-land.'

'I never meant to bring you so far out of your way,' Merrick said. 'And I've kept you away from home all night.'

'Some sixth sense, popularly supposed to reside in primitive peoples, persuades me you may be worth it,' Shepherd said. 'Frida's shown you how to cross a merse, yes? Keep right behind me.'

It took them twenty minutes to travel perhaps half a kilometre. Sometimes the ragged grass hissed and foamed, sometimes clicked, crackled, crunched. When they reached the far side Shepherd said, 'Keep to the headlands – the hedgerows – then you won't trample the crop.'

'A crop at this time of year?'

'That's winter wheat, not grass,' Shepherd said. 'How the hell do you people survive?' He held out his hand. 'I'll be hearing from you, I suppose. If you're so sure you're under surveillance, call me Harrison.'

'Why Harrison?'

'That was our family name before we took to herding those mythical sheep you find so hilarious.'

'Call me Cordwainer,' Merrick said.

'You mean you—?'

'That was our family name before we cut ourselves down to size in order to fit.'

'We had Cordwainers here, once.'

'But not any more? Then I'll be the only one, won't I?' He pressed the hand he was still holding, let go and walked away towards the headland that would take him safely to Eavrey. Shepherd did not speak again or call him back, and when Merrick turned at last to look he saw the twirling quant of a fen vaulter returning to his element.

This time when he called Amandine he wondered if she lived with her brother. Such an unlikelihood would not have entered his head had he not discovered, in his visits to Briease, that whole families lived together in purpose-built houses. On the whole only students lived together, and that in order to share information facilities rather than for sociability; and it was cheaper.

Amandine answered in person. 'Who?'

'Merrick Korda. I work with your brother. I took you to the theatre.'

'Oh, I *heard*.' Her voice was breathy with distress.

'Heard what?'

'About the department being under threat. Rémy called.' They didn't share, then. 'I'm *so* sorry. And you lost your skeleton. That's *awful*.'

Anyone listening in might misconstrue it as more than awful. To lose your job, bad; but to lose your skeleton . . . ?

'We're very disappointed.' Be the unemotional

academic. 'I'm trying to cheer myself up. Would you like to have a drink?'

'Oh. Yes. All right. When? Where?' She sounded surprised, which was reasonable – she hardly knew him – but not reluctant.

'How about the Central Parc?'

'Won't it be cold?'

Not what I'd call cold. 'There's an indoor café there. Or we could try the Ayckbourn bar.'

'Oh, I *like* the Ayckbourn. Yes. Let's meet there; twenty-one hundred?'

'Can't we make it a bit earlier? Nineteen-thirty?'

'Yes; yes, all right. I'll meet you inside.'

From what he remembered of the Ayckbourn bar it would be heaving from 19.00 to 19.45, then empty out in time for the performance at 20.00, very conveniently. He wanted a good long run at Amandine.

What a giddy social whirl he was entering: coffee with Turcat in the Senate bar, drinks with Joris Tieltman and now a rendezvous with Amandine at the Ayckbourn, where it had all begun, in a way; the theatre visit, the meeting with Frida afterwards – if he had not met her then he would never have spoken to her on the monorail – and his first acquaintance with Orlando Mirandola, who never remembered who he was.

Or did he?

But then, he reflected, none of us is very memorable to look at. Our skins are flawless, our teeth are straight, our vision is perfect. We do not go bald, we do not stoop. We do not shrink from osteoporosis or become twisted with arthritis. We don't live for ever but we are still young at fifty. It was not always thus. Once we were like the Oysters, who are as unlike each other as it is possible to be for people who are all the same colour. No wonder if Mirandola never recognized him. He himself must have seen the objectionable little turd half a dozen times now but he could not recall a single distinguishing feature apart from his haircut, whereas Ed Shepherd had left every line of his pockmarked face engraved on Merrick's memory. And Frida, with her scarred cheek and overcrowded teeth; he had known her again immediately, after only one meeting.

We were all like that once.

He remembered Mirandola because he loathed him.

On the way to the Ayckbourn he called in at Waldemar Height. Joris might stall if approached in advance; better to beard him at home unannounced. Luck was with Merrick, although Joris did not seem overly delighted to see his visitor.

'I won't waste time,' Merrick said in Joris's viewing room, where all four walls and the ceiling were tuned to an underwater experience, surrounding them with blue-lit shoals and sharks. Perhaps he had interrupted an exciting bit. 'Remember *Tabanus bovinus Rex*? I'd like some eggs.'

'*What?*'

'I'd like some *Tabanus* eggs. More precisely, I want one female – *Tabanus bovinus Regina*, wasn't it? – hungry for blood, and perhaps a couple more for back-up in case it turns out she's not biting.'

267

'You're out of your mind,' Joris said. 'What are you planning? Why not have some smallpox and start an epidemic?'

'Just an experiment, a stringently controlled experiment. *T. bovinus Regina* will die the minute she's finished her lunch.'

'An experiment? On whom? By what authority?'

'I want to know what effect those horsefly bites had.'

'On a skeleton? It would have to be a skeleton in your outfit.'

'Abscesses formed between the bones, didn't they? Not so much abscesses as concretions.'

'You know that much? How can you conduct an experiment if your department's closed? And how controlled would it be?'

'It's not closed yet,' Merrick said, 'and anyway, I don't need a department for this. All I need is a human body; one I can control absolutely.'

Joris squinted at him. 'A human body; yours?'

'Yes, it's my own property. I can do what I like on my own property.'

'You guys have got a *very* odd reputation, you know that?' Joris said, as a flotilla of pilot fish crossed the ceiling. 'I'm beginning to see why. Scientists have always experimented on themselves, but *archaeologists*? Why not mummify yourself while you're at it?'

'Archaeology's a science too,' Merrick said. 'Or it was once.'

'The lost science,' Joris said. 'Frankly, I'm not surprised it got lost.'

'We could make it live again.'

'By reintroducing the bloody flux, I suppose – under controlled conditions. Very scientific. Look, if you think I'm going to let you loose with *Tabanus* eggs, a species which officially no longer exists, you must be even madder than I thought. I told you that vaccine was synthesized. I can synthesize the venom.'

'No,' Merrick said. 'I appreciate the trouble you're prepared to go to but I must have a horsefly. All experiments are recorded. If I stick a hypodermic probe in my arm all it proves is that I've stuck a hypodermic probe in my arm. I want to be bitten by *Tabanus bovinus Regina* on cam.'

'This will be a lot more trouble,' Joris said. 'I'll incubate you *one* female – and the only reason is that the thing isn't contagious. I'll let you know when she's ready.'

'It's got to be a breeding female.'

'This is illegal. What do I get out of it?' A hammerhead smiled over his shoulder.

'The pleasure of furthering scientific inquiry?'

'Sod that. If you manage to grow a pearl you can give it to me and I'll retire on the proceeds. I take it you've heard that one – that people used to buy the things.'

'You don't say. What a sick joke.'

'A necklace of abscesses,' Joris said. 'Might as well have a necklace of gallstones.'

As he had hoped, the Ayckbourn bar was full. From the other side of the Central Plaza he saw the tall lighted windows throwing down on to the paving

269

shadows of people socializing in unaccustomed proximity. It was that, as much as the novelty of seeing live theatre in a traditional playhouse, that drew them there in such numbers.

Glancing up from street level he saw Amandine on a stool at a high table, looking uncomfortably compressed against the window with a glass in her hand. He waved, but she was not looking downward and he stood, dark-clothed, in the dark. Giving up trying to attract her attention he went into the foyer and walked up the curving carpeted stairs; there were no elevators here, all was as it might have been three hundred and fifty years ago at the beginning of the twentieth century: carpets, wallpaper, dense insanitary velvet and brocade fabrics, a thick red rope instead of a handrail against the concave wall of the staircase, and all the fittings, lamps, brackets, door handles cast in heavy unidentifiable alloys.

It was 19.30. It might take him until 19.45 to reach either Amandine or the bar, which had revived the tradition of making people buy their drinks at it from serving staff, and stand in a line to do it, all very Aboriginal. He insinuated himself through the crowd towards the end window, fortunate in having located Amandine from outside.

'*Was* this such a good idea?' Amandine drooped a petulant lip. 'I'm *crushed.*'

'Well, it is called a crush bar. They'll all go away in a minute, then I'll get you another drink. It's really nice when it empties out, and the performance starts soon.'

Amandine looked doubtful. 'Why did you want to meet here? There are *thousands* of places.'

'You wanted to be warm.' He could hardly say, Because this is a place where we're unlikely to be overheard and since they are playing that hoary old favourite, Osborne's *Look Back in Anger*, which has no parts for Oysters in it, we are unlikely to run into Mirandola. He said, 'I sort of fell in love with the place the first time I came here with you, to see the ballet.'

If she chose to translate that as a declaration of sentimental feelings, so much the better. He wanted unforced confidences this evening, even if they were going to be talking about bones. Amandine did not know they were going to be talking about bones.

A bell rang and there was a rapid drainage towards the glazed double doors.

'What are you drinking?'

'It's a hock and seltzer – that's what it says at the bar. Fizzy wine, I think.'

He fetched fresh drinks and returned. 'We don't want to perch here, let's find a sofa.'

The sofas, in crimson plush, were more comfortable and well away from the windows. No one down in the plaza would be able to see them. He asked himself if he really believed that anyone was taking an interest in his movements. Even though most people seemed to be unaware of his existence, nevertheless he did exist and many of his movements were easy to check up on. But taking a drink with a pretty girl – and were not all girls pretty? – what could be a more unexceptionable way of passing the evening for a

271

good-looking young man, as good looking as all the others. Rémy Turcat must be all of ten years his senior but they could easily be exact contemporaries.

He thought of a place where the men were plain and the girls were not pretty and ten years made an enormous difference.

They had the bar almost to themselves now, save for one or two couples and the barman, passing among the tables to collect glasses. Merrick was wondering how to set the conversation going when Amandine solved the problem by asking, as if she really cared, 'What will you do now if the department closes? Will they throw you out?'

'No, that's all being seen to. Considering how they must be feeling, your brother and Ehrhardt have taken care of things wonderfully. Ehrhardt's absorbing us all into the history faculty, though there aren't that many of us. I'll be supervizing. The students will be reassigned to subjects of their choice. There's nothing to stop them studying palaeontology, or early archaeology, come to that. It was a very short-lived discipline, late nineteenth century to late twenty-first, barely two hundred years.'

'Really? Didn't people excavate before that?'

'Yes, on a freelance basis. They called themselves antiquaries; grave robbers, more or less.'

'Like Parizo Man?'

So Turcat had been discussing his work with his little sister and Amandine, bless her, was steering their talk in the right direction again.

'Parizo Man was a robber, pure and simple.

Antiquaries told themselves that they were contributing to the sum of human knowledge – which they were, in a way. The trouble was, they chucked out more than they contributed. They only kept the bits that shone.'

He must not let his enthusiasm for his subject lure him off the path he meant to follow, divert him into telling Amandine about Ehrhardt's dream of founding a new museum, named in honour of the father of scientific archaeology, Pitt-Rivers.

'They'd never have bothered with Parizo Man,' he said adroitly, turning back on course, 'a skeleton with no gold or silver in it – valueless.' He said nothing about the pearls; he did not think Turcat would have mentioned them. 'Tell me, how did you stumble on him?'

'It was the most amazing coincidence,' Amandine said. 'We were checking the wave barrages – after the hurricane, you know – and it was a lovely morning. Philippe said—'

'Philippe?'

'My boss, Philippe de Harnac, he said, "Let's go up the coast a bit," just for the ride, you know. And when we came ashore—'

'Why did you go ashore – just there, I mean. It *was* an amazing coincidence, wasn't it?'

'Well, there's that sticky-out jetty thing, and Philippe said he wanted to see if the Oys— the – oh, *you* know, if they'd lost their turbine. In the high wind. He's a sweetie, really. I say, I couldn't have another of these fizz things, could I?'

At the speed she was downing them he would have to draw a fine line between making her loquacious and getting her pissed. How much loquacity could he take? He was used to people of few words but he had never before come across anyone who could deploy so few words across so much conversation. He stood at the counter while the barman mixed the hock and seltzers. The wall behind the bar was mirrored, with rows of bottles and glasses ranged against it. He saw himself gazing moodily at himself. Lighten up, Korda.

'Well,' Amandine hosed in a mouthful, 'we walked up the beach and it was black! All black and slimy, foul, and rubbish all over it, birds' bones and feathers and . . . *rubbish*. And then Philippe said, "Oh god, what's that?" and I mean, *I* knew at once, but I mean, I'm used to bones. *You* know, what with Rémy, even when we were children.'

'You don't mean he was digging up skeletons as a kid? He'd have been put in corrective therapy.'

'Oh no, but he was always looking at *pictures*, and since he started at the department, showing me things. I mean, it didn't bother *me* when I saw what we'd found, but Philippe was, you know, really shocked. I don't think he'd seen one before.'

'What could you see?'

'Well, just the top of the head – what do you call it, *crandulum* – and the top half of the eyehole thingies, and that was worse because when he, Philippe, bent down to look, this jellyfishy thingy was in one of the eye *sockets* – that's it, that's what you call them, isn't it?'

274

'Most people do,' Merrick said.

'Like an eyeball. And Philippe just stood there *looking* at it, and of course, I was thinking, that could be a whole *skeleton*. Rémy would give his eye teeth to get that out, and I didn't like to say anything because, you know, Philippe's never actually said as much, because well, *you* know, I think he likes me – as a person, you know – but I don't really think he approves of what Rémy *does* – not just Rémy, the whole department, archaeological thingy-thing – and I thought if I said Rémy would like to see it – well, he'd be *mad* to see it – he, Philippe, might say I was being unprofessional or something, or that it was an Oyster skeleton because of the Briease thingy, it was their bit of beach and we'd be breaking the law, but then he *said* it.'

Merrick, frantically trying to extract a coherent sentence from the dependent clauses, almost missed their arrival at the point he'd been aiming at.

'What did he say?'

'Well, *he*, you know, Philippe, said it for me. What I'd been wondering if I could say. He said, "Wouldn't your brother be interested in this?"'

'That *was* a stroke of luck,' Merrick said.

'Wasn't it? I'm going to get another – no, my turn.'

'I'm fine,' Merrick said. He was deliberately restricting his consumption. 'You go ahead.' So it had been de Harnac who had found the skull, because he just happened to be passing Parizo Beach the day after it came to light; de Harnac who had pointed out that Rémy Turcat would like to know about it.

275

Amandine returned, navigating between the tables with unwonted caution.

'Nice of him,' Merrick said noncommittally.

'What was?'

'Nice of de Harnac to think of your brother – when he doesn't really approve of what he does.'

'Oh, I *know*. I mean, he was really touched, him even thinking of it. And then he said of course it would have to be classified as an ancient death first, but the Politi wouldn't care what happened to it after that, and I said what would happen if it was on Oyster territory and he, Philippe, he said he didn't think it was and if they minded so much they should mark their boundaries.'

Merrick, listening avidly, had been picturing the scene: the sea, the sloping peat bed, the dunes. Even from the top of the dunes, he was sure, it was impossible to see the Briease turbine when the trees were in leaf.

'But,' Amandine said happily, 'the *biggest* coincidence was me being there. I was supposed to be in the office, monitoring breakdowns. He said, Philippe said, I deserved a treat. Wasn't that the most amazing luck?'

Given what had happened as a result of that piece of amazing luck, Merrick wondered if Amandine was purely stupid or talking through the effects of the hock and seltzer. No one these days could be *that* stupid.

'What does your work usually involve?' he asked with sincere interest, staring into her eyes. 'What would you have been doing if you hadn't gone to Parizo Beach?'

She told him, at length. He did not hear, he was too intent on watching the disparate tesserae turn and fit into his mosaic. De Harnac had taken a trip to a place he did not need to visit, where he stumbled by chance on something that would be of tremendous interest to the brother of the woman who was with him and who was supposed to be somewhere else at the time. How very good of Philippe de Harnac to suppress his natural disapproval, possibly revulsion, at the activities of Rémy Turcat in order to deliver into his hands an ancient death, a skeleton which had providentially surfaced on Parizo Beach after the hurricane.

If he hadn't buried the bloody thing himself then someone must have made sure he knew where to find it.

During the interval the bar filled up, emptied again, and Amandine talked unstoppably, sinking hock and seltzers. Only one thing of note stood out from the torrent of non-information: the fact that she was madly in love with de Harnac and he did not know it. Merrick thought that almost certainly he did know it and had, at least once, found it very convenient. 'Come up and see my wave barrages.' All he wanted to do was go home and examine his mosaic, all those little pieces that were fitting so snugly together, but having asked the girl out for a drink – seven or eight drinks at the last count – he could hardly get up and leave her on the grounds that she had nothing else to say that he wanted to hear.

The premises closed as the performance ended and the barman, whose performance was also over, sent out a robot to clear the tables.

'Shall I see you home?' It was not the kind of thing one normally offered to do but Merrick doubted if she could manage alone.

'Oh, would you?' Amandine walked down the stairs as if they were coming up to meet her. 'What's this stuff called?'

'Carpet.'

'Horrible. Like walking on sand.'

It was unexpectedly cold outside. Amandine shivered and paused while her coat adapted.

'Do you want to take the souterrain?' He did not even know where she lived.

'No, it's only a few minutes away, Atlantic Height.'

Just across the plaza, then. They set out slowly, into the wind. Amandine clung to his arm.

'I've been an awful bore.'

'No, it's been fun.'

'It hasn't.' Her voice shook. 'I feel terrible about Rémy's work. I wish I'd never found that thing – everything's going wrong at the moment. I've been talking and talking, it's the only way to stop thinking. I haven't said anything I shouldn't, have I?'

'Not at all,' he assured her.

'I only – I'm so miserable about – about—'

De Harnac, he supplied silently.

He went up in the elevator with her and delivered her to her door. In Atlantic Height the apartments were built around three sides of an atrium the full height of the tower, each one opening on to a balcony planted with trees and creepers to keep the greenery going, in stages, up to the roof level. The elevators rose through glass columns, but too fast to appreciate the view. He had once entertained ambitions of some day living in a place like this, stepping out each morning into a fragrant garden instead of the sweaty utilitarianism of the ball court; forget about that.

'Will you be all right?' Merrick asked as Amandine fumbled to find a hand to wave at her scanner.

'I'll be fine.' The door opened anyway, it knew her voice. 'Don't tell Rémy I'm worried. He'll only worry about *me*.'

'Wouldn't he be glad to know how concerned his sister is?'

'No, please. Oh, you *will* be loyal to him, won't you?' she burst out.

'Loyal? But of course.'

'He's going to need it. He *trusts* you, did you know that? He said to me, "Korda's all right. Half the time I forget he's there, but you can say that about your own heart"—'

'*What?*'

'– or did he say brain?'

'Brain,' Merrick said firmly. 'Or maybe kidneys.'

'Don't laugh. He needs you.'

'You mustn't worry about those death threats, they didn't mean anything – *really* they didn't.' That was truer than she knew. 'No one's going to lay a hand on him. They'd have done it by now, don't you think? He's quite safe . . . No, don't cry.'

Amandine sniffed and remembered her manners. 'Thank you for seeing me home. Would you like to have sex?'

He would, now she mentioned it, but he doubted if she meant it and you would have to be a Visigoth indeed to take advantage.

'No, thank you. Go to bed.'

Merrick went back down in the elevator hoping very much that Turcat had compared him to his brain rather than his heart. Walking the short distance to Admiral Height he rehearsed what he had learned from Amandine; what was supposition, what was certainty, but even the certainty was not confirmed. Still: the skull appears on Parizo Beach on, or soon after, the night of the hurricane. Unless someone knows it is already there, which is virtually impossible, this is the first sighting.

Two days later de Harnac makes an unnecessary journey along the east coast, northwards, and lands exactly where the skull is waiting. Why, he might almost have co-ordinates. He has brought along the sister of a man who, de Harnac knows, would love to dig up a skeleton – assuming that there is a skeleton attached to the head. It is de Harnac who proposes that Turcat should be informed, keeping everything legal by informing the cops as well, aware that Turcat will not dare to excavate illegally since he can't do it in secret.

It is a certainty that once Turcat knows about the skull he will want to excavate. The Oysters don't seem to know or care about it. The Politi definitely don't care, it's an ancient death, none of their business – even if it isn't very ancient.

So Turcat excavates and no one tries to stop him until Mirandola turns up out of the blue, on Parizo Beach, when it is too late to stop.

Another certainty: Mirandola knew about the skull. If he had not seen it himself then someone had told him about it. Someone, possibly Mirandola, had told de Harnac, and the rest was history.

Next day, after another night of quite decorous rioting, in the battle-scarred bastion of Millennium House Professor Ehrhardt assembled his archaeology department and formally disbanded it.

Chapter Ten

Having joined Turcat's department immediately after his degree was awarded, Merrick had never known the joys of teaching students. As the winter began to bite he felt the tedium eating into his bones while he sat daily in his slip of a room auditing the undigested data of the second-year European history undergraduates. Long ago someone had said, 'Information is not knowledge.' Whoever it was had been uncannily prescient, speaking before the time when students sought their information from identical sources and processed it into identical presentations. You could tell these bat-brains that the Australias had been discovered accidentally by Galileo while mining X-rays to build the first neutron bomb and they would ingest it unquestioned. The stuff went in and came out unmetabolized. It was like eating grass.

Turcat all but vanished, reputedly engaged on research. It was generally agreed that this was what someone of his standing ought to be engaged on rather than grubbing about in the mud. If he were relying on Merrick as his brain Merrick was not aware of it. Even when officers of the court came to order the removal to a place of safekeeping every last thing the department had ever excavated, it was left to Ehrhardt to supervise and catalogue. When the cherished hoard was packed there was pitifully little of it to show for fifteen years' work. Had Incunabula ever doubted if it was getting its money's worth?

He did not meet Amandine again; she did not get in touch. He half-hoped for a message from the Moss, from Harrison-Shepherd – not news, just a friendly word. His message bank was no emptier than it had ever been, but now he noticed the emptiness. He was almost excited to find a single communication in it when he came home from work shortly after the midwinter break, head creaking with information overload; information, he was beginning to notice, that was not merely repetitious but exiguous to the point of being misleading.

The message was brief: 'Regina is ready for lunch.' Joris had incubated his horsefly.

Merrick called back. 'Where would she like to eat?'

'I'll drop in tomorrow evening. We'll make it a threesome.' Joris did not want Merrick showing up at his apartment or at the laboratories, where his presence would feature in the Tieltman data.

Another message followed: 'You'd better decide where you want it.'

Tabanus bovinus Regina was much larger than he had expected, all of three centimetres long, viciously striated in black and yellow and waiting for him in a glass tube.

'Still sure you want to go through with it?' Joris said. 'You'll notice I'm not pressing you for details. If this kills you it's nothing to do with me.'

'I didn't know it could be lethal.' Even Ed Shepherd had not suggested that Oysters died *acquiring* their pearls.

'Ordinarily speaking, no, it wasn't, just unimaginably painful. You don't know what you're in for, do you? Neither do I, but people like us aren't equipped to withstand what's going to happen to you. We hardly know what pain is. We're protected against everything, we have no natural immunities. If you're recording all this, by the way, keep the lens on your wrist and off my face. I don't want even my *hands* in the picture. Do you know what allergies were?'

'No.'

'Physical reactions against something which normally had no effect on the system: strawberries, peanuts, pollens, wasp stings. Some people were violently affected; if they didn't get treatment they died. It could just happen to you, but with insect venom it was usually the second attack that was fatal – anaphylactic shock. There'll be no second bite for *T. bovinus Regina.*'

'Supposing it doesn't work the first time?'

'You'll have to look elsewhere for your next date. I'm not prepared to take the risk. Now, did you decide where you want her to go in?'

Merrick held out his left hand with a red circle carefully drawn around the hollow between the magnum and scaphoid carpals.

'My, we are picky,' Joris murmured. '*Exactly* there? Are you sure about this? I'm assuming you're right-handed but don't you occasionally need lefty here?'

'I want it where I can get at it,' Merrick said.

'Well, given your morbid interest, I can see that you might want to watch developments.'

'It's not that – well, partly it is – but you can . . . *handle* a hand without anyone noticing; not like a knee or a foot, covered in clothes, maybe out of reach; just what I said, I can get at it.'

'I think all you're going to want to do is cut it off,' Joris said. 'However, that's your decision. Sit at the table, put your arm on this towel with the wadded part under the wrist. Keep it flexed.'

'Will this hurt?'

'Not half as much as it's going to. No, you'll hardly feel anything, not enough to make you flinch. That's the trouble, really; if the victims had felt themselves being punctured they could have brushed her off before any harm was done. It was the withdrawal that set things going.'

While he was speaking he had upended the tube, removed whatever was sealing it and placed it over Merrick's bent wrist, so that the lip encircled his red circle. *Tabanus bovinus Regina* ambled unhurriedly down the tube, settled for an instant on the skin she had instinctively been expecting, and without prelim-inaries for so momentous an act, began her meal.

'I told you to keep still – you're trembling. What she is doing,' Joris explained, 'is sinking her proboscis through your hypodermis in search of blood for her egg-laying. If she were operating on your buttock, for instance, you would end up with the aforementioned tennis ball. Your gluteous maximus has no articulating parts – it's a muscle, before you ask. But that proboscis is almost a centimetre long; as you planned, it is now down among the bones of your wrist. Look at her go. Can you feel anything?'

'Yes, slightly – I can't describe it. Not quite a sting—'

'That will come later, don't worry – don't move. Don't disturb her before she's finished. We want her to do as much damage as possible – you do, at any rate. Ah *ha*, here she comes. You may feel something as she pulls out but keep still. We don't want her loose in here.'

Merrick felt a shadow of a sensation as the fly withdrew her proboscis, not even a sting, a *frisson* of discomfort compounded by the fatalistic knowledge that he had begun something he could not stop.

'If I wanted to, could I take an antidote?'

'Second thoughts already?'

'No, I just wondered.'

'If you wanted you could take an antidote now – not that I have one. The usual analgesics will help but not for long. If you become desperate you can always have recourse to surgery – no, not amputation; that's what you'll wish for, but a medic could remove the concretion at any time – after it's started growing, that is.'

'How long will it take?'

'A few weeks, months. It has already begun you know. You can move now. Within the hour there will be a raised inflamed area just about fitting inside that circle you so thoughtfully described. It will itch – put any kind of emollient you like on it. That will give some relief and have absolutely no effect upon the subcutaneous infection. If you manage to get an unbroken night's sleep you will wake tomorrow in considerable pain. Take pills, they may dull it somewhat. The inflammation will be worse and things will continue thus for a week. You may be feverish. Then the swelling will subside and for a time you will feel nothing. You may forget all about what has happened, but all this while the pearl is forming, tiny, like a grain of oolite, a single codfish egg; and then it begins to grow, and then you will remember it.

'It must, you see, displace the little bones to make room for itself. You're hatching a cuckoo in your nest. The pressure may damage nerves, cause temporary or permanent paralysis in one or more fingers. After a time – and remember, I personally have never seen this happen; I doubt if anyone alive has seen it – after a time a swelling will reappear. As well as the internal pain, the pressure is now upwards to the surface, burning, aching, itching; again, any palliative you find effective, if any exists. Eventually you will not be able to resist rubbing it, scratching it, even biting at it perhaps, as animals do with their injuries. And all the while the pearl grows and the day comes nearer and nearer, inexorably, when it will rupture the epidermis and break out.

'It's almost like being pregnant!' he concluded, with a burst of happy inspiration.

*　　*　　*

287

Merrick did not get an unbroken night's sleep. After recording the promised inflammation he went to bed early and lay awake until after midnight, haunted absurdly by the small murder he had brought about.

'I could release her somewhere,' Joris had said. 'In a humid house at the botanical dome, or an atrium – not out of doors, the cold would finish her off. She is breeding out of season but of course she doesn't know that. If I'd thought to provide her with a husband she could lay her eggs and a whole new cycle might begin. But that would be unethical.' He had wrapped the glass tube in a fibre towel and crushed it under his heel.

Meanwhile *T. bovinus Regina*'s legacy was at work in Merrick's wrist. The itching had begun. He anointed it and felt the numbness spread around the bite. It was all on the surface.

At three in the morning he woke with the certainty that someone was driving a metal spike through his wrist. Putting on the light he saw that the red ring no longer contained the swelling, which was hard, but encircled it like a coronet. He took pills which, as Joris had forecast, dulled the pain somewhat, enabling him to sleep for a few hours. When the alarm roused him to go to work the spike recommenced its endless penetration; his whole hand ached round it and while he rose and dressed and drank coffee, filaments of pain began to explore his fingers. The swelling grew larger almost as he watched. He recorded it faithfully.

He could not let anyone see it and put an athlete's brace around his wrist, which gave it some support while hiding it and at the same time constricting it cruelly. He felt feverish; this was the result of the lack of immunities Joris had warned him about, and Joris had hazarded a week of it.

In his office the history presentations drilled through his head; he could see them, the facts, an endless snaking toothed wire sawing between his ears. He did not know if what he was hearing was correct – he had assumed it would be because the system allowed for no margin of error. If you found the correct sources all you had to do was redirect them. Only the most halfwitted could fail to find the correct sources and there were no halfwits any more.

Except for him, perhaps. The suspicion that the facts were no longer as he remembered them persisted. They were so many fewer, skewing the conclusions; not *suggestio falsi* but *suppressio veri*, the truth, but not the whole truth.

He could not concentrate. He wanted somewhere to put his hand, preferably somewhere that was not attached to his arm. He laid it on the desk, tenderly couched on his folded jacket, and enjoyed a few minutes' relief. When that was over he raised it, balanced on his elbow. The pain receded, then rallied and returned. He let it dangle, bad mistake, rested it on his lap, tucked it into the front of his shirt, and each time the tide of pain ebbed, then, as he relaxed, surged back again and flooded his excavation. There was a sour metallic taste in his mouth. The room, not having been a room for very long, was without drinking facilities. When he reached the stage where nothing he could do would ease the pain he rose and floated out through the storage area and into the corridor.

Someone said, 'Good grief, what have you done to yourself?'

He focused, with an effort, on something that was not his hand. Turcat.

'I slipped,' he said, imagining that Turcat had seen him clutching his wrist.

'Slipped? What into, boiling oil? You're running a fever. Hadn't you better get to a clinic? You should never have come to work in this state. Did you pick up something in that swamp – god knows what they've got flourishing there? You haven't been at the toxic frogs, have you? No, seriously, you must get medical attention. I'll call—'

'No.' Not that, not now. Turcat might be personally concerned for the health of his auxiliary vital organ but his priority was the prospect of a possibly infectious disease breaking out in Millennium House. Merrick did not know how he was looking but he could tell that he was running a temperature, sweating, conditions now so rare as to be unknown to most people; enough to set up the spectre of contagion. He knew he was not contagious; how to convince Turcat?

'It's happened before,' he lied and cursed himself for not being ready with a cover story, but Joris's comment on the possibility of fever had not prepared him for this. 'I react very violently to muscle strain. When I was a child—'

'What muscle have you strained to bring this on?'

Merrick, conversant with all two hundred and six bones in the human body, was hazier about muscles. Which ones operated the hand? No, that didn't matter, Turcat had not noticed the brace. Why hadn't he pretended to cut himself? He named the only muscle he could remember. 'Gluteus maximus.'

'That must be hell, anything in the sacral region . . . but there's no need to suffer like this.'

'If I rest it I'll be over it in a few days.' Joris, you'd better be right about that.

'You don't have to rest it for a few days. Go to a clinic now and you'll be fine by tonight.'

'No, I won't, I promise you I won't. Six days at most.'

'Are you delirious?'

At this rate he soon would be. 'Amandine said you trusted me.'

'What's Amandine got to do with this?'

'We met for a drink. We talked. She says you trust me.'

'Yes, I do. Though just at the moment—'

'Trust me now. Give me the week off. I'll get over this.'

'It's not muscle strain, is it?'

'No.'

'Can I ask—?'

'No. Trust me.'

'Well' – Turcat walked in a despairing circle – 'whatever you're up to, and I can't begin to guess, it can't put us in a worse position than we're in already. Has this got anything to do with . . . anything?'

'Yes. It's an experiment.'

'You want to find out how it feels to die?'

'Something like that. Can you get me a ride home?'

'Not in a public vehicle – they'd run you straight to the nearest clinic before you start an epidemic.'

'This isn't contagious, I promise.'

'I said I trusted you, didn't I?'

After three days things began to improve. He awoke on the fourth morning to find that he could move his fingers and the pain had subsided to a throbbing ache from shoulder to fingertips. He stopped the cam and reran his experiment from the moment he had staggered home from work on Wednesday, his waxen face basted with sweat, to call Joris.

'Can I take narcotics?'

'Of course you can, you fool. Didn't I say so?'

'No.'

'Well, take them, take anything, take poison. And don't call again, I'm not here.'

He remembered nothing of the subsequent seventy-two hours and watched with interest as he ripped off the brace, thrust his fiery wrist in front of the lens, scrambled about mainly on hands and knees, undressing, swallowing tablets, falling asleep on the floor.

The rest of the record was more of the same. He sped through it, skipping the boring parts, the embarrassing parts, halting to look occasionally at close-ups of his hand. He was rather touched by his devotion to the project, in that he had been sufficiently aware at intervals to make sure that the progress of the bite had been recorded. On Thursday evening the swelling had reached his elbow; by Friday morning his shoulder was engulfed; twelve hours later his hand resembled an inflated glove, on Saturday a bloated scarlet udder.

He had been expecting a tennis ball but then, as Joris had said, people like him – which was, after all, most people – had no natural immunities, no defences against invasion. The gates of the city had been swept open, the barbarians had broken in.

He started the cam again and gave it a good look at his arm. The styloid processes at the wrist were not yet visible but he could at least feel them, with gentle pressure. His knuckles were re-emerging and the inflammation had localized to a livid areola around the bite, which manifested itself as a tiny dot, still encircled by the ring he had drawn before his encounter with *Tabanus bovinus Regina*.

Which reminded him that it was Sunday and he had not washed since Wednesday morning, but before he could do anything about it his balance failed again and he fell back on the bed, asleep before he hit it.

The sepsis vanished as suddenly as it had developed. On Monday there was little to show the cam but a pink stain on his skin, slightly raised, tender but not really painful. The initiation was over, he had survived it. He could do nothing now but wait for the object of the exercise to make its presence felt, if it ever did. He had gone through all this and there was still no guarantee that he would get his pearl of great price. At the same time he knew that in the last few days he had discovered pain and sickness, the lost afflictions. He felt weak but he must have come out of the ordeal strengthened, morally if not physically. But he had not been brave, resorting to every chemical intervention available. How would he acquit himself when the pearl did begin to make itself felt?

Until it did it was going to be an effort to remember to record all those uneventful days on the cam. He decided to log on to it as soon as he got up and before he went to bed, every day, so that it became habitual, like the first piss and the last.

Showered; ate; drank; felt less like Parizo Man. Having watched his own week on the screen the day before, he settled down to see what had been happening in the world at large. Many of his fellow Europeans had little idea of where the world at large was. Since national borders had become state lines, many continentals had trouble envisioning the shape of their own country. Only the inhabitants of the Rhine Delta Islands had any sense of outline, intensified during those years when the perimeter had decreased so dramatically, the memory of the old woman on her pig. Australia, Asia, Africa, the Americas languished on the periphery. Russia, fermenting on the border, sometimes got a look-in on home news, but at the moment home news was mainly taken up with its own fermentation and, like the grit in the mollusc, there he was unnoticed at the heart of it.

Throughout the Union all archaeological activity had been suspended on the grounds that it was stirring up racism, separatism and anti-federalism. It was suspected that all those seemingly innocuous academic institutions had been secretly funded by elements inimical to the stability of the Union, subversively encouraging Europeans to question the status quo and to begin to rethink themselves as French, Magyar, Polish and, of course, Inglish.

Could it be coincidence, the speaker asked, that so many of these so-called academic institutions got all or most of their money from outside the parent universities? Could it be coincidence that all of them had come into existence since 2240? Now we're getting there, Merrick thought. Could it be coincidence that the first of these debatably 'academic' institutions had been in the RDI, the same hotbed that had spawned the first instance of a secessionist group demanding and being cravenly granted the right to claim Aboriginal Status? Could it be coincidence—

'*No, of course it fucking isn't*—'

– that these same Islands had traditionally been the most obstructionist, retrogressive, contentious and disruptive of all the states of the Union?

There were now twenty-three states which had given legal credibility to the dubious notion of Aboriginal identity. How many of the reserves were receiving support from the same sources that supported the archaeologists? How many of them, while appearing to adhere to federal legislation, were in fact breaking the laws on, say, weaponry? Were we going to wake up one morning, in those twenty-three states, to find ourselves facing armed insurrection? And did each of those *soi-disant* Aboriginal reserves mysteriously arrive at consensus by coincidence, or was there some nationwide conspiracy bent on imposing a New World Order?

Put like that, in the hectoring rant of the broadcaster, it sounded ludicrous. Everything that went wrong, including the hurricane, was ascribed to one conspiracy or another. But, Merrick thought, hadn't he himself asked where Incunabula got its money from? Hadn't he asked who proposed the idea of an archaeology department, Bilderdyk of Incunabula or Ehrhardt? He *hadn't* known that Ehrhardt had been the first. No wonder they were the first to be investigated – or was it no wonder? What had started the whole business; the resurrection of Parizo Man; and how had that come about?

At which point Orlando Mirandola appeared on the screen.

Merrick's reflex was to tune him out – he did not want Mirandola in his living room. The little bastard was there on a special errand, to plead the cause of his Aboriginals, his own particular private Aboriginals in the Briease Moss, beleaguered, suppressed, aghast at the result of their natural desire to claim what was theirs, the ancestor, the body on Parizo Beach, on their own land, that archaeologists had summarily dug up and made off with. How could they possibly be accused of conniving with these desecrators? All they asked – he almost had tears in his eyes – was to be left alone, to live as they chose, in the ways of their forebears. They had struggled, suffered for this right. If opportunist nationalists had hitched a ride in their wagon for their own nefarious ends, could they be blamed for that? Must they suffer again?

He could say what he liked now, Merrick thought savagely. He and the presenter were reading from the same script, a script that Mirandola might well have written himself. It no longer mattered what anyone said. Mirandola had set the ball rolling and it had gained its own momentum. He had betrayed and used the very people he had been appointed to protect.

Merrick tuned out the volume as the presenter was issuing dire warnings about the possible need for mobilization of federal Anti-Insurgency Forces. He had never heard of any such forces and he paid more attention to the news than most. The general public would no doubt be nodding sagely: Ah yes, the Anti-Insurgency Forces, good to know they're there when you need them; now we can sleep easily even if millions of heavily armed Hungarians rise up in the night to slaughter us in our beds.

The powers that be, presumably the federal government, were already talking of armed response to a threat that very probably did not exist. How could a situation so potentially devastating have evolved in a matter of weeks?

Were Ed Shepherd and his fellow Oysters at Briease even now bringing out their fire power? It would be desperately out of date, like everything else there: tanks, perhaps, artillery, tactical nuclear missiles.

He had asked for a week off on Wednesday, he remembered that much. He had two days left; Turcat would be pleased to see him back early, if he were around to notice, although they both knew that a machine could audit the presentations just as efficiently, if not more so. A machine would ask no questions. And he had laughed at the Oysters seeking ways to employ themselves.

Merrick set his ancillary robot to cleaning the room and the bed, and righted furniture and fittings that he had overturned or brought down, thrashing about in his half-drugged sleep. Had he dreamed at all? If not, what a waste of so much febrile energy. He ought to have had wild psychedelic dreams, but if he had he could not recall any of them. He had seen from the cam record that he had woken up only to swallow more pills; everything else, visits to the lavatory, to the water supply, to the cam itself, appeared to have taken place while he was unconscious. The place stank, as he discovered coming in again after a brief foray into the courtyard to see how light-headed he felt walking about.

He would take the cam to Millennium House with him. Nothing much was likely to happen in the next few weeks but even nothing had to be recorded and dated, and given the turn events were taking it seemed likely that someone might feel the need to look at his accommodation. He must keep the existing record capsules with him; without them the last horrible days would have gone for nothing, with only Turcat's testimony to back up his assertion that the bite of *Tabanus bovinus Rex* was violently painful, and he had yet to confess to Turcat about that.

The last thing he saw as he closed down the screen

was a surtitle above Mirandola's head, informing him that Professor Ehrhardt had been taken in for questioning again, along with one Peter Bilderdyk, in connection with certain revelations about a certain publishing house.

This sent him skiing across channels to the commercial sites. The Incunabula hoarding, which normally listed its current publications and backlist, was blank. SITE VACANT, it said. No word of what had occupied it.

He moved to the classified ads and posted one of his own, informing interested collectors of antiquities that a small quantity of mollusc derivatives of Inglish origin might shortly become available, and inquiring, as an afterthought, what the going rate was likely to be.

Turcat eyed him thoughtfully when he returned to Millennium House.

'The agony has abated?'

'Absolutely.' He set aside thoughts of the agony to come. 'Any chance of meeting for a drink later?'

They both knew that not long ago such a suggestion would have come from neither of them, certainly not from Merrick, but the peak from which Turcat had overlooked Merrick's trough had suffered a tectonic shift. They were more or less on the same level now, in the trough, with only the merest incline between them; Turcat harassed, suspect, departmentless; Merrick in possession of something Turcat could not even guess at.

He put in an hour with the presentations, not even

bothering to listen; if someone had entered a disquisition on frog-licking he would not have noticed, and then Turcat looked in and asked if he would like to come across to the library with him.

Out in the cold, iceless plaza Turcat said, 'What was the last you heard?'

'Ehrhardt's been arrested again.'

'Called in for questioning – and you may still refer to him as Professor Ehrhardt,' Turcat said acidly. 'Anyway, he's back. They've finished with us, having finished us.'

'What did they get out of him?' Merrick's bluntness did not surprise even him. Professor or not, in the current situation Ehrhardt's eminence put him scarcely higher than either of them on the incline.

'They wanted to know about Incunabula first of all.'

'Did he approach them or did they approach him?'

'What makes you say that?'

'Who funds Incunabula?'

'You worked it out. Bilderdyk approached Ehrhardt – but only after Dieter had got permission to go ahead in the first place, which does not look good. Well, they're now pursuing Brandenburgers through the undergrowth, as it were. Since they are mostly elderly and sedentary this should not be difficult. The latest question is, who is behind Brandenburg? Most of Dieter's visit to the Feds was to explain and identify every last thing we've dug up since we started. If you'd been at work you'd have noticed that I've been missing too. I got called in to corroborate everything separately. We went through the items, we went through

300

the records. Seeing one's much younger self skipping around is deeply depressing.'

'You couldn't have looked so very different.'

'The *enthusiasm* . . . They have hours, days, years of video-logs. The game is to stop suddenly and say, "This is such-and-such a dig, Dr Turcat. What were you hoping to find?" Then they produce a toenail. "And what did this tell you?" First there was young Dieter, then little Rémy. Latterly, of course, there was the boy Merrick. Even you've changed in five years. Oh, you look the same but the iron has entered your soul. But even if you hadn't suggested that drink I'd still have invited you over to the library. Everyone who has assisted at a dig is on record, a face to a name. You feature prominently. They know who you are.'

'Up till a few weeks ago I sometimes wondered if you knew who I was,' Merrick observed.

'You were always more than a useful pair of hands,' Turcat said.

'Now you tell me. A liver— No, forget I said that.'

'Why else do you imagine that I used you so much? I thought you were going places.'

'None of us is going anywhere now, are we?'

'I'm telling you this because whatever it is you're up to is going to cause suspicion. We've served our purpose; they're after the big boys now. I don't think anyone has the slightest interest in our activities, and what we've been accused of is patently nonsense. We were used by Incunabula, by the Brandenburgers, by whoever, if anyone, is pulling the Brandenburger strings, and now we're being used by the government, but I don't think anyone seriously believes that *we* had a nationalist-separatist agenda. That won't save the department but it will probably save us, if we keep our heads down. You haven't been keeping your head down, have you?'

'Am I under surveillance?'

'I don't think you have been more than anyone else has, but you are becoming conspicuous by your absence. You are on record at most digs over the last five years. The only reason no one connects you with Parizo Man is because the records were impounded with the skeleton, and the only reason you haven't been questioned yet is because you haven't been around to question. Next time they ask for you, be here. I'm running out of excuses.'

'All right, you've told me what you wanted me to know – now tell me something I want to know. This was my treat, remember, or it will be if we ever get to a bar – and we aren't going to the library, are we? What did you do with the artefacts and related material from Parizo Beach?'

'I handed them over – once I saw there was no chance of hanging on to them.'

'But not the pearls.'

'No, I didn't hand over the pearls, I've told you that.'

'Why not?'

'I wasn't asked for them.'

'I'd have thought,' Merrick said, 'that the pearls would have been of enormous interest. You said they were down to itemizing toenails.'

'No one is itemizing anything to do with Parizo Man. You, I, we keep saying "they". We ought to define our terms. They who have been giving Dieter and me so much grief are Federal Investigators. Parizo Man, with his artefacts and related material, was impounded by a local magistrate who has them sealed up somewhere pending further court proceedings. The Feds aren't interested in Parizo Man – he served his purpose, as we did. He stirred up a row. Safely sealed away with him are the records of his excavation, on the beach and in the lab. Eventually, perhaps, someone will get around to looking at them. They will not, however, see you finding the pearls. That part of the record went missing.'

'How—? Oh, I see. Why?'

'Let's face it,' Turcat said, 'they were the sole interesting thing about Parizo Man.'

'Isn't being shot in the eye interesting?'

'Only if it's your eye.'

'I meant of interest to other people.'

'You know the kind of people who are interested in moss pearls. If they knew we had any there'd be a queue around the block.'

'I wonder if you know just *how* interesting.'

'Tell me.'

They had found their way to the parc. On the other side of the arboretum lay the lake, unfrozen, where grateful wildfowl took advantage of the warm water, and on its farther shore the café bar. In summer, tables were set out between it and the lakeside. These had all been taken away and those few people who felt the need to move beyond their own heights for relaxation could sit indoors looking out over the approximation of nature in the raw. There was nothing to stop the foolhardy taking their drinks outside. Merrick and Turcat settled on a log artistically arranged near the water's edge. Merrick had sat here before. For the first time he noticed that it was not a real tree trunk. The simulation was masterly, but when he ran his thumb along the fissures in the bark, nothing came away.

'You were saying . . . I don't understand just how interesting the pearls might be.'

'Parizo Man was robbing graves to steal moss pearls. He only attacked new graves because he knew how fast the body deteriorates.'

'Are you still riding that hobby horse?'

'It's a real horse. He did have pearls, didn't he?'

'They were in the abdominal cavity, in a glass phial. He was obviously hiding them when he was discovered. We know he swallowed them, either on purpose or—'

'I didn't say they grew in *him*.' Merrick was not sure now how much he wanted to tell Turcat, or how little.

'Good. There's not the slightest evidence that those things grew in human bodies. It's one of those ugly stories put about to discredit Oysters – the things they're supposed to get up to in that swamp of theirs.'

You don't know the half of it, Merrick thought. He said, 'There is proof. There must be. Scientists believe it.'

'We're not scientists?'

'Zoologists. The pearls grew as a result of horsefly bites.'

'Why are you so interested in this?'

'Why *aren't* you interested? Suppose we could prove—'

'It's too late to be interested,' Turcat said.

'You can't mean that. You'll just turn off the tap? No more intellectual curiosity? It's only practical archaeology that's being suspended.'

'No, it won't be. I said you shouldn't stay away so long. Any activity which leads to inquiry into racial and national origins will be banned.'

'Along with the original reasons for the Aboriginal Status Act?'

'Even the history syllabuses are going to be inspected and overhauled.'

'Given the crud I've been hearing from the second years, I'd say they'd been overhauled already, decimated, one fact in ten taken out.'

They drank in silence, staring out over the lake, wondering independently if the man on the far side who had been loitering for so long among the trees had anything to do with them.

'So, where did you put the pearls,' Merrick said finally, 'and the missing records?'

'I didn't put them anywhere,' Turcat said. 'You did.'

'I did?'

Turcat got up and began to walk away. 'Work it out, that's what you're good at. And make sure you're back in your office this afternoon. Come back a different way.'

If only events had not moved so fast. If he had known what Shepherd and his undertakers were going to do with the recovered bodies he would have begged to save the one in the coffin they had opened in the chancel at Briease. A simple test would have proved that the pearl had grown in the Oyster; Bilderdyk could have paid them in kind, for once. Now the body was gone beyond recall, and so was Bilderdyk, by the look of it.

But he knew, without having to work it out, what he had done with the Parizo pearls. They were in the library stacks, in the Vanderkerckhove treatise on mummification, in the only place they could be, since it was the only place he had not looked at, that convenient tunnel between the spine and the binding. It might be a sensible move, in the near future, to find them some other reading matter before someone else thought of it.

One afternoon he stood in his office talking to a bewildered student who had come along to question the need to misremember certain facts about the years following the Anarchy. The woman, forgiveably resentful at having wasted perhaps ten minutes of her valuable time, made it a prolonged interview, clinging to the rare opportunity to talk face to face with a human tutor. The office was small. Merrick, having given her the one chair, had spent far longer than he had intended leaning against the desk. He did not care to risk sitting on it; it looked, and moved, as if it might be of the same vintage as the building, and after a while he rested his weight on his hands.

When the argument was over he stood up to indicate that his visitor might usefully leave. Both wrists ached, but in the left one there was a lingering discomfort, very small, very localized, very internal, like a pinprick, but in a place no pin could reach.

It faded, with the ache, but in the morning when he unthinkingly levered himself out of bed, he felt it again. It might be a real strained muscle this time, but he was fairly sure that no muscle or tendon attached just there, so far in. He rotated his hand. The sensation grew no worse and by the time he reached Millennium House he had forgotten about it, but over the next two days it recurred more frequently and it was becoming, almost imperceptibly, more insistent. He could not call it a pain yet, but on the third day he knew that it could not be long before it did become painful. He had chosen his left wrist because he was right-handed and he had chosen a wrist because, he remembered telling Joris, he wanted to be able to get at it.

That had been a misapprehension; he could not get at it. Rubbing, scratching did not shift it. Massage at first relieved, then exacerbated it, but still it was not yet a pain.

He would have liked further consultation with Joris, but knew what kind of a reception he would get if he proposed a meeting or even a conversation. It was quite possible that Joris had held something back. It was equally possible that he knew precisely as much as he had told Merrick in which case, Merrick reflected, his knowledge was miserably inadequate. He had not known the whole truth about the pearls and whatever he did know was more than Merrick could find out. There was no reference to moss pearls on any information site. Pearls were exhaustively described and illustrated: Pacific pearls, Mediterranean pearls, cultured pearls, freshwater pearls; not even a nod in the direction of the Briease Moss, where pearls had grown for a while in humans, been cultured in humans, vile heritage of *Tabanus bovinus Rex*.

There was nothing about *Tabanus bovinus Rex* either.

Or accounts of the petitions and proceedings that had resulted in the Aboriginal Status Act; it might have been handed down by god in the garden of Eden before records began. This was how to create a myth, he realized: expunge every shred of documentary evidence that proves the truth. The only source of information reposed in the collectors of antiquities to whom he had addressed his advertisement and they were never going to reveal themselves, although the sums they were offering were revelatory.

He ransacked the library catalogues. It seemed there was nothing in the stacks about moss pearls, horse-flies or early Aboriginal legislation. Many books had been taken out on extended loan, which was unusual. However, Vanderkerckhove's *On Mummification* was still there. After all, the stacks did contain a little information on moss pearls. It was time he went down there and did some research on Parizo Man, or all that they had left of him.

The chief advantage, if it could be called an advantage, of his experiment, was that the project was

confined to such a small space, one currently undetectable. Only Joris, who was sedulously distancing
himself from the whole thing, was in a position to lead
anybody to it. Merrick kept the records and the cam
on his person wherever he went. They were with him
when he went down to the library stacks.

As usual he found himself alone there with the
sliding humming shelves, the subdued lighting.
Vanderkerckhove was where he had left it. He considered taking it out to a reading desk, but there was just
sufficient illumination between the shelves for what
he needed to do. The related material and record
capsules were where he had guessed they would be,
in the tunnel between the stitched spine of the book
and the leather binding, in a flattish oiled-cloth
package, barely two centimetres across and ten long.
Only someone searching for it, or someone who knew
it was there, would have found it. He hooked it out,
replaced Vanderkerckhove and looked for a fresh
repository.

It had to be a book with no recent trail leading back
to Turcat, and a book that would arouse no interest
outside the faculty, that only people like himself,
perhaps only himself, would be likely to remove. There
was an even chance that any book down here might
remain undisturbed for years, or eternity, but it was
safest to stick to his own subject. Since no one knew
that anything was missing from the Parizo collection
no one was going to come looking for it, but there
might be curiosity alerted by his visits. He selected a
volume on the British railway system, a safely neutral

subject although as exciting, in its way, as the decline and fall of the Roman Empire, and reburied his treasure. The book, balanced on his open left hand, was heavy. The discomfort in his wrist did not go away for a long while.

Chapter Eleven

There was no swelling. There was nothing at all to be detected externally. Merrick regarded his flawless complexion in the glass and wondered what effect protracted suffering was going to have on it. No one suffered protracted pain – his appearance when *T. bovinus Regina* gave him the fever had been enough to frighten Turcat, although that was only fear of contagion. Would he, when his hand began seriously to hurt and go on hurting, and on, find his face incised like Shepherd's with its swags of bruised flesh beneath the eyes, the broken veins, the scars?

It was growing among his bones, and would one day emerge if he could bear to keep it so long. He daily and nightly recorded its progress in spite of the fact that there was nothing yet to see, no swelling, no discoloration, not even stiffness. He regularly added a word of voiceover, detailing how it felt, but this was partly mere conscientiousness, partly ground work for what he feared was coming. Joris and Ed might not have their facts right – possibly the fever following the bite of *T. bovinus Regina* could turn out to be the worst of the experiment, but he doubted it. When the records were reviewed he might be accused of faking the symptoms, but not those of that week. When the thing started to come out, no one would be able to accuse him of faking.

Then he received the summons to present himself at the Assembly complex for an interview. On the face of it this was no cause for concern. Other graduate assistants had been called, lightly grilled and sent back to work. He grilled them again; what sort of a mood were the questioners in? What were they asking? What were they really after?

'They wanted to know how Welsh I felt,' Tudor said.

'How Welsh do you feel?'

'More Welsh than the guy who was asking the questions. His name was Powell, he didn't know why.'

The more he heard the more convinced he became that no one expected to learn anything of value. It was a formality, a furthering and completion of a process that had already achieved its end the moment it began; the furnishing of an excuse to clamp down on nascent nationalism before whole states started claiming Aboriginal Status.

Who needed to know anything? All that was needed was visible proof. Archaeology had been seen to stir up nationalist feelings; root it out and everything else could be rooted out with it. Turcat clung to his hope of clinging to palaeoanthropology, but they all knew that they no longer mattered. An ancient murder in the right place was all that had been required; all that had been required of them was to dig it up. The pearl round their own personal piece of grit was now so large that they had no comprehension of its circumference.

'So tell me,' the Inquisitor said, 'what was your own interest in the subject?'

Merrick could not help but think of her as the Inquisitor although she was perfectly friendly and coffee had been provided. Her name was Selma Rasmussen, but whatever the designation of her office he had not been informed of it.

'I majored in history,' he said. 'This seemed a natural progression. So much has been lost, especially in the RDI; history is the recovery of the past by reading it. Archaeology is the recovery of the past by seeing it. Palaeoanthropology is of course prehistoric.'

'What is your personal interest in the past of the RDI?'

'I live here, I was born here. I'd go anywhere if the opportunity arose but for now I work where I happen to be.'

'How do you think of yourself?'

'As a European citizen.'

'As Inglish?'

'No.'

'But you *are* Inglish.'

'How can you tell?' he said sharply, but she did not answer. That something about him, as Ehrhardt had elegantly put it. Or they had checked his lineage as they had checked Tudor's.

'Do go on.'

'My ancestors were Inglish. I've no especial interest in my family history.'

'Why is that?'

'It doesn't seem important.' He had been right, this was all so much rhubarb. He was being interviewed because everyone was being interviewed. These were the questions everyone was being asked, however intrusive. And if he were privily conspiring to restore the British monarchy he was hardly likely to say so over a cup of coffee. Unless Rasmussen was planning to spring something on him she was going to conclude the interview knowing exactly as much or as little as she had known when they began.

He tossed in a small bomb of his own. 'For instance, when we excavated on Parizo Beach I wasn't looking for evidence of Inglishness, rather the reverse. Parizo Man might have been the victim of a shipwreck for all we knew; he could have been African.' Like the casual remark about Incunabula's funding this was not something he had thought out beforehand.

He could tell by her face that she had not expected him to mention Parizo Man unprompted, was probably thinking that *he* was relieved that she had not raised the subject, but she would not rise to the bait.

'Many people, the majority, consider the investigation of human remains as offensive,' she said.

'That was true a couple of centuries ago,' he said. 'I find it hard to credit that many people do now. We have so little regard for the body that we vaporize it. Is there any reason why a knowledge of the skeleton should be the preserve of the medical profession? The Parizo body was the first time *I'd* seen a whole—'

314

'So it was simple prurience that led you into this discipline?'

Parizo Man sank back into the sand which had hidden him. Either the inquisitors truly had no interest in him or they were so interested that they would get the court order lifted and conduct their own investigation into the dig. Merrick doubted that anyone would bother and doubted that by mentioning it he had raised the stakes against himself. The department was going to join its subject in oblivion, with all the other departments, big and small, and the faculty of the mighty Paris-Sorbonne. It might well have been Paris-Sorbonne that they had been after all the time, but out on the fringe of the Union a fortuitous discovery by an insignificant bunch of academics in a state with a long reputation for intransigence had come at exactly the right moment. The names of Ehrhardt, Turcat and Korda would never be associated with Parizo Man. They were all, he thought poetically, as Rasmussen showed unmistakable eagerness to draw the interview to a close, doomed to sink into the sands of time.

At home, when he raised his hand to salute the scanner at the ground-level entry, a sharp pain shot through his wrist, like an instantaneous sprain. It went away immediately and did not return, even when he repeated the action at his own door, but as he lay in bed that night, on his left side, the hand draped inactive across his shoulder, he felt the pearl lodged among his carpals; something was there that had not been there before.

'Like being pregnant,' Joris had said. This then was the quickening, the moment when the mother felt the baby move for the first time and knew that she carried a living creature. This moment was nowhere near so joyous – what he carried was not alive – but this was his first consciousness of something being in there, beginning to displace the bones it grew among. If he was lucky it might wax no bigger than a seed, but he had seen larger ones, much larger.

In the morning he felt nothing and thought he had been fantasizing, until he held up his hand for its morning record, and then he felt the bones crepitate and knew what was going to happen. However smooth the pearl might be, it was going to force those bones against one another until there was no more room, and then it would begin its journey to the surface.

'Why are you doing this?' he asked himself one evening, when the crepitus was, he thought, audible enough to be picked up. He was measuring his wrist on cam now, against the day when it would begin to expand to accommodate the cuckoo in his nest. He looked at the cam eye as he spoke, seeing himself tinily reflected, and answered his reflection.

'There is no one alive to whom this has happened. There is no proof that it did ever happen to anyone, and now there is no hope of finding proof, except this. This is proof.

'Proof of what?

'Before there was organized labour, workers were exploited. When they formed trades unions people

316

resented their power, forgetting why they had been necessary.

'Before the people of the Briease Moss won Aboriginal Status they were exploited. Now they have the right to call themselves Inglish the government and who knows else resent their autonomy and fear their potential. No one remembers why Aboriginal Status was necessary. They may have been wrong-headed in insisting that they were different, but there is nothing inherently dangerous about being different. Moss pearls grew in the human body, reputedly causing terrible pain. I am in the process of finding out if this is true.'

He intended to continue, but having begun with no clear idea of what he was going to say he knew he was sure to dry in the middle of what ought to be an important spiel. And what came next was something for which he had only Ed Shepherd's word and no proof. Joris, if gripped warmly by the throat, or subpoenaed, might confirm that moss pearls were human. Merrick was, as he had just announced, in the process of proving it. But only criminals and very suspect antiques dealers would know, although they might not admit it, that there was a market for moss pearls among people who knew where they came from. There was no proof at all that anyone had ever deliberately caused the infection that caused the pearls to grow. Sooner or later Parizo Man must be liberated, with the visual record of his iniquity. If the courts refused to release him to a private citizen, which was all Ehrhardt and Turcat would be, an Oyster might be able to recover

317

him, going to law on his own behalf and on behalf of his people, without requesting that the representative act for him. The present representative might agree to act; he was unlikely to let himself succeed.

That evening, outside Millennium House, he stood on the steps and tasted the wind. It was bitingly cold and there were few people about, most preferring to use the souterrain transit, but he walked, because he was used to walking and he must school himself to disdain mere discomfort in the light of what he would have to endure. But crossing the Central Plaza he saw the lit facade of the Ayckbourn Theatre and had a sudden need for the dusty warmth of wallpaper, curtains and the carpet that had so disgusted Amandine Turcat. The drinks there were appallingly expensive but you were paying for the ambience, and it was after all the ambience that attracted the clientele. He quickened his pace as he changed direction, but even through his gauntlet gloves he felt the cold probing his bones and freezing his pearl. How could he have lived so long among bones and yet remained unaware of his own *memento mori*?

The Ayckbourn affected posters behind glass instead of screens. One of them announced that the House Ballet Company had re-formed for a limited season by popular demand; Frida Mason was appearing in certain roles. The last night was scheduled for Friday. Frida would surely be going home to Briease after that. When he was settled with his drink in a corner he called poor useful Amandine.

'Did you know Frida was dancing at the Ayckbourn?'

If Amandine was surprised to hear from him again she did not let her voice betray it. Quite likely she had no memory at all of their last meeting.

'Yes, I went on the first night.'

He might have guessed that. 'Well, the last night's on Friday. There are still a few seats, I checked. Do you want to go again?'

'Oh, yes, *thank* you.'

Cheap at the price, dear, don't thank me, he thought as he made his way over the carpet – and, yes, it was like treading on soft sand – downstairs to the peculiar glass-fronted booth where those nostalgic for a past they had never known could purchase real tickets to retain as keepsakes. Who would make a better cover for a meeting with Frida than Philippe de Harnac's employee, even if she was Turcat's sister. He really ought to have got to know Frida better himself; at least gone to see her that last time he was in Briease, especially after asking the way to her house; but he had been too busy chasing a skeleton. That said a lot for his human relationships.

As he waited for Amandine in the foyer two evenings later, Merrick wondered how she was getting on with de Harnac, whether he appreciated her mute devotion now that she had ceased to be of any use to him. All of them now, including Mirandola, were no more than ants pursuing their own frantic but infinitesimal concerns around the feet of giants.

Now it was all going on at a higher level, in state legislatures, regional assemblies, upper and lower

319

houses, in Brussels, in the civil service departments, in ministries, the debate on the move to abolish Aboriginal Status throughout the Union, to modify it, to allow it to continue in certain states. The RDI, tired of being regarded as the seat of all unrest, was the most vociferous in arguing against the last suggestion. It had been the first state to recognize it, it was happy to be seen as the first to abandon it; no special pleading for once. Mirandola bobbed up daily on newscasts, pleading most especially for his beleaguered bogtrotters. No one found this strange – he had always been loudest in defence of their interests; wasn't he the one who got their skeleton impounded for them?

Thinking of which Merrick was horribly startled to see Mirandola's spherical head a couple of metres away.

For all his duplicity he might be a real fan of Frida's dancing, or he might find it politic to be seen at her performances, reaffirming his adherence to the cause. He was unlikely to show up at Briease these days, after all. Mirandola saw Amandine before she saw Merrick and attached himself firmly, yakking proprietorially in her ear, and Amandine noticed Merrick a fraction too late for him to vanish into the crowd and reappear at the last minute when there would be no time to get into conversation.

'You know Orlando, don't you?' Amandine said, drawing the three of them together.

'We've met,' Merrick said.

'I wasn't aware that you were a devotee of the *danse*,' Mirandola said.

'The first time we ran into each other was here,' Merrick said. 'The *Sea Witch* ballet, back in October.'

'So it was.' Mirandola, like Merrick himself, was, Merrick suspected, thinking of all the other things that had transpired in October, and since.

Fortunately he was sitting some distance from them, down at the front. Merrick, having booked late, had only been able to get seats to the side, in a loge. The dance drama was an old one, *The Sleeping Beauty* which, according to the programme notes, was danced on the point and required command of very specialized techniques – which was why Frida had been called in again, he supposed, thin, light and relatively short. Few Aboriginal societies had gone to the lengths the Oysters had to keep themselves pure, but they tended to be smaller in comparison to the rest of the population. On the programme notes they were identifiable by their listing as guest stars, Frida at the head of the list.

What would become of the Oysters if they were forced to accept federal health and development programmes, the screening out of what the Union perceived as defects and they regarded as identity? And what would become of the South Turf Bankers, the undertakers, the true Oysters, guardians of the dead? And what would become of the dead? He could not begin to grapple with the ramifications of authority discovering the truth about Briease burial practices. How deeply unjust that against the threat of nationwide insurrection a small group of deviants should lose their jealously preserved way of life and, particularly, their way of death.

The house lights dimmed and the curtain rose. He was not familiar with the ballet, although he knew the folk tale it was based on, but however much the company claimed to be recreating an original he could surmise enough to appreciate that the only original elements were those danced on the point by Frida and her kind. The others were just too big, too heavy, to spring in the air and be caught, lifted and land hideously upon their toes.

Frida was dancing the title role, Aurora, the girl who cut herself on a piece of antiquated textile equipment and fell asleep, cursed by a bad fairy. Her face larded with the masking make-up she twirled about the stage like a member of an anthropoid species, not fully human—

Subhuman?

One number required her to balance on her pointed toe for fourteen interminable minutes while a succession of large men offered her roses. The first gasps of admiration were, by the middle, mingled with sympathetic sighs and murmurs of distress which took on undertones of disgust by the end. It was unnatural.

Subhuman?

No one should be doing that in public.

After what seemed like several hours an interval occurred, then another, two days later. Merrick accompanied Amandine to the bar for the first; by the second he was finding it difficult to stay awake except that his hand, lying across his knee, was hurting, a persistent, nagging hurt that he tried to ignore by telling himself that Frida's toes must be hurting far more. When

Amandine left her seat he made his excuses and stayed put, leaning over the edge of the loge to see what Mirandola was up to.

He was socializing, the round black head bobbing like a ball in a fountain. With a little effort Merrick could have spat on it. What kind of people socialized with a schmuck like Mirandola?

Admittedly, very few people were in a position to know what Mirandola had done, but Merrick saw nothing at all in him to like. His voice was affected, his very appearance annoying. Why would anyone seek his company? Or was it subliminally accepted that his was the company to be seen in?

If Merrick could only persuade Ed Shepherd into court, complete with Turcat's evidence and his own, the Oysters might yet preserve themselves. Even if they lost their precious status the exposure of what had once been done to them might cause enough feeling to draw attention to their outrageous betrayal by the man appointed to represent them. All legal proceedings were broadcast; no one could interfere with that. They must have their day in court.

Leaning on the rail of the loge his left wrist bore his weight and was pierced as if by a nail. The Christian god had been traditionally portrayed with nails through his hands even after it was known that to support the weight of his body on the cross the nails must have passed through his wrists.

Amandine returned.

'Will you go backstage to see Frida again?' he asked her as the lights went down.

'Oh, *yes*. Do you want to come?'

That had been the intention. He prayed that Mirandola still maintained that it would spoil the magic.

The ballet ground its way to a conclusion. The applause at the end was generous, but Merrick discovered after clapping his hands together twice that the jarring shock ran up to his shoulder. He could only tap the right against the left feebly and hope that in the uproar Amandine would not notice. Frida and the other point dancers received ovations but he sensed that a certain warmth was withheld, unlike the last occasion he had seen her dance. People were beginning to ask themselves if this sort of thing ought to be encouraged. They might have expected to see it done well but they did not wholly want to see it done at all, and they would take care not to see it again.

There was no stampede to go backstage and the maze of passages was echoing and empty. As the première dancer Frida had her own dressing room now. By the time Merrick and Amandine arrived she was sitting in a wrap, face mercifully scraped clean.

'It was marvellous,' Amandine cried, descending large and glowing on Frida's small pallid person. 'Amazing, that *adagio* . . . Oh, do you remember Merrick Korda?'

'I met you once before,' Merrick said swiftly, 'after you danced the Sea Witch.'

Frida, quick on the uptake, nodded and said with well-feigned cordiality, 'Oh yes, of *course*,' contriving to imply that she could not remember him at all but was covering up politely. Under that cover went subsequent meetings.

'Another wonderful performance,' he said sincerely. 'We don't see enough of this kind of thing.' He sounded just like Mirandola.

'The way things are going you're not likely to see much more,' Frida said.

Amandine gasped. 'You're not retiring!'

'I'm not, nor are any of the others as far as I know. We've a few years left in us yet.' She flexed her ugly toes. 'But if the repeal of the Act goes through there won't be any more little ballerinas. We'll all be great big girls like you. And none of those great big men will be able to lift or catch us; their centre of gravity is too high. That'll be the real end of ballet on the point. Judging by this evening quite a lot of people won't mind a bit.'

Amandine looked anguished. Merrick watched them in the mirror that reflected Frida's sound profile: spare, hard, sharp, unyielding. Amandine by contrast was all curves and contours, as near perfect as genetic intervention could make her.

But she is so *nice*, he thought, and was almost sorry that he had found her passion for dance no more than convenient.

'Will you come and eat with us?' she asked. 'You'd be able to tell us *everything*,' she added piteously.

'Not much to tell,' Frida said. 'It's all on the newscasts – except the search for arms.'

'Searching, at Briease? Oh, that's terrible. You haven't got any arms.'

'Of course we have, we're meat-eaters, remember? We shoot to kill, kill to eat. House-to-house searches and every hunting piece checked and catalogued.'

Amandine sniffed. 'But in *Briease*!'

'Why does that seem so terrible? You've never been to Briease, have you? Or did you make a guided tour?'

Had the weapons search extended into the Moss? Probably not. Merrick found her bitterness hard to forgive when it was directed at Amandine and Amandine was so obviously, genuinely moved. But what do we know? he thought. Frida thinks Amandine associates with her because it's a kind of liberal chic, or that's what she told me. And no matter how outraged and indignant we are on their behalf it costs us nothing.

'No, I won't join you,' Frida said. 'Usual reason. Must get properly warm and exercised. Thanks anyway, stay in touch,' she said dismissively, but all the same Amandine bent to kiss the disfigured cheek before turning and going out through the door that Merrick held open for her with unseemly promptness. Without looking back he extended his arm and felt Frida take from his hand the letter he had written to her Uncle Ed, on paper, in an envelope, just as the Oysters liked it. His handwriting, he had found, was quite as appalling as Turcat's.

The shallow pit between the magnum and scaphoid carpals was a pit no longer. Something lodged there now, something as hard as another bone that was not bone, while the bones that it had dislocated in its growth ground agonizingly against each other. The joint was less swollen than misshapen, but not to any degree the uninformed eye could see. It showed on the gauge, however, when he measured it twice daily in front of the cam.

He had chosen, sacrificed his wrist because it would be easy to get at; too easy. He could not leave it alone, continually pressing his right index finger into the hollow that was daily less hollow, feeling under his skin the new thing that was growing there. The hope that, his wrist being fairly lean, the pearl would have to exit while it was still small, had been misconceived. It was going to be a big one.

The reply to his letter to Shepherd had been laconic, a brief message in the bank: 'You're welcome any time. I'll be ready,' by which he understood that Shepherd had responded favourably to his suggestion that the Oysters file an application with the court to recover the skeleton found on and illegally removed from Parizo Beach, in order to give it a proper burial in accordance with their customs.

And you must bury it if you get it, Merrick had written, *in earth. That way diverts attention from the fen and the South Turf Bank. You wouldn't want him lying with your people anyway, would you? We have to do this before there is any definite move to repeal the Act.*

Parizo Man was going to be far more useful in death than he had been in life, as the sole existing proof, once reunited with his related material and records, that he had been robbing graves for moss pearls.

Merrick regularly cursed Shepherd for his over-zealous disposal of the evidence which would have furnished them with a second reunion, the body with the pearls from the coffin. DNA tests, however illicitly obtained, might have linked Parizo Man's pearls with the remains in the other coffins. Instead he had had to provide his own proof, which no one was going to be able to refute, with no matter what ingenious sophistry, and if anyone disputed it he could demand forensic testing as a legal right. Even if he died tonight the pearl was there, and the lewdly avid replies to his advertisement. Without in any way condoning Parizo Man's enterprise he at least understood it now. With the pearls they had between them, Shepherd's trio, Turcat's five, and his own, the three of them could live like gods for the rest of their lives. Merrick could not begin to calculate the value of his own pearl, shortly to erupt fresh and gleaming, its origin authenticated, of great price and of great size.

He touched it in its wincing bed, and the unwelcome thought came to him that while he carried it he too was of great price. If someone knew what he was incubating he could be seized by the greedy, the immoral, the ruthless; not abducted but stolen. Thieves, wreckers had once severed the fingers of their victims to get at their rings. The ruthless but patient would watch him in his extremity until the pearl hatched in its own time. The greedy would simply gouge it out or, to expedite matters, cut off his hand. Perhaps Joris had not been joking when he said he would take the pearl in exchange for begetting it, and

Joris was the only person who knew it might exist. Joris had rejected the idea that anyone would pay cash for the equivalent of a gallstone, but that could have been bluff.

He contacted him. 'Do you still want my pearl?'

'I told you, I'm not here. And don't be disgusting.'

He was not entirely convinced.

Turcat came in one afternoon while he was auditing presentations. Although the days were noticeably lengthening now, his nook at the end of the corridor was still drear with wintry gloom.

'Come to cheer me up?'

'Good news first, or bad news?'

'Good, please. Is there still any?'

'In small measures. The study of palaeoanthropology has been reinstated on the curriculum.'

'Up to and including the Neanderthals?'

'Don't let's push our luck, you know how contentious the Neanderthal issue was. We stop in the Olduvai Gorge for now.'

'And the bad news?'

'The university library is going to be inspected and recatalogued.'

'The Feds?'

'No, not officially, this is internal; we have a week's notice. All borrowed volumes are to be returned immediately. If you've left any favourite bookmarks you'd better hurry up and get them back. Don't bugger off afterwards, there's a departmental meeting at seventeen hundred.'

'Which department?'

'European history and— Why do you keep doing that?'

'Doing what?'

'Prodding your wrist. You haven't strained another muscle, have you? You're not going to start collapsing again?'

'I twisted it.'

'Really? You do have bad luck, don't you? In the five years you were excavating for me, really heavy labour, I don't recall your suffering so much as a cut finger. Now you spend your days sitting in an office—'

'It's the lack of exercise, obviously,' Merrick said. 'I've grown soft and vulnerable. Just look at these, would you?' He had on the table a manifest of the offers to purchase mollusc derivatives. 'We can provide our own funding in future; start our own department.'

'We could start our own university on this.'

'The smallest one would pay for court proceedings.'

'A hundred times over. What court proceedings?'

'To recover Parizo Man.'

'We'd never get him.'

'*We* wouldn't. The Oysters.'

'Do they actually want him?' Turcat said doubtfully.

'I want him in court. We don't stand a chance of getting him back because officially we no longer exist and even if we did, no one would trust us with him. We wouldn't even be allowed to petition. But the Oysters would.'

'And we would pay for it. Why?'

'Because I want to nail Mirandola. In court the truth would come out and only in court. It would be seen live. If only *one* person saw it the truth would come out.'

'Truth may perhaps come to the price of a pearl,' Turcat said.

'Very appropriate. Is that original?'

'Francis Bacon, the sixteenth-century essayist and statesman and early experimenter with refrigeration. He died of a chill sustained while stuffing a chicken with snow.'

'A dead chicken, I hope.'

'What a foul mind you have,' Turcat said. '*Truth may perhaps come to the price of a pearl, that showeth best by day; but it will not rise to the price of a diamond or carbuncle, that showeth best in varied lights. The mixture of a lie doth ever add pleasure—*'

'No wonder Mirandola always looks so pleased with himself.'

'You look quite cheerful yourself, come to think of it.'

So pain had not yet marked him. Turcat was writing on the edge of the manifest. Merrick could just translate the wavering beetle tracks: *We shouldn't be talking like this in here. I'll see you after the meeting.*

In his insularity, the insularity that they all shared, that had sprung all this upon them, he had expected to have the stacks to himself, but half of the history faculty seemed to be down there, supposedly returning borrowed volumes, apparently renewing acquaintance with old favourites or perhaps saying farewell to them in case the recataloguing, which excuse fooled no one, should result in their removal or loss. Representatives from other disciplines must be there too, but they were less likely to consider their books under threat. The whole faculty had been tainted by Turcat's fall from grace.

The stack he wanted was closed and he had to wait until sufficient space opened up elsewhere before activating it, watching the shelves slide apart to reveal the white light glowing at the far end that indicated the presence of the book he had requested. As he headed for it he glanced up on a momentary impulse to look at Vanderkerckhove's *On Mummification*, and did not see it. He knew exactly where it ought to be and it was not there.

He went back to the console at the end of the stack and recited the code.

Extended loan.

The inspection had not begun. The book, as a work of information, could be of little interest to anyone outside the department, and yet it had been removed on extended loan. This, to the innocent eye, looked more reassuring than *Removed from stock*, but unless a lone pervert was hoping to make a mummy of his own, the book, he was sure, had been removed because Turcat was known to have borrowed it. It could have been gone for weeks . . . and then relief hit him so suddenly that he had to lean on the shelf for support. Had he not made his visit after that walk in the parc with Turcat, the Parizo material would have gone with it.

By the white light he knew that *The History of the*

332

Permanent Way in Great Britain 1821–2017 was still there, but was *The Permanent Way* alone in its slip cover? The light was flashing now: *Hurry up.* He strode down the gangway again, grabbed the book, which was at shoulder height, and opened it far enough to expand the tunnel in the spine. The treasure dropped into his hand, it was done in a second, the hand went into his pocket and came out empty.

Someone passed the end of the stack and paused to look in.

'Just coming!' With the place so full it was ill-mannered to keep a shelf open longer than was strictly necessary, but he ought to look as if he were there for some purpose other than the real one, especially as Vanderkerckhove had vanished so suspiciously. He carried the book down the side aisle to a reading desk, noticing as he left the gangway that a metre-long section of volumes relating to the Anarchy, almost a whole shelf-full, had been removed. This too must have happened since his last visit. If such a length of shelving had been empty then, he would have remarked upon it. Space was at a premium down here although that congestion was likely to be relieved in the near future. No one person would have borrowed the entire archive, and the only department likely to want it was his own present one, European history. They did not have it.

He walked down the hangar past the shelves that hummed and glided together and apart, their seem-ingly effortless motion belying the enormous weight of steel and books. It felt warmer than usual; the unaccustomed numbers and the increased activity of the shelves must have overtaken the temperature controls. All the reading desks were occupied. He was about to replace *The Permanent Way*, which was uncomfortably heavy, with the excellent excuse that there was no room to read it in comfort and no scanners free for taking notes, when he noticed that the English liter-ature shelves were open. The screen informed him that the *Essays* of Francis Bacon were in residence so he went and had a look at what else Bacon had to say about truth.

A cursory reading revealed that Bacon was substan-tially more concerned with untruth. *The mixture of a lie doth ever add pleasure . . . the lie that sinketh in and settleth . . . that doth the hurt . . . There is no vice that doth so cover a man with shame as to be found false and perfidious* – Mark that, Mirandola. He skimmed. Bacon on revenge, *a kind of wild justice*, on gardens, *God Almighty first planted a garden . . .* The man knew how to grab his reader; he was a master of the first line.

A discreet cough; he was hogging a gangway again. Merrick replaced Bacon and went back to the history stack which, for a wonder, was open, the green light shining where *The Permanent Way* must be returned. As he placed the book on the shelf three things happened simultaneously. The green light went out, the hanger was filled with a raucous desperate braying, and the stacks began to close.

The sound was the flood alarm, and the aisle at the end of the gangway was a blur of departing readers. His shout went unheard in the uproar.

Before he had taken two paces the shelves had him pinned by the shoulders. He twisted sideways and, as they sighed together as gently as lovers, compressing his back and chest, he had just time to stoop and slither into the gap where the Anarchy archive had been removed.

The shelves stopped moving without a sound and shut out all sound, even the blaring of the alarm. He was lying on his side, occupying the empty shelf and a few centimetres of the one that faced it, feet pressed against the upright, head jammed against books, his right arm wedged along the top of the volumes in the facing shelf, the left cramped under him. There was no possibility of a flood. The alarm was for practice or had gone off by accident. Soon the readers would be back, the stacks would open. He tried to shift to a more comfortable position while he waited and discovered that he could not move at all. Books pressed against his back, his head; his face was forced against the shelving. He could clench the fingers of his right hand; every other part of him was clenched by books. He might have been lying in a coffin.

And as the sense of self-congratulation at his quick thinking subsided, and the rush of panic with it, he had the leisure to consider his entombment. The waterproof shelves sealed themselves hermetically; he had access to just as much air as was sealed in with him, must control his breathing, make every shallow lungful last. Shallow lungfuls were all he could manage. The phrase 'no room to breathe' was no mere saying; breathing involved expansion of the chest; there was no room to expand his chest. If he could only turn a little . . . but he could not turn and his right shoulder was beginning to complain, but that discomfort was nothing to what was happening to his left hand, cruelly trapped beneath his hipbone, bearing his weight that he could not shift.

He could not move, he could not breathe; all he could think of was that fine opening line from Bacon's essay: *What is truth? said jesting Pilate, and would not stay for an answer.*

It was so dark, darker than the Briease Moss at night, and so hot, so airless. Where was he and why was he in such pain and why could he not move? Why was it so quiet?

The answers came to him all at once. He did not know how long he had been here in his steel coffin lined with the wisdom of the ages. *Don't panic. Panic needs oxygen.* He could not remember the time of day he had entered the library; it could have been closed for the night, it might be hours, days, before anyone opened this stack again. This time it was terror as much as carbon dioxide that stifled him.

They were digging him out of the peat, scraping and brushing his poor twisted bones and wondering what kind of a death would so contort the skeleton.

'Died screaming,' Ehrhardt said.

'The face in death is no guarantee of the manner of that death,' said Turcat, taking his jaw by the symphysis and moving it up and down. He tried to tell him

336

to stop but he had no tongue, no throat, no lungs—

Turcat was still speaking. 'Korda, where have you got to? We have a meeting, remember? Seventeen hundred. Get your arse back here at once.' It was his ear stud, intimately nagging.

'I'm here,' he said. '*I'm here*,' but he had no tongue, no throat, no lungs. And where was he? His left hand was numb, he could no longer feel the pearl swelling malignly in his wrist, but the moving fingers of his right had kept the circulation going and that arm felt as if it were being slowly torn away at the shoulder, while his flexed knees were ground into gravel, his wrenched spine unstrung and the vertebrae scattered like a necklace of pearls, and his own pulse boiled in his ears. He would die here; this was his coffin, history.

'Where are you? Goddamn you, why aren't you answering?'

Moonrise. He lay in a cutting in the darkest heart of the fen. Crooked branches pinned his knees and elbows, a great stone lay on his chest, but it was so quiet down here in the gateway to the next world, so cool, so peaceful. They need not have pegged and weighted him down, he had no desire to move ever again. The moon, hanging overhead, grew pale as ice formed over his pool and sealed him in.

This is not happening this is not happening this is not happening this cannot happen to me . . .

*   *   *

A smashing blow that clove the coffin lid and his forehead at the same time. The lid was torn away and a heavy fleshy face looked down on him. 'This one's ripe,' said the fat red lips, and took his left hand and began to hack and slash at the skin and sinew and bone, gouging, jabbing, until the knife point found what it was looking for and out came the pearl, the size of an eyeball.

'Where the hell are you? Why don't you answer, you skiving sod? Merrick, where are you? You're just doing this to annoy me, aren't you? *Merrick!*'

The ceiling of the laboratory was so close, he seemed to lie only centimetres below it on the light table. Turcat lifted his cranium and set it carefully on the lower mandible. Now he could look down the length of his body, and what a length it was, seven, eight metres, spread out for analysis with a space between each bone and the next, his ribs arranged tidily on either side of his dorsal vertebrae, the tesserae of carpals and tarsals and phalanges in each hand and foot placed with scientific precision. Something was missing. He saw the graduate assistant, Merrick Korda, the Inglishman, walking alongside the table with a cam in his hand.

'Don't move,' said Korda. He could not move. 'Where is my pearl?' he said, but he could not speak because his mouth was full of pearls.

This is the end, I haven't even begun . . .

* * *

Turcat was pushing the phalanges around with a spatula and singing: '*From stirrup to stirrup I mounted again and on my ten toes I rode over the plain.*'

When the stacks vibrated softly and slid apart he did not know it, until his right arm fell free, swinging him over, and he rolled off the shelf onto the floor a metre below, to lie there whooping and retching and then at last, with his aching lungs, screaming aloud as he attempted to move, although no sound came out.

No one came. He lay, trying to hear voices, footsteps, above the whirring of his exhausted heart.

Nothing.

Whoever had done this would not expect to find him lying there, half-suffocated but whole. He had seen death, lying compressed in the darkness, but he was supposed to *be* dead, crushed flat between the stacks, mangled probably beyond recognition. Forensic techniques would be required to identify what was left after that inexorable pressure.

At first deafened by the silence of the tomb, his hearing was returning. The air was alive with little clicks, electronic hoots, squeaks. Lights flashed. By kicking at the lower shelves he managed to lever himself into a sitting position. The stacks were designed to close and seal themselves when the flood alarm went off, to protect the books, but they were not designed to close while anyone was between them. He knew that; he had caught his coat in them once and they had stopped moving at the merest resistance but – *anything that can go wrong will go wrong*, the first law of engineering.

339

Or else, someone had overridden the fail-safe.

Why did no one come?

Someone was approaching. Down the gangway, bleeping peevishly, came an inspection robot, antennae scything the air ahead of it. When it blundered against him it emitted a high-pitched squawk and went into reverse.

At the end of the shelves, back-lit from the aisle, a figure appeared; standing; walking towards him.

There was only one person who knew he was here.

And one person who had guessed?

'Rémy?'

Turcat lived in Caledonia Height, in a corner apartment that overlooked the university district and the parc. Now all that could be seen were lights, like a star map laid out across the city.

Merrick could not take his eyes off it – so much space, so much air. He had a confused recollection of being dragged out of the library into the souterrain, arguing all the way, Turcat insisting that he sought medical attention instantly and Merrick, all too aware of what a physical examination would expose, pleading in a despairing hiss to be taken home at once, for both their sakes. He had meant his own home and he could not remember how they had reached here, thinking all the way that they were bound for Admiral Height. It was only when he took in the size of the place, and the view, that he knew where he must be.

It was greatly to his credit, Merrick thought later,

that Turcat did not at once ask if his visit to the library had been to recover the Parizo material, and if he had been successful. It was only when he was slouching on the divan, drinking whatever ardent cordial it was that Turcat thought would do him good that he remembered it himself. It was somewhere about his person, he knew. He began fumbling nervelessly at his clothes.

Turcat, sitting on the floor, his back against the window glass, watched him unhappily.

'Look at your hand.'

Merrick looked. It was puffy, blue-white, unbearable to touch.

'We're not designed for this,' Turcat said. 'Your degenerate Oyster can take any amount of punishment and shrug it off. We're part of the controlled environment. If you carry on like this you'll kill yourself.'

'I doubt if I'll have the chance. Someone else will get there first.' He forgot what he had been looking for and cradled his hand. No doctor or clinic would have any notion of how to treat this ailment.

'You don't think it was an accident?'

'Murphy's Law: anything that can go wrong will go wrong. A fault in the design will manifest itself in the performance. If an accident like that could happen, it *would* have happened already. I wasn't alone down there, there must have been forty or fifty others, but I was alone in that gangway when it happened. The rest of the time there were people in and out. When the alarm goes off the stacks are activated to close, but not instantaneously. There's a lag while people have time to get out, you know that. I saw them getting out. My stack started to close the moment the alarm sounded. If I hadn't noticed earlier that the Anarchy archive had been moved I'd have been crushed within – I'd guess five seconds. The shelves ought to have stopped moving as soon as they sensed an obstacle – me. They didn't. I had just enough time to get on to that empty shelf. If I were any taller or the Anarchy had been any shorter, I'd be dead by now. I'm supposed to be dead. How long was I there?'

'I don't know, although we could check and find out. You left Millennium House at sixteen-o-five – that is, you left *me*.'

'Yes. I went there straight away.' He began to remember. 'You wanted me back for a meeting.'

'At seventeen hundred. You didn't show. Dieter asked where you were. I said I thought you'd gone to the library; Tudor said that you ought to be back because the stacks had been closed; the flood alarm had gone off, or been set off.'

'It wasn't a practice?'

'No, and it wasn't a flood. Then someone said she'd been there and they weren't going to reopen because they would have to investigate the fault, if it was a fault. I couldn't raise you on the earphone or at home. And knowing of your questionable activities of late it occurred to me that you might have been up to no good and got stuck down there. I didn't realize *how* stuck. Why didn't you answer?'

342

'I couldn't breathe, much less talk. Who opened the stack?'

'They wouldn't let me in at first when I got there. The surveillance system was down as well. I said I was after essential research material but I don't rank very highly these days when it comes to bending rules. I had to call Dieter and get him to exercise his professorial authority. *Then* I was allowed down. It must have been nineteen-thirty by then.'

Three hours in the tomb . . . three days . . . Lazarus.

'It was crawling with robots, half the panelling was off the end wall. Nice to think that they go to all that trouble for a pile of books, although the suspicion did cross my mind that when it's been recatalogued out of existence the Senate may have other plans for all that lovely space. Faculty ball courts, for instance.'

'*Rémy*: who opened the stack?'

'I did. When I went in I looked at the reading area first – it was the only place you could be. That is, I thought it was the only place you could be. As I went up the aisle this robot was grovelling along the other way, you know how they move, especially the inspectors – like caterpillars. When I came back it was up on its hind legs, scrabbling with the controls on the history stack. There seemed to be something wrong and I – I – do *you* ever speak to them?'

'Robots? Well, yes. You know, if you meet one in a doorway they always sense you and move aside. You can't help saying thank you.'

'This one was – it looked as if it were on tiptoes,

343

not quite up to the job. I said, "What's the matter, can't you reach?" and activated the release, and it toddled off down the gangway. I didn't see you, I wasn't looking for you there – well, obviously I wasn't looking for you there. I was on the way out when I heard it squawking and all the others came worming along to have a look.'

'You realize,' Merrick said, 'that if you hadn't I should have suffocated. I nearly did. I owe my life to a man who talks to robots.'

'We all do,' Turcat mumbled.

'You took pity on it . . . you know, you are so nice really. It must run in the family. Amandine—'

'I ought to call her over, she could look at your hand.'

'The woman's touch?' Merrick said. 'Don't be so quaint. She's no better equipped to look at my hand than you are.'

'What were you trying to tell me in the souterrain? Why wouldn't you let me call for help – I thought you were dying—'

'So did I.'

'"For both our sakes,"' you said.

Merrick raised his arm. Whatever he was drinking had detached it. The pain was there but it was all on the far side of the window, out in the soothing darkness. 'No one could do anything about this, and no one must know about it. Do you know what I've got in here? No, of course you don't. Guess.' He giggled. 'Go on, three guesses.'

Turcat looked at him sharply. 'Not tonight. None

of this is making any sense. Go to sleep now, you'll be all right on that couch. Do you need anything?'

'No, I'm fine, absolutely unscathed . . . but I think I had a dream. You were digging me up and I was taking pictures.'

'I hope I'm doing the right thing or I'll be burying you too,' Turcat said.

The lights went out in the apartment, leaving only the star map beyond the window and the stars themselves in their winter brilliance.

Through the silent Moss the funeral boats glided, each freighted with a pall-draped coffin, each poled by a hooded silent Banker at the stern. At the prow stood another holding a flaring torch and ahead of them, on the silent streams, drifted candles set on frozen leaves. The punt where he sat lay in a parallel cut, waiting to follow the cortège, which seemed endless, for as one boat faded into the murk another passed and a third came into view, preceded by its floating guide light.

'Now it's our turn,' Frida said, standing up with the quant in her hand.

'It's not our turn. The dead are still passing.'

'You are the dead.'

She drove the quant into the bed of the cut but the punt did not move. He was mooring it by a nail that was driven through his left wrist into a tree trunk, and now that there was nothing to prevent him from screaming he screamed and screamed and screamed and the scream made no sound but rolled coiling and

345

twisting among the reeds and birches like white vapour, and Frida did not stop and the dead continued in their silent passing through the fen.

Chapter Twelve

The jaws of the backhoe swooped upon his grave and clamped his ribs and he jumped awake. The hand had not been bitten off after all, it was lying on a cushion near his face. The swelling had gone down but there was a gathering redness where *T. bovinus Regina* had taken her first and only drink.

Turcat was standing by the window wall, looking out over the city where the sun, not yet high enough to illuminate the ground, shone golden red and full upon the crystal spires and heights. Merrick sat up, found that he felt no worse than hung-over, and lurched across to the window.

'Do you see sunrise *every* day?'

'When it's clear.'

As they watched, the sun reached a level where on the ground it would be seen to rise, and the blue dusk beneath them was flooded, a tide of light sweeping across the city.

'Oh, it's beautiful.'

'There speaks a man who didn't expect to see another dawn,' Turcat said. 'Coffee?'

'It *is* beautiful. If you see it every day I suppose you stop noticing.'

'No, I never stop wondering at it, but it must seem especially wonderful to you – this morning.'

'It isn't just the sun – the buildings, the glass . . . have you ever seen those old twentieth-century fictions of what cities would look like in the future? Filthy, cramped, crowded, aerial traffic jams ninety storeys up, roving gangs, summary justice, *always* raining, fog . . .'

'Ah, but they were American,' Turcat said, 'petroleum-based dystopias. Look, skip the coffee, go and shower, revive yourself. Anything of mine should fit you. First door on the left. *Then* we'll have breakfast.'

In the shower room, which was not much more luxurious than his own, he took a long hard look in the mirror and saw Lazarus: grey skin, greyer lips, purple crescents under the eyes, nose pinched, a face that would look perfectly at home in Briease but was likely to arouse concern in the city environs. Anyone could be forgiven for making the same mistake Turcat had made once before, and having him apprehended as a likely source of pestilence. You'd *have* to be near death to look like that, they would reason. How contagious was terror?

Would he ever be able to enter the stacks again? Would he run, howling with panic, next time he opened a book?

He told himself that it was misleading to let the cam see him like this – after all, his appearance had little to do with the pearl – and confined his record to a close shot of the red patch on his hand, as much to see if the cam was still functioning after being crushed in the stacks. His upper arm bore the impression of it, indelibly bruised into his skin. Then he reconsidered, stepped back and recorded himself full length, naked, in the mirror.

'Yesterday someone tried to kill me,' he said, matter-of-factly, and cut out, seeing his ashen face flush at the melodrama of the announcement.

Turcat had laid out fruit and coffee on a table by the window. Merrick went over and said, 'Wasn't there something you wanted from the library?' He placed the oiled-cloth strip on the table. Turcat sat and stared at it for several minutes without saying anything. Then he looked up.

'Not worth dying for, Merrick.'

'Parizo Man thought it was.'

'Do you think that's why—?'

'No, I don't. There's something I didn't tell you.'

'Only one thing?'

'Shut up. I'm telling you now. A few weeks ago I went to the library and took down the Vanderkerckhove – and found these. I knew you'd put them there, you'd as good as told me. And as you were on record as having borrowed it I took them out and found them another book.'

'Without telling me?'

'As you said, there's a lot I haven't told you. When I went to get my – what did you call it? My favourite bookmark yesterday I found that the Vanderkerckhove had gone; extended loan.'

'Who?'

'I didn't have the chance to find out. I'd put this stuff in a history of railways. I got it out and I was just replacing the book when the alarm went off.'

'It must have been an accident – how could anyone know when you'd be in the library?'

'I've thought more than once recently that I was being followed. Once the news that the recataloguing was scheduled I'd be sure to go there – everybody's going there. Anyone with a basic knowledge of the system could work out how to override it and set off the alarm at the same time; to cover the sound of crunching bones, I suppose, while emptying the library. Very well thought out.'

'But what a horrible way to do it.'

'Needs must – virtually undetectable. Leaves no trace – no one laid a hand on me – no one went anywhere near me. Once the forensic team had hosed me out of the shelves there wouldn't have been a whole lot left to go on.'

Turcat sat twisting the cloth tube in his fingers. 'The only evidence of what this contains is inside it: a bone sample, the pearls and the record of you and me finding the pearls. How could anyone know?'

'No one knew.'

'Anyway, why kill you for them? As far as anyone else is concerned Parizo Man is irrelevant now. If someone knew the pearls were there why didn't they just remove them? Or get them off you once you'd taken them out of the library? A quick ambush, dark corner, no one need have been hurt.'

'Next time I want a job done I'll come to you,'

Merrick said. 'Rémy "the Neck" Turcat, muggings a speciality. No, seriously, Parizo Man had nothing to do with this – well, only indirectly. Remember when we found the pearls in his pelvis?'

'Of course I do.'

'I've found others – hey, I suppose it wasn't you?'

'What wasn't?'

'Tried to crush me to death. Rémy the Neck. You were suspiciously quick on the uptake – first on the scene.'

'You *shite*,' Turcat said. 'You ungrateful turd. If you weren't such a wreck I'd smash your teeth so far down your throat—'

'Just making sure before I tell—'

'– you'd need a proctologist instead of a dentist.'

'Only an archaeologist would tell a joke that old,' Merrick said. 'Most people wouldn't know what a dentist is.'

'Do you know what a proctologist is, arsehole?'

'Look, I'm not really joking – yes, yes I am. I didn't really think it was you. But only you and I and Ehrhardt know what we found. I'll assume Ehrhardt wasn't interfering with the stacks last night. Three of us; only two people, as far as I know, have any idea of what I'm about to show you, and one of them's me. You'll be the third.'

'You said you'd found other pearls.'

'Yes, I have, in another skeleton. I tried to tell you and you told me I didn't know what I was talking about. Well, I did know; there were pearls and they were in a skeleton – no, it's no good, we'll never find it again, I've tried. But they were the pearls Parizo Man was after; when the Oysters dug on Parizo Beach they turned up his axe and nine coffins. Four had been smashed open. We opened a fifth.'

'Who did?'

'I did, with an Aboriginal colleague. You were right, they didn't know what to do, but they learn fast. We opened the coffin that Parizo Man was sitting on when whoever caught him shot him. He hadn't got into it, but he must have plundered at least one other that night. What he'd found he had in his mouth.'

'And his killer didn't realize?'

'Obviously not. It was probably dark. He must just have filled in the grave again with its new occupant and vanished into the night.

'When we opened the coffin we found a skeleton, with pearls in its joints – not in its pelvis, not in a glass bottle. You still think it's a myth, don't you, that moss pearls grew in human beings? It isn't. They did – they do. We found three, one in the ankle, one in the knee, one in the wrist. There's no doubt, Rémy, they grew there. The bite of a species of horsefly, *Tabanus bovinus Rex*, set up an infection. The pearls formed round it.'

'Are you surmising?'

'No. If there was any co-operation between disciplines we'd have known about this. I checked with an entomologist, it's true. And because these pearls were so rare, and so unspeakable, people paid huge sums for them. They still will, if they can get them. I showed you the answers to my advert.'

'Oysters . . .'

'There's worse to come. Because the bog dwellers were especially susceptible, certain people deliberately infected them, then gathered the pearls, from corpses if necessary. That's what Parizo Man was doing. And that, as much as anything, was what won the peoples of the Briease Moss Aboriginal Status, and the protection that went with it – of which there now seems to be no record, except perhaps in the library. If so it won't be there much longer, will it?'

'You want to prove this? Match the DNA of the pearls with the skeleton? But you said the skeleton was – what, lost? Destroyed?'

'The skeleton is no longer available. Don't ask why, *please* don't ask why, I can't tell you. I had to get my own proof.' He held out his hand, palm down.

'You don't mean what I think you— Oh, my god. Oh no, how could you? You're growing one of those hideous things.'

'You didn't think they were hideous in Parizo Man. Think how much it's worth. Touch it.' He laid his hand flat on the table. 'Think how much *I'm* worth. Go on, touch it, where the red mark is.'

Turcat put out a quivering finger and made a fastidious tap at the swelling.

'*That's not touching it!*' Merrick gripped the finger and jabbed it into his wrist, letting out an involuntary yell. 'Feel it?' He ground the finger against the pearl. 'Feel it? Feel it? It's a myth, is it?'

'Let go!' Turcat tore his hand away and they fell back in their chairs. 'You lunatic!' Merrick, doubled over, rocked backwards and forwards, hand clutched to his chest. 'Maniac. Who let you out? Who let you into my department? You're a pathological specimen, even without your pearl. They'd have had you pickled in a bottle once. You're the kind of freak people used to queue to see in museums.'

He sprang up and strode round the room.

'Why, in god's name? *That's* why you were so ill – how long have you had it? Why?'

Merrick chose to interpret this outburst as a sign that Turcat was profoundly moved by his suffering. It did not lessen the suffering but it rallied him.

'Truth may perhaps come to the price of a pearl.'

'Oh, *shut* it. You'll be blaming me for giving you the idea next. I didn't, did I?'

'Only by saying it was a myth. No, I came up with this all by myself.'

Turcat sat down again, poured coffee and leaned his elbows on the table, head in hands. 'How did you do it?'

'Inter-faculty collaboration – what we don't do enough of. I said one other person knew, someone who had access to eggs of *Tabanus bovinus Rex*. The species is extinct, allegedly. We incubated a female and she bit me. I chose my left wrist so I could keep an eye on it.'

'Did you know what would happen?'

'Not exactly; I expected a fever – actually you have no idea what happened and neither would I have if I hadn't got the whole thing down on record. I asked for a week off, remember? I needed five days, but, oh, *did* I need those five days! You can watch it, if you want.'

'And since then you've been cultivating this thing. How long has it been hurting?'

'Quite a while; badly for about ten days. It's worse this morning because I was lying on it in the stacks; that's why it was so swollen last night, and I couldn't move. I couldn't move *at all*, I couldn't breathe—'

'It hurts because you've just jammed my finger into it,' Turcat said, moving swiftly to lay his revenant horror. 'How long have you got till you . . . give birth?'

'I can't tell. It's on its way out now. It grows among the bones in the joints. It grows until the bones can't accommodate it any more, then it exits. That red mark's the first sign that it's starting to come to the surface. I don't know how big it is. I don't know quite how it comes out, either; whether it's a clean eruption or a gigantic suppurating boil.'

'And me without a spoon,' Turcat said regretfully.

'I'm hoping it's out before Shepherd goes to court.'

'Who's Shepherd?'

'Haven't I ever mentioned him?'

'No. But then, of course, there's a lot you haven't mentioned.'

'He's the mayor of Briease, the – the colleague I told you about, who opened the coffin with me. *He* knows where moss pearls come from.'

'And was he the colleague who brought in the backhoe?'

'No.'

'No?'

'Definitely not. Anyway, he's the one who'll petition to recover Parizo Man.'

355

'Yes, I see,' Turcat said, 'but I don't see much. That's what I meant to ask you about after the meeting last night. You want to show the world that Oysters are entitled to their protected status because they were so shamefully treated. Fair enough. But what did you mean about nailing Mirandola? What's he done – apart from the obvious?'

'Think about it,' Merrick said. 'Mirandola knew the skull was on the beach before we did, but he made damn sure he was too late to stop us excavating. I think – I'm certain – that he arranged for us to find it and get it out.'

'Why would he do that?'

'He's a government agent,' Merrick said. 'I wouldn't mind betting that there's one of him on every reserve in the Union and they've all been waiting for an excuse to cut up rough about an archaeological discovery on Aboriginal land. What started our troubles? Mirandola going public about Inglish Aboriginals losing their Inglish skeleton, at which point the Feds stepped in, hunting for nationalists – you follow? Bilderdyk, Incunabula, Brandenburg.'

'You certainly can't prove any of this.'

'No, but Mirandola shafted the very people he was meant to protect. Why should he get away with it? De Harnac didn't *find* the skull, he was told where to look. Ask your sister what happened that day on Parizo Beach.'

'I don't want Amandine involved in this. If what you suspect is—'

'You don't have to involve her, she was just the short

cut to you. She was used, we all were. But Mirandola, he's the operator. Well, let's see how he operates in court facing top-of-the-range lawyers.'

'Top of the range? And you're going to sell your pearl to pay for all this?'

'No, I am not. One of Parizo Man's pearls will more than cover the cost, as you said yourself. My pearl's for another purpose. I've got every stage of it on record, from the bite onwards. If we have nothing else we'll have undeniable proof that these things are human, and if people refuse to believe that there was a market for them, we've got proof that there's surely a market now. Can you conduct the sale and record it?'

'Why not you?'

'I have to get out of here,' Merrick said. 'What happened last night was no accident. Someone was trying to destroy the evidence.'

'The Parizo pearls?'

'No,' Merrick said. 'My pearl, and me with it. I'm dead. I'm going where the dead go.' Turcat did not hear the last words, nor was he intended to.

He took the souterrain transit to the most remote of the monorail stations on the city loop to change at Metro for an express north. He had planned to go at night.

'There'll be fewer people about. Easier to see if I have a tail.'

'I thought you were dead.'

'You are so literal,' Merrick said. 'Those history

357

stacks are in constant use right now. Once the system's up and running my mangled remains will become conspicuous by their absence – even if we weren't seen leaving the premises.'

'If you go by an early morning service it'll still be fairly quiet but it'll be easier to lose yourself if you have to. I can cover your back. If I think there's anyone attaching themselves I can warn you.'

'What will you say at Millennium House?'

'That you are ill. Given the way you've been carrying on that should surprise no one. Dieter will make sure that it's taken no further.'

'What sort of ill? No one's *ill*.'

'Present company excepted. It must have been something you contracted in the Briease Moss.'

'And what are you going to tell Dieter?'

'How much do you want him to know?'

'Of course,' Merrick said, 'I trust him absolutely . . . tell him everything, but not this.' He patted his hand. They had contrived a kind of double splint out of strips of contour-cloth that could hide in sleeve and glove, giving support without pressure.

'Three of us know about the pearl; let's keep it at three, for now. One of them I'm not sure of.'

'The eggman?'

'Yes. The eggman.'

Joris would not have arranged that lethal booby trap, why should he? But Merrick could not think of any reason, other than the pearl, why anyone should want to eradicate him. Yet only Joris could have told someone else about it. Why would he do that?

The answer came to him as he sat in the car in the early-morning twilight. By incubating *T. bovinus Regina* Joris had broken the law, not just university regulations. Merrick seriously doubted if Joris had any kind of a conscience about the infringement or that he was so gnawed by remorse that he had been driven to confess. *T. bovinus Regina* had been terminated before she had laid any eggs and Merrick was past help the moment she bit him. Confession would salve nothing but Joris's sinful soul, if he had one.

But someone might have known of their meetings. The first and second had been open, the third covert. If he had had a tail and Joris had been questioned about the association, Joris might have had a momentary qualm about spilling the beans and then told himself that the greater good was at stake, and as he had not, after all, sent the idiot Korda away infected with smallpox he might as well admit to what he had done.

Especially if he had been leaned on: *We know what you did. Korda has told us everything. This needn't go any further.* Joris might well be feeling resentful that Merrick had got him into this mess.

And when they knew that the idiot Korda was walking evidence of an ancient crime, a crime that no one wanted to know about, why then, all they had to do was get rid of the evidence; a horrible accident in the library stacks.

He drew his elbows against his chest and let out a soft whimper of distress. The man opposite looked at him curiously. He turned it into a yawn. The memory

359

of those stifling hours was waiting for him every time he stopped thinking about something else. Last night, sleeping again on Turcat's divan, he had choked in quicksands on the seashore, dug himself a grave in the dunes and felt his mouth and nose and lungs fill up with sand; lain on an embalmer's bench while the Egyptian priest who had drawn out his viscera and extracted his brain filled his carcase with natron and spices and wound it in bandages until his breath was stopped for ever.

The embalmer had been singing a dirge while he worked: '*Took my heart in my hand, to keep my head warm* . . .' But it was Merrick's heart that he held in his hand. It was still beating.

They were coming into a station, Metropole. No word from Turcat yet. He had travelled on the transit to the Galleria Interchange, cased the platform and then run back down to the souterrain for the tram to Metro. Merrick saw him now on the southbound platform, trudging up and down to keep warm, as one might suppose, and watching to see who left the car, crossed the platform to the express line and boarded the northbound service with Merrick.

They did not look at each other and no word came through the earpiece. The car arrived; he boarded and sat at the end, near a door. In the tail of his eye he saw Turcat, still mooching, and felt a twinge of guilt at having deceived him yet again. Turcat thought he was going to Briease Town, via Norge.

Two men boarded as the doors were closing and sat, one in the middle of the car, one at the far end.

Still no word from Turcat, who could have seen nothing to arouse his suspicions. Turcat's sympathy and concern had touched him but he could not begin to tell him what had happened in the stacks. He had not been crushed to death, he had escaped suffocation by a hair's breadth, physically he was relatively undamaged. He would never be able to tell anyone that he had been nearer to death from fright in the dreadful hours of silent solitude, unable to move, unable to call out because he could not breathe deeply enough, unable to weep, afraid that every breath he took would use up the very last of the dwindling oxygen, the unyielding shelf at his face, the unyielding books at his back, the absolute darkness, the smothering silence. He had been buried alive. He had never feared death, he did not fear it now, but he knew that for the rest of his life he would fear being put alive into the tomb. The memory of his living death would be with him all his days.

Anyone who followed him into the Briease Moss would never follow him out.

There was no one behind him at Eavrey Sound, but this did not mean that he would remain alone. Turcat the cloistered academic, although become daily more exposed to life's little excitements, had not imagined that his innocent stratagem might be employed by others less innocent. He had supposed one tail, not a possible network of followers, all in communication with each other.

There was no one behind him as he left Eavrey and

struck out across the fields of winter wheat, hidden now beneath snow, hugging the lee side of windbreaks where there was no danger of leaving footprints, under the wide white sky of the Anglian peninsula.

At the edge of the merse, where he had taken leave of Shepherd, he found something that he had not even thought of hoping for. Lying beneath the hedge was a quant, three metres long and shiny about the middle section with years of use. Could it be there by chance or had Shepherd, remembering that he had spoken of needing another way into the Moss, left it on purpose? One day he would return it.

He had no intention of trying to vault across the merse, but with the pole he could test the ground ahead of him, doubly treacherous now that it was frozen. What might have taken several hours, delicately probing the snow with each step, might now take less than one. He located the place to which Shepherd had brought him, betwen two birches, but only because he knew where to look. That was what he must head for, no matter how many zigzags he made in the process. Lifting the quant he brought it down ahead of him; it struck firm ground and for five paces he advanced in a straight line. But at the sixth stroke the quant cracked ice and sank in. He had to cast about in a full semicircle before he found the way and made his sixth step.

Halfway across he looked back and saw his trail, the zigzags, and with a pleasing flash of comprehension saw too why they were called zigzags. He had made a series of Zs in the thin driven snow; and then realized that anyone else who saw them would know exactly where he had gone.

But even as he thought it the white sky leaned down towards him and snow began to fall in his footprints. Covering my tracks, he thought, before he understood that the snow would literally cover his tracks. So many of the casual clichés that they shuttled back and forth must once have referred to matters of life and death: covering the tracks, no room to breathe, I feel it in my bones.

With the quant to guide him he took his next step towards the birch trees. The snow fell lightly. Before the Flood, before the Gulf Stream turned away, whole winters at these latitudes had passed without snow. Most city dwellers would have known how it looked from the media; few would ever have stood in falling snow, on fallen snow, and marvelled at the smell of it.

His hand hurt so badly it was a distraction, it spoiled his joy in the snow and deterred him from gripping the quant securely. This made him grip it all the harder, in honour and memory of those oppressed Inglish who had acquired their pearls by accident, and then by design, never by choice, but had nonetheless lived and worked and, as Turcat had put it, shrugged off the pain, because they had no alternative and could trust no one to succour them. He would endure his pearl as they had endured theirs. He saw it all, now, as he punted himself across the frozen merse. They had lost faith in the medicine that was promised to cure them because it had done no such thing. Therein must lie their determination to rebuff all offers of help in future, no screening, no prophylaxis, no cures. They would deal with what they knew. The unknown would never be visited upon them again.

At the far edge of the merse he found no firm ground to cross the last three metres. With the quant he could touch the nearer birch trunk; with a short run he could jump the distance, but there was nowhere around him, by the scramble of his last footprints, to make that run.

The snow fell thicker now; he thought he heard voices, saw indistinct figures, knew it was illusion; but he could not stay there. Hidden by the snow a monorail car swept by, reminding him that as soon as the snow cleared he would be visible from a distance. He made a decisive stab with the quant and it went in only fifteen centimetres or so. It was worth the risk – there had to be a first time for everything. He raised it, stabbed again, drove it down and swung up, over; the pole sank under his weight and threw him off balance, but when he landed, stumbling and rolling on his back by the birch trees, he had pulled it free and still held it.

The channel where Shepherd had brought the punt lay frozen at his side. He could follow it for a while but once he came to a diversion he would have nothing to follow but his nose. With the waterways under ice, candle floats would be useless, but now it was snowing the temperature must have risen. A thaw might be coming. If not he must rely on the evidence of senses that had virtually atrophied: the sight of the sun rising on his right, the scent of peat smoke that would tell his proximity to the South Turf Bank, and the stones of the burial grounds. To his left the monorail cars passed by, drawing their threads of sound behind them.

In the Moss little snow reached the ground. Leaving no tracks he trod over a frozen pudding of churned leaves and arcing briars and everywhere the pale friable reeds. The sporadic trickle of snowflakes had ceased before he reached the first cross-cut, and he had to decide which course to follow. He did not want to meet the Bankers, especially after his funeral dream based not on fact or even heresay but on god alone knew what memories and imaginings. To go straight ahead would be madness; it was madness to be here anyway, but less mad now that he knew the surroundings. He blessed Frida for scaring him so thoroughly on that first journey; now he properly understood his foolhardiness. If he turned always to the left, he would not stray too far from the western fringes of the Moss. The sound of the monorail would guide him. Sooner or later he would come to Herigal Staithe and before night fell he was sure to find a turf lodge.

Meanwhile he had to cross this cutting. He aimed the quant at the farther bank and swung himself over, landing on his feet but giving his wrist another painful wrench. He badly wanted to unwrap it to look but Turcat had secured the splints firmly with metres of bandage. He would not be able to replace them with one hand and he needed the support. The pearl was throbbing now; not the pearl itself but the tortured bones and tissue round it. When he found Ed

Shepherd he could ask how it would come out and hope that Shepherd's reliance on oral tradition was not misplaced, so that he might be prepared. Another car passed, its busy hum stitching between the trees. How sound carried in the stillness; how incongruous to hear it at all in that wilderness. Through the twigs to his left he saw a pallid sun and knew that in spite of his early start it was past noon. It had travelled to the zenith of its shallow winter arc and was on its way down again. He ought to eat. When he reached and crossed the next cut he would stop – no not the next, the one after that. Each vault must be more accomplished than the last.

The cut after the next brought him to an eyot, where he sat and forced down bland high-protein concentrates, craving sugar and fat, but he carried nothing that would not fit into the pockets of his clever but hopelessly inadequate city coat. The stillness wrapped him, the cold sedated him; he might have dozed, but in his hand the pearl beat its fiery rhythm like a second heart.

As the sky darkened it became harder to judge distance among the encroaching trees. He slipped and tripped more often, once almost lost the quant, more than once almost failed to make the farther bank, although the cuts were not wide. The distances that defeated him became shorter, his hand was so swollen in its splints that he thought they must crack. He found his turf lodge by running up against it.

It was a very small one, not much above waist height

and just long enough to lie down in. He stooped in at the door, grateful to shut out the louring night, and saw at once what ironic chance had led him to. Once the door was closed he might as well be in a coffin. He could not risk a light unless the door was closed. Within seconds he was gasping, fumbling and thrashing about in the darkness. Then he found his torch and the small light brought small relief.

In the corner was a hurricane lamp that would give warmth as well as light, but he was already sweating so hard he could, he reflected grimly, probably keep himself warm with regular panic attacks. There was water and, its being winter, a blanket. The hurricane lamp smoked and stank, the small space became rapidly airless, his breathing laboured. The only remedy was to brave the cold as any degenerate Oyster would do without a second thought, douse the lamp, open the door and hope to sleep. After a day of hard physical exertion he ought to fall asleep at once, but it was so dark, the roof was so low, the walls so close, that as soon as he closed his eyes the lodge shrank around him and he was back in the stacks, entombed in books; books at his head and feet, books at his back, books above and beneath him, his face pressed against the steel divider.

It was not steel but glass, the glass of Turcat's glorious east-facing window. He saw the sun rise, not over the horizon but from out of the parc, a glowing red ball the size of a pearl. But that is impossible, he told himself. The pearl is 150,000,000 kilometres away and the sun is in my hand. The morning was cool and beautiful, summer trees as tall as the highest height were in full leaf. The city stirred in the sunshine and he yearned to be out there, down in its lovely streets and clean air, but he never would be for he was dead, crucified between the double panes of Turcat's window like a leaf trapped in ice. A Christian came along and cut off his hand to carry away for a holy relic.

In the end he slept heavily and late. When he woke the sun was cold on his face and burning in his hand.

He travelled carefully all day, resting often, using the quant as a rod and staff to comfort him, keeping to a minimum his experimental vaults across the cuttings. He was not getting any better at it and the pearl needed all the rest he could afford it.

He had been right about the thaw. The air was milder, the going softer, the ice in the cuts was thinner. The only sounds were of the birds, dithering among the branches, and the intermittent rush of the mono-rail cars. He kept the sound always ahead of him and slightly to his left, steering inland.

In the afternoon he almost met his first human, an upright figure gliding through the trees. Lying flat he saw that the man was in a punt proceeding smoothly between reeds, passing only a dozen metres away. He heard the soft plash of the pole in ice-free water and almost at once a sound that at first he could identify only as a faraway flood alarm, before he translated it as the lowing of cattle. At a discreet distance he followed the punt, and when he lost sight of it the westering sun guided him through the thinning trees and he came at last to Herigal Staithe.

He had been there only once before in early autumn, in sunlight after a day of rain, leafy and fragrant. Now it was as stark as the Moss itself but he saw the cottage roofs first and then the staithe itself, the row of eight wooden posts and, in the channel beside them, seven punts. The man he had tried to follow earlier had moored and gone home. His must be the last punt in the line.

Merrick looked all round warily before stepping down into it. It was not simply the punt he wanted but to take this opportunity to announce his presence to the only one who would recognize the message so that, whatever happened, somebody would know what had become of him. He had to think hard before he could remember what day it was although he knew the time. He picked up the slate by the post, found a chalkstone and wrote, *17.50 Friday: Cordwainer to Briease Town by the Vyzel Cut,* amended *17.50* to *3.50 p.m.* and turned the slate over. As he was casting off, curiosity made him look at the slate by the vacant post where the punt had been taken by the last person to leave Herigal. *13.25 Thursday: J. Smith to Briease Town by the Decoy.*

The Decoy. He did not like the sound of that but had an idea that originally it had been a means of trapping wildfowl. He had heard someone mentioning it, Ed or Frida, and retained the certainty that it was a long way in, central. Had they passed it, or near to it on the way to the Hazel Carr and the burying grounds?

Then he looked again at the slate. J. Smith sounded like an Oyster, but no Oyster used the twenty-four-hour clock or European time. Only a few hours after he had entered the Moss yesterday, someone else had entered it too; someone who had been informed of the ways of Aboriginals, but not too well. He was not alone.

Merrick pushed away from the bank into the channel. From here he would have to try to retrace his journey, made so long ago with Frida, in the dark. He seemed to remember that it had taken an hour or so along the Herigal Channel, and then a single turn to the – to the *left*, into a narrower way which had brought them to the turf lodge on its eyot; nearly two hours all told, propelled by Frida's steady experienced poling.

'Shall I take a turn?' he had said.

'Do you know how?'

'Is it difficult?'

'If you don't know how.'

Since then he had learned how with Shepherd, but on that occasion he had had two good hands. Now he was virtually operating with one, using the other only as a last resort when he dug the pole in too enthusiastically and could not pull it out. His left arm ached from shoulder to fingertip; favouring it had kindled a compensatory pain under his right shoulder blade, which had not recovered from its mauling in the stacks. In its splints and wrapping the pearl blazed on;

he wondered that he could not see the illumination through his sleeve.

His first test was approaching; the channel turned and branched; which fork should he take? He was sure it was to the left. He walked to the prow of the punt and looked down at the black water. The few leaves on the surface seemed to be going nowhere. He had not yet reached running water, if the creeping streams here could be said to run. The temperature had dropped with the sun; only now, when he stopped moving, did he notice how cold it had become, and at that moment the sun slid wholly below the horizon that he could not see, out there somewhere west of the Moss, and the blink of the last ray showed him where the turf lodge stood.

He took up the quant again, steered into the right-hand cutting, and headed confidently towards the eyot where he had spent his very first night in the Briease Moss.

In the small hours the pearl woke him by driving white-hot wires up to his elbow, down under his fingernails. 'The pressure may damage nerves,' Joris had said, 'cause temporary or permanent paralysis in one or more fingers.'

He had not told this to Merrick until after the poison had entered his system. He could feel his nerves being damaged as the wires burned through them, and the constriction of the splints became unbearable. In the darkness he tore off the bandage, hearing the splints fall. His arm must be monstrously swollen. He crashed out of the half door, scrambled to the edge of the eyot and, lying full length, plunged his arm into the freezing water. Freezing but not quite frozen; as he lay there, face almost touching the surface, he saw a light on a level with his eyes, flickering off, on, off, irregularly, in the distance.

Foxfire? Ignis fatuus, the self-combusting marsh gas? No, it was definitely moving, moving towards him, but how far away was it?

Not far; as he judged the distance he saw what it was: a disc of candle on a float of some kind, sent on ahead to light the way, a pathfinder on the current. If anyone were following it he could not hear them, but it might be dangerous to move. He lay there, his arm up to the shoulder in the water, his hair trailing in it, eyes fixed on the little point of light as it turned and drifted, now shunted into the reeds by a twig, now curling out again, now close enough to make out the bud of yellow flame; still he remained motionless, following it only with his eyes as it drew nearer, level, passed him within millimetres of his hair.

He watched it to the end of the eyot, where it spun and passed out of sight, to the right, reminding him of the way he must go in the morning. Still he did not move, eyes swivelled upstream again in readiness for the boatman who might be following the light; but no one came. When his hand was so numb that he thought the pearl must have shrunk to nothing, and he so shaking with cold that his teeth rattled, he withdrew his arm, inching backwards on his belly like a snake, and crept into the lodge.

He had nothing to dry his arm and sodden sleeve with; water trickled from his hair down his face, down his neck. In the end he swaddled his arm in the lodge blanket and wrapped his coat around himself. One steady star shone through the upper half of the door and he pictured the other little star on its solitary voyage along the black waterways in the darkness, journeying onward through the night, into the dawn.

No one was following it. How long had it been burning? It must have gone ahead of the one who set it floating when he stopped for the night. It might have been caught in reeds or debris or even frozen in for a time, as it twirled and dawdled with its small flame burning ever upright.

But it could not have been burning for very long. Whoever had launched it could not be very far away. He was travelling by water, not vaulting overland. If Merrick were to stay ahead he must leave as soon as it started to get light. He ought to have left immediately, following his star along the currents to the Vyzel Cut.

It was quite possible that the sender of the candle was an innocent traveller or Moss dweller, but he did not think that a Moss dweller would be caught out this late. Only idiots like him did that.

He knew the etiquette: if you came upon an empty punt moored in a cutting and blocking the thoroughfare, you moored your own punt and took the other; all property held in common. It was a practical, civilized scheme, but he did not want anyone, friend, enemy or neutral, coming up behind his punt. He did not want to meet anyone in the night.

He spread the blanket on the floor of the lodge to air, inserted his left arm into his coat sleeve with his right hand, and stepped down into the punt, taking up the quant with a stoical determination that he shared, he was sure, with the Oysters. At the end of the eyot he steered to the right and set off again in pursuit of his star, which must have burned out long ago in the thin light of dawn.

He had forgotten what came next. There was no sunrise, but as the sky lightened the trees thinned and the punt skimmed into that flat and featureless stretch of marsh where the only verticals were himself and the quant. Even the running water was freezing now, although the ice was fragile, the going easy; but he was moving very slowly on the sluggish stream, barely able to sustain any momentum with his one aching arm.

With the bandage he had fashioned a sling for his left hand. The pearl had caught fire again but he was dourly amused to see that in spite of his sick fancy that the whole limb was monstrously swollen, he had nothing to show for his torture but the pearl itself; and it did show, almost a hemisphere, proud of his wrist, hard and hot. It did indeed show best by day.

'Eventually you will not be able to resist rubbing it, scratching it, even biting at it perhaps as animals do with their injuries.'

He had not come to that yet but he could not resist touching it to his lips every so often, to marvel at the heat. Joris had not forecast that he would be kissing it.

Each time he bore down on the quant he looked back. The crossing with Frida had not been exactly rapid but it had been straightforward. The farther he travelled, out into the open, the more he felt sure that this was not the way they had come. Either he was in a different merse or on a different waterway, or both. Miserably exposed, he knew he had reached the point of no return, as far from the sheltering trees he had left as from the ones he was approaching, which never seemed to come any closer, for this stream ran in loops and bends. Each time he looked there was nothing to see but the marsh and the trees, the serpentine curves of the stream. Then, between one backward glance and the next, a punt had appeared from among the trees behind him. He disengaged his hand from the sling, grabbed the quant and drove it into the stream bed, feeling the punt surge in response and the hot wires frying his tender nerves.

The other punt drew on. It was too far away for him to tell if it were gaining on him, but he did not see how it could fail to if the punter had the full use of both hands. No one hailed him. An Oyster would call a greeting, surely, supposing him to be a fellow Moss dweller. No voice came from the following punt, no hand was raised. It was not someone looking for Cordwainer, but it might be someone looking for Korda.

It *was* following him, and whoever was in pursuit was obliged to stay in the punt. A Moss dweller in a hurry would be fen vaulting by now, spinning across the snow to catch him in minutes. If he could only maintain his lead, however diminished, until he reached the trees, he guessed his pursuer would have scant advantage in the alien terrain of the peat cuttings; except that he would have two hands.

In the old fictions about the horrors of the future, cops, warriors and members of the public had been armed with preposterous weapons of enormous size and weight, improbable range and awesome fire power. With these they had destroyed buildings, cities, spaceships, planets and each other, singly and in multiples. The other punt was gaining on him; where were the fast cars of the old fictions? This must be the slowest chase in the history of the world. Merrick wished devoutly for a preposterous weapon of improbable range and awesome fire power with which to take out his adversary. In a society where no one went armed, no one was prepared for a situation like this.

And as he thought it, he heard a shot.

He had never heard a shot before, in real life. Shots belonged to the old fictions, to the time of Parizo Man. Oysters used firearms for hunting; this was no Oyster and the quarry was not food.

But he had almost reached the trees. The man behind – he could see him clearly now – was redoubling his efforts, having failed in what he must have hoped to achieve before Merrick got in among the peat cuttings again. He would never make it now. Once Merrick was out of plain sight he stood as much chance as the other in the labyrinth of the Moss, on the water or on foot. His pursuer might lack even his poor knowledge of the landscape. He must be the one who had let his errant float get away.

Now the trees overhung him and he had the chance to make use of his small advantage. The man in the punt must have assumed he could overtake Merrick in the open; it was only bad luck or misjudgement that he had not, and his lack of practice with a firearm. Where were the Oysters when you needed them? a friendly fen vaulter with a quant at his disposal or, better still, a punter coming the other way. Merrick knew what to do in these situations; perhaps the other did not. He and the punter would exchange greetings, and punts, and continue in opposite directions, Merrick in the knowledge that the way behind him was temporarily blocked. It would slow the bugger down at any rate.

Or he could block the way himself. An eyot was coming up. No turf lodge stood on it but there was an unusually thick growth of scrub and briar at the nearer end. Merrick poled to the far end and left the punt, swinging the mooring rope around a sapling on the other bank as he went, and reached the scrub in three strides. Crouching down he held the quant vertical, like another sapling trunk. All the while hearing the plash and dip of the other punt drawing close, he fitted his left hand around the pole and bound it there in a figure of eight with the bandage. Whatever happened, however much it hurt, he could not let go.

The second punt came into view; the occupant, in fur-fabric hat, long coat, gauntlets, looked so like himself that Merrick was unable to tell if he had ever seen him before or not. As he came through the reeds he saw the empty punt blocking the way in front of him. By the turn of his head Merrick knew he was looking at the mooring rope and assuming that that was the side on which he had disembarked. The stranger walked the length of his own punt, stepped into Merrick's and stood in the prow, clearly making up his mind what to do next. The gun was held ready at his side. Merrick stood up, gripping the quant to swing it over and down. It was all he needed to do; his hasty plans for a lancer's charge or a pool shot went for nothing. The other end of the pole came down on the man's head with a reverberant thud, almost tearing his hand off and yanking him forwards with an anguished roar. When he sat up, grinding his teeth to keep from yelling again, all he saw was the two punts resting companionably in the cutting. The punter had gone.

Merrick unwrapped his hand and edged to the bank. He had heard no splash, nothing but his own bellow of pain. The quant had not come down that hard, it was not that heavy; the guy had been wearing a hat as thick as his own. If he had been knocked off balance and fallen into the cutting, where was he? Why was he not climbing out?

Then Merrick saw him and saw why he was not climbing out. He was lying in the water, water so shallow that he was barely below the surface, and level with his head, in the undergrowth of the far bank, was a stone. He must have gone over forwards, struck his head in falling and turned as he hit the water. There were signs of contusion above his eyes, his open eyes.

In the time of preposterous weapons and awesome fire power, mass murderers murmured a derisive epigram and sauntered on to further mayhem. Merrick knew of no appropriate epigrams. He knelt by the stream and said aloud, 'I killed him.' In the quiet of the Moss it sounded as vainglorious as his address to the mirror in Turcat's bathroom. 'Yesterday someone tried to kill me.'

That failed assassination had been calculated, callous beyond belief; this death was an accident, but he had made it happen. He did not know now what it was that he had intended to do in those last frantic moments between leaving the punt and making his wild swing with the quant. He supposed he had entertained some vague notion of fending off an attack; he could not remember. How easy it had been to laugh at Turcat for his ignorance of the world. Two visits to the Moss and he had thought he knew—

All this while he had been looking at the stone that had done his murderous work for him. Not much of it was visible, which was why he had not noticed it as he moored the punt, but it must stand forty centimetres clear of the earth in which it was bedded. No casual observer would have noticed it, but few casual observers came this way. People who came this way would have been on the lookout for it. He had seen such stones before and knew he had blundered into the undertakers' territory.

He stood up and looked around. There was another stone, and another, a little way off. He could not continue the way he had been going for two reasons.

To do so would take him intrusively among the reposeful dead, and he would have to punt over the man he had just killed. He could not get him out, he could not even try, and the corpse was, horribly, at least in the right place.

He took up the quant, stepped into the punt that the dead man had travelled in and steered it away from the eyot, and as he went, saw another stone at the mouth of the cutting which he had overlooked in his race to escape. He had already trespassed. God knew what he had plunged the quant into.

He had no idea where he was going. There was no sun to guide him, no sound; all he wanted to do was get away from the stones and they were everywhere. *Row, row, row your boat.* Through the unforgiving afternoon he blundered among the cuttings, seeking the open merse, the way back to Herigal, the Vyzel Cut, any escape from the fen, while the snow fell again to confuse him further. Once he thought he smelled peat smoke and backtracked. The Bankers might help him, they might recognize him, he could call out, but the Moss oppressed him, he had no right to be here; the stones threatened. He was the desecrator now, Korda the Desecrator, Korda the Killer.

The cold blueness that heralded nightfall was descending through the trees. The snow had stopped falling, the water was beginning to freeze. The stream ahead of him divided; he saw a stone on the bank, an abandoned punt and a white face staring up at him from beneath the curdling ice, as if through a window, the mouth a little open, asking for help. His blind fear had driven him in a circle and brought him back to face his crime. The poor devil might have meant no harm after all, the shot might have been no more than a warning, he might not even have been the one who fired it. Dressed as a city dweller – why not? Merrick stood gazing down at the man who gazed back up at him, who had lived and breathed not centuries but hours ago. Here was another aspect of the truth he was so anxious to uncover. To this must we all come.

He would not retreat from it a second time. He moored the punt and with the fires of hell in his hand sat up all night, to wake the dead.

Chapter Thirteen

When dawn was still a pale-green promise in the east he had to move on. While he kept his vigil the heavy skies had cleared, the branches overhead became sequinned with stars and the temperature dropped until he knew that if he stayed where he was he would freeze where he sat.

The cuttings were already frozen, the ice so thick that he could not see the face beneath it, even when he dared to cast a light on the place where he knew it would be watching for him, and the two punts were so firmly fixed that they might have been set in cement. Only the constant passage of travellers had kept the waterways open before; he doubted if anything would be moving today. He must go forward on foot again, abandoning the punts for the next passers-by to find and make of them what they would. The man below the ice – what condition would he be in when he was found? In the cities the interval between death and the vaporarium was never more than twenty-four hours. To his shame Merrick, who knew what millennia did to the human body, had no idea what days could do.

The monorail was out of earshot now, but with the sky lightening to his right and a honed moon declining on his left, he set off north-easterly, away from the stones, following the watercourse he would have taken in the punt. The quant was a support, nothing more. When he came to a cutting he walked across, trusting the ice to bear his weight, and although it creaked under him it did not break. The pearl was tucked into his shirt, drumming against his breastbone. No sleep, little food; unless he came to Briease soon he might as well have stayed where he was and joined his assailant under the ice.

Sometimes he thought he heard bells, clean strokes that cut through the crunch of his footsteps and the rasping of his breath. *Ding-dong bell, pussy's in the well* . . . Bells did not go ding-dong, he knew that – unlike most people he had actually heard a bell quite recently—

He was not imagining it. A new red star flared through the trees ahead of him as the sun ignited the bird on the tower of Briease church and its clock struck the quarter. A moment later the sun itself came up, rouging the white expanse that lay in front of him beyond the trees. He had come to the mere that he had crossed with Ed Shepherd on their way to the South Turf Bank. On the far side were the lights and snow-covered roofs of Briease Town. By the time he had skirted the mere to the staithe and retraced his way to the lane behind Shepherd's house, the lights were out and his shadow was long behind him. The latch of the gate was loud in the snowshine and before he could walk up the path Ed Shepherd had his back door open.

'Cordwainer from Herigal Staithe by the Vyzel Cut. Where the hell have you been?'

'Three nights out in the fen,' Shepherd said, in the cosseting comfort of his living room. 'Madness. You'll catch a chill.'

'No,' Merrick said. 'We don't, remember?'

'Well, you look terrible. You ought to take—'

'I don't want any of your eye-of-newt, toe-of-bat concoctions,' Merrick said. 'I'm not going to be ill from exposure. I shan't even sneeze. If I look terrible it's not because of that.'

He had an additional reason for looking terrible, but he was not prepared to share it with Shepherd or, indeed, with anyone.

'And what's wrong with your hand?'

'I'll tell you in a minute. First bring me up to date.'

'I've had your boss in touch, three times,' Shepherd said. 'He said you'd told him not to call you and then went into a great sweat because you hadn't called him. You'd better see to that when you've thawed out. He hadn't taken into account your vanishing off the face of the earth for three days. We have a date for the hearing – in ten days' time. He's got his evidence, he says, and I've got mine, so where's yours? He told me you'd be bringing it with you.'

'I don't know what you're going to say about this,' Merrick said. 'You'd noticed I'd hurt my hand.'

'The only excuse for losing a punt,' Shepherd said severely.

'You lot never get frozen in, I suppose. Well, that's the evidence.'

When he had offered his hand to Turcat there had been little to see. He had seized Turcat's finger and made him probe for the hidden treasure. There was no need for that now. As he unwound the filthy bandage the excrescence on his wrist was so large and inflamed that he would not have been surprised to see it split ripely open as they watched.

Shepherd stared at it. 'What is it? What have you done?' He put out a sympathetic hand but Merrick, seeing it coming, flinched away.

'Don't touch it, for Christ's sake.'

'I thought you people didn't have things like this, chills, boils, haemorrhoids . . . *Is* it a boil? We can cure that.'

'It isn't a boil.'

'A carbuncle?'

A diamond or carbuncle, that showeth best in varied lights.
'No, Ed, not a carbuncle. It's a pearl.'

'Oh, good. Very good,' Shepherd said. 'It was a mistake to let you see that skeleton.' He was not smiling.

'You think I'm joking? I nearly died for this. Someone tried to kill me – I've ki— I – I—' He swallowed a rage he did not know he had.

'You *have* to be joking.'

'No. Go on, touch it if you must.'

Shepherd did not move. 'How?'

'In the good old-fashioned way, with a horsefly. And

385

don't tell me it was a mistake to show me the skeleton. If you hadn't handed it over to the Bankers I'd never have had to do this.'

'Had to?'

'The pearls and the skeleton together would have proved that those pearls weren't a myth. In court we would have been entitled to forensic tests. The only person I know, apart from Aboriginals, who believes it thinks they were abscesses. No one can deny *this* when it comes out.'

'How soon will it come out?'

'Very soon, I hope. You cannot imagine what it feels like, especially after the last three days.'

'Will it be out in time for the hearing?'

'Christ, I hope so. Pragmatic doesn't begin to describe you.'

'Wasn't that the idea?'

'Yes, but it's me that's carrying it. I've carried it for weeks and before that there was the fever after the bite. It's all recorded. We have to have it out in ten days or it will all have been for nothing.'

'Poultice,' Shepherd said.

'What's that?'

'A dressing, to draw out poison. It'll draw out anything. Perhaps that's what we used to use in the last stages. It will relieve the pressure and the pain.'

'I could use all sorts of things to relieve the pain,' Merrick said, 'but I haven't.'

'More fool you then. We always did.'

'I had to know what it was like.'

'Why?'

'The price of truth, I suppose,' Merrick said. 'Would you care to know just how much I'm currently worth?'

'Is that why you were followed into the fen?'

'I don't know.'

'You said someone tried to kill you – the same person?'

'I don't know that either. Is paranoid a word you use?'

'When we can get our faltering tongues around it.'

'For weeks I thought I was being followed. I broke the law to get this pearl started, and I got someone else to break it. I'm pursuing a subject that's been banned. I was nearly crushed to death in a library – that doesn't happen often enough to be an accident. That's why I came here secretly, but someone *was* following me yesterday. I discovered the price of antique pearls by advertising, but I never mentioned this one and anyway, no one knew where the ads were coming from. Until I showed the pearl to you only three people knew about it – officially. Unofficially, I'm not sure. I thought that if my eggman had told anyone – oh, I'll explain about the eggman later – if he admitted to what we'd done I might be wanted by the Feds, not just for breaking the law but for proving where the pearls come from when no one wants to know. But the guy who followed me yesterday, it could have been the pearl he was after, not me at all, except inasmuch as I'm carrying it.'

'Then you were lucky to get away. Did you lose him in the fen?'

'Yes,' Merrick said, 'I lost him in the fen.'

'Has it been born yet?' Turcat whispered in his ear as he lay in the upper room at Shepherd's house. Other voices were murmuring downstairs but Ed was keeping visitors at bay.

'No, I'm still in labour. We've poulticed it, what looks like a slurry of boiled paper, to draw the thing out.'

'Will that work?'

'We hope it'll work in time for the hearing. Ed reckons twenty-four hours.'

'How are you feeling?'

'Very relaxed. These people have the most amazing selection of smokes.'

'Yes, you sound as if you've been enjoying yourself.'

'Traditional remedy; you light this little pellet in a dish and let it smoulder.'

'Remedy? Hah!'

'It dulls the pain, and you see some extraordinary images.'

'I *was* going to ask you what you got up to in the Moss for three days,' Turcat said, 'but by the sound of it I doubt if you can remember.'

Merrick's head cleared instantly. 'I was discovering my true worth,' he said.

He dreamed of mermaids, little things the size of herring, rainbowhued, that swam in the limpid waters of a fen transfigured by spring and basked on stones among the flowering eyots. They had long pale hair, like Frida's.

Next evening the pearl was still with him. Shepherd examined the swelling. 'It doesn't seem possible. You realize this is bigger than anything I've ever seen. It's

388

certainly going to be bigger than the one we found in that woman's knee.'

'Due to my excellent physical condition, no doubt,' Merrick said. 'My diet supplies me with an abundance of calcium.'

'Whatever; you're the most valuable person I've ever met. Didn't I tell you I had a feeling you'd turn out to be worth the trouble you were causing?' He applied a fresh poultice and strapped it on while Merrick made his ritual recording. 'How much do you think you'd fetch on the open market?'

'Don't sound so eager. It's a very closed market.'

'I suppose you wouldn't like to cut—'

'No, I would not. I'm carrying this to full term.'

'I was only thinking how it must feel. Bad?'

'Very bad.'

'Yet you are perfectly well otherwise? Remarkable.'

'It's very tiring,' Merrick said, sensing that Shepherd was almost disappointed by his robust constitution. 'And you should have seen me after the bite – well, you *can* see. All the records are here.'

'I've got something stronger for you tonight. You'd better sleep down here. I don't want you drifting around in the dark and falling downstairs.'

'No, it would be a pity to lose your material witness at the last moment. It must come out tomorrow, surely. I've been saying that for days. Maybe I'll still have it when we go to court and I can . . . *express* it, right there in front of the magistrate.'

'Shall I put the screen on? What would you like to watch? Something soothing?'

'I don't need the screen; this stuff has much better pictures. I think I dreamed of Frida last night – where is she? I thought I might see her – in real life, I mean.'

'Maybe tomorrow,' Shepherd said. 'Now, make sure you inhale; get the best out of it.'

The magistrate's court in Norge was made entirely of glass. Merrick had not realized that the hearing had been transferred to Norge until they arrived. He had no memory of the journey from Briease.

But the room set aside for their case was small and windowless. He was annoyed, having hoped that there would be sunshine for his pearl, which showed best by day. They sat in the front row of chairs, Ed Shepherd with a skeleton on his knee, Rémy Turcat carrying his evidence in a large wicker basket, Merrick with his pearl, facing the bench where the magistrate would preside. He had the unpleasant impression that the room was getting smaller, the side walls softly sliding together, and in the airless silence Merrick could hear his pearl mark the passing seconds, a discreet regular ticking. The magistrate came in, extravagantly robed with a billowing fur train that continued to arrange itself in swathes on the floor after she had taken her place at the bench, expanding in one direction, contracting in another, like an amoeba. It crossed his mind that it might not be fur at all but some living organism that had been persuaded into the form of judicial robes for the occasion.

People began to speak from somewhere behind him. Was that Mirandola's voice?

'Well, now we've got this far it might as well come out on its own. We don't want to damage it.'

'It can only be a matter of hours. *Look* at it.'

He turned round, indignant at being discussed as if in his absence, to see who was talking about him, but the rows of chairs were no longer there. The rear wall of the courtroom was at his back, a steel shelving unit filled with books.

'We'd better take him down now.'

'Get that thing out of his ear first.'

'It's not in my *ear*,' he said. 'It's in my hand. Look—' But there was in truth a sudden very severe pain around where his ear must be if he could only see it.

'Are we going to watch him?'

'Him or it?'

His ear? How could it have been in his ear, when his hand had been hurting for so long? It was still hurting.

'Look in at intervals, I'd say. After all, he won't be going anywhere.'

'Suppose he swallows it?'

'Strap it up – no, behind him, where he can't get at it.'

The courtroom was now so small that all the lights had gone out and he was lying on the magistrate's train, which was less furry than it had looked. This was not what was supposed to happen – where were Shepherd and Turcat with their precious evidence? How could they have abandoned him with the pain in his hand, the pain in his ear? They were his *friends*. Somewhere close the pearl ticked on.

* * *

It was so dark, darker than the Briease Moss at dead of night and it was no dream. The pearl was still pounding in his wrist and the pain in his ear was so raw that he feared to touch it in case the whole thing had been sheared off, like his arm. He could still feel the pearl but his arm had gone, torn away . . .

'Light,' he said, but no light came on. '*Light*.' Nothing. Then he remembered that he was in Ed's living room and the lights were manually controlled. If he pressed his good hand to the wall just above the head of the sofa—

There was no wall above the head of the sofa. There was no wall behind the sofa; he was not on the sofa but crawling about on the magistrate's train – no, not that; what was this called? Carpet. He was in the Ayckbourn Theatre. There ought to be lamps in those strange heavy yellow metals. The carpet was writhing under him and it was dark, no light; no light meant no air, but there was air, very very cold air. He madly clapped his hand to his face and the pain sawed through his earlobe as he touched it. His fingers came away sticky. The ear was still there; the communication stud in the lobe had been cut out.

Get that thing out of his ear.

This time he really did wake up.

Jottings from his dream began to assemble themselves into joined-up writing; he could see the writing, white on black, Turcat's ramshackle cursive.

Take him down now . . . get that thing out of his ear . . . he's not going anywhere . . . Strap it up, where he can't get at it.

Take him down? He was already downstairs, he had fallen asleep in the living room with its tables and sofas, the window, the unlocked door that led out into the street. *Take him down.* Could the house have a cellar? Were the Oysters mad enough to build their houses with basements so close to the sea which might at any moment surge casually over the dunes and wash them out?

His left hand was in a sling again, but up against his back *where he can't get at it.* That wasn't how Ed had left it. What had happened in the magistrate's court? No, he had never been in the magistrate's court, waiting before the bench with Ed and Rémy. He had been in Ed's house the whole time, on the sofa in the living room and now, down here, wherever here was. It must be a room if it had a carpet, although the carpet was as clammy as sea sand when the tide went out, and smelled of mould. His tentative hand found the edges of the carpet – it could be no more than a couple of metres each way; beyond it lay damp porous tiles. Very carefully he stood up and advanced to the edge of his eyot, from where he could touch the walls, also damp and porous, cold, and the ceiling, only centimetres above his head, a low Oyster ceiling. There was a door in the corner and it had no handle. He knew it was a door by running his hand around the frame.

Footsteps were descending beyond it. Not knowing which way it would open he stepped back and a light shone in.

'Turn round,' said the voice behind the light.

'What's happening?' He did not turn round. Someone turned him round, face to the wall.

'Don't be a nuisance.' There was a second presence in the room, holding a thin blade near his eyes. The man with the light was busy at his back, fumbling with the sling, not deliberately rough but not careful.

'It's still there.'

'Where's Ed?'

'He's busy. He's the mayor, remember. Very busy.'

'Is this his house?'

'No.'

'Then why am I here?'

'Why do you think?' Something was thrown over his shoulders. 'Here's your clever winter coat. You'll need it.' The light receded, the door closed.

Now that the pearl had been revived he could feel its heat again, and the effects of whatever had put him to sleep were wearing off. He sat down on the carpet. He was not in Ed Shepherd's house; did Ed know where he was? Did anyone? Would anyone ever find out? He knew now what had happened to his communications stud; too impatient to dismantle it properly his abductors had slit the lobe and torn it out, leaving him isolated and silenced, unable to get in touch, untouchable.

Not abductors, thieves; as he had foreseen, he had not been abducted but stolen; he was no more than the case that carried the loot; they wouldn't risk damaging that by cutting it out. He would be left, safely under lock and key in the good old-fashioned Oyster manner, until the precious thing that he carried had been delivered. How long would that be? Oh god, how long? And would they kill him then, when he was worthless, and lay him in still water as he had dreamed? He had grown it in his hand so that he could get at it and now he could not get at it to comfort it. *Eventually you will not be able to resist rubbing and scratching it, even biting at it perhaps as animals do with their injuries.*

Joris, were you questioned? Did you tell them *everything*?

Suppose these bastards want to know how to get hold of *Tabanus* eggs so they can start growing their own.

Was he perhaps dreaming again? The lifetime of dreams he had thought he did not have had been put out at interest and now it was paying dividends. Of course he had never remembered his dreams; what had he ever done that was worth dreaming about? He was one of the sullen Inglish, a malcontent, that lifetime passed in a slough of resentment, unloved, unliked, unappreciated. He was appreciated now all right. The noble Oysters, backs against the the wall, feet in the mud, maintaining their right to be Inglish in life and in death, were no more high-minded than any other Europeans, the politicians, the Senate and librarians of the University of New Cambridge, the hitman who had pursued him through the Moss, the unknown other who had tried to kill him in the stacks. No higher minded than Rémy Turcat, who could have had nothing but base motives originally for refusing to hand over the Parizo pearls and the evidence of their origin. Turcat might have redeemed himself since but it was miserably obvious now that his first intention had been to sell them.

Only Merrick Korda, the useful idiot, had had a higher purpose: to uncover the truth that might perhaps come to the price of a pearl, and his moment of truth was imminent. Mirandola had spoken in his dream but in their treachery the Oysters had left Mirandola far behind. *If you murdered me now and buried me on your land, would I be yours?*

Yes, apparently.

Stay awake this time. Stay awake. Stand up, walk, walk round the carpet, walk round the walls, make sure they stay the same distance apart. Don't panic. Talk.

I have been down into the dark three times: when *Tabanus bovinus Regina* bit me, when I went into the stacks, and now, down here, wherever I am. When you go down for the third time you don't come up again.

No, don't think, *talk.*

'*This little piggy went to market, this little piggy stayed home, this little piggy had roast beef . . . Come you not from Newcastle? Come you not there away, oh saw you not my truelove?*' Scraps of fragments, songs, Inglish songs, long suppressed. '*My truelove, a truelove of mine. Tell her to buy me an acre of land, between the salt water and the sea strand—*'

Between the salt water and the sea strand, a grave on Parizo Beach.

> '*Tell her to plough it with a ram's horn,*
> *Parsley, sage, rosemary and thyme.*

396

And sow it all over with one pepper corn,
Then she'll be a truelove of mine.'

He was singing now – he had hardly known he could sing, there had never been much call for it.

'*Met the king and the queen, that was called*
a grey mare,
A-walking behind, a-riding before.
In Nottingham Town, on a hot frozen stone—'

He did not hear the door open again, thought he was still alone until he saw the light, not a probing beam as before but the wan glow of a hurricane lamp. He backed into a corner, both hands behind him, as the lamp approached.

'What have you got to sing about?' Frida said.

He could hardly speak for shock, relief, disbelief. 'It's that or scream.'

'Pain? Let me see.'

'I can't. It's somewhere . . .'

'Behind you? Oh, that wasn't kind. Turn round.' He felt her fingers unfastening, unwrapping. What had she to do with this? Should he knock her down and run for it?

'Did you really grow this yourself?'

'Yes, I really did.' You know what it is, then, do you?

She lifted his hand to examine it coolly, put it to her cool mouth. He expected balm but the touch was hot iron.

'Where are we?'

'It doesn't matter, we're leaving.'

'They're letting me go?'

'I'm letting you go.'

'What's happening, Frida? Who's doing this? I won't ask why.'

'You know why.'

'We were going to court.'

'No, I don't think you were ever going to court, not once we'd seen your evidence. Come on.'

Was not the prince supposed to resue the sleeping princess? He followed the light she carried out into a long echoing space, green-stained walls, vaulted ceiling. He knew at once where he was; this was what he and Turcat had been delving for at the cathedral site, an undercroft, a crypt. They were in the foundations of the church, treading over gravestones.

'Isn't anyone keeping watch?'

'Turn and turn about. It's my turn. I'm keeping watch.'

'How did you—?'

'Don't talk now.'

How did you get involved with this? he had been going to ask, but as he must not talk nor she answer he had time as they climbed the stone stairs to work it out for himself. And he had given her that letter – for Ed Shepherd – trusting them both.

'Not everyone is happy with things as they are,' Ed had told him. 'Some younger ones are quite desperate to get away.'

You could get a very long way on the price of a pearl.

'Is your Uncle Ed in on this?'

'Be quiet. Especially now.'

Frida opened a door at the head of the steps, putting out the light, but not before he saw, looking down, or thought he saw, a figure lying on the floor below him, sprawled on the stones at the side of the stairs, as though fallen from a great height.

He had been imagining that they would come out into the glassy brightness of the church, but on the other side of the door was an arctic darkness. The air was electric with stinging sleet, the ground slithery, and when he flung out a hand against the wall to steady himself, it skidded on a laminate of verglas. It was his left hand. He could not stifle a sharp cry. Frida wheeled and smacked her palm across his mouth. His lips were mashed against his teeth, the savage cold scalded his mutilated ear and the pearl shrilled on a high white note.

Twenty paces into the freezing furnace of the wind and then they stood in the lee of buildings, houses, he saw warm lighted windows. The Masons lived here by the church, didn't they?

'Are we going to your house?' He whispered this time but the wind dispersed his words. They were not going to her house. Frida's gloved hand took his ungloved hand and steered him. He longed for the reassuring comfort of flesh upon flesh but he could not ask her to bare her hand to the blast, although she was wrapped in a heavy hooded cape and he had only the clever city coat.

He did not know where they were going although

he knew what would happen if he asked, but she did, walking surely into the darkness. Lighted windows became fewer, the wind assaulted them unimpeded by buildings, and the ground beneath them changed from icy pavement to shingle, to frozen grass. They were heading into the fen, across the merse. Something more feral than intelligence told him that this would be his last journey through the Briease Moss. He listened for the sea but heard only the roaring wind; if he tried to speak now he would drown in it. All he could do was follow as the hand drew him on, sightless, deafened. After a while he stopped even thinking; a vessel of ice that carried the seething pearl.

Something came between them and the wind. Twigs scraped against his face, the ground became slippery again. They must be treading along a frozen waterway, a narrow ditch, frozen solid. Frida said, 'Nearly there.'

'Where?'

'A little place I know.'

She made it sound like an intimate overnighter favoured for assignations, furtive dalliance. Dalliance was not what he wanted; he wanted to lie down here in the ditch, fall asleep and not wake up again, but the gloved hand never slackened its grip.

'That first time you brought me into the fen – why?'

She paused. 'Oh, devilment, I think. I wanted to scare you.'

'Why, you didn't know me. We'd only met once.'

'Anyone would have done. Europeans come here on tours to gawp at us. I wanted to see one all on his

400

own, see what he would do. And when I knew what you were—'

'What am I?'

'An archaeologist; not just any old archaeologist, the Parizo Beach archaeologist – why are you mumbling?'

'My mouth's bruised.'

'Yes, it must be. Don't ask so many questions, they all begin with Ws.'

He risked another. 'Why are you doing this?'

'Would you rather have stayed in the crypt?'

'Were they going to kill me?' *Are you?*

'I don't think so. They'd have kept you until the pearl came out; once you'd healed they'd have let you go. What could you prove?'

'I have all the records.'

'Ed has the records, Merrick.'

She stopped without warning. 'Here we are, up this bank – no, I know you can't see it. Just keep following; remember how easily I can lose you. Wasn't that the first thing I taught you?'

She transferred her grasp to his collar and hauled him up the side of the ditch, on across grass among unseen masonry and over rubble until they were stooping in the shelter of an overhanging arch. This must be one of those fallen buildings Shepherd had told him of, where the undertakers mined their lyke stones, a ruined fenland church.

A light sprang up where Frida was bending over a ledge, a little disc of candle such as travellers in the Moss sent on ahead to find their watery paths in the dark.

'That won't last long,' he said.

'We don't need long,' Frida said. 'Lie down.'

There was a rug or blanket underfoot, dankly redolent of the magistrate's train, but he stretched out on it gratefully. Frida, kneeling, was arranging a hanging across the low aperture where they had entered from the howling night. When she was satisfied she turned, still kneeling, and spread herself over him in her heavy cloak that was lined with real fur . . . sheep fur . . . wool?

'Oh, poor Merrick, is that better? Your clever city coat's no match for our weather, is it? No hat, no gloves—'

'Whose fault is that?'

'Not mine. Oh, your poor hands, one so cold, one so hot. Never mind, never mind – do you want to have sex?'

'*What?*'

'That's what you people are always asking me.'

'It's a courtesy, that's all.'

'A courtesy?' She laughed, low and unamused. 'It never sounds very courteous to me. A refusal often offends.'

'Having my ear half-torn off offends. Who did that?'

'I don't know, but it was a sensible precaution, wasn't it? They couldn't have you calling home, now could they?'

'Did Ed have anything to do with this?'

Her hands were inside his shirt, fingers wandering. 'You like Ed, don't you? Your friend. No, he wasn't so very willing, but what could he do? Once people knew

402

what you were carrying, once you told him how *valuable* you were. It's the first time you've ever been valuable, isn't it? Oh, Merrick, those little dried pitted things we found in the coffin, you told Ed how much *they* were worth. And then yours . . . so *big*, and fresh and *moist* . . . won't it shine? I wonder what colour it will be. How does this feel? This? Where did you get the eggs?'

'Eggs?'

'The horsefly; so you could grow your pearl, your lovely pearl, how did you get hold of them?'

She *couldn't* mean what he thought she meant. 'I can't get any more. There aren't any more. Frida, please—'

'How do you like this?'

'Oh, not now—'

'Not now? I thought men were always ready. They always seem to be. You are a man, aren't you?' Her mouth came down punitively on his. 'How does that feel? Does it hurt? Does it hurt terribly? How about here?'

Her teeth closed on his earlobe. At every touch he shuddered and bucked beneath her tensile dancer's body, the steel-sprung, crab-claw limbs. 'Oh, you like it *really*, don't you? That's what they all say, "Oh, you want it really, don't you? You like it *really*, you know you do." How about here? No, stop struggling, you'll like this, you will like it, *really*.'

One hand was in his hair, stroking, the other on his belly, kneading, exploring, down, down, but her mouth was on his wrist, at first licking, then kissing, sucking, *biting*—

'Aaaah!'

Two climaxes, simultaneous. The light went out.

A little boat, not a Banker's funeral punt but a clinker-built dinghy rocking gently like a cradle under a loving hand; a figure sat in the stern, propelling the craft across the black water with a single oar. Merrick, lying with his head to the prow, saw over the oarsman's shoulder the spires and heights of New Cambridge, fiery in the morning sun. There was no sun where he was going. He could not turn his head to see the farther shore but he sensed the radiant chill, the encroaching dark and felt, under his tongue, the pearl that someone had put in his mouth to pay the ferryman.

During the night the wind had torn down Frida's makeshift curtain but the ice storm had blown itself out. The view he had seen over the boatman's shoulder was not New Cambridge, not the sun shining on a thousand windows but the sun shining on a million crystals welded to branch and twig, dazzling; life after death.

His ear was still sore but a fingertip investigation located a healthy scab. On the back of his hand, between the magnum and scaphoid carpals was a small bloody crater no larger than his little fingernail, glazed with plasma and already healing at the circumference. The joint ached, not unpleasantly, the ache of deliverance and relief.

'I never saw it,' he mourned, for his lost pearl, his

outraged trust, the price he had paid to learn the truth, but try as he might he could not cry. Too bad that he should have been the target for Frida's wild justice, her cold revenge on all Europeans. She had at least saved him, only leaving him marooned here in the Moss when she could have left him pillaged and dead in Briease church like the body he had seen at the foot of the steps in the undercroft. How could he sit in judgement upon her? He too had killed his man. And after that, he supposed, she had fled alone with her plunder, leaving her confederates to think they had escaped together. They must have believed that he had gone with her or they would be here now, searching for him.

Perhaps they were. When he came out of his niche he might find the shining fen alive with waiting Oysters who knew he would have to break cover eventually. It might as well be now.

He advanced, on hands and knees at first, then stood upright amid the sparkling chandeliers of ice. There was no ambush, no one appeared from the blue and white woodland. The ruined church stood on a grassy hummock, roofless, the tower collapsed, but the high narrow windows pointed skyward. On the walls were memorials to the truly ancient dead, scrolled cartouches, cunningly engraved, and by his arch was a slate tablet, older than all the others, with the figure of a skeleton incised, head and shoulders.

All you that do this place pass by,
Remember death, for you must die.

405

As you are now even so was I,
And as I am so shall you be.

He traced the lines of the *memento mori* with his finger. 'I know,' he said. 'I know.'

The sun was still low in the sky and he saw it through the trees; he must be close to one of those open merses. He did not hear the sea but, now that he stopped to listen, he could hear *something*, not the slow percussion of the waves on shore, but a steady, rhythmic swish. Leaving the mound of the church he began to walk towards the source of the sound, noticing, as he went, that there were no cuts or channels here; under the crisping grass the ground was firm.

Beyond the birches stood thicker uprights, great white tree trunks; surely no birch ever grew so stout; and then he came to the edge of the woodland and saw where he was: on the boundary of the Parizo wind farm. He walked on, limping but heedlessly confident now, through the thundering grove, feeling the solid earth shaken beneath his feet by the stunning thud of the blades. Ahead, the irregular crest of the dunes bisected the verticals, but still he did not hear the sea save as a distant agitation in the ears, and when he came to the last of the turbines and scaled the frost-bound dunes, he saw why.

All along the coast from north to south the sea was frozen, a white turbulence of peaks, troughs, plateaux and crevasses, cols and cwms. Far out the glittering spray was dashed upward where ice floes jostled in the

406

open water. He stumbled across the snow to the foothills of the miraculous mountain range and laughed aloud at the wonder of it.

Under the sun, to the south, the Nox rose out of the horizon and marked the mouth of Eavrey Sound, where the tramlines ran. He could walk there in two hours, less perhaps. Frida had spoken darkly once of quicksands; well, she had also warned him of vipers in the dunes and there had been no vipers; not in the dunes. If he encountered quicksand he would bypass it, scaling his own salt-sea Himalaya.

Gloveless, hands in pockets, he set off towards the sun, a little haltingly at first while his abused joints and tissues adjusted to normal use, but purged of poison, safely worthless again, he soon established a rhythm and fell into an easy gait, the fearless step of a man with no one at his back. He could not foresee what lay ahead of him, but there was nowhere else to go.

'Who knows what I know?' he had once asked Turcat, and answered himself: 'No one does.' And now no one ever would. In a few days the flesh of his wrist would bear no sign of trauma. Whatever Joris had confessed to, the only proof of it was in the hands of the Oysters, probably already destroyed. He had offered them salvation, the truth purchased at great price, and they had rejected it. If he wanted the truth he was welcome to keep it, and keep it was all he could do. No one else wanted it.

He would have to carry it alone for the rest of his life, and it would be a long life, but at least he would be free of the burden of trust. Trust had been left behind last night, in the Briease Moss. Striding angrily now, he found himself singing as he paced along the frozen shore, in a voice that surprised him by its depth and power; the half-remembered song that had come to him as he lay suffocating in the stacks and returned last night in the undercroft; confusedly ominous then, now comfortably meaningless.

'In Nottamun Town not a soul to be seen,
Not a soul would look up, not a soul would look down,
Not a soul would look up, not a soul would look down
To show me the way to Nottamun Town.'

How could he have hoarded such nonsense when so much that made sense was so hard to remember?

'I rode a big horse that was called a grey mare,
Grey mane and grey tail, grey stripes down his back,
Grey mane and grey tail, grey stripes down his back,
There weren't a hair on him but what was called black.

She stood so still, she threw me to the dirt,
She tore my hide and bruised my shirt;
From stirrup to stirrup I mounted again
And on my ten toes I rode over the plain.'

Had it ever meant anything? If he hadn't known the tune he would never have remembered the words. The icy air bit at his ear. Torn hide? Not so meaningless, perhaps . . .

'Met the king and the queen and a company of men
A-walking behind and a-riding before.
A stark-naked drummer came walking along
With his hands in his bosom a-beating his drum.'

He had never understood a word of it, but under
the circumstances it made as much sense as anything.

'Sat down on a hot and cold frozen stone,
Ten thousand stood round me and I was alone.
Took my heart in my hand to keep my head warm.
Ten thousand got drowned that never were born.'